OASIS

Patricia Matthews

Thorndike Press • Thorndike, Maine

Library of Congress Cataloging in Publication Data:

Matthews, Patricia, 1927-
    Oasis / Patricia Matthews.
    p. cm.
    ISBN 0-89621-857-0 (lg. print: alk. paper)
    1. Large type books. I. Title.
[PS3563.A853027   1989]   88-36823
813'.54--dc19   CIP

Large Print edition available by arrangement with
Harlequin Enterprises B. V.

All the characters in this book have no existence outside the
imagination of the author and have no relation whatsoever
to anyone bearing the same name or names. They are not
even distantly inspired by any individual known or unknown to the author, and all incidents are pure invention.

Cover design by James B. Murray.

OASIS

One

The white Rolls glided to a cushioned stop before the concealed entrance to the two-storied, sand colored building that sprawled amid drought-resistant landscaping as if it had grown there.

The veil and the long, beige linen coat, did little to disguise the true identity of the woman who emerged from the vehicle. Although Lacey Houston was thinner than usual, a little haggard and drawn, the fabled beauty of the actress's face was still there, ghostlike behind the smokiness of the veil.

Lacey nodded to the tall black chauffeur holding the door open for her. "Thank you, Theodore. Will you see that my jewels are taken to my room?" she asked in a voice that was little more than a husky whisper.

"I'll take care of it, Miss Lacey," Theodore Wilson replied. "And I have a room at the Holiday Inn for the duration. I'll be available if you need me for anything."

Lacey nodded and entered the Heinman Medical Center. She shivered a little at the contrast between the air-conditioned interior and the dry scorching heat she'd experienced momentarily outside the building. Clutching the loose coat more closely around her, she paused just inside the door, uncertain how to proceed.

Then she saw a man striding toward her down the long corridor. He was dressed casually, without a tie or jacket, his sport shirt open at the throat. He was of medium height, slightly stocky, and moved with an athlete's grace. As he drew nearer, Lacey saw that he had thick, unruly black hair. Intense black eyes stared back at her from a strong, Slavic face.

And then he smiled, an enchanting smile that changed the severity of his features.

"Miss Houston! Welcome to The Clinic," he said in a deep voice. He took her hand in both of his. His grip was strong, reassuring. "I'm Dr. Noah Breckinridge."

Lacey laughed somewhat nervously. "I wasn't sure who . . ." She gestured. "One expects a doctor to be wearing a white coat or . . ."

"Or a suit and tie?" He ran one hand through his already ruffled hair, a gesture curiously boyish. "We tend to be somewhat informal here. After all, this is laid-back Southern California."

"I talked to you on the phone, didn't I?"

"Yes, you did." He took her overnight bag in

8

one hand and her elbow in the other. "We have no reception desk at this entrance, but I'll see you directly to your room."

He was interrupted as a shrill scream resounded off the corridor walls. Lacey froze, then half turned, ready to flee back to the safety of the Rolls.

"It's all right, Miss Houston," Breckinridge said, exerting a gentle pressure on her elbow. "It's nothing to be alarmed about. Occasionally a new patient wakens from medication, finds himself disoriented, in surroundings he doesn't recognize, and screams without thinking."

Damn, Noah thought, why did it have to happen now, right this very instant? He was sure he knew who had screamed. Billie Reaper, the little prick. Reaper let loose a scream now and then, not from pain or fright, withdrawal or even disorientation, but simply to cause an uproar, to bring a nurse running so he could vent his frustration at his confinement. Noah cursed the day the rock star had been admitted to The Clinic.

He turned his attention to the woman by his side. He felt her arm tremble in his grip, and he sensed that she was on the verge of losing control. She was one of the world's most famous sex symbols, perhaps a fading one, but still beautiful enough to be desired by half the men in the world — envied by almost all of the women. And yet she was afraid and vulnerable, her arm fragile beneath his hand.

He said again, "I assure you there's absolutely nothing to be alarmed about, Miss Houston."

"Does . . . does that happen often?" she said in her husky voice.

"Not often, I promise. We don't torture people here."

She gave him a nervous smile. "Perhaps you don't, but people in this situation go through their own private torture. This isn't my first time, you know."

"I know. But you made the decision to come here on your own. That's the important first step, and a very brave one."

"Brave? Not really, Doctor. If I had real courage, I would do this on my own, without help."

With a sweep of her hand she removed the veil, and Noah saw the heartbreaking beauty firsthand. His breath caught. It was one thing to see her face on film or reproduced in magazines and newspapers, but it was something else entirely to be within inches of the legendary beauty. Lacey Houston was not the first actress to seek the services provided by The Clinic, but more often than not, Noah found them pale imitations of their photos. But in Lacey's case the camera didn't lie – if anything, it understated. Since she was in her forties, Noah figured that she'd probably had a facelift, but if she had, it had been a damn good job. The ravages of drugs and alcohol were there, yet they somehow managed to enhance her beauty. And that shining dark hair and those huge green eyes, which one journalist claimed were large enough to swim in — yes, Noah concluded, he did feel a tug, an impulse to dive in and to hell with the consequences!

"Do you disapprove, Doctor?"

"Disapprove?" he said, at a loss.

"Famous beauty, adored movie star, in and out of four marriages, plenty of money, known far and wide for her collection of jewels, having to undergo treatment for drug and alcohol abuse."

"It's not my job to make moral judgments," he said somewhat stiffly. "My job is to treat."

"Come now, Dr. Breckinridge. You must feel some scorn for a wreck like me."

"You're far from a wreck, Miss Houston." He let his face relax in a slight smile. "I admire your candor. Most patients admitted here deny that they need treatment, deny they have an alcohol or drug dependency. Or they say they're agreeing to be admitted to The Clinic because they badly need a rest."

As Noah opened the second set of doors and waited for Lacey to walk inside, he noticed that she had paled and was badly trembling. He let the doors shut and stepped to her side. "Are you all right, Miss Houston?"

11

"I'm fine." Then she laughed shakily and looked at him. Perspiration gleamed on her forehead. "No, I'm not. I feel like I'm about to scream, just like the person we heard a moment ago."

"When did you last take drugs of any kind?"

"Last night. No, I won't lie to you." She took a deep breath, those fabulous breasts rising and falling only inches away from him. "I snorted two lines of coke in the hotel in Los Angeles this morning. But God, the way I'm feeling it could have been days ago!"

"Good for you! That's the first lesson you have to learn − never lie about your dependency. I've had people come in here smelling like a distillery, swearing they haven't had a drink in days." He squeezed her hand. "Just hold on." He turned and raised his voice. "Kathy!"

A slender girl in a starched uniform, a tumble of brown hair tied up with a ribbon, came rustling toward him. "Yes, Doctor?"

"This is Lacey Houston. She'll be in room 112. Would you please escort her there and get her settled in? And then give her . . ." From his pocket he took a pad and scribbled a prescription for a tranquilizer on it, tore the sheet off and gave it to the nurse.

Kathy Marlowe glanced at the paper. "Yes, Doctor. Would you come with me, Miss Houston?"

12

As the nurse started to lead her away, Lacey held back. "Doctor?"

"Yes, Miss Houston?"

"My driver, Theodore, will be coming in shortly with my trunk. Will you leave instructions so that he can find me?"

"Your trunk?" he said blankly. "Miss Houston, I really don't think you'll need that many clothes. This isn't a social club, after all."

"Oh, it doesn't hold my clothes. It's my jewels."

He stared. "Your *jewels?*"

"Of course, I never go anywhere without them."

Lacey turned then and followed the nurse, without giving Noah a chance to respond. A moment ago he had been feeling some admiration for the woman's candor and spunk. Now this! Checking into a drug treatment center with a fortune in jewels! He had read about Lacey Houston's fabulous collection — who hadn't? — and now he also recalled mention of the fact that the jewels always went with her, no matter where she traveled. He vaguely recalled a TV interview where the interviewer had quipped that the jewels must be her security blanket. Lacey, instead of denying it, had retorted, "That may be true enough, but those jewels were acquired through much hard work, sweat and tears, and I like to have them where I can see them."

Noah's respect had never been high for most of the celebrity guests at The Clinic, but now and again one would fool him, and for a moment there he had thought that Lacey Houston was one of the rare exceptions.

He came to with a start, hurrying after her. "Miss Houston?"

Lacey and the nurse paused, waiting for him.

"We have certain rules here, and there can be no exceptions. You can't have your jewels with you in your room. I'm sorry."

"But why not?" she demanded. "What harm can it do?"

"It will be a distraction. There can be no distractions. No books or magazines. No TV, newspapers, except at certain hours. No telephone calls, no visitors except by approval and then only on weekends. This all may sound harsh to you, but experience has taught us that it's necessary."

She looked crushed, and Noah felt sorry for her, but he hardened his heart. As he watched her walk away with Kathy, he wondered what she would think when she learned that she would have to share a room, when she found out that she had to make her own bed.

Noah found the memo from Sterling Hanks, The Clinic's director, when he returned to his office. Hanks had an inflated estimate of his own worth, and because of his theatrical shock of silver-white hair, those at The Clinic who disliked the man — and there were many — called him Sterling Silver.

Noah disliked Hanks intensely, mainly because of his ego and pomposity. Hanks wasn't a medical man and disdained any knowledge of the inner workings of The Clinic. Noah grudgingly admitted that he projected a good PR image — smooth, suave, at ease with VIP patients — but he did not concern himself with the methods of treatment, unless they clashed with the image of The Clinic that he worked so diligently to protect. He was only interested in the end result, when he could announce publicly that so-and-so had emerged rehabilitated, a tribute to The Clinic's efficiency.

Noah was grateful that Hanks rarely interfered with the day-to-day operations, yet the two men constantly clashed over two things. One was represented by the memo in Noah's hand. The other was Hanks's scorn for the lesser mortals accepted for treatment. If Hanks had his way, *only* celebrities would be admitted. Noah didn't begrudge the celebrities their opportunity for rehabilitation, but he was also concerned for others, those who were not affluent and famous. It was working with these people that justified his presence at The Clinic.

He scowled at the square of white paper. Hanks almost always handed down his edicts and orders by memo, ignoring the telephone as if Alexander Graham Bell had never been born. Noah had once accused the director of using memos so that he could always provide proof of communication should the need arise. Hanks had not bothered to deny the charge, which had goaded Noah into saying, "You could get the same results by recording all phone conversations."

Hanks had assumed a look of shock. "My dear Dr. Breckinridge, that is not only unethical, it is illegal."

However, it was not the memos themselves that raised Noah's ire; it was their usual content. He read it.

Dr. Breckinridge,
A new patient will be honoring us with his presence within the next three days. Governor William Stoddard. I received a telephone communication from the governor this morning and advised him to get in touch with you.

"Goddammit," Noah said aloud.

It had been said of Noah that he had the combined bedside manners of Dr. Marcus

16

Welby and young Dr. Kildare. It was both a curse and a blessing. Dealing with the highly volatile patients at The Clinic required the patience of Job, plus the tact of a diplomat. The latter was the curse. When Hanks had learned of Noah's ability to deal with people, he made a move so adroitly performed that Noah hadn't realized what was happening until it was too late.

Noah was now expected to handle all the important patients personally – greet them on entrance, as in the case of Lacey Houston, shepherd them through all the preliminaries, and then personally supervise their treatment. In Noah's opinion, it was nothing more than public relations. He was a *doctor*, dammit! He had selected this field of medicine for personal reasons, to treat *all* alcoholics and drug abusers, not just the rich and famous. Aside from the fact that the chore was distasteful to him, it limited his time with the other patients.

He had strenuously objected to Hanks about it, to which the man had blandly responded. "Your peculiar talent is valuable to us, Dr. Breckinridge."

"But I am a doctor!"

"Your medical expertise is not in question. You are the best doctor on staff here, undeniably. However, The Clinic is unique, certainly more famous than the Betty Ford Center. Our reputation is known worldwide and deservedly so. Because of that reputation, we attract notable people. To a large extent that is due to your efforts. The patients coming here know of your talents, and they expect personal attention from you."

"Notable? Notorious, you mean," Noah muttered darkly.

"You are entitled to your opinion," Hanks said severely, "so long as you keep it to yourself. You will continue as before, Dr. Breckinridge."

Noah had appealed to the board of directors for relief from the onerous chore and had been told curtly that all such matters rested entirely in the hands of Sterling Hanks.

He had even thought of appealing to Karl Heinman, founder of The Clinic. But who could find *him?* Heinman was a man of mystery, jokingly referred to by some as the Howard Hughes of Oasis.

Still staring at the memo, Noah tried to peg the name. It tickled a memory. . . . Then he had it. William Stoddard was the governor of one of the most populous states in the nation. Noah grimaced. Next to movie stars and rock stars, politicians were his least-liked patients. They were usually a royal pain in the ass. A number of politicians had been at The Clinic, including an ex-president of the country, the current vice-president and numerous senators.

This was the first governor, to Noah's knowledge. The politicians expected, and received, total anonymity. Show business stars, although they claimed they did, really didn't object all that much to publicity; but politicians really wanted secrecy. The voting public would not look kindly upon a drug or alcohol abuser running the affairs of state. So far, with a great deal of trouble, Noah had been reasonably successful in keeping the politicians' visits a secret; only twice had the identity of a political inmate leaked out. One had been defeated in the next election, while the second, pleading born-again status, had been reelected handily.

As if some psychic emanation had sped halfway across the nation, Noah's outside phone rang, breaking his concentration on the piece of paper in his hand.

"Dr. Breckinridge," Noah said into the receiver.

"Yes, Dr. Breckinridge, this is Governor Stoddard." The voice was subdued, with little of the confident resonance Noah remembered hearing the few times he had listened to the governor speak. "I spoke with your director earlier today."

Noah suppressed a sigh. "Yes, Governor. Mr. Hanks informed me of your call and your intentions."

"He told me to consult you regarding entering The Clinic without being recognized."

"That can usually be arranged, if you follow

19

instructions carefully."

"I am in your hands, Doctor, and I promise my full cooperation."

That will be the day, Noah thought. Aloud, he said, "First, which members of your family will know about your being here?"

"None, absolutely none. You must understand my situation, Doctor. I'm up for reelection three months from now. I will be candid with you. I have brains enough to realize that I can no longer control my consumption of alcohol, and that I might get drunk while campaigning, make a fool of myself and blow the election."

"That is commendable of you," Noah said in a dry voice. He was getting a double dose of candor today. "But that still doesn't tell me why you aren't informing a relative. You do have a family, as I recall."

"A wife and three children, and I love them dearly, yet I don't dare trust them. If they let anything slip, even inadvertently, it could mean the end of my political career."

"Governor, it is our firm policy that someone know of your presence here. While it is not a risk situation, accidents can happen. A heart attack, for instance. There must be someone we can notify if something should occur."

"My executive assistant will know, no one else. I trust him completely. If he lets word leak, I can, and will, fire his ass. A fact that he damned well knows."

"Very well, Governor, if that's the way you want to play it," Noah said slowly. He proceeded to advise the governor of the best means by which he could arrive at The Clinic unnoticed and unheralded.

Two

Susan Channing breezed into the kitchen without knocking and on into the atrium where Zoe Tremaine sat over a late breakfast. The birds in the hanging cages set up a great clatter, and Madam, the large, elegant Triton cockatoo, scolded angrily. Zoe caressed her feathers, calming her.

"Zoe, listen to who just checked into that place now!" Susan said in disgust as she waved a copy of the *Insider*.

Zoe knew what "that place" meant — they rarely called The Clinic anything else. She scowled at Susan affectionately. "Can't you even say good morning first?"

"Good morning, Zoe." Susan tossed the tabloid down on the table before Zoe, then poured herself a cup of coffee.

Making a face, Zoe picked up the tabloid as gingerly as if it had just been removed from one of her bird cages. "This scandal sheet! Why do you pay good money for it, Susan?"

"Because I naturally love gossip," Susan said cheerfully, sitting across the table from the older woman. "Read Cindy Hodges's column, 'Cindy's Scoops.'"

With a sigh, Zoe read aloud.

"Guess who checked into The Clinic this week, kiddies? Everybody's favorite movie goddess, Lacey Houston. According to my reliable source, our Lacey has been imbibing too heavily and having trouble with her pretty little nose. This same reliable insider told me that Lacey was about to start her latest flick, *Heartsong.* On the first day she was caught sniffing two lines of coke, and the director, Don Sparr, who won't stand still for such behavior on his pictures, swore that he would walk if she didn't straighten up. It seems she couldn't swing it on her own. Hence, The Clinic, where she is in the hands of that cute doctor, Noah Breckinridge . . ."

With a snort, Zoe threw the paper down. "Out and out garbage! I never could figure out how she, and her scandal sheet, escape being sued for libel."

"They have been, many times. It only increases the paper's circulation." Susan took a sip of coffee. "This time she happens to be telling the truth. I was driving past The Clinic on

Monday, and I had to stop as a white Rolls made a left turn in front of me, through the guard gate at the side entrance. It had to be Houston's. I've seen pictures of it. It sailed along the street like a big white yacht. Or a white whale, whichever you prefer."

"How does Hodges get her information?"

"Pays for it, I understand. Informants. This time she may have seen Lacey with her own eyes. Cindy's staying here, you know."

"Here? In Oasis?" Zoe Tremaine, the matriarch of the peaceful desert community, was surprised that she hadn't heard this bit of news earlier.

Susan nodded. "Yep. She seems to be making The Clinic her regular beat. You'll notice that she mentions it in almost every column. Apparently her readers are panting to hear which one of the rich and famous check in next for treatment."

"The idle rich providing diversion for idle minds."

"The arrival of Lacey Houston should be the occasion for a party, don't you think?" Susan asked casually. "On a scale of ten, for popularity, I'd think she should rate at least a nine."

"You're right, Susan!"

Of course, Zoe seldom needed a reason for a party. At the mention of one, she became animated. Not that she wasn't always full of energy,

Susan thought. Zoe was seventy, but didn't look a day over fifty. Behind the quiet elegance that she projected was a mind that worked faster and was more complex than people half her age.

Susan studied Zoe as the other woman gazed out at the swimming pool, shimmering in the heat. She was still an attractive woman with upswept gray hair and strong facial features. Zoe loved giving parties and was something of a social leader, if Oasis could be said to have one.

She was also something of a mystery, at least in regard to her past. She never talked about it, and as far as Susan, or anyone else in Oasis was concerned, Zoe's life might have begun fifteen years ago when she first came to town.

Susan had met Zoe only two years earlier, when she had attended a public meeting Zoe had arranged to discuss The Clinic. They found they had many things in common, beside their dislike of The Clinic, and had soon become fast friends. Susan recognized the fact that she looked upon the older woman as a surrogate mother, and she suspected that Zoe saw her as a surrogate daughter.

However, despite their deep bond of affection, Susan had never been able to isolate the exact reason for Zoe's deep hatred of The Clinic. Susan opposed it because her father had been instrumental in having The Clinic built, and Otto Channing corrupted everything that he touched. The rest of Zoe's followers thought that The Clinic demeaned the town of Oasis, brought in an undesirable element and thrust their city into notoriety through too much media attention. Also, there had been a couple of bad incidents. Once, a male patient had escaped The Clinic; higher than a kite on smuggled drugs, he had raped a woman. The second time, a female patient had slipped out of The Clinic and committed suicide by throwing herself in front of a speeding car on Broadway, one of the town's main streets.

Zoe shared all these feelings, yet Susan had a hunch that there was more to the older woman's dislike of The Clinic, much more. . . .

"I think I'll invite this Hodges person to the party," Zoe said, breaking Susan's thoughts. Her eyes had that mischievous twinkle that the younger woman had always associated with her own peers until she met Zoe. "That should spice up the stew, don't you think?"

"More than spice," Susan said gravely. "Having her there is likely to burn a few tongues."

"All to the good. A good party must have the proper mix or it becomes dull as dishwater."

"Maybe I should show her the pictures I took Monday of Lacey Houston's white Rolls."

Zoe arched an eyebrow in surprise. "You took pictures?"

Susan nodded. "Not that I believe for a minute that Houston would mind. But others would, can't you see, Zoe? If I stood outside The Clinic with my trusty camera and snapped pictures of some of those patients trying to sneak in unnoticed, it might discourage others."

Zoe shook her head. "Harassment, girl. That's about all it would amount to."

"Well, even so, if it only discourages a few, it will be a victory for our side."

Zoe looked at Susan thoughtfully. Archetypal California golden girl. Tall, athletic, sun-streaked blond hair, blue eyes – the works. Yet, despite her good looks, there was a bright intelligence behind the pretty face, unlike so many of the airheaded beach girls Zoe had encountered. Susan was serious, dedicated, and at twenty-four, very much on her own. Estranged from her father since the death of her mother four years earlier, she had yet to find a direction for her life. She had plans to become a professional photographer, but so far she had done little more than play at it. When Zoe's campaign against The Clinic had heated up, Zoe found that she needed a secretary to handle correspondence, and she had employed Susan. She was inordinately fond of the girl. She reminded Zoe so much of . . .

Zoe winced at the thought and directed her attention at Susan, who was speaking again.

"If Cindy Hodges does come to your party,

Zoe, maybe I *can* interest her in using some of the pictures in her column. That should cause a flap!"

"Do what you think best, dear. Heaven knows I'm for anything that would damage that place, but that won't close it down, and that's what I want to see." She smiled slightly as a blue jay flew overhead, scolding something on the roof. The jay reminded Zoe of Mayor Charles Washburn. "I think I'll invite the mayor. He's always scolding me about my opposition to that place, and a little scolding always puts me on my mettle."

"How about Dick Stanton?"

"Of course! What would a party be without Dickie? Besides, his feelings would be hurt if he couldn't help plan it." Zoe took a long thin cigar from a tin on the table by her elbow — Cuban panatelas smuggled in at great expense. She lit it — her first of the day. "And I was thinking . . . The only person from the Clinic I've ever had at a party of mine is the director. What's-his-name, Hanks? And he's such a pompous ass, it's no fun to poke at him. The most important doctor there, I suppose, is this Noah Breckinridge that Hodges mentioned in her column. I think I'll see if I can get to come."

"Well, Hodges says he's cute. Of course, I've never met her. She may think any male under the age of sixty is cute."

28

"I'll invite him and we'll see." Zoe's laughter was hoarse, raspy, from age, cigars and other abuses. "It should make for an interesting mix."

Jeffrey Lawrence read the column over breakfast at the Beverly Hilton Hotel. He read it with interest, especially the bit about Lacey Houston. Jeffrey always read Cindy's column, no matter where he was. She detailed the doings and the whereabouts of the celebrities, and Jeffrey had a vital interest in the movements of the famous and wealthy.

Jeffrey was a jewel thief by profession; if not the best, certainly *one* of the best. Now in his early forties, he had been a professional thief most of his adult life. He had never served a day in jail, had never even been arrested, which had to say something for his skills at his chosen profession.

He had four unbreakable rules: never be greedy; never do a job until the money from the last one was almost gone; never use the same MO twice; and never steal from anyone who couldn't afford the loss — which was the reason he confined his activities to the rich. Jeffrey liked to think that these rules were responsible for his success and for the fact he'd never been arrested.

Jeffrey Lawrence wasn't his real name, of course. He always changed names, complete with a full set of forged identification papers, after each job. At the moment, he was strapped for money. The last job, the theft of the jewels of a Beverly Hills socialite, had gone sour at the last minute; or at least the vibes had been all wrong, and he had backed off. Jeffrey trusted his instincts, and they had yet to fail him. He always planned things so that he had enough money to finance his next job. But because the last one had not gone down, he had only a few dollars left. He needed to find a banker, which was something he hated to do. If he was bankrolled, he was in hock, obligated before the caper even began to roll. But this time, he had no choice.

He read the item in the *Insider* again. There was no mention of Lacey's jewels. It wasn't necessary; it was there between the lines. Everybody who followed Lacey Houston's career knew that she never went anywhere without her jewels. Jeffrey recalled a comic's line in a Vegas show. "Lacey never even goes to the john without her sparklers."

Jeffrey had read various estimates as to the jewels' worth; from two million all the way up to five. A pleasant tingle sped down his spine and his adrenaline began to pump.

He called for the check, paid it and went outside to the taxi rank. Cab fare was out of sight in Los Angeles, Jeffrey knew; it would almost empty his pockets to cab it to Hollywood. But he'd be damned if he would ride a bus. Jeffrey Lawrence always went in style.

Twenty minutes later, he got out of the cab at Hollywood and Vine. He walked east for a few blocks, then suddenly stopped at one of the stars set in the sidewalk. Lacey Houston. He laughed aloud, traced the letters with his toe, then walked on. Was this a good omen? He wasn't superstitious, yet he knew that a man's luck was important. More than once a turn of luck had saved his ass.

After another few blocks, he turned left onto a grungy side street and stopped before a small storefront. The glass was so grimy that the contents of the window were scarcely visible — a display of rings, watches and other pieces of cheapjack jewelry. A small sign over the entrance to the shop announced Bernie's: Jewelry Bought and Sold.

As Jeffrey pushed the door open, a cowbell clanged over the door. The store was crowded to overflowing with glass cases, which looked as if they hadn't been dusted for years. The items on display, Jeffrey knew, were all pawned, cheap stuff, nothing more than a hundred dollars, although Bernie would charge whatever he could get, depending on the gullibility of the buyer. Bernie kept all the good stuff under lock and key in the back, and it was only for sale to special customers on his list.

Jeffrey heard a wheezing sound coming from

the rear, behind the dingy curtains hanging over a doorway. Bernie Kastle soon emerged from the back. Bernie always reminded Jeffrey of Sidney Greenstreet at his most sinister. He was enormously fat, his face as round as a pumpkin and about the same color, but somehow menacing for all that; and he had the same wheezing laugh Greenstreet had often displayed in his roles as a villain.

Bernie was a pawnbroker, but more importantly, he was a fence, one of only three in the country with whom Jeffrey did business.

Now Bernie saw him and smiled widely. "My boy! It's good to see you."

"Hello, Bernie."

Bernie's eyes, buried deeply in fat, were as shrewd as a ferret's. "Business or pleasure, my boy?"

"Business, Bernie."

Bernie wheezed a sigh. "Always business. Nobody ever comes to see old Bernie to chat about the good old days," he said mournfully.

"Now, Bernie, you know you wouldn't have it any other way," Jeffrey said with a grin.

Without responding, Bernie waddled to the front door, locked it and turned the cardboard sign around to say Closed for Lunch.

"It's a little early for lunch, isn't it?" Jeffrey commented.

"My regular people know it means a deal is

going down and I don't care to be disturbed. As for the others, to hell with 'em. Besides —" he patted his huge belly "—I eat out of a paper sack. Cottage cheese and yogurt. I'm on a diet."

"You've been dieting ever since I've known you, Bernie."

"I'm a determined man, my boy."

With a wide beckoning gesture, Bernie waddled toward the back, pushing through the curtain. Jeffrey followed, into an untidy room. The only thing that showed any care was a large vault built into one wall, the steel gleaming in the dim light.

Bernie pushed some boxes off a straight chair and went over to sit sideways at an ancient rolltop desk, whose pigeonholes were crammed to bursting with papers.

As Jeffrey sat down, Bernie dry-washed his plump hands, his small brown eyes glittering with greed. "Well, boy, what do you have for me this time?"

"Nothing right now, I'm afraid. The hit I was planning went sour before I'd even moved. It didn't have the right smell."

"Always the cautious one, huh, boy?"

"That's why I've never spent time in the slammer, Bernie."

"Well, I'm sorry to hear it went sour on you." The fat man sighed. "Then what's this about?

You mentioned business."

"I'm thin in the pocket. Flat, to be truthful. I need some backing on a new scenario I have in mind."

Bernie arched a pale eyebrow. "That's a switch. You've never come to me for money before."

"I've never found it necessary before."

"I might be able to accommodate you, but I'll need a few details. First off, how much are we talking about here?"

"I figure forty thousand should set me up."

"Forty thou!" Bernie wheezed. "This is a big one."

"If I bring it off."

"Who's the mark?"

Jeffrey hesitated. Bernie Kastle was honest, within his concept of the word. And he was closemouthed. He had been arrested once in New York for fencing and had served time, but he had never made a deal with the cops. And he always, as far as Jeffrey knew, gave an honest count on fenced goods. Still . . .

"I trust you, boy," Bernie said. "You're the best in the business. But you can't expect me to back a caper completely blind. I have to at least know the target."

Jeffrey took a deep breath. "Lacey Houston."

"The movie broad!" Bernie whistled. "She's got the stuff, there's no denying that. But

34

there's such a thing as being too visible. I understand she never lets the goods out of her sight. Lifting from her would be like stealing the crown off the queen of England during the coronation ceremony!"

"I'm sure I can do it," Jeffrey said steadily.

Bernie stared at him. "Well, it would be a hell of a score." His laughter wheezed. "Probably put you in *The Guinness Book of Records*, boy. And maybe it's best I don't know too much about it. What kind of a time frame are we talking about here?"

Jeffrey thought for a moment. "Three weeks, maybe a month."

"Seeing as the odds are stacked against you, I'm going to have to stick you with a stiff vigorish."

"How much?"

"Ten percent. Per week, boy."

Jeffrey was outraged. "Shit, Bernie, that's highway robbery!"

A wheezing chuckle worked its way past Bernie's diaphragm. "That's the sort of business we're in, ain't it?"

"Bernie, if it does take me a full month, I'd be owing you nearly sixty grand!"

"Good with figures, ain't you, boy? And that comes off the top, before we dicker over the goods. Look at it from where I sit. It's a high-risk caper you've got here."

35

"That's right. If I don't score, you may never get it."

"That's why the stiff vigorish, and I'll get it, boy, sooner or later. You're about the best there is. You'll make a big score. If not this time, the next."

"If I get caught, there may not be another time." Now why did I say that, Jeffrey thought as a chill coursed through him.

"Oh, you won't get caught. You're the cautious type, remember?" Bernie's eyes suddenly went cold and hard. "You'd better not get caught, boy. I may not be able to collect from you personally, but I've got friends in almost every joint in the country who would be happy to do me a little favor. Keep that in mind while you're spending the forty."

Back in his room at the Hilton, forty thousand in cash in his pocket, Jeffrey put in a call to The Clinic. When it went through, he asked to speak to Dr. Noah Breckinridge.

While he waited for the doctor to come on the line, Jeffrey underwent a startling change. He had once taken acting lessons for a year, something that had allowed him to adopt different personas in the pursuit of his profession. A teacher had said to him, "With your looks, the way you walk, the way you carry yourself and wear clothes, that voice of yours, plus your natural acting ability, you should definitely take up acting as a career. It's a tough life, and you need the breaks, but I'm convinced that you could make it."

Jeffrey had toyed with the idea, but in the end he had discarded it. He liked what he was doing, was candid enough with himself to admit that he was hooked on the danger and excitement of it. However, his acting ability was a handy talent in his profession.

As he waited to connect with the doctor, he began to tremble, his hand shaking so badly that he could hardly hold the phone. With his free hand he scratched himself. Even in his mind he became an alcoholic, desperate for a drink, just this side of delirium tremens. . . .

"Hello. This is Dr. Breckinridge."

In a high scratchy voice, Jeffrey said, "Doctor, I am an alcoholic. I know that this is very short notice, but I'm desperate. I must be admitted to The Clinic. . . ."

Todd Remington read the Hodges's column without a great deal of interest, his gaze blurred by the drinks he'd had before noon. He had met Lacey Houston a couple of times during the past few years, had once even been considered for a part in one of her movies, but he didn't really know her. He doubted that anyone knew Lacey well. After twenty-five years in pictures, moving with the Hollywood crowd, he had learned that the truly beautiful woman had few intimate friends. Lovers, yes, but few friends. There was something about great beauty that rebuffed friendship.

But then he didn't feel sorry for Lacey, not even for the fact that she was checking into The Clinic. She could damned well afford it. Rem was also going to The Clinic, but he could *not* afford it. He was in hock up to his eyebrows, and had had to borrow the eight thousand to pay for a month at The Clinic. There were other, cheaper alcohol treatment centers he could have gone to, of course. But The Clinic might be a shot at stopping a career on the long slide into oblivion. A long shot, granted, but worth trying, to Rem's present soggy way of thinking.

At the very least, he should get some publicity out of it. Maybe even a paragraph in Cindy Hodges's column, he thought sardonically. In earlier days, any mention at all in a scandal sheet like the *Insider* was anathema; and any smudge on a star's private *or* public life could mean an abrupt end to a career, or temporary exile, as had been the case with Robert Mitchum and marijuana, Ingrid Bergman and infidelity.

Nowadays, Rem couldn't seem to get *any* publicity, no matter what he did; probably his death would rate only a line or two in the obituary column of the *Los Angeles Times*.

For fifteen years, Todd Remington had ridden high in the saddle, the star of Western after Western. Rem had the lean, leathery look of the cowboy, and such roles had been tailor-made for him. The sudden demise of the Western had ended all that. Some of his colleagues had gone on to other types of roles; Rem hadn't been able to hack it. Other Western stars had retired to ranches and lived off shrewd investments made in their heyday. One had even gone into politics. But Rem had spent the money as fast as he had earned it, and he couldn't afford to retire. During the past ten years, he had scratched out a living any way he could, even resorting to earning a few dollars as an extra, but even those days were pretty well over. The costs of filmmaking had really escalated and producers were employing fewer extras; mob scenes were mainly in the past. So he made a buck here and there — and drank, drank to forget. The trip to the bottom of the bottle was endless.

After his last big drunk, Rem had regained consciousness in a hospital, and the doctors had warned him that he had one choice left to make — stop drinking or die.

Once out of the hospital, he found that he couldn't stop on his own. The thought of simply drinking himself to death crossed his mind, but whatever else he might be, Rem wasn't a quitter.

He scrambled around for money, straining old

friendships and getting a second mortgage on the last piece of property he owned, a run-down horse ranch just outside of Thousand Oaks. He finally scraped together enough to pay the fees at The Clinic. If the treatment was successful and he managed to get a little publicity out of it, maybe, just maybe, it could catch some producer's eye and he would be given a second chance. He wasn't thinking of a lead, not anymore, but he would be more than content to have a shot at a character role, like a Walter Brennan part. All he needed was a goddamn chance!

He refused to think about what would happen if he spent all his money at The Clinic and nothing happened.

Dick Stanton read Cindy Hodges's piece sitting in Zoe's kitchen, over a cup of coffee and a cigarette. Finished, he snorted and sat back, looking at Zoe across the table out of brown eyes as innocent as a babe's. "I'll bet this Cindy Hodges is a real bitch, love."

Zoe drew on her thin cigar and gave a noncommittal shrug. "Perhaps, perhaps not." Her lips curved with faint amusement. "Not all successful women are bitches, Dickie."

"Anyone who peddles dirt to get that success is."

Zoe smiled at him tolerantly. Dick Stanton was a pale thin man of forty-two, as lean and tense as a whippet, and a bundle of energy when it came to anything but his writing. Once a very successful novelist, Dick had fallen on bad times. Nowadays, he had to psyche himself up to write even a few paragraphs, which always ended up in the wastebasket.

Zoe had never even been able to understand how one man could make love to another; but, as she often said in her blunter moments, "I never knock anybody's transportation." Of course, in the old days, she had felt that such relationships were a threat to her financially.

However, she did like Dick Stanton. He was a good and loyal friend, he was amusing, and he was an ardent convert to her cause. He had candidly confessed his reason for opposing The Clinic. During the years of his success as a writer, he had enjoyed a beautiful relationship with his roommate in San Francisco, but when he encountered writer's block, or whatever it was that had choked off his creative juices, he had started to drink heavily. This continued for three years until Dick was a stone alcoholic. Meanwhile, the relationship with his lover deteriorated, until one day, the roommate simply moved out.

Dick had moved to Oasis after that, and he had stopped drinking. He was still sober, yet he had to battle daily with the urge, and he was absolutely terrified that he would one day start drinking again and end up in some place like The Clinic. It held all the horrors of an insane asylum for him.

"But this party of yours, that turns me on." Dick got up to prowl the kitchen restlessly, his lean face aglow. "I like the mix at your parties, love. They sometimes remind me of all your birds." He swept a slim hand around. "When one of them gets upset and starts squawking, soon they're all yodeling. The only difference is they can't get at each other like your guests." His face lit with a mischievous grin. "Wouldn't it be a kick to have your guests all caged up sometime and listen to them yawp in frustration? Some of those people can't talk unless they're right in your face, within easy spitting distance."

"Now, don't be catty, Dick."

Dick was quite familiar with the widespread belief that gay men liked to have an older, motherly woman for a close friend. Like so many clichéd beliefs, there was an element of truth in this one, but Dick had managed to escape the trap. And, although now a close friend of this woman, he figured he had still escaped it. By no stretch of the imagination could Zoe Tremaine be called motherly! Beneath the elegant exterior was the calculating heart of a shrewd business-woman.

He had told Zoe most of his secrets, yet one he still hugged to himself. While it was true that most of the writing he did now was worthless, fit only to be shredded the instant it left the typewriter, he did keep a journal into which he scribbled from time to time – thumbnail sketches of the people he met, friends or not – and these sketches he retained. For what reason, he wasn't quite sure.

Zoe was one of his favorite characters.

Woman of mystery. Never talks about her past. Could have been born a hundred years ago, a month ago, yesterday. One senses a deep tragedy. Yet she has a rich, bawdy, ironic sense of humor, a keen eye for the ridiculous. A strong face, almost masculine in its strength, with the eyes of a hunting falcon, undimmed by age. In another time, could have been a monarch, ruling with an iron hand. A queen for the ages. No pun intended.

Now Zoe said, "I'm thinking of adding to the mix, inviting Otto Channing."

Dick's gaze sharpened. "Susan's father? You know how much she hates the man."

"That makes it that much more explosive, wouldn't you say?"

Dick shook his head. "Sometimes, Zoe, I think you're the queen of malice."

"Not so. Susan can easily avoid Otto – it's a

big house. And she must learn to deal with unpleasant situations. I think I'll invite all three of the unholy triumvirate, so we can all take potshots at them. Channing, Mayor Washburn and our dear chief of police, should add an interesting element to the party."

Billie Reaper read his copy of the *Insider* in his room in the detox section of The Clinic. He had bribed an attendant into smuggling in copies of both Hollywood trade papers and the *Insider*. So far, he hadn't been able to arrange a fix of any other kind in the damn place, but at least he could have his show business gossip.

He read the Lacey Houston item with interest. So, she was in this gilded cage with him. He had never met the fabled Lacey — they traveled in different circles — but he had seen her flicks. Despite the fact that she was no spring chicken, she was a foxy lady, enough to make a man's blood boil. And it seemed they shared a little something in common, after all. Cocaine. Billie wondered if she snorted, freebased or shot it right into the vein.

He shivered. Shit, what he'd give for some crack right now, dreaming on the water pipe, waiting for that incredible rush. The rush from the needle was far better than snorting or freebasing, better than coming with any lady he had ever banged; but he was spooked by the needle – the search for a vein, the pain of the needle prick, and the drawing of blood. Besides, he knew that a guy could pick up all kinds of diseases from the needle – hepatitis, strep infections, even blood poisoning and AIDS. When he was in a group, he snorted – it was the "in" way, for socializing; but when he was alone, Billie always freebased.

He moved restlessly on the bed, wanting nothing so much as to break the hell out. Man, it was just like being in the slammer. He'd awakened in the place three mornings ago, with little memory of how he'd gotten there. At the first opportunity, he had made a dash for the door. It had taken two guards and a hypo in the arm to subdue him.

When he'd come to the second time, he was in this room, steel mesh on the door and the window and a dead bolt that was shut every time someone came or went. They'd been giving him Valium daily, or some shit, which was about as much help as pissing on a burning building.

During the past two days, Billie, with the help of his manager, had gradually pieced together the events that had brought him to The Clinic. He had been appearing at an outdoor rock festival at Irvine Meadows, along with four other groups, and the Reaper fans in the audience had gone totally apeshit when Billie took hold of the microphone.

If Billie had appeared first, the whole thing probably would never have happened. But he was third on the bill, and by that time, he had crashed. Through experience, Billie had devised a workable routine for a concert — sniff a couple of lines of coke about fifteen minutes prior to going onstage. The rush usually lasted from fifteen to thirty minutes. But on this occasion, the time schedule was screwed up, and it was almost an hour before Billie and his group were called. By that time, he was crashing, plunging into depression, down, down. . . .

He had a couple of jolts of vodka, which usually helped when he began to crash. But not this time. He simply couldn't go out and perform. Billie knew that the drummer mainlined coke, and as much as he feared and detested the needle, he needed the jolt. Two minutes before they were to go onstage, the drummer stuck a needle into Billie's arm and shot the white magic straight into the bloodstream.

The rush was just beginning when Billie strode to the mike, walking ten feet high, on top of the world, the welcoming screams of the kids out there giving him an extra high.

He began to sing, handling the guitar as though it were an extension of his body, and the kids in the audience rocked and swayed with him. Then he was really into it, his voice soaring high over the heads of the crowd. He was up there also, riding his guitar like Slim Pickens riding the nuclear warhead in the movie, *Dr. Strangelove.*

Somewhere in there he lost all memory, since the next thing he knew was that he was in The Clinic. His manager, Joe Devlin, helped piece together the missing parts for him. It seemed that Billie had hallucinated, leaping right off the platform, truly crashing, and would have been badly injured if the fans hadn't been so tightly packed together that they cushioned his fall. Billie had been unhurt, but one fan suffered a broken arm, another a concussion, and both were suing the shit out of him, according to Devlin. It had been Devlin who had checked him in to The Clinic. Billie had already decided to fire his ass, once he was free of the place.

Devlin claimed that Billie was totally dependent on cocaine. He was a drug abuser, at age twenty. Not only was he endangering his health, he was putting his career in jeopardy. Another episode like that one at Irvine Meadows and he was finished.

All according to Joe Devlin. And all total bullshit, according to Billie Reaper. He could handle anything. He had handled the sudden fame, the big money, the ready supply of broads, hadn't he? He could handle the coke, as well. Dammit, he needed a boost to get him up for a performance. Nobody understood that but another performer. To perform at the pitch of frenzy demanded by his fans, Billie needed an upper.

But it looked as if he was in here for the duration. Devlin had shown him the papers, the admittance forms with Billie Reaper's signature on them.

With a shrill laugh, he reached over to thumb the call button to summon someone from the floor. They wouldn't give him anything, but at least he could hassle them a little, relieve the boredom.

Suddenly he thought of one of the nurses he'd seen once or twice. Kathy something or other. Nice tits and ass.

Billie began to grin lasciviously, rubbing himself. Maybe he could get a hand up under her starched skirt. He couldn't be too far gone if he still desired sex.

Governor William Stoddard read the *Insider* item in a diner thirty miles from Oasis. Someone had left the tabloid in the booth.

The governor had been nipping steadily on a thermos of chilled Jack Daniel's since they'd left the Los Angeles International Airport. A few miles back, Reed had finally commented on his employer's behavior. "I know you can handle the juice pretty well, Governor, but I would suggest that you take it easy. I don't think it would look

48

too good for you to check into that place drunk."

Stoddard had grunted. "Bobbie, I'm going into this place for a month while they dry me out, and there sure as hell won't be any booze in there. So get off my back, okay?"

"I'm thinking of you, Governor. You do have an image to maintain, and I happen to think you should be halfway sober when checking into the treatment center. Must I remind you that this whole thing was your idea?"

"Sorry, Bobbie. I didn't mean to sound sharp with you." Stoddard looked with affection at the short, dumpy man at the wheel of the rented Ford. It was hard to believe by looking at him that Bobbie Reed had the finest mind of any man Stoddard had ever known, and a political sense that was uncanny. Stoddard was willing to give credit when deserved, and he knew without the slightest doubt that he would not be governor of his state without Bobbie Reed's guidance. "Bobbie, you know how much I've been drinking these past few months? A quart a day."

Reed gave him a startled look. "That much? Damn, I never realized."

"Well, it's true. That's why I decided that I had to dry out, had to get off the sauce completely. It's going to be a rough campaign this fall, you said that yourself. I've never been comfortable campaigning. It's boring as hell, and when I get bored, I turn to Jack Daniel's for comfort."

Reed swung out to pass a slow-moving truck. When he moved back into the right-hand lane, he was frowning. "I'm still worried about this, Governor. A whole month. That's a long time for you to be out of touch. People are going to wonder."

"Let them wonder. The state legislature is home for three goddamned months! I haven't had a real vacation for the whole of my term. I deserve a month to myself. A mountain cabin, hunting, fishing." He grinned fleetingly. "Chopping wood, like the President. Hell, Myra and the kids swallowed it. There'll be no important bills to sign.

"And if there is an emergency, you know where I am, and I'll be talking to you almost every day. This Dr. Breckinridge at The Clinic said that I'd have a private line to use, and any call from you will come directly to me, not through a switchboard. Think about it this way, buddy." He touched Reed on the shoulder. "In a way, you'll be governor for a whole month. Doesn't that kind of turn you on?"

"No way," Reed said with an emphatic shake of his head. "I'm perfectly happy being what I am, helping you in any way I can."

"Well, you've helped me a hell of a lot, in case I haven't told you lately. Help me through this rough spot and I'll owe you yet another one."

Stoddard brooded on the thermos in his lap. Suddenly he rolled down the window, ignoring the blast of hot air, and upended the thermos, dumping out the rest of the whiskey. Then he rolled the window back up, corked the container and tossed it onto the back seat. "Maybe they can dry me out good in The Clinic and teach me to stay that way. Let's stop at the next truck stop, Bobbie, and pour some black coffee into me."

And that was where he had found the *Insider*. Waiting for their coffee, he leafed through it idly. It was the first copy of the scandal sheet he'd looked at in years. Reed screened all his reading matter, and the rag wasn't on the list. Then, just as he lifted his coffee cup to his mouth, Stoddard froze, his gaze riveted on Cindy Hodges's column and the mention of The Clinic.

He had encountered the woman before, when he was running for governor. She was just starting with the paper and had been assigned to cover his campaign. She had a sharp tongue, a vicious, slashing writing style, and the true scandalmonger's nose for dirt. She had been like a mosquito, buzzing around him, occasionally stinging. After a while, he had tried to ignore her, but the woman was impossible to ignore. Later, Stoddard had decided that it had been hatred at first sight. Maybe it wasn't mutual, maybe she used that vitriolic typewriter on everyone, but he sure as hell despised her.

He started to mention the column to Reed, then changed his mind and drank his coffee. Reed was concerned enough about the stay in The Clinic as it was. And this Dr. Breckinridge has assured Stoddard that if he followed instructions to the letter, no one would ever learn of his presence in The Clinic. He was registered under a false name, the car was rented under yet another false name, but only two people at The Clinic knew his real identity: Dr. Breckinridge and the director. It was certainly not to their advantage to leak word that Governor William Stoddard was a guest there.

Stoddard smiled slightly. If the electorate ever found out that he had used a false identity, he would probably lose some votes, but that was the least of his concerns. Cindy Hodges, she was the one he had to watch out for. If *she* found out, then the game was over. His political career, maybe even his marriage, would have to be sacrificed.

Three

Cindy Hodges scooped up the ringing phone. "Hello?"

"Cindy Hodges?"

"Who is this?"

"This is Zoe Tremaine. Perhaps you don't know who I am. . . ."

Cindy's brain clicked like a computer. She never forgot a name; it was part of her job. "Oh, yes, Miss Tremaine, I know who you are. We've never met, however."

A husky laugh sounded on the line. "I hope to remedy that. I'm giving a little party this Friday evening, and I would like to invite you. This is short notice, I realize, and you may not be free."

"For a Tremaine party, I will see to it that I *am* free."

The husky laugh again. "I am indeed flattered, Miss Hodges. Cocktails are at six, and a buffet dinner will be served at eight."

"I will be there, Miss Tremaine, and thank you for inviting me."

As Cindy hung up, her mind totaled up the few facts she knew about Zoe Tremaine. Independently wealthy, something of an eccentric, the social lioness of Oasis, an ardent opponent of The Clinic. Also, there was something of a mystery, it seemed, about her past. Cindy loved mysteries involving people, important people. Solving them often made good copy for her column.

She shivered suddenly in the chill of the air conditioning. She had just stepped out of the tub when the phone rang. Cindy had decided only three months ago to spend a part of every year in Oasis, and had recently purchased a condominium there. Eventually, she would have a telephone installed in the bathroom so she wouldn't have to run to answer it every time it rang. She had an answering machine, although she never switched it on when she was at home. Much of her material came from telephone tips, and she had learned early that a great many tipsters were spooked by answering machines, and refused to leave a message, or to call back.

Cindy started toward the bathroom, which was still warm and steamed from her bath. She detested the furnace heat of Oasis in the summer, yet she had found The Clinic to be such a rich source of material for her column that she had recognized the value of establishing a base in Oasis, for at least a few months out of the year. Thank God all the buildings were air-coditioned!

In the bathroom, she wiped the full-length mirror clear of steam and examined herself in it. She was rather pleased with what she saw: tall, slender, with long, lustrous black hair — her best feature — and cool gray eyes. She kept herself in good shape, swimming every day, tennis, a workout at a gym at least once a week. Not bad for someone of thirty-five, she thought, winking at her reflection in the mirror.

Cindy knew that most men found her distant and somewhat cold, and while that turned some men off, it challenged others. She usually had her pick of escorts.

Shrugging into a robe, she went into the small room she used for an office, clicked on her word processor and sat down at it. She had to finish next week's column and have a courier service pick it up in the morning.

Yet she sat for a moment, thinking of something else. Should she dig up an escort for the Tremaine party? She didn't know many available males in Oasis as yet, perhaps a half dozen. She quickly ran down the list in her head, discarding them one by one.

To hell with it! She would go alone. If Tremaine has the right mix at her party, Cindy thought, maybe I can meet an attractive, interesting man. The decision made, she reached for the stack of file cards by the word processor. The cards contained scribbled notes. Now all she had to do was weed out all but the juicier ones, put them together in her chatty style and fill her column.

She felt a sense of power, like a sexual surge, as she began to transcribe some of the names onto the glowing screen. The names represented famous and powerful people, and yet, by just the use of her fingertips, she, Cindy Hodges, could manipulate them at will.

As he returned to his office from an afternoon session with Billie Reaper, Noah was seething. The rock star was a compulsive liar; he was tricky, vicious, and he refused to admit that he was a cocaine addict, refused to even admit that he was in any way dependent on the drug. He did admit to freaking out at the concert, but he put it all off to stress and overwork. He refused to cooperate at all. If Noah was to follow his inclinations, his instincts, he would discharge Billie as incurable or, at the very least, turn him over to another doctor to handle. Yet Noah was stubborn by nature, especially when it came to a patient. He had encountered difficult patients before – although none as impossible as Billie Reaper – and he had stuck it out, usually successfully.

And yet, the pity of it was, Noah was convinced that even if he succeeded in getting through to Billie, the kid would be back on cocaine within days of his discharge. It had happened with others, even with some who desperately wanted to be cured. It was a discouraging aspect of his work. But Noah knew that if he didn't do everything he could, he would be disappointed with himself.

Recidivism was something he expected in his field. He could only give it his full effort and hope for the best.

Melancholy replacing his anger at Billie Reaper, Noah sighed and went around behind his desk. And then his anger flared up again when he spotted yet another memo waiting for him.

He snatched it up and read it.

Dr. Breckinridge,
Zoe Tremaine called and invited you to a party at her house this Friday evening, starting at six. Since you were unavailable to take her call, I accepted the invitation for you.

Sterling Hanks

Dammit to hell! Noah slammed the flat of his hand on the desk. Hanks had the gall of a burglar and none of the finesse when it came to

57

dealing with his staff.

Noah picked up the receiver and started to punch out the number of the director's office. Then he changed his mind and hung up. The phone wouldn't do; he had to face him directly.

Scooping up the memo, he rode the elevator up to the second floor, where Hanks's office was located. He paused at the receptionist's desk. "Anyone with him, Nancy?"

She looked startled at the anger in his voice. "No, Dr. Breckinridge, he's alone. But I don't think he wishes to be disturbed. . . ."

"Well, he's damned well going to be!"

Noah strode past her desk and opened the office door. Sterling Hanks was turned away from his desk, staring out the big picture window. The desert, beginning where the outskirts of Oasis abruptly ended, stretched away to the low treeless hills to the north.

The office was opulent, with the huge desk, custom-made chairs, a low couch and a gold carpet with ankle-high nap. The walls were papered with pictures of a smiling Hanks posing with various celebrities.

Those pictures are his medical certificates, Noah thought bitterly; the only ones he's qualified to possess.

At the sound of the door closing behind Noah, Hanks swiveled his chair around, a slight smile curving his thin lips when he saw who it was. "Well, Doctor, you look like a thunder-cloud about to rain on somebody." He made a steeple of his fingers and rested his dimpled chin on the apex. "Did we have an appointment?"

Noah was already striding across the room. He let the memo flutter to the desk before the director. "This is my appointment."

Hanks didn't even glance down. "Ah, yes, Miss Tremaine's party. I assumed you might be somewhat upset. But your girl told me that you were with a patient and left word not to be disturbed. So . . ." Hanks let his shoulders rise and fall. "I accepted the invitation for you."

"You had no right to do that. You may be The Clinic's director, but you're not my social director!"

"Anything having to do with The Clinic is my business."

Noah stared. "What the hell does this party have to do with The Clinic?"

"Try not to be naive, Doctor," Hanks said with a sigh. "This Tremaine person is a bitter foe of The Clinic."

"If that's true, why does she want one of us there?"

"Zoe Tremaine is known as an eccentric. She likes to have guests at her parties with opposite points of view. She seems to thrive on controversy. It will be your job at the party to present

59

us in the best light possible."

"A PR snow job, you mean," Noah growled. "That's your department, Hanks, not mine."

"She had me at her last party." Hanks's smile increased. "This time she wishes to have the famous Dr. Noah Breckinridge present. Evidently you are unaware of how your fame has spread."

"You didn't let me talk to her for fear that I'd turn her down."

"That thought crossed my mind, yes."

"Well, I'm not going," Noah said obstinately. "You accepted for me, now you can call and tell her I broke a leg. Tell her anything."

Hanks leaned forward, his voice turning hard. "Now you listen to me, Doctor. You *are* going to Tremaine's party. I put up with your maverick ways because you are valuable here, but there are limits."

"But why me? Why not one of the other doctors? They'd probably be delighted to go."

"Two reasons. First, because Miss Tremaine invited *you*. And secondly, because of your bedside manner."

"I told you, that's bullshit."

"Is it?" Hanks was smiling again, a smile tainted with secretive malice. "I must confess that I don't understand it, but I'm constantly being told by patients prior to graduation about the bedside manner of the marvelous Dr. Breckinridge. Apparently they then go forth from here and spread the word. Don't be modest, my dear doctor. You must be aware of how well-known you have become. You were even mentioned in 'Cindy's Scoops' in the *Insider* this week."

Noah sliced the air with the edge of his hand. "I never read that rag. It's garbage, pure crap."

"Perhaps it is, but it's also widely read, especially among the people who may someday need our services."

"Yeah. Celebrities, show business people."

Hanks held up a staying hand. "Now, please, Doctor, I would prefer not to hear that refrain again. Your feelings on that subject are well-known to me. I will remind you once more that these patients pay the freight, as the saying goes, for the other, less fortunate people who so engage your sympathy. Many treatment centers receive grants, or raise money through funding drives. Mr. Heinman himself told me that we must pay our way. The celebrities you claim to despise, and the attendant publicity, keeps us comfortably in the black."

"Heinman? How'd you manage that? I thought he only spoke to God."

Hanks wore a smug smile. "I am in Mr. Heinman's confidence, you may be sure."

"Good for you," Noah muttered. "Be that as it may, public relations is not my job."

"Public relations is the job of everyone who works here, all the way down to the cleaning people." Hanks steepled his hands again, probing the dimple in his chin with forefingers pressed together. "Attending this party does not interfere with your duties here. I would never ask you to do anything that takes you away from that. But you are going, Doctor. You know why? You have no choice."

"I do have a choice. I can . . ."

Hanks was nodding. "Resign your position here. There is always that alternative, but do you want that? This is your chosen field, and I am well aware of your dedication to it. I am sure you could find a position elsewhere. But what other treatment center can offer you the facilities we provide here? There are none even comparable, and I am sure you are well aware of that fact."

Noah was silent. Although it galled him to admit it, the director was right. Noah had considered leaving The Clinic any number of times, but when that happened, he also thought of the good he was doing here; and there was no place where he could make the kind of money he earned at The Clinic, although he liked to tell himself that was unimportant. Hanks was also correct in something else. Even if he, Noah, didn't care for most of the celebrity patients, they had the same right to rehabilitation as anyone else.

Hew felt suddenly weary. How many times had he had this argument with Sterling Hanks? Too many. And always Noah knew he was as loser going in.

"Well, Doctor? What is your decision?"

"You know very well what it is, Hanks," Noah said dully. "I'll attend your damned party."

Hanks beamed a smile at him. "Good, good! One more word of advice. Try not to let that thorny temper get out of control. Try to exercise your bedside manner, as you would with a difficult patient."

Noah turned away toward the door. As he reached for the doorknob, Hanks spoke again, as Noah had known he would. "Dr. Breckinridge?"

Sterling Hanks was what Noah thought of as a "last worder." In every confrontation, even a simple conversation, he always tried to maneuver himself into having the last word. Noah was strongly tempted to push on through the door as if he hadn't heard. Then he sighed and turned back, facing that smile. "Yes?"

"Look at it this way. The possibilities at the party might very well be to your liking. You might meet a beautiful young lady there. Who knows what that might lead to?" His smile became taunting as Noah's face tightened. "You should really get married. It doesn't become a doctor of your renown to have — what do they call it nowadays? — one-night stands. Oh, yes, I am aware of your sex life. There's very little I don't know about you, Doctor. I make it my business to know."

The unholy triumvirate was meeting — to discuss their invitations to Zoe Tremaine's party. All three were charter members of the Oasis Country Club, and as such, had the privilege of having lunch in the Green Room, a private dining room overlooking the sweep of lawn leading down to the golf course.

The three men at the table were a study in contrasts.

Otto Channing looked what he was — a promoter. He was in his fifties, had styled blond hair, an open face just beginning to show the ravages of dissipation, and guileless blue eyes. His manner was as smooth as butter, and he had an actor's ability to adopt a persona to fit the occasion. Right now he was unhappy, and since he was with friends, he could let it show.

Mayor Charles Washburn had the appearance of a beardless Santa Claus. He was short, with a protruding belly, a thatch of white hair and a round red face that was normally filled with smiling good cheer, just in the event a camera or a voter's eye caught him unaware. At the moment, he was glum.

Thad Darnell, Oasis's chief of police, was an even six foot, sinewy, with cold black eyes, a tough weathered face and black hair that didn't have a touch of gray. He had served in the marines for the full twenty years, joining Oasis's small police force immediately upon retirement. The police force had tripled in size during the years Darnell had been a member, and he had been its chief for the last five of those years. He kept himself in excellent physical condition, and his mind was as tough as his body.

He despised the two men in the room with him, yet they had tempted him and he had succumbed. He was as corrupt as they were, and he hated himself as much as he hated his partners. Greed, blind greed, had been his downfall.

He listened in stony silence as the two men bickered.

Mayor Washburn finished his bourbon in a gulp, short plump fingers digging a long brown cigar out of his pocket. He waved it in the air like a baton. "I don't know why I have to go to this damn woman's party, Otto."

"For the same reason I do, Charles, and I don't like it any more than you do."

"That still doesn't tell me why. Just so that blasted woman and her pinko liberal cohorts can pick at us, call us despoilers and exploiters. And all just because we allowed Karl Heinman to build The Clinic in Oasis. You'd think we had sold out or something."

Otto Channing watched the mayor snip off the end of his imported cigar and light it with loving care. He was such a damned whiner! And what a convenient memory he had. They *had* sold out. Channing knew that and had no qualms about it. In exchange for Washburn's wheedling the city council to steam roller a secret vote granting Karl Heinman the permit to build his clinic, Channing and the mayor had gotten an inflated price from the multimillionaire for the land.

That was only one deal in which Channing, the mayor and Thad Darnell had wheeled and dealed to their financial advantage, making all three relatively wealthy men. And the majority of the deals were on the shady side of legal. But the moment they were completed, the money divided up, Mayor Washburn conveniently forgot the illegal aspects. It somehow seemed to ease his spongy conscience.

Now Channing said smoothly, "If we don't attend, they'll think we're afraid to face them."

"Why should we be afraid of them? Bunch of do-gooders. Pests, that's all they are," Washburn said petulantly. "What I don't understand is what put the burr under their saddles in the first place."

"Well, there was the guy who escaped from

66

over there and raped the girl," Channing said. "And then the other time when a girl slipped out and threw herself under a car. That's around the time it all started. At least, that's when Zoe Tremaine got involved."

"That's just a handy excuse," Washburn responded. "Besides, what should she, or the others, care about a couple of freaky drug addicts? From the way she carries on, you'd think we had allowed a prison to be erected in Oasis, instead of a treatment center that does good for a lot of people."

"And also brings quite a bit of money into Oasis," Darnell said dryly.

The mayor turned on him. "And what's wrong with that, I'd like to know? Hell, ten years ago Oasis was nothing, a watering hole in the desert. Then Otto and I teamed up and started things stirring around here. Now people with money to spend have vacation and retirement homes here. And you . . ." He narrowed his eyes. "What are you complaining about? You've made a bundle for yourself."

"Oh, I can't deny that, Mayor," Darnell said in the same dry voice. "We're all in it together."

Channing was looking at him thoughtfully, a little surprised at such loquaciousness. Three words at a time was usually the limit for the chief. "Are you worried about something, Thad? Something we should know about?"

"Nothing you don't already know, Otto. And I'm not actually worried, but that clinic has always made me a little nervous. It's not like having a prison here, true, but some of the inmates don't have both oars in the water, else they wouldn't be there in the first place."

"I never knew you felt that way," Channing said slowly.

"That director assured me that there would be no recurrence of the kind of thing that happened before," Washburn said.

"Sterling Hanks is an asshole," Darnell said with a grunt. "And if it happened twice, it can happen again."

"I hope to hell you haven't been talking like that around other people," the mayor said nervously.

"I'm not a fool, Mayor. I know which side my bread is buttered on." Darnell stared at Otto Channing.

Channing returned the look for a moment, then was forced to glance away. He had noticed of late that the chief of police was getting itchy about something, but he had ignored it. After all, there was nothing the man could do; he was tied in with them. If he opened up to somebody, he would bring them all down together, and he was certainly not fool enough to do that. Channing admitted to himself that he was afraid of Thad Darnell; there was a vein of violence in the retired marine. Channing had seen that violence erupt on occasion, had seen suspects that Darnell had beaten into confessions.

Channing cleared his throat and said, "Well, we're getting off the subject here. We're all three invited to this party, and I think we should go. I'm certainly going, but it would be better if we presented a united front."

"Oh, I'll go, I'll go," Washburn said in a grumbling voice.

"Well, I'm not," Darnell said flatly. "I have no time for such nonsense, and I won't put myself in a position of ridicule from that bunch. You two go." His sardonic gaze switched from one man to the other. "You're the talkers. I'm not. I have a police force to run. Sure, I've given you guys a hand down over the years, and have been well paid for it, but I'm not paid to socialize with people I don't like."

Four

Zoe Tremaine had looked over a lot of property before she picked Oasis as the site for her retirement home.

Fifteen years ago, Oasis had barely been a spot on the map, with a population of about two thousand; mostly well-to-do retired people who valued their privacy and the peace and beauty of the desert. It was just what Zoe had been looking for.

Land was cheap then, and to ensure future privacy, Zoe had bought two acres, situated on a slight rise, with a beautiful view of the mountains to the west and the north.

She had her house built to fit her own desires and needs, supervising the construction from the ground up. With her usual thoroughness, she filled her mind with construction details and drove the contractors crazy. A day never passed that she didn't spend some time at the site. But her money was good, and she never quibbled over costs, so the various contractors put up with her interference.

When the house was finished, it was exactly what Zoe wanted. Sprawling over almost a half acre, it was built in the Spanish style, with thick stuccoed walls and a red tiled roof, to keep out the desert heat. A deep veranda circled the front and protected it against the sun's glare. The huge inner atrium, around which the house was built, was an oasis of its own. In the center was a large fountain, and bright Mexican tile covered the ground. Flowers and plants were everywhere; the special misters had cost a fortune, but they were necessary for the effect Zoe wished to sustain, and for her tropical birds.

The birds were Zoe's hobby and passion. Although each bird, or pair of birds, had its own ornate cage, Zoe often let one or two out at a time, for the atrium had a sturdy wire netting overhead. There were two golden conures, a yellow-naped Amazon, a redheaded Amazon, a pair of blue-front Amazons, and Zoe's favorite, Madam, the Triton cockatoo. She loved them as if they were her children.

Whenever Zoe gave a party, all the birds were kept caged, for the atrium was a favorite spot for party guests. It was right off the enormous party room, where the bar, pool table and entertainment center were located. There was also a large swimming pool on the east side of the house, situated there so it would be shaded in the late afternoon.

The house had been built with entertaining in mind. Although Zoe desired privacy — when *she* wanted it — she also enjoyed people, and loved to observe them.

It hadn't taken long for her to become known as the "hostess of Oasis." She provided nothing but the best liquor, the food was exquisitely catered, and she always invited an interesting mix of people.

Even before The Clinic became a matter of controversy in her life, she wasn't averse to inviting adversaries — their clashes provided a pleasant diversion. If a confrontation threatened to become a nasty scene, she would move in and break it up. She was good at that.

Although liquor was always plentiful, Zoe had one inflexible rule — no drugs provided and none used, not even marijuana. She would tolerate drunkenness to a certain degree, but if a guest became too loud or quarrelsome, out he or she went.

Although Susan Channing had her own small apartment, one of the four bedrooms at Zoe's was always available to her; and because she was helping with the preparations, she spent the night before the party there.

Susan, Zoe and Dick Stanton spent much of the day getting things ready. Dick was in his element, arranging flowers, flicking at an imaginary speck of dust here, another there, and generally harassing Juanita Romero, Zoe's housekeeper and cook. A widow, Juanita's age was as indeterminate as Zoe's. She didn't care for the hot rich spices of her native food, and was as thin as a rail. The Mexican woman was accustomed to Dick's heckling, and good-naturedly ignored him most of the time.

The caterers and the bartender arrived at five, and Susan and Zoe left Dick to zero in on these new targets, while they retired to shower and change into party clothes.

By the time Susan emerged from the bedroom wearing a cool white off-the-shoulder dress, adorned with one large red rose at the neckline, a few early guests had arrived. Since they were compatriots of Zoe's in the good fight, Susan knew all of them. She took a glass of white wine from the bar and circulated, saying her hellos. The ages of the people varied; from young people willing to join enthusiastically into any fight, to the retired people of the community who were opposed to The Clinic because it disturbed the quiet tenor of the lives they had envisioned for themselves when they had moved to Oasis.

Susan was talking to one of the older couples in a corner of the living room when she saw Zoe, looking regal in red, greet a newcomer, a casually dressed young man with a strong face and unruly hair. The face wasn't familiar to Susan, but she liked it.

Excusing herself to the older couple, she casually worked her way into the party room and over to the bar, where Zoe had led the new arrival. Susan stood at Zoe's elbow, studying the stranger. There was an air of competence about him, and she had noticed that he moved with an athletic grace. His face was set in a scowl, and she could almost feel his displeasure at being there. A reluctant guest, undoubtedly.

As the young man accepted a Chivas Regal on the rocks from the bartender, Susan touched Zoe's arm.

Zoe turned her head. "Oh, Susan! I'd like you to meet someone. Dr. Noah Breckinridge, this is Susan Channing, my very good friend and girl Friday."

The doctor held out a blunt-fingered hand and gazed into Susan's eyes. "How do you do, Susan?"

He had a strong handshake, and Susan found that the impact of his intense dark eyes made her feel uncomfortable. She tried to shake off the discomfort by being flip. "The *cute* Dr. Breckinridge?"

He looked nonplussed. "I beg your pardon?"

"I take it you don't read Cindy Hodges's column?"

"Not if I can help it."

"She mentioned your name in this week's column. That 'cute doctor, Noah Breckinridge,' were her exact words."

Susan felt a bit of a fool. Why on earth had she blurted out such nonsense? It was an inane remark to make. Maybe he was one of those serious men — after all, he *was* a doctor — and would now think she was some kind of a bubblehead.

"Cute!" His eyebrows climbed, and then, suddenly, he began to laugh, and Susan watched in fascination. When he laughed, his whole expression changed, and he looked younger and more vulnerable.

"Cute?" he said again. "Do you think I should sue?"

Susan felt herself relax. He had a sense of humor, at least. "I wouldn't advise it, since you don't have a leg to stand on. You'd lose."

"I'm not sure whether I've just been complimented, or not," he said, fixing her with those intense eyes.

He took her arm and, as if by mutual consent, they moved away from the bar. "Shall we go into the atrium?" Susan suggested.

The atrium was particularly beautiful in the light from the hidden fixtures, which were positioned to illuminate the plants, the fountain and the colorful birds. Dick had arranged

75

small groupings of tables and chairs, and Susan led the doctor to one of them.

As they made themselves comfortable, Noah watched Susan covertly. He thought she was one of the most wholesome-looking young women he had ever seen, and yet there was a sexiness about her that exerted a powerful pull on him. He had arrived in a grumpy mood, determined to stay for maybe two drinks at the outside, then sneak away. Now he decided that he might stick around for a while, after all.

Cindy Hodges had a rule — never arrive early at a cocktail party. Usually the first hour was a waste of time. Even if the guests she wished to worm information out of were there, it was always better to wait until alcohol had lubricated tongues and dulled minds.

Consequently, it was after seven before she left her condo for the Tremaine house, which was a couple of miles across town. On the way, she decided to drive past The Clinic, something she did almost every day anyway. There was always the chance she might spot a well-known face going in.

Zipping along in her Porsche, she hummed to herself. She was feeling great. Things were going splendidly for her. It had taken five years of scratching and fighting, using every means at her command, to get where she was —

She slowed suddenly, and then stopped, glancing up into the rearview mirror. Behind her, the tall figure of a man in a Stetson, jeans and cowboy boots was shambling along the sidewalk, carrying a small bag. Something about the figure struck a familiar chord in her mind. The Clinic was only four blocks away, yet it seemed unlikely that anybody important would be *walking* to it. Still, she remained where she was, studying the weathered face. Her computer memory for names and faces went into full gear. Then she had it. But was he important enough to bother with?

"What the hell," she said aloud.

As the figure drew abreast of her, she leaned over and opened the passenger door. "Hi, cowboy!" she sang out.

The man stopped and leaned down from his great height to peer in at her.

"Aren't you Todd Remington?"

"That's me," he drawled. "I'm surprised anyone would recognize me way out here."

"It's my business to recognize people like you. I'm Cindy Hodges."

His face brightened. "Hey, Cindy! I'm a faithful reader of 'Cindy's Scoops.' "

"Well, faithful reader, could I offer you a lift?"

"But I'm only going . . ."

She nodded. "Four blocks, I know. The Clinic."

"Now, how did you know that?" He was already folding his long length into the car. "But I reckon my reputation has preceded me."

"As the aroma of bourbon precedes you into the car now," she said, wrinkling her nose.

"Terrible, ain't it? But I figure a long dry spell is coming up, and so I stopped in a saloon and knocked back a few. They may not approve at The Clinic, me showing up half-bombed. But what the hell! They know I'm a stone drunk, or I wouldn't be coming here in the first place."

Cindy had started the Porsche moving again, and Rem glanced over at her as she geared up, wondering at his good luck. Was it expecting too much to hope for a mention in her column?

"You've pretty much dropped out of sight these past few years, haven't you, Rem?" she stated matter-of-factly.

"Not really. I've been around, but I might as well have dropped out of sight. Whenever I run into some producer, he looks right through me, as if I wasn't there."

"Well, Westerns aren't being made nowadays."

"But they're going to make a comeback, ain't they? I've heard rumors."

Cindy shrugged. "The industry thrives on rumors — you should know that."

"Yeah, I guess you'd know if anyone does. But then, I figure it's time they came back. Pictures go in cycles, you know. Of course, I don't have my sights set on a lead. I'm a little long in the tooth for that, and I've been out of sight for too damned long. But I could handle a supporting role, and . . ."

He was rambling now, and Cindy suddenly realized that he was angling for a mention in her column. Eagerness was coming off him almost as strong as the whiskey fumes. The poor sucker! A has-been, and a drunk at that.

Then she had an inspiration. "Rem, I'm on my way to a party here in Oasis, given by a woman named Zoe Tremaine. Do you happen to know her?"

Rem glanced over at her, resentful at being pulled out of his ramblings. "I don't know a soul in this burg."

"Well, I don't have an escort for this evening. Why don't you come along with me? It might be fun."

They had stopped in front of The Clinic. Rem stared at the structure. Despite the elegant landscaping, it made him think of a prison and, for an instant, his imagination superimposed bars on the windows. He shook his head to clear it. "I'm supposed to check into this place sometime tonight."

"What will another hour or two matter? Tell

them you were delayed for one reason or another." She placed a hand lightly on his knee. "Well?"

He hesitated for a moment, then nodded abruptly. "Why not? But I shouldn't stay long."

"You can stay for whatever time you like," she said with a shrug. "I understand the Tremaine place is only a few blocks from The Clinic."

As she put the car into gear and moved away, Cindy was wondering at her motive for taking this has-been to the party with her. But she had remembered that Todd Remington sometimes became quarrelsome when he'd had too much to drink. A good brawl always livened up a party, in Cindy's estimation, and more often than not, it resulted in a juicy item for her column. This guy was aching for a mention in "Cindy's scoops"; maybe she could accommodate him.

"When my brother came back from Vietnam," Noah said, "I was in premed. He was back in Denver for a month before I saw him. And when I came home during Christmas vacation, I was appalled at how he looked. Rand had been an athlete in college, a football lineman, made all-American two years in a row. He was a bear of a man, weighing in at two-fifty when he left for Vietnam. When I saw him that Christmas, he was down to a hundred and fifty."

"What happened to him?" Susan asked softly.

Noah took a sip of the Scotch. The ice cubes had long since melted. "He had been through hell over there, but then, of course, he wasn't alone in that. I tried to get him to talk about it, having the notion, then, that talking it all out would free him of the horrors he'd seen. He laughed at me, if you could call it a laugh. You know what he told me?"

"What, Noah?"

"He said that if he told me about all the things he had seen, I'd probably go mad. He did tell me of one incident, the last thing that happened to him over there. It was when we began to use napalm to defoliate some North Vietnamese territory. Rand saw a village catch fire. Men, women and children were burned alive. He tried to rescue some of the children, and did save a few, before he was almost burned alive himself.

"And you know something?" Noah laughed harshly, forgetting Susan for a moment, his mind in the past. "You would think Rand would have received a citation for that, wouldn't you? But no, after he was discharged from the hospital, he was sent home as unfit for combat. Not because of a physical disability, but because he had given aid and comfort to the enemy by saving children."

Susan was deeply moved. She let a moment pass before she spoke. "How did your brother die, Noah?"

"He OD'd. He came back from Nam an addict. Like so many of his buddies, he got hooked on heroin. They tell me you can buy it easier than alcohol over there. That was what was wrong with him that Christmas, and I was too stupid to realize it. He was practically living on heroin."

"I've read that a lot of Vietnam veterans came home addicts."

"Yes, thousands of them."

"And that's what decided you to get into the drug treatment field, your brother's death?"

He hesitated, staring down into his empty glass. "That's a large part of it, but something else happened. My mother couldn't cope with Rand's death. She began to drink heavily, and she never could handle alcohol. My father did everything he could. He tried to talk her into going to a treatment center. She wouldn't do that — she said it would shame us all." He laughed curtly. "And then, one night, while Dad was out, she really got loaded and got into her car. There was an accident. Luckily no one else was involved. She ran head-on into a bridge abutment. Dad and I never could decide if she did it deliberately or not."

"Oh, Noah, how terrible for you!" She

reached out to touch his hand. "I am so sorry."

"Anyway, that's when my life changed direction. Instead of going into general medicine, I went into the drug and alcohol treatment field. I couldn't save Rand or my mother, but I thought I could save others —" He broke off. Susan was staring off with a blank look. "Hey, Susan, I've lost you somewhere."

"Oh." She gave a start and faced him. "I was just thinking. We have something in common."

"And what might that be?"

"My mother died of alcoholism. Not a quick death, but slowly, over the years. And one other thing was different." Her mouth got a bitter twist. "*My* father didn't try to help her at all. He just let her drink herself to death. In fact, he was the reason she drank in the first place."

Noah shook his head, smiling slightly. "No person can drive another person to drink, Susan. That's an old wives' tale. Without intending to slight your mother, her trouble lay within herself. She had psychological problems. True, an event, or another person, might trigger heavy drinking, or drug abuse, but the fault lies within ourselves."

Susan bristled. "Does that apply to *your* mother? Or your brother?"

"As much as I hate to admit it, yes. Alcoholics or drug abusers feel they can't cope with their problems, they feel inferior, so they resort to drugs or alcohol. Strange as it may sound, this applies to people who are very successful. On the surface, they may appear confident of themselves, but they are not."

"Does that apply to your Lacey Houston?"

Noah put down his glass. "I never discuss my patients, Susan."

Susan plunged on, "And the others in that place, the rich and the famous. Is that how you treat them, cure them? Take them apart and expose their weaknesses to them?"

"I don't much care for the way this conversation is going, Susan."

She leaned forward, openly angry now. "Tell me something, Dr. Breckinridge, doesn't it ever bother you that you're spending your life coddling rich drunks and drug addicts? Aren't there others out there who need your help badly?"

Stung, he retorted, "Of course, there are! And they receive the same treatment as anyone else. I don't discriminate —" He broke off, running his fingers through his hair.

"Oh, don't you! I don't believe that. The movie people, the jet-setters! I don't for a minute believe that you don't pamper them. Otherwise, they wouldn't all flock here, coming to get cured of their indulgences, polluting our town!"

"Polluting? How do you arrive at that?" He began to withdraw from her, physically as well as mentally. "I believe I'm under attack here. Is that the reason I was invited?"

Susan felt herself flushing, and her burst of temper receded. "Of course not. You were invited because you work at The Clinic. Most of us here today are against it, and Zoe thought we could have a productive dialogue."

Susan listened to a playback of her words in her mind, and she wanted to cringe. How pompous she sounded!

They sat staring across the table at each other, both breathing heavily, as though they'd been running. The one person I thought I could connect with, Noah thought, and look at what we're doing. He was considering making a quick exit when a voice broke into his thoughts.

"Here you are, Susan! It's not nice of you to monopolize our honored guest."

Noah glanced around to see Zoe Tremaine approaching, with two men trailing her.

Susan relaxed with a rueful laugh. Without looking around, she said, "I am sorry, Zoe. I'm afraid I'm not only monopolizing him, but he feels he's under attack. And perhaps he's right. I apologize for that, as well, Doctor."

Her face had broken into such a charming smile that Noah was completely beguiled, his irritation gone as if it had never existed. "Apology accepted, Susan. After all, you said nothing that I haven't heard before, many times."

Zoe said, "Dr. Breckinridge, I understand that you haven't met Mayor Washburn and . . ."

Susan whirled around in her chair, her glance going to the two men. "Zoe, you had no damned right!" she said in a trembling voice. "You had no right without telling me!"

She bolted from her chair and into the house, giving the two men a wide berth.

As unperturbed as though the outburst hadn't occurred, Zoe continued, "And Otto Channing." She indicated the second man, dressed in Western attire, with pointy-toed cowboy boots.

"Gentlemen, this is our guest of honor this evening, Dr. Noah Breckinridge."

As Noah got to his feet to shake hands, his curious gaze rested on Otto Channing. Was he any relation to Susan?

Mayor Washburn shook his hand and chirped, "I'm delighted to meet you at last, Dr. Breckinridge. You're doing great work, Doctor, great work!"

Zoe said, "If you gentlemen will excuse me, I'll tell Juanita to come out and take your drink orders."

Zoe found Susan in the bedroom she always

used, sitting on the bed, her back rigid, hands braced on either side of her, staring blankly at the wall.

"Dear?"

"Go away, Zoe. I don't want to talk to you!"

Zoe moved around the bed. "Susan, you're behaving childishly."

"Childishly? You know how I hate that man, and yet you invited him here. I've told you how he treated my mother."

"Yes, you've told me. Wait now, don't explode." Zoe held up a staying hand. "I suspect that your father is fully capable of that, as well as other unspeakable things." She sat down and took Susan's hand. "But there are a great many unpleasant, unspeakable things in life, and we all have to face up to them sooner or later. Otto Channing is one of the things we're fighting. It's better to fight a serpent that you can see than one hidden under a rock somewhere."

Susan had to smile a little at that. "Is that another Zoe Tremaine aphorism? I've heard better from you."

Zoe shrugged. "Off the top of my head, dear. What can you expect from an improvisation? Are you going to hide in here for the duration of the party?"

"No, I'll be out in a bit," Susan said with a sigh. "Just give me a few minutes alone."

Zoe nodded and left the bedroom, making

her way down the hall and back to the party. She saw that a few late arrivals had put in an appearance while she'd been gone. She worked her way through the throng, greeting the late-comers. As she went into the party room, her gaze was drawn to the bar, where a tall man and a black-haired woman were getting drinks, their backs to her. Dick Stanton was with them.

Zoe started over, and then stopped short as the pair turned around. A wave of shock raced through her, and it took all her willpower to regain her composure. Dear God, it had finally happened! Her greatest fear for years had been that a familiar face from her past would show itself; but it hadn't happened in the fifteen years she had been in Oasis, and she had gradually relaxed her guard.

Dick spotted her and waved. "Where have you been, love? A hostess shouldn't disappear like that. Meet two new guests. Cindy Hodges and Todd Remington, your hostess, Zoe Tremaine."

Zoe had never once removed her gaze from that leathery face, but there was no flicker of recognition. Then he swayed and she realized that he was quite drunk. It *had* been a long time, so maybe the time element, combined with the alcohol, would work in her favor.

She winged a silent prayer up to a deity she had never believed in, and then said brightly,

"Hello, Mr. Remington, welcome to my home."

She turned the smile on Cindy Hodges. "Welcome to you, as well, Miss Hodges. I must confess that I never read your column, but my assistant does, religiously."

Zoe hadn't intended the remark as censure, but it had come out as such. The presence of a face out of the past had shaken her to the core, shattering her usual sense of tact.

Cindy Hodges recognized the slur, but ignored it as was her habit. So long as people recognized the name, she cared not a whit whether they liked her *or* her column. She took a sip of white wine and said, "I've heard a lot about you, Miss Tremaine, *and* your parties. I feel privileged."

"The privilege is all mine," Zoe said graciously.

"I hope you don't object to my bringing along an escort?"

"Not at all. It's a pleasure to have Todd Remington in my home. I'm an old fan of his." God, Zoe thought, now why did I say that? I only called attention to myself!

True to form, Todd Remington, like an old fire horse reacting to the smell of smoke, came out of his fog at the word *fan.* "Thank you, ma'am. I'll treasure that. I didn't think I had any fans left."

"Well," said Zoe, anxious to get away, "I must

mingle a little. Enjoy yourselves."

As Zoe moved off, Rem stared after her, blinking. There was something about this regal woman that struck a chord. But his thoughts were too fuzzy to make a connection. With a shrug, he took a pull at the bourbon in his glass.

"I'll take you both around, introduce you," Dick offered. "Maybe you can uncover some tidbits for your column, Cindy."

"I fully intend to." She gave him a cool look. "That's the only reason I attend parties. Otherwise, I wouldn't waste my time." Then she smiled and tucked her arm into his. "This is very nice of you."

"Just playing the surrogate host," he said merrily.

As they moved into the press of people, Cindy pressed close against him, and Dick could feel the firm curve of her thigh against his. He liked the feeling.

Since Ken had walked out on him, Dick had thought very seriously of trying to go straight. It seemed to him that it would solve most of his problems. Other men had done it, he knew. True, most of them backslid, but not all. If others could do it, why couldn't he?

He had surveyed the available women in Oasis, but none had really appealed to him. This one was different. The cool directness of her gaze, the tartness of her tongue, the subtle curves of her slender body — all reminded him of Zoe. This would probably strike most people as incongruous, he supposed, since there was probably thirty-five years' difference in their ages; yet there was the same air of self-assurance about Cindy that Zoe possessed.

The more he thought about it, the more he was intrigued. It would take time and careful effort; he hadn't courted a member of the opposite sex since his teens. . . .

Cindy spoke suddenly, "Dick Stanton? I thought that name rang a bell. Didn't you write *Images of Fortune?*"

Damnation! That blows it, he thought. He said stiffly, "Yes, I wrote *Fortune.*"

"I loved it!" She squeezed his arm. "It was a bestseller, if I remember correctly."

"Ten weeks on the *New York Times* list."

"And you had other bestsellers before that.

"Before that, but not after," he said, plunged into gloom. "Not a bloody publishable word since *Fortune.*"

"Writer's block?" she said in what seemed to be genuine sympathy.

"Something, I don't know what."

"You know what I always think of when I hear of writer's block?" Her voice dropped to a whisper. "Constipation."

He darted a look at her to see if she was

having him on. But her eyes were guileless. All of a sudden, Dick found himself laughing helplessly. "It feels like it, too. Take my word for it."

"Oh, I don't have to take your word for it. I know the feeling very well."

Writer's block doing a gossip column? For a moment, Dick feared he had spoken aloud.

Cindy seemed to read his mind. "Oh, I don't mean my column. I once tried to write a book."

"A novel?"

There was a brief hesitation. "Yes, of course, a novel." She squeezed his arm again, with a low, intimate laugh. "Oh, we're going to get on famously, Dick Stanton."

"I certainly hope so," he said, considerably buoyed by the developing rapport between them.

Noah was bored out of his socks.

He had been pinned down at the patio table by Mayor Washburn for nearly an hour, and the mayor had a nonstop mouth on him. He had covered the statistics of the town's phenomenal growth, the advantages of having The Clinic in Oasis, and the country club and golf course. "Finest damned course this side of Los Angeles." None of which would have existed but for Mayor Washburn, according to Mayor Washburn. Now he was well launched into his grand plans for the future of Oasis. And all the while waving a smoking cigar in Noah's face.

Wisely, Otto Channing had escaped most of it, leaving them with the excuse of getting a fresh drink. He never returned.

Being cornered like this was one reason Noah had been reluctant to attend. At least he had escaped the heckling of The Clinic haters, except for Susan. He supposed he should be grateful for that.

Noah picked up his empty glass. "Excuse me, Mayor, I think I'll freshen my drink."

"Now, Doctor." With a sly grin, Washburn shook his finger in Noah's face. "You have to watch it. That's how you become an alcoholic. Who should know better than you?"

Noah couldn't remember when he had so longed to smash his fist into another man's face. He was spared a reply by a sudden eruption of sound from inside – glass breaking and voices raised in anger. Seizing it as an excuse, Noah got up and strode quickly into the house.

People had crowded back, leaving a space cleared around the bar. A tall man in cowboy boots and faded jeans, Stetson pushed back on his forehead, stood swaying, one hand braced against the bar. Another man stood down at the end of the bar, a handkerchief pressed against the corner of his mouth. Blood was seeping through the handkerchief.

"I may be a has-been," the tall man said loudly, his words slurred, "but, by God, nobody calls me that to my face!"

"I didn't say you were a has-been," the other man said around the handkerchief. "I just said you were a faded Western star. . . ."

"What the hell! I may be drunk, but I'm not stupid. In my book, 'faded' means the same thing."

Someone was trying to push past Noah, and a voice said angrily, "I'll put up with most things at my parties, but not fighting. He goes. Now!"

Noah took her arm, holding her back. "Who is this guy, Miss Tremaine?"

She glanced at him. "That's Todd Remington."

Noah said, "Shit, he's one of ours. He was supposed to check in this evening. What's he doing here?"

"All I know is that he came with Cindy Hodges. But now he has to go."

"Let me handle it," Noah said dourly. "After all, handling drunks is my job."

"But you can't go yet," she said in dismay. "The party has hardly begun. The buffet will be set up shortly."

"A doctor's first duty is always to his patient, Miss Tremaine. Thank you for inviting me.

94

Will you . . . ?" He hesitated. "Will you tell Susan goodbye for me?"

"Of course."

Noah moved toward the bar, approaching Todd Remington warily. He touched the man's elbow. Remington's head whipped around, and he glared at Noah out of reddened eyes. "Who're you, fellow?"

"I'm Dr. Breckinridge, Mr. Remington," Noah said in a low voice. "From The Clinic."

The actor slumped back against the bar. "Hell, I'm supposed to be there, ain't I?"

"That's right. Now, why don't we go along and I'll check you in."

Todd Remington went with him without protesting. Just inside the front door he stooped to pick up a small bag, and would have fallen on his face if Noah hadn't supported him. Once inside Noah's small car, the actor sat staring bleakly through the windshield. After a few moments, he said, "I screwed up, didn't I?"

"I guess you could say that. How did you happen to be there, of all places?"

"Oh, I got sidetracked. Cindy Hodges gave me a lift and invited me to the party. I went, thinking I might run into a producer. I'm always thinking I'll run into a producer. Hell, for all I know, the guy I hit might have been one. When I get sloshed, I always get a cob up my ass and usually wind up making a fuss. Doctor . . ." He suddenly clutched at Noah's arm, causing the car to swerve. "Do you think you can do me any damn good?"

Noah shook his hand off. "We can only try. We've helped people worse off than you, if that's any comfort."

"I don't know how any fool can be worse than me," Rem said morosely.

He lapsed into silence. Then, a block away from The Clinic, he sat up with an exclamation. "Hey, I remember her! I thought I knew her from somewhere."

"Remember who?" Noah asked without much interest.

"That woman back there. She's May Fremont. I haven't seen May in eighteen, twenty years now."

Five

Mayor Washburn, a smoking cigar in one hand and a drink in the other, came up to Zoe. "You should thank your lucky stars, Miss Tremaine, for the likes of Dr. Breckinridge. He prevented a nasty scene here. And you're so against The Clinic!"

Zoe shrugged. "I'm grateful for his help, of course, but that has absolutely nothing to do with my opposition to The Clinic."

The mayor shook his head. "You're a strange one. I never have been able to figure you out."

"I'm a woman," she said with a slight smile. "Men aren't supposed to understand women."

"That's not what I meant," he said irritably, waving his cigar around. "And you know it."

"Isn't it?" she asked innocently. "Then what *did* you mean?"

"Your confounded opposition to The Clinic. And your damned no-growth initiative. If your kooky followers and you have your way, Oasis will sink back into the Dark Ages. The Clinic is the best thing that ever happened to this town. It really put us on the map. This town is ripe for development — the whole country knows about us."

"Oh, I certainly agree with that. We're famous, all right. Mention Oasis and people immediately think of drug addiction and alcoholism."

"And what's so wrong with that?"

"There's a great deal wrong with it."

"The Clinic provides a needed service."

"I would much prefer that service be provided elsewhere." Usually, Zoe enjoyed jousting with Mayor Washburn, but tonight the zest was missing. The thoughts of Todd Remington lingered in her mind like a menacing shadow. "As to the reason for my opposition to The Clinic, I've spoken enough at open meetings about it. As to our group's no-growth initiative, that also speaks for itself. We don't want our sleepy little town to become a bustling metropolis. And I'm confident that the voters will agree in November. Mayor Washburn, I chose Oasis as the place to spend my so-called golden years. In peace and quiet. Now look at it. It's as bad, or worse, than Palm Springs."

"And what's wrong with Palm Springs? There's big bucks there. If I have my way, we'll outdo Palm Springs," he said boastfully.

"And if I have my way, *you* won't have your way."

Otto Channing, carrying a plate of food, drifted over. "Charles, if you want something to eat, you'd better get in there before it's all gone."

Washburn grunted, opened his mouth to speak again, then clamped it shut and marched away.

"Thank you, Otto," Zoe said with a sigh of relief.

He smiled charmingly. "Charles a bit windier than usual?"

"Not really, but it was a little more than I feel up to coping with just now."

"Charles does natter on."

"Is that any way to talk about a crony?"

"Crony?" Channing arched an eyebrow. "I haven't heard that word lately. It's usually used in reference to politicians and ward heelers."

"Then I would say I used it accurately enough. Wouldn't you?"

For just a moment Channing's eyes darkened with anger. Then he shrugged, smiling urbanely. "One can't always choose one's bedfellows, Zoe."

There was something about his manner that was confidential, as if he were sharing secrets with an old friend. Zoe tensed inside, reminding herself that Otto Channing was the enemy.

He could be so damned charming, so plausible, that it was sometimes difficult to remember just how ruthless and corrupt he really was. They had been antagonists long before Zoe ever met Susan, but Zoe had never truly disliked him personally, only what he stood for. When Susan first talked of how he had treated her mother, Zoe was inclined to disbelieve most of it. Yet when she came to know the girl better and realized that there wasn't an ounce of deceit in her, Zoe began to look at Channing more carefully. Yes, there was a streak of cruelty there, perhaps even sadism, a tendency certainly to disregard the feelings of others. She realized that he was amoral, viewing everything in respect to his own benefit.

In the open doorway to the party room she caught a glimpse of Susan looking out. At the sight of her father, the girl turned and disappeared back inside.

Channing had also seen her. "My daughter has avoided me all evening like I had the plague," he said with a sadness blatantly false.

"From what I gather, she has reason."

"What has she been telling you?" He transferred his gaze to her face. "Talking about her mother, I suppose. She blames me for her death. She makes no bones about that."

"And from what Susan told me, again, she has reason."

"The girl exaggerates." Unperturbed, Channing shrugged. "My wife was a hopeless drunk, Zoe. I did everything I could, but it was useless. I tried to get her into a clinic, like that place you hate so much. She wouldn't go. They might have helped her."

"According to Susan, that wasn't the way it was. She claims that you never really wanted your wife to receive treatment, that it would have been a disgrace for the wife of a man of your stature to become known as an alcoholic."

He stiffened, spots of color on his cheeks, and Zoe knew that she had scored.

In a low, furious voice Channing said, "That's a lie, goddammit! That makes me out to be some kind of a monster!"

"Well?" she said composedly.

He glared at her, "Thad Darnell warned me that I was foolish to come here tonight. You're a troublemaker, Zoe Tremaine, a nosy old busybody, and you'll never be anything else. You delight in stirring things up. I think you get off on it. I saw some kids once, poking with sticks at a den of scorpions so they'd sting each other to death. That's you, old woman!"

She said coolly, "Perhaps that analogy has some truth in it, Otto. But if it does, what does that make you?"

With an indrawn breath, he broke off his glare and strode off, his boot heels drumming

101

an angry tattoo on the tiles.

Zoe stared after him, suddenly depressed. Perhaps he was right. *Was* she just a trouble-maker, a meddling old woman, stirring up a fuss to no good effect? Certainly she had accomplished very little in the past three years. The Clinic was still there, still thriving, its fame now worldwide. Common sense should tell her that it was invulnerable to her puny attacks.

And yet she knew that she would continue. To stop now would be a betrayal of her friends, and she had her own private reason to keep up the fight.

She arranged a smile on her face and went into the house to see her guests.

By eleven all the guests had departed; even Dick and Susan had gone home. Zoe was finally alone.

She poured a glass of cognac and went into the atrium. The cages were all covered, the birds asleep. Zoe uncovered one, opened the door and held out her arm. Madam, the female Triton cockatoo, chirped grumpily but settled on Zoe's arm.

Zoe sat down with her drink, moving the bird to her shoulder. She fired a thin black cigar, exhaled smoke and took a sip of cognac. The cockatoo scolded angrily; the bird didn't like it when she smoked.

"It's all right, Madam," Zoe said gently. She stroked the brilliant-colored feathers. "You can endure it for a bit, then I'll put you back on your perch. I feel the need of a little friendly company about now."

Zoe had named the bird Madam as a private joke, but she never used the name around other people. Juanita and Susan were the only ones who knew, and Juanita hated all the birds equally and had no interest in what they were called.

Zoe closed her eyes, letting her thoughts drift back into the past, back to Todd Remington's account of their first meeting.

"Cut! That's a print. And that wraps it up."

Todd Remington breathed a heartfelt sigh of relief. Mel Connors, the chubby director, came bustling over to where Rem stood in the saloon set, where the last scene of *Sunset Raiders* had taken place.

"Great work, Rem!" Connors stuck out his hand. "It should do well, and it's been a pleasure working with you."

"Same here, Mel," Rem drawled.

"Maybe we can work together again some-time. You heading back for L.A.?" the director asked.

"Nope. I thought I might run over to Vegas

for a couple of days, since we're so close here."

"Try your luck at the tables?"

Rem shook his head. "Naw, I'm not much for gambling. I get rid of my dough fast enough as it is, and I like something in return. I thought I'd take it easy for a few days, maybe catch a few shows, check out the broads."

Connors cocked his head. "Professionals?"

"Whatever." Rem shrugged. "There are some good-looking hookers in Vegas, and sometimes they're easier and cheaper in the long run."

"There's a place I know that's outside of town, a real class operation. All clean as a whistle, no dopers, juicy, good-lookers all, and they treat a man like a king."

Rem lit a cigarette. "Sounds interesting. I might check it out."

"It's called the Heavenly Retreat."

Rem laughed. "The name has a nice ring to it."

"It's aptly named, believe me. It's on Highway 95, a few miles beyond the city limit north of town. Tell May that Mel Connors sent you."

"May?"

"May Fremont. She runs the place."

Rem had taken Connors up on his suggestion, but he'd been too tired for much of anything the first night after checking into the Flamingo. It had been a couple hours' drive into Las Vegas, and they had been shooting from dawn until dark on the picture every day for a month. He wanted nothing but a few drinks, a good dinner and a soft bed.

He slept until noon the next day, had lunch, and then spent the afternoon around the pool. By evening his batteries were recharged and he was ready to cruise. Except for one quick episode with the script girl on the picture, he'd been celibate for a month. He mulled over what Connors had told him, then decided to check out the action around the casino first.

A tall blonde came on to him in the bar, and it looked promising. He bought her drinks and dinner, and tried to steer her up to his room. She balked. It was then that he learned she had blown every dime at the crap table, and she wanted him to back her. "Let's have a little action at the tables first," she said silkily. "Then I promise you some fine action later."

"You strike me as a loser, babe," he said bluntly. "So, you could turn out to be expensive. No, thanks, but I'll pass."

He left her fuming and went out to his Cadillac in the parking lot. Angry at the blonde, angry at himself, he burned rubber out of the lot and headed for 95, the highway to Reno. Once he'd passed the city limits of Vegas, he began looking for a sign.

After spending time on the Strip, he was expecting a blatant neon sign, probably in flashing red. But he had driven past it before he realized — a cluster of house trailers off to the left, almost hidden in a grove of trees. It had to be the place.

Rem slowed the car, looked both ways, executed a U-turn and drove back.

The trailer park was isolated, no other buildings within a mile; and there was the sign, illuminated by only a single white bulb. The Heavenly Retreat.

The sign was on the side of the largest trailer, which had an even smaller sign over the door spelling out Office. There were only a few cars in the graveled parking lot, but then it was a weeknight and still early.

Rem got out of the Cadillac and mounted the two steps. The door stood slightly ajar. He rapped, waited, then pushed it open. The front third of the trailer had been turned into an office, with a desk, chairs and filing cabinets. The office was empty. Lights were on in the other part of the trailer, and he could hear the tinny sound of TV voices.

"Hello?" he called out tentatively.

The TV clicked off, and a throaty voice called, "Be right there."

In a moment a tall woman, with a full figure, dark eyes and long hair, as black as a raven's wing, came toward him. She was dressed tastefully, in virgin white. Rem judged her to be in her early forties. Those piercing eyes studied him intently, giving Rem the eerie feeling that she had passed a reasoned judgment on him in those few seconds.

"It's a little risky, ain't it, leaving the door open like that?" he asked.

She was moving with a fluid grace around behind her desk. "There's no crime out here," she responded.

Rem thought that a rather strange remark, considering the nature of her business. "Mel Connors recommended this place."

"That was considerate of him. How is Mel?"

"Fine, the last I saw of him." He chided himself for mentioning Mel. Now she'd know he was in the movie business.

"What may I do for you?"

Taken aback, he said, "Well, hellfire, this *is* a cathouse ain't it?"

She gestured with one long-fingered hand. "That's a rather crude way of putting it, but I suppose the term would apply."

Shit, he thought, what kind of a place *is* this? "Then you know why I'm here."

She had pulled a scratch pad toward her, pencil poised over it. "What is your drink preference?"

He stared. "I drink bourbon. Bourbon on the rocks. But I fail to see what that has to do with why I'm here."

She made a note on the pad. "We provide all services here. Even food can be supplied, if required."

"What about the reason I'm here? Don't I get to see . . ." He'd been about to say "merchandise," but her level gaze had come up, and he changed it to, "Don't I get to pick and choose?"

"Not here," she said calmly. "I do the choosing, and I'm rarely wrong. If I am, you may complain afterward."

He began to grin. "It'd be a little late for that, wouldn't it?"

"Not really, not if you've gained satisfaction," she said pointedly. "Most of my clientele is composed of repeat customers, or referrals, such as yourself. And we are doing well, thank you." She became brisk. "The fee is fifty dollars an hour, or three hundred dollars for the night."

He started to complain about the price, then held his tongue, suddenly certain that he was about to receive his money's worth. Without a word, he took out his wallet and counted out a hundred dollars onto the desk.

She nodded, punched a button on the intercom on her desk and spoke into it, "Marilyn, you have a client." She looked up at Rem. "Trailer number seven, down the line to your right. You're expected."

He drawled, "My lucky number."

As he started to turn away, she spoke again, "One more thing. I impose limits here. No drugs of any kind permitted. No S and M. Nothing kinky. And absolutely no physical abuse of my girls."

"Hellfire, what do I look like?" he snapped, nettled. "I *can* fuck them, I hope?"

"That's what you've just paid for," she said composedly.

Rem went out, deliberately slamming the door. What the hell kind of a place was this, anyway? It was the strangest cathouse he had ever visited; still, he very well knew that some weird types patronized such establishments. And underneath the annoyance was a sneaking admiration for the woman in the trailer. She gave the impression that she could handle just about anything that came along. Rem wasn't unfamiliar with whorehouses — he'd gone through three marriages and several expensive mistresses since becoming a star, and he'd found that pros were less expensive and far less trouble.

He found trailer number seven, knocked on the door and was told to enter.

He entered directly into a dimly lit boudoir, with a thick shag rug, a small table with a bottle of Old Crow and a bucket of ice cubes — all dominated by a huge round bed. And standing beside the bed was a tall statuesque blonde in high spiked heels, black silk stockings sheathing incredibly long legs. Garters ran up under a short negligee, so sheer that her nipples were clearly visible.

Rem felt a quickening arousal. He spoke past the thickening in his throat. "You waiting for me, honey?"

She had a round face, scrubbed clean of makeup, and looked to be about eighteen, yet her brown eyes were pools of calculated sensuality. Full lips parted, and a pink tongue darted at him.

"I'm waiting for you," she said in a husky voice.

Two hours later, half-drunk from sex and liberal doses of Old Crow, Rem stumbled from trailer number seven, still tucking his shirttail in. As he made his way toward the parking lot, he considered this one of the best times he had ever experienced.

He noticed that the lot held several more cars now. He started past the office trailer, then veered toward it. The door still stood ajar.

This time she was sitting at her desk, smoke drifting lazily up from the thin cigar in her mouth.

"Just thought I'd tell you that I'm a satisfied customer." He chuckled. "So you don't have to refund my money."

She took the cigar from her mouth and said

in a dry voice, "I'm glad to hear it. I was worried."

"Tell me something, May Fremont . . ." Rem knew that he wouldn't have said it sober, but he said it anyway, "If I make a return visit, what would I have to do to get a date with you? Call ahead and reserve the time?"

"No way, Mr. Remington," she said flatly. "The day is long past when I have to make a living on my back."

Rem was uneasy. "You know who I am?"

"Of course. I'm a fan of yours. I'm a sucker for Westerns, good guys versus the bad guys. In the real world, the white hats don't always win." She smiled fleetingly. "Don't worry, Mr. Remington, no one will ever know you were here. Along with other services, I sell discretion here."

Todd Remington visited the Heavenly Retreat sporadically through the years, and Zoe got to know him very well. She came to like him. After the first visit, he had shown her more respect, and his visits continued even after Zoe closed the Heavenly Retreat, moved to Los Angeles and opened a place on the edge of Beverly Hills. Her clientele grew then to include a great many of the people in the movie industry. She provided a class operation, charged outrageous prices and accumulated a great deal of money.

Before she finally decided that she had enough money to be able to live more than comfortably for the rest of her life, Zoe was saddened to see Rem's career languish as the popularity of the Western declined. His visits became less frequent, and his drinking increased to the point where he was often in a drunken stupor when he came to her place. Zoe came to dread his visits.

Without warning to any of her clients, she sold her establishment for a very good price and disappeared from the Hollywood scene.

Coming back to the present, Zoe shook her head fiercely and snubbed out her cigar.

But now someone else knew she was here. There was one slim hope. She knew that people who drank heavily had blackouts during a certain stage of intoxication. If she was lucky, perhaps Rem wouldn't remember seeing her tonight. Certainly, there had been no indication of recognition.

Following Zoe Tremaine's party, Otto Channing drove his Lincoln downtown to the police station. Beside him in the passenger seat, Mayor Washburn chattered away, fouling the air with his cigar. Channing only grunted a time or two, scarcely listening.

He pulled up before the police station located

downtown on Broadway. The station was two years old, a modern cubistic structure of two stories. Its facilities were up-to-date, with half of the second floor taken up by cells. The station had cost far more than was necessary for a town the size of Oasis, but it had been planned for future growth. "Besides, nothing gives affluent, solid citizens more reassurance than a good, efficient police force," Mayor Washburn had said at the time. "That's one of the first things they will look for when thinking of moving here."

As Channing parked, Washburn stirred and looked around. "Why are we stopping here, Otto?"

"I want a few words with the chief."

"But it's late, almost eleven. He may not be here."

"If he's not, then we'll go to his condo," Channing said grimly. "Besides, the odds are he'll be here. Thad practically lives here. He has no family. The force is his family."

"But I don't understand. Why do you have to see him *now?* Can't it wait?"

"No, it can't wait." Channing was already getting out of the car. "I have to talk to him tonight."

Naturally, the new police station provided a private office for Chief of Police Darnell; a spacious room with a private bathroom. The budget to furnish the office had been generous, but Darnell had chosen a Spartan look, patterned after his old barracks office in the marines. There was a desk, with nothing on it as a rule except an intercom and a telephone, a swivel chair behind it and two chairs for visitors.

True to Channing's prediction, Darnell was in, browsing through the day's reports from his officers. He glanced up with a frown as Channing and the mayor came in.

There wasn't even a carpet on the hardwood floor, and Washburn voiced his usual complaint. "I can't figure you out, Thad. You could at least carpet the damned office and hang some pictures on the walls. This room gives me the shivers. It's as cold-ass bare as one of the cells upstairs!"

Unsmiling, Darnell said, "That's the way I want it. I want the people I usually have in here to feel uncomfortable." His glance was directed at Channing, sensing that he was the source of this unexpected visit. "What can I do for you, Otto?"

Channing sat down before the desk. "I've decided it's high time we do something about Zoe Tremaine, the meddling old bitch!"

Darnell's lips twitched in a thin smile. "I gather she gave you a hard time tonight? I warned you you'd be better off not going."

Channing made a dismissive gesture. "The

only thing that happened tonight is that I tried again to get her to back off. But there's no reasoning with her."

Darnell's gaze was direct. "So, what do you expect me to do?"

"Dammit, man, you're the chief of police!" Channing said explosively, then got a grip on his temper. "There are several things you can do. You have the facilities and the authority to do them. For instance, we know nothing about her before the day she showed up here. She's hiding something in her past, I can just feel it. Run a check on her. Find out who she really is, where she came from, what she did *before* coming here. Here." From his coat pocket he took something wrapped in tissue. Placing the object on the chief's desk, he carefully unwrapped it. "This is an ashtray I took from her house. I saw her handling it, so it has her fingerprints on it. Run a check on them."

Darnell looked at the ashtray with distaste. "I can't do that," he said obstinately. "She's broken no laws. I have no cause to investigate her."

"*Cause!* Thad, she's giving us nothing but trouble! If you can find out something about her past that she's hushed up, we can club her with it."

"No. I won't do it."

Channing locked stares with the other man, his insides churning. He knew that what he

115

was about to do was dangerous, but he had to do it. He felt sweat pop out on his forehead, but he forced himself to speak casually. "You know, I've kept records of all our dealings from the beginning. Records of monies received and divvied up. I have copies of all the documents. All stored away in a safe place."

Darnell leaned forward, hands flat on the desk. "What are you trying to say, Otto?" he said in a soft voice.

"I'm trying to say that I need your cooperation!" Despite himself, Channing's voice was shrill.

"It sounds to me very much like blackmail," Darnell said in the same soft voice.

"Blackmail!" Mayor Washburn, who hadn't been following the conversation too closely, suddenly sat up. "What's going on here? Otto, what is this?"

Both men ignored him, never once looking away from each other.

"Call it what you will, Thad," Channing said. "But I'll get your cooperation, one way or another."

"What will you do if I don't bend? Take your documents to the media? You do that, you're right in the same shit pile with the mayor and me."

"I don't see why you're fighting me on this, Thad. What's this damn woman to you? She's a pain in the ass to the three of us. I'd think you would want her out of your hair."

"She's nothing to me, of course." Darnell relaxed a little. "I just don't like to be threatened, is all."

Washburn spoke up. "Otto's right, Chief. If you can stop her, for God's sake, do it!"

Darnell didn't even look at him. The mayor was afraid for his own neck, and Darnell couldn't care less. He was trying to decide if the matter was worth locking horns over with Channing. He wasn't particularly surprised at the bastard's veiled threat; he had been halfway expecting something like this for some time.

He finally said, "I suppose I can initiate a quiet investigation of the woman. You said 'several things.' What else did you have in mind?"

Channing relaxed with a smile. It was going to be all right. "Oh, nothing hard. Just pass the word to your men to keep a close eye on the Tremaine woman. And Susan. If they step out of line the least little bit, ticket them, arrest them, whatever the offense calls for." His smile grew conspiratorial. "You know how many piddling little laws there are on the books, Thad? Spitting on the sidewalk, things like that. Pressure, that's what I want on them."

Darnell started. "Susan? Your own daughter?"

"I no longer consider her my daughter,"

Channing said harshly. "She gave up that right long ago. And since she's allied herself with Tremaine, she deserves the same treatment all those nuts do."

"Well, if that's the way you want it," Darnell said with a shrug. "I'll pass the word along to the men to keep a sharp eye on them."

Channing leaned forward to speak again, then changed his mind. He'd been about to tell the chief to trump up a charge if nothing else worked, but he decided he'd pushed the man far enough for the moment. He'd come at him again another time. He got to his feet. "Well, we won't bother you any longer, Thad. Sorry if I sounded like I was hassling you. I'll admit that I was upset when I came in here. Come along, Charles, let's leave the man to his duties."

Darnell said nothing, but his hard, uncompromising stare made Channing uneasy. He had to force himself to stroll out instead of hastening his step.

As the door to the chief's office closed behind them, Washburn said, "What was that all about in there, Otto? Would you really do what you threatened?"

"No, of course not," Channing said with false laughter. "I was just running a bluff. Sometimes you have to do that with Thad. I would never do something like that." He clapped the mayor on the shoulder. "Come on, Charles. Join me in a nightcap."

Hands laced together so tightly that the knuckles shone white, Thad Darnell stared unseeingly at the closed door. He was so incensed that red dots danced before his eyes. That slick son of a bitch! Someday he was going to teach Channing a thing or two. How dare the corrupt bastard threaten him like that!

Gradually, he calmed down. After all, he had known the kind of men Washburn and Channing were when he went into cahoots with them. He had nobody to blame but himself. But after years of Spartan living in the marines, the temptations dangled before his eyes had been too much to resist. He had to admit that he enjoyed the money and the power. Most of all, he relished the power inherent in his office. He had shaped an efficient police force in Oasis; in his estimation the best in the state. He ruled with an iron but fair hand, he thought, and he could do pretty much as he pleased.

The corruption he had succumbed to had stopped at his desk; he had not passed it down the line. His men were straight arrows. He had let them know in no uncertain terms that if he ever caught one taking so much as a free meal, he was out on his ass, with no recommendation.

A wintry smile touched his lips. How could he reconcile that with his agreeing to alert his men to keep a sharp eye on Susan Channing and Zoe Tremaine? He had done this type of thing before. Occasionally, Oasis had been visited by a retired criminal or a Mafia type. Darnell always told his officers to hassle them when they committed even the smallest infraction of the law.

Of course, Zoe Tremaine hardly fit that description. Darnell admired her in a way, admired her intelligence and spirit. She was one gutsy old broad. And when she held a demonstration or spoke at one of their meetings, she adhered strictly to the law. She would not stand for any unruliness, and never once had the police been summoned.

Yet there were often innocent casualties of war, and he had his orders. Darnell had followed orders to the letter during his years in the marines, even orders given by incompetent officers, men he detested.

And he would follow these orders — at least for the time being.

Six

"Doctor, I don't think I can face a group therapy session." Lacey was obviously distressed by the thought. She nibbled on a fingernail as she talked, those huge eyes wider still with apprehension. "Not just yet."

"That's fine, Lacey," Noah said soothingly. "We won't rush it. We'll make do with individual therapy for another day or so."

"Are the group sessions absolutely necessary? Baring my soul in front of all those strangers. . . ." She shivered.

"Well . . ."

Noah looked out the window of his office while he marshaled his thoughts. This was Lacey's third day at The Clinic. The first two days she had been on tranquilizers and had undergone extensive medical tests, including urinalysis, which had shown recent, heavy cocaine use. Noah had spent four hours with her so far, questioning her about her drug use.

121

"Dr. Breckinridge? You started to say something."

"Oh! I'm sorry." He turned to her, his smile flashing. "I got distracted for a moment. You asked if group therapy is necessary. In my opinion, it is. In individual therapy it is one-on-one, just the therapist and you. The primary purpose of therapy is to seek out the underlying problems that lead to drug or alcohol abuse, and for you to develop your coping skills and a better self-image. That can all be done much more effectively in a group of people, from a half dozen to perhaps ten at the most. A sort of group structure forms. These people have the same general problems. In the group, you can interact with others, and you learn that others have the same problems. You're not alone in the world —" He broke off, spreading his hands. "I realize that I sound like I'm lecturing to a student. But in a way, you *are* a student, learning about yourself."

Lacey was frowning. "You said a better self-image. What do you mean by that?"

"Well the greatest problem with drug addiction, Lacey, is not the physical, but the psychological addiction. The physical addiction can be cured easily enough. In most cases, that is," he amended, thinking of Billie Reaper. "But if we don't uncover the underlying cause, the patient will soon revert to the same pattern of drug abuse after leaving here. And more often than not, the root of the problem is a poor self-image. From what I've already learned about you, Lacey, that is the problem with you."

She was staring at him in disbelief. "A poor self-image? Forgive me, Doctor, but I find that hard to believe. I have appeared on stage, made numerous public appearances, and I'm seen by millions in movies and on television." She gave a self-conscious laugh. "Forgive me for putting it like that. I know how it sounds, but it happens to be true."

"I realize that, yet buried inside you some-where is the belief that you're not worthy of all the attention, of all the adulation. You fear that you will be found out and it will all stop without warning." He smiled gently. "I categorize coke users into five classes. Recreational users, routine sniffers, performance users, stress users and the hard-core coke abusers. I differentiate between the first four and the last because many of the first four may never become confirmed addicts, since cocaine isn't as physically addictive as heroin, for example. A coke abuser could very well progress through several stages, or he might become an addict with the first initial use of cocaine.

"Recreational users, those who use the drug in social situations, may never become true addicts. The same does not apply, however, to the other four categories. A routine user doesn't employ cocaine for recreational purposes. He takes cocaine at regular intervals in order to cope with what he considers a difficult work situation. He takes it to provide energy, not euphoria. Of course, if he continues use over an extended period of time, he would certainly become an addict."

"Then I suppose you classify me as a performance user?" Lacey said thoughtfully.

He nodded. "That's the way you began, yes. But let's not soften it, Lacey. You're an addict now."

"I still find your theory about me hard to accept. It *is* true that I've always felt that I've been incredibly lucky to get to where I am, and I sometimes worry about what will happen when my luck runs out."

"And that's part of your problem, you see. From the little I know of you so far, I'd say that luck had only a small role to play in your success. Landing the right role at the right time, for instance. But you are enormously talented, Lacey, and you are a very beautiful woman. In my judgment, you use cocaine to bolster your low self-esteem. Your self-esteem has never equaled your success. You're always on the line and your fear of failure is perpetual and self-perpetuating. And each achievement always exceeds your self-evaluation.

124

"Our culture is partially responsible for this. We're brought up to believe that we must always be a winner, always be the very best at what we do." He looked at her intently. "I haven't had time to do much digging into your background, yet. I do recall reading that you started in the movies at an early age."

Lacey shrugged. "I'm afraid that mine isn't a very original story, Dr. Breckinridge. I suppose you could call my mother a show business mom. I was born in Orange County, an only child. My father owned a liquor store, and worked long hours. One of the first things I can remember is my mother reading movie magazines. As far as I know, she read them all. They were the only things she read. When I was about seven, my father remarked that I was 'a budding beauty.' From that moment on, my mother became obsessed. When she was a girl, she had dreamed of becoming an actress, but she got pregnant with me and had to marry my father. She was bitter about that and always blamed him for holding her back. She finally left him when I was ten.

"Anyway, she transferred that ambition to me. It's a story that you must have heard a hundred times. My days were filled with endless rounds of the casting agencies. Mother worked as a waitress at night to support us, so she could make the rounds

125

with me during the day."

"That must have been hard on you," he said sympathetically. "What about schooling?"

"Catch-as-catch-can," she said with a shrug. "I remember we had to move from time to time to escape the wrath of the school authorities. Luckily, schoolwork was easy for me. I was usually able to keep up —"

"There's that word *luck* again. If what you say is true, you have to have been an exceptionally bright child. But let's leave that for now. When did you start getting parts? I don't recall that you were a child star."

"I wasn't. I did some modeling, a few commercials and a couple of bit parts. I didn't get my first real role until I was seventeen."

"And you were seven when she started with you? That's ten years. Your mother didn't discourage easily, did she?"

"I don't think anything could have discouraged her."

"I assume that you rose pretty quickly after you got your first role?"

"Yes, I had my first starring role when I was twenty."

"And your mother, was she happy about that?"

"Not really. Oh, I suppose she was pleased enough, yet she was never satisfied. She was always after me to do better, to live up to my potential." Lacey's voice turned sour. "I have never received an Academy Award, you know. I was nominated once, but didn't get it. I doubt that she would have been satisfied even then." She took a breath. "Mother died nearly two years ago, around the time of the breakup of my third marriage."

"And that's when you started on cocaine?" he asked casually.

"Not too long after that."

"How did it happen?"

"I was in the middle of doing a movie. The one before hadn't done too well at the box office, and I was determined to do better. And the breakup with Ty had been messy." She wasn't looking at him now. "I was working my tail off — I was emotionally and physically exhausted. I had started an . . . an affair with Kurt Johns, who played a supporting role in the film. I was so wrung out that I couldn't enjoy making love with him. One night he showed me two grams of coke he'd just bought. He told me that he'd used it off and on for years. He swore that it wasn't dangerous, and would give me an incredible high. I had always been terrified of drugs, but I had been drinking heavily since the death of my mother, and had always handled that well. And I had used cocaine once before, with Ty, and it had been a rather pleasant experience.

127

"I figured that I had nothing to lose. I was so depressed, and scared to death that the movie wouldn't do well. So, I sniffed two lines. I felt an immediate rush, I was full of energy, I was on top of the world and the sex was fantastic."

"And so you began using it daily during the movie?"

She finally looked at him, without surprise this time. "That's right. I sailed through my scenes with confidence, and I think my acting was the best I've ever done. The movie was a smash."

"And you kept using cocaine?"

"Yes. It gave me the boost and the courage that I needed."

"But you had to keep increasing the amount and frequency of use?"

She glanced away, nodding glumly.

"And each time you crashed, came down after a high, you felt worse, depressed and listless?"

"Yes, and I desperately wanted to sniff more, but I usually managed to resist. I tried vodka, I tried Valium, but nothing helped to get me over the crashing. Nothing but another line of coke."

"During this last movie, it got away from you, didn't it?"

She shivered, hugging herself, her face bleak at the memory. "It was awful, Doctor. I found that I couldn't get through the first day without sniffing several lines, every two hours or so. I even became paranoid, imagining that everyone on the set was staring at me, talking about me in whispers behind my back. I got to the point where I simply couldn't function!"

He nodded. "That is a typical pattern. You had passed over the line. You became a hard-core addict, Lacey." He glanced at his watch, started to get to his feet. "Well, that's enough for today. I have another patient in a few minutes. . . ."

"Wait, Doctor!" She leaned forward. "What happens now?"

"Well, you're over the worst of the physical withdrawal." He sat back down. "Actually, you had an easier time of it than most. But to answer your question, we continue with therapy. A daily session, more if necessary."

"And that's it?"

"No, not by any means," he said with a smile. "You'll be on tranquilizers for a few more days. And I want you to start what I call a Coke Book."

She drew back. "A Coke Book! What's that?"

"It's a log, a daily journal. It will become your constant companion, not only while you're here, but after you graduate. But I want you to start it now, get accustomed to it. It will become your security blanket, if you will.

It will serve several purposes.

"First, I want you to go back into your past, back to the first time you ever used cocaine. List the reasons you started, how you felt and how you felt afterward. Be candid, be honest with yourself. Unless you wish, no one aside from myself will ever see what you've written. Then, over the next few days, bring the log up to date.

"Next, start two parallel lists, one titled 'The Good Effects of a Cocaine High,' then a second column titled 'Bad Effects.' For example, under column one you might write confidence, in the second list, sinus irritation. Under one, great sex. Two, uncomfortable and painful crash. Do you get the idea?"

She simply nodded, looking intrigued.

"This all probably sounds simplistic to you, but believe me, it works. As I said, you will continue to keep the log after you leave here. Then, anytime you feel an urge to binge on cocaine again, look in the 'Bad Effects' column. It will cause you to stop and think. Carry this diary with you wherever you go. The best thing is probably a notebook that you can easily carry in your purse.

"Also, I will give you assignments from time to time. For instance, to start off, I want you to write down how it feels to be an addict, day by day, and how you think it affects the people close to you.

"There are a number of other things involved in your treatment. I'll eventually mention all of them. Contracting, the buddy system —" he grinned faintly "— even blackmail."

She gave him a startled look. "Blackmail?"

"Yes. You could write a signed letter to me. Or to any therapist, for that matter. In the letter you confess to using cocaine excessively, or confess to something else you've done — something you're heartily ashamed of. Then you leave the letter with me, and agree to regular urine tests. If the tests show cocaine use, I am free to mail your letter to the newspapers. Or perhaps even better, you will forfeit certain of your jewels. They will be sold and the proceeds will go to charity."

"Oh, no!" She shook her head violently from side to side. "I could never, never do that!"

Noah cursed himself silently. He had made a mistake, a mistake any reasonably intelligent doctor would never make. "I'm sorry, Lacey. I wasn't thinking."

"You didn't mean it?" Her voice was little more than a whimper.

"No, Lacey, I didn't mean it," he said gently. "Besides, the letter, or anything to do with your jewels, could never be done without your consent."

She drew a shaky breath. "I know what you

must think of me, Doctor, clinging to something like jewelry. I know what it means. I've been in analysis a couple of times. The analyst told me what they represent to me. A security blanket."

"Just put it out of your mind. We all need a security blanket of one kind or another," he said inadequately. "Why don't you go to your room now? Try and get some rest. We'll talk again tomorrow."

Noah berated himself soundly as the door closed behind Lacey. What happened to your famous bedside manner, Doctor? You really blew that one!

Rem tried to smile at Dr. Breckinridge, but it was more a grimace than a smile. He didn't really feel like talking; he felt more like weeping. He felt as weak as a baby. For two days he had been vomiting constantly. Nothing would stay in his stomach. Imaginary insects had crawled on his skin, and he had scratched until he bled. Snakes and dragons appeared and reappeared in his bed. Every time he fell asleep from exhaustion, he would awaken with a scream dying in his throat.

This wasn't the first time he had experienced delirium tremens, but this time was by far the worst. It struck him as a minor miracle that he had survived.

He looked at Noah with pleading eyes. "Am I over the worst of it, Doc?"

"You should be, but you'll still have the dry heaves from time to time, and the shakes, probably continued nightmares. Do you remember the physical examination yesterday?"

"Vaguely."

"You're in bad shape, Mr. Remington. Your liver is almost destroyed. I don't know how you're still alive. Another binge and you're dead. That should be enough incentive right there to make you stop drinking."

"I know. The last time I was in a hospital, the doctor told me I'd buy the farm if I didn't stop."

"But you didn't."

"I tried. I couldn't hack it."

"You're going to have to."

Rem didn't answer directly. "You put some Antabuse down me yesterday, didn't you?"

"Yes."

"I thought that's what it was. I've had an experience with Antabuse before. The worst time in my life."

Noah smiled slightly. "But you have no craving for a drink right now, do you?"

"God, no." Rem shuddered violently. "But I didn't think it was used in a place like this. I remember one doctor telling me that it was only a crutch."

"It went out of fashion for a while, true. But

some of us are employing it again. Antabuse has stood the test of time. It's been in use for thirty-five years. And it's a useful tool in the treatment of alcoholism. That phrase 'Antabuse is a crutch' is nonsense. Any therapeutic tool, including a cast for a broken leg, can be called a crutch. But you're evading the issue here, Mr. Remington." Noah looked at him sternly. "You are an alcoholic. That's the first thing you must face, admit to yourself, before you can hope to be cured."

"Oh, I know I'm an alcoholic, Doc." Rem shrugged. "But alcohol is the only thing that helps me through the day. And the night."

"The thing we have to do is structure a new life-style for you," Noah said briskly. "One that will allow you to exist without alcohol once you leave here."

"How can I develop another life-style, Doc?" Rem asked in an agonized voice. "I've done nothing else in my life but star in movies. Well, I'm no longer a star, and they don't want me for minor roles, either."

"Other people have had their careers come to an end, for one reason or another, and yet they manage to cope without alcohol or drugs."

"Other people ain't me, Doc." Rem jabbed a thumb at his chest. "I rode high in the saddle for too long. Now, I miss it. Without it I feel like shit. I need to get it back.

That's the life-style I want."

"Well, I hardly think that drinking yourself into the grave will help."

Rem thought of telling him the real reason he was here, but he stopped himself in time. If he mentioned that he hoped to catch the attention of a producer by checking into The Clinic, he would likely get tossed out on his ass. Instead, he said, "You know what I even considered? When they started making all the porno flicks, I thought of starring in a few. They're shit, but what the hell, a movie is a movie, and they pay good bucks. But you know why I didn't? My age and too much booze. I couldn't get it up anymore."

"Another good reason for stopping. Or would you rather be dead?"

"Sometimes I wonder if I wouldn't be better off," Rem said with a twist of bitterness.

"Tomorrow, we'll move you out of the detox wing. That should help you to feel better."

Suddenly, Rem was seized by a paroxysm of coughing. He almost strangled. Then he began to heave. Noah held the bedpan for him. Nothing came up. It was painful; he had heaved so much that his stomach muscles were sore.

He finally stopped, eyes streaming tears, and Noah eased him back down onto the bed.

"We're going to have to get some food into you. Along with everything else, you're suffering from malnutrition."

"Food!" Rem groaned. "And have it come right back up again?"

"No more Antabuse. And we'll start with soft stuff." Noah grinned. "Baby food."

Rem groaned again. "Baby food! What am I doing here, reverting to childhood? I'm a steak and potatoes man."

"We'll come to that. First, we take it a step at a time."

Sterling Hanks, dimpled chin resting on his steepled fingers, was contemplating his favorite vista — the desert stretching into the distance beyond his office window. There was really nothing to see, but Hanks's imagination visualized acres of condos out there. He owned several of those acres. It was nothing but sand now, inhabited by lizards and rodents, but soon the building boom would see his acres gobbled up. He had paid a pittance for the land, but soon it would be worth a fortune. . . .

The intercom buzzed behind him, shattering his dream. He grunted, swung around and thumbed a button. "Yes?"

"Mr. Hanks, I just had an urgent call from Bud Long, the guard at the front entrance. He says you should come right away."

"Did he tell you what it's about?"

"No, he just said something is happening

that you would want to see."

"I'll be right down."

Although he sensed the urgency of the summons, Hanks took his time. It would never do to let any of The Clinic employees see him hurrying. In an institution such as this, one never showed panic, under any circumstance. It could easily throw the whole place into an uproar.

At the front entrance he found several employees grouped around the pudgy figure of the guard. At the sight of the director, they scattered, going back to their jobs, leaving Hanks alone with the man.

"All right, Long, what is this all about?"

Bud Long, a retired Los Angeles cop in his fifties, stepped back and gestured outside. "See for yourself, Mr. Hanks."

Hanks stepped up to the glass entrance doors. The glare of the midday sun off of the white gravel borders of the flower beds blinded him for a moment. Then all he could see was a young girl in white slacks leaning against a red VW parked at the curb. A camera hung from a strap across her shoulder.

Hanks looked at the guard. "All I see is a girl with a camera. Is she waiting for somebody?"

"I didn't see anything wrong at first, either. But she's been out there almost an hour. I started watching her more closely and finally caught on to what she's up to."

"Well, what *is* she up to?"

"She's taking pictures of everyone who comes and goes out of these doors!"

"What!"

"That's right, sir. Luckily, there have only been three patients. One check-out, two check-ins."

"Why haven't you called the police and had her arrested?"

"Well . . . I thought I should check with you first, Mr. Hanks." Long scrubbed the back of his hand across his chin. "Besides, the sidewalk out there is city property. It doesn't belong to us. And also because of who she is."

The director looked at Long hard. "Who is she?"

"That's Otto Channing's daughter. Of course, I've heard that they're on the outs. Still, he might not take too kindly to having her rousted."

Hanks pondered for a long moment. "You might be right," he conceded. "Keep a eye on her. I'll be back in a few minutes."

Hanks strode over to the reception desk. "Beatrice, page Dr. Breckinridge. Have him down here on the double."

Noah heard the page on his way to see William Stoddard. "Dr. Breckinridge, report to the reception desk in the lobby immediately."

"Shit! Now what?" Noah stopped in his tracks, thinking for a moment. Finally, he swung around and headed for the lobby in lunging strides.

When he saw Sterling Hanks standing by the desk, his step slowed, and he almost turned away. Then he saw that Hanks had spotted him and was beckoning imperiously.

With a sigh, Noah continued to the desk. "What is it, Hanks? I'm busy with rounds."

The director jerked his head. "Come with me."

Unwillingly, Noah followed him to the front entrance.

Hanks leveled his finger like a pistol barrel. "Look out there."

Blinking against the glare, Noah looked. He saw Susan Channing leaning against the VW, arms crossed over her chest. Head shaded by a floppy straw hat, she looked cool in white, impervious to the heat.

Noah caught himself smiling. Dammit, she *was* lovely! He felt his pulse beat accelerate. Puzzled, he turned to Hanks. "So?"

"Do you know what that is?"

"Sure, that's Susan Channing. I met her at the Tremaine party. But I fail to see what the uproar is about. I don't know what she's doing standing out there in all this heat,

139

but there's no law against it."

"The camera, Doctor!"

"Camera?" Noah looked again and finally saw the camera. "I still don't . . ."

"Dammit, man!" Hanks snarled. "She's standing out there snapping pictures of patients coming and going!"

All of a sudden, Noah wanted to laugh. One would almost think that she had a smoking bomb in her hand, instead of a camera slung over her shoulder.

"What are you grinning about? I fail to see anything humorous! Suppose she's planning to sell those photos to some scavenger sheet, like the *Insider?* Or she could be scheming a little blackmail." Hanks sliced the air with one hand. "But no matter, I want you to march out there and put a stop to it!"

"Me?" Scowling, Noah raked his fingers through his hair. "Why me?"

The director's face reddened. "Why do you always ask that question when I give you an order, Dr. Breckinridge?"

Glaring, the two men stood toe-to-toe for a long moment. Noah thought of many things he could say, but he suddenly experienced a feeling of utter weariness. How many times had they gone through this? And the result was always the same. He always faced the same option − obey the orders or resign.

Without another word, he spun on his heel, pushed through the doors and strode toward Susan.

She saw him coming and straightened up warily. A small smile touched her lips. "I was wondering when they'd be sending someone out to hassle me, but I didn't expect you, Dr. Breckinridge. Are you their errand boy?"

"Susan, why are you doing this?"

"I should think that would be obvious. If some of your celebrities learn that they'll have their pictures taken, they may quietly fade away. And others may have second thoughts about coming here. They might not like their pictures published in the *Insider*."

"Are you the *Insider*'s errand girl?" he asked quietly.

She colored. "Of course not. I don't work for that rag. But I'm sure they would be interested in pictures of some of your celebrities. Like Lacey Houston."

"I'm sure they would be. But the whole world already knows that Lacey is here. Cindy Hodges has seen to that."

"There are others in there." Her mouth had a stubborn set.

"A great many of them don't give a damn, Susan. And those that do come here in secret. You could easily destroy their lives if you're responsible for publicizing their presence here."

She tilted her chin. "That's their problem."

"Susan, you don't really mean that," he said with a sigh. "This is all demeaning, beneath you."

She flared up. "Not nearly so demeaning as this place and its inmates."

"I credited you with more intelligence than to make a remark like that. Now, why don't you just go along home?"

"I'm not leaving here and you can't force me!"

He studied her for a few moments. "No, I suppose I can't." All of a sudden his grin flashed. "Look, I'll make you a proposition. Let me take you on a tour of The Clinic."

Susan couldn't have been more astonished than if it had suddenly started to snow. "You'd do that? But what would that prove?"

He shrugged. "Maybe nothing. On the other hand, it might, just *might*, change your mind about a few things. You can see how we operate, meet a few of the . . . 'inmates.' Those who are willing to meet you, that is."

Susan was still suspicious of his motives. He could be so damned charming, so persuasive, when he turned it on. In that respect, he reminded Susan of her father. Otto Channing could also be utterly charming, when he chose to be. With her father, however, it was all surface; underneath, he was evil, always avoiding the light of scrutiny.

"No tricks?" she asked.

"What tricks?" He spread his hands. "What would I gain by trying to run something past you?"

"A great deal, but what do I have to lose?" She stepped away from the VW. "All right, a guided tour it is."

"Then shall we proceed?"

Noah held out his arm, and Susan tucked her arm into his.

As they approached the big entrance doors, Noah was smiling to himself, anticipating Hanks's reaction.

He was not disappointed. When the doors swung open, Hanks stared at them with his mouth open. It was the first time Noah had ever seen the director lose his control.

"Director Hanks, this is Susan Channing," Noah said breezily. "I'm taking her on a tour of the facilities. I'm sure you have no objection, since Susan is the daughter of one of our most prominent citizens."

Hanks gulped. "You're taking her . . . on a tour?"

"Yep. Oh . . . Here, you hold this." Noah deftly unhooked the camera from Susan's shoulder and gave it to Hanks. "Keep it safe now. She'll be wanting it back when she leaves."

As he walked off with Susan, Noah reflected that it was the first time he had ever gotten in the last word with the director.

Seven

Lacey Houston lay relaxed upon the bed in her room. The sedative Dr. Breckinridge had prescribed for her had put her in a pleasant state, half awake, half dreaming.

She was certainly well rested. In the three days she had been here, she had been averaging about ten hours of sleep a day.

She knew that most people experienced disorientation in a place like The Clinic; they felt fear, even panic, for they were terrified of such a controlled, restrictive environment. It was just the opposite with Lacey. She knew from previous experience that she always felt a great relief once she was officially checked into a drug treatment center, for then *her* problems were no longer *her* problems, they belonged to the doctor. She realized that this was a dangerous self-delusion. The underlying difficulties that had made her a drug dependent, that had brought her here, still existed, but for the moment, she felt safe and protected in the hands of Dr. Breckinridge.

What a nice, understanding doctor he was!

The brief foray with Dr. Breckinridge into her past had left remnants of memory floating in her head. Safe in bed, nothing threatening her at the moment, she drifted back into the past, the immediate past, to the events that had triggered her last coke binge.

It had really started a year before she had signed to do *Heartsong*. It had begun with the breakup of her marriage to Ty Medina – Houston the Third, as the snide press had labeled him. That sobriquet had always galled him. Ty wasn't accustomed to playing second fiddle. Handsome, dashing, virile, Ty was a part-time soldier of fortune, part-time in that he only went adventuring when he needed an excitement fix. He had been left a fortune by his father, and for a few years he had run with the so-called jet set; but when the life of a playboy paled, he would find a small war somewhere on the globe and sell his services to the highest bidder.

Ty cared nothing for the causes he fought for. He cared only for the excitement, the challenge of pitting his mental and physical skills against those of other men. Spending the monies earned in such a fashion always seemed more satisfying to him than spending his inherited fortune. In his late thirties, he was still in top physical condition, and some of his employers referred to Ty Medina as the "ultimate fighting machine." He was the perfect embodiment of many male fantasies.

Lacey Houston met Ty Medina under circumstances that could have been taken from one of Lacey's movies.

Lacey was in Acapulco, recuperating from the rigors of her last movie. She had rented a house and hired a small staff. The actress had opted for privacy, and it was almost total. None of her friends knew where she was.

The only person who knew her whereabouts was Tobe Breen, her business manager; and it was necessary for him to know, since he made the arrangements for renting the house. But he had been forbidden to tell anyone, even her agent, where she was.

She spent the next two weeks lying on the beach and swimming, trying to bake out the fatigue under the blazing sun. But despite the sun and the gorgeous panorama of sand, sky and the multihued sea, two weeks alone and she was climbing the walls. She longed for the company of her friends.

Consequently, she was delighted when Tobe called at the end of the second week. "Lacey, I know you wanted complete isolation down there, but I thought I should pass this one on. Besides —" he chuckled "— knowing you, I figured you'd be chewing on the wallpaper by this time."

"Not the wallpaper, Tobe, but my nails are down to the quick. What's up?"

"Jason has been bugging me about getting in touch with you." Jason Quimby was her agent. "I finally told him that I'd pass on a message. If you don't want to act on it, fine."

"What's the message?"

"Well, Cliff Van Horn keeps a penthouse suite down there, as you probably know. He's one of the richest men in the world, as you probably also know. At least, he's in the top ten. He's backed a few movies in his time. He's got a new script and a director all lined up, but he needs a star. He's been talking to Jason about you, Lacey. Van Horn is giving a party this Saturday. He passed on an invitation through Jason. Since you don't have anything lined up in the near future, I thought . . . Well, I've passed on the message. What you do about it is up to you."

"I think I'll go," she said without hesitation. "I'm going soft in the head here. Tell Jason to let Van Horn know I'll be there. A party is what I need right now, and I *would* like to get back to work."

At eight the following Saturday, wearing a green gauze dress that bared her newly tanned shoulders and complemented her emeralds,

148

Lacey got on the elevator at the ground floor of Van Horn's building. The elevator was empty when she got on, but just before she pressed the Up button, a man came hurrying across the lobby. She held the doors open for him.

As the doors sighed shut, he said in a deep voice, "Thank you."

"You're welcome."

As the elevator began its rapid ascent, Lacey studied him openly. He was tall, muscular, dark and certainly handsome. He had a dimpled chin and what Lacey always thought of as an Errol Flynn mustache. Come to think of it, he looks a bit like a young Errol Flynn, she mused, only darker.

His eyes, which he now turned on her, were a deep black. "Forgive me. I'm Ty Medina."

"And I'm Lacey . . ."

The lights went off, and the elevator came to a jarring halt.

"Oh, hell!" Ty Medina said. "The power's gone."

"It happens often here."

"How long does it usually last?"

Lacey shrugged in the dark. "Usually not too long. But on the other hand, it *could* last all night."

"I don't much fancy being stuck in here half the night."

She heard the rustle of clothing, and then a

small light blossomed. His cigarette lighter.

"Let's see what we have here." He held the light up, his face upturned.

"I'm sure someone will investigate soon. There are bound to be other people wanting to use the elevator."

He grunted. "Maybe. Maybe not. I don't like to take chances. I tend to get claustrophobic in small, confined spaces." He reached a hand up. "Ah, there we go!"

He had found a panel in the roof of the elevator. Ty pushed against it and it raised. He manipulated it up and out of sight, exposing an oblong hole.

He held out the lighter. "Would you hold this, please?"

She took the lighter, then said incredulously, "You're going to . . . ?"

He grinned lazily, his teeth ivory white in the dim light. "Why not? I certainly don't intend to stay in here."

He reached over his head with both hands, caught the edge of the hole, and began pulling himself up Within seconds only his feet could be seen. He made it seem so easy.

Then his feet disappeared, soon to be replaced by his smiling face. He dangled a hand down. "The light, please, ma'am."

She handed him the lighter, and he disappeared with it, leaving Lacey wondering what kind of a crazy situation she had gotten involved in.

Shortly, his face appeared in the hole again. "Yep, I can reach the door on the next floor up. We're stuck about halfway between floors." He stretched one hand down, beckoning. "Come on, I'll pull you up."

"I don't believe this, I simply don't believe this."

"Up to you, lady. I can get us out. But if you want to stay down there, in the dark, it's okay with me."

"But isn't it dusty, greasy, up there?"

"A bit."

"My clothes . . ." She gestured. "I'll get all filthy, and I'm on my way to a party."

"So was I. Cliff Van Horn?"

"Why, yes."

"Same here. Cliff won't mind. He's a touch weird, you know. He'll probably get a kick out of it. Hell, he may even suggest that everybody strip down to their shorts so we'll all be equal."

She laughed. "I think you're a touch weird, yourself."

"I won't deny it. But I have more fun than sane people." He grew impatient. "Well, are you coming? This isn't exactly the best place for clever repartee."

"Oh, all right," she said resignedly. "What do I do?"

"Let me put this lighter aside . . ."

Lacey felt a heartbeat of panic when she was plunged into darkness again. All of a sudden, she was anxious to get out of there.

"Stretch your arms up."

Dimly, she could see his hands hanging down. Strong, capable hands. She extended her arms. She was seized by both wrists, and then she was off the floor. Ty was amazingly strong. He lifted her easily, and almost before she knew it, she was through the hole and standing beside him. Above her was the elevator shaft stretching into darkness beyond the pale flicker of the cigarette lighter. She drew in her breath and clung to him, glad of his reassuring strength.

"Here, hold the lighter while I see if I can get the doors open on the next floor."

He left her alone and pulled himself up to a tiny ledge no more than a few inches wide. Inserting his fingers between the rubber edges of the door on the next floor, he began to force the doors apart, until there was enough space to jam one foot between them.

Slowly, the doors widened — one foot, two feet. Then his body was between them, holding them open. He called down, "You'll have to climb up now. Between my legs. Come on, move it, lady! I can't hold them open forever."

Lacey reached between his spread legs. Her

fingers searched for something firm to grasp. "There's nothing to hold onto!" she cried.

"Hang on to my legs."

"But I may pull you off."

"I'll manage. Just do it!"

She gripped his ankles with both hands and began to pull herself up. For a few moments she didn't think she could do it, and once she was sure she felt his right leg begin to slide back into the elevator shaft. Then his foot shifted slightly, becoming rigid again.

Desperately, Lacey exerted her waning strength. Then she was through, over the top and sprawling into the hall. "All right, I'm in now!"

"It's about time."

He stepped into the corridor, and the doors whooshed shut. What little illumination the lighter had provided was gone, and the darkness in the hallway was total.

Lacey got shakily to her feet. "I'm sorry about your cigarette lighter. I'm afraid I left it down in the elevator shaft."

"No big deal. . . ."

The lights came on without warning, and Lacey could hear the elevator in motion again.

"My God!" She clapped a hand to her mouth. "I just thought of something! What if the power had come back on while we were still inside the shaft? We would have been killed!"

"But it didn't," he said in a reasonable tone. "Life is full of what-ifs. If we let our lives be ruled by them, we'd never get out of bed in the morning." He extended his arm. "Shall we go to the party now? I feel badly in need of a drink."

Lacey looked down at herself. The pale green dress was filthy, dusty, and had a large grease stain across the front. One stocking was laddered.

"Oh, I couldn't possibly go now, not looking like this."

"I tell you Cliffie won't mind, he'll think it a hoot," he said impatiently.

"Well, *I* mind. And he may think it's a hoot, but I sure as hell don't."

He tapped a thumbnail against his teeth, eyeing her appraisingly. "I happen to think that you're rather attractively mussed. But if you feel that way, I have an alternate suggestion."

She eyed this wild man warily. "And just what might that be?"

"I have an apartment not far from here. It's not quite up to the Van Horn standard, but it'll do. I have the best liquor available, some Russian caviar and probably the best jazz collection around. Collecting old jazz records is a hobby of mine. Do you happen to like jazz?"

"Oh, and it is your idea that we strip down to our 'shorts,' so we'll be equal?" she asked dryly.

"What ever turns you on."

Lacey felt her blood quicken pleasurably. She hadn't been sexually attracted to anyone for months, and she sensed that it might be one reason for her restlessness during the past few weeks. "As it happens, I love jazz. But I do have to call Van Horn."

"There are telephones in the lobby," he said with a slight smile.

After walking down to the main floor – she had refused to trust herself to the elevator again – Lacey used the lobby telephone to ring the Van Horn penthouse. As she listened to the phone ring, she gazed at Ty Medina, who stood a few feet away, smoking a cigarette that he'd had the doorman light. Even standing perfectly still, he seemed to tilt forward slightly, as though he were on skis, challenging a dangerous slope.

A man's voice said in her ear, "Van Horn here."

"Mr. Van Horn, this is Lacey Houston. Something came up. I'm very sorry, but I can't make your party."

"That's really too bad, my dear," the faintly British voice said. "I especially wanted to see you. I don't know if Jason told you, but I have a movie in preproduction. It has a role written with you in mind."

"Some mention was made of it, yes. And I would like to get back to work again."

155

"I have a shooting script all ready. Would you like to see it?"

"I would very much like to see it. Would you messenger it over to me? I'm staying here for another couple of weeks."

"I would be most delighted. Just give me your address."

Thirty minutes later Ty Medina let Lacey into his apartment. It was not a penthouse, but it was certainly expensive.

"I don't know about Van Horn's place, but this one isn't too shabby," Lacey commented.

"It'll do," he said with a shrug. "I only spend a few months a year here."

"And the rest of the time?"

"Here and there." He looked at her with those piercing black eyes. "I just came up last week from Central America. There's a small war going on down there."

"A war?" she asked, faintly startled.

"Yeah," he said casually. "I'm a mercenary. I fight for hire."

"Which side?"

"Whichever pays the most bucks. There's a bathroom that way, if you want to clean up, shower maybe." He pointed. "And in the hall closet next to the bathroom are several bathrobes. I'm sure you can find one to fit." His bold gaze dared her to question him about the robes.

As she went down the hall to the bathroom, Lacey was wondering exactly what she had gotten herself into. A mercenary? She almost turned back to ask him if he also charged for his sexual maneuvers, but decided to let it go.

She stopped and slid back the closet door, revealing a half dozen robes of various sizes and colors. She laughed softly. Did he run a harem through here?

Some fifteen minutes later she emerged from the bathroom, rosy and tingling from the shower, one of his robes draped around her.

Ty was in a robe, as well. He was busy at the glass-topped coffee table. In the background, music was playing softly — Bix Beiderbecke on the horn. As Ty stood and stepped back, Lacey stopped short, staring.

It was all laid out — four lines of powder as white as sugar, and two red-and-white straws three inches in length.

Ty said proudly, "I brought this back with me from Central America. The best coke, almost pure."

The white lines both drew and repelled Lacey. She had never used cocaine. What harm could it do, just for tonight? The misery of the past few weeks could be wiped out in an instant.

She laughed a little wildly. "What, no silver

spoon? No hundred-dollar bills?"

He gave a careless shrug. "Who needs all that fancy paraphernalia? It works just as well this way." He bowed ironically. "After you, my lady."

Lacey fell to her knees before the low table. She placed a finger tightly over one nostril, put the end of the straw into the other, and sniffed a line of coke, just as she had seen so many of her friends do. The sensations came immediately — a burning high in her sinuses under her eyes, and a bitter taste dripping down the back of her throat. She repeated the process with the other nostril, then sat back with her eyes closed as Ty squatted beside her and snorted his lines.

The rush came within minutes. It spread over her nerves like a soothing balm. She felt her energy level expand. She knew that the man beside her desired her, and that was an added bonus.

"Come along, Lacey."

Ty was standing, holding out a hand. She took it and let him draw her up. He folded her into his arms. Her robe fell open. His mouth teased hers, his hands fondled her breasts. Her skin felt extremely sensitive. She could feel his pulsing hardness against her thigh.

He led her into a bedroom. Lacey had only a hazy impression of a round bed covered with black satin sheets, and little else. She was at the peak of an incredible high now, and she knew it would only heighten the sex with this man.

Before she knew it, Ty was undressed. His body was exceptional, and it was evident that he took inordinately good care of it.

From a small container on the nightstand beside the bed, he dusted his palm with cocaine, then rubbed it on the head of his penis. Lacey knew that this was supposed to prolong a man's pleasure, delay his orgasm, but she had never seen a man use coke that way before.

Now he reached for her, and they fell across the bed together. Dreamily, Lacey watched as he worked on her body. He had almost arcane knowledge of her erogenous zones, and soon she was at a high pitch of arousal.

As Ty rolled her onto her back and entered her, Lacey abandoned herself to the combined pleasures of sex and cocaine. And she learned that what she had heard about the deadening effect of coke on a man's organ was correct. After her first shuddering orgasm, Ty remained hard. He continued to pound into her, driving her to a second orgasm within minutes.

Even after Ty finally came, he was still hard inside of her. "Great sex, babe," he said as he moved off her.

Lacey was slowly coming down off the high, but she wasn't at the point of crashing yet. Her nerve ends still thrummed with pleasure, and from time to time she spasmed slightly, as though coming again.

Sometime later she dimly heard his voice. She twisted around to look at him. He was sitting up. "What did you say, Ty?"

He was bending over the glass-topped nightstand. He dumped out a mound of coke, then began to shape lines with a safety razor blade.

"I asked if you're ready for another snort."

His question triggered a guilty response in Lacey. In a few minutes' time she had shattered all her firm resolutions to never indulge in drugs of any kind. From what she had read about cocaine, she knew that she would be coming down soon; the guilt and remorse would be heavy. She would sink into a slough of depression.

All that could be avoided with a couple of lines of cocaine.

"Well?"

"No, Ty. I think I'll pass," she said.

He shrugged. "Suit yourself."

Taking a straw from the drawer, he sniffed both lines. "Ah-ah, good stuff!" He lay back down on the bed.

"Ty . . . do you use cocaine regularly?"

"Am I hooked? That's what you mean, isn't it? The answer is no. I only use it on occasions like this. If I got hooked, I'd screw up my life royally. In my line of work you screw up your head, you don't live long, babe."

Ty let a hand fall on to her naked breasts. He tweaked a nipple gently. "What's the rest of your name? Lacey what?"

She was startled. "Didn't I tell you, back there?"

"Nope." He grinned. "Only the first name. And considering what we've been up to, maybe you should introduce yourself properly."

"Maybe I should," she said dryly. "I'm Lacey Houston."

"Lacey Houston." He rolled the name around on his tongue. "It has a nice sound to it."

She stared at him, nonplussed and not a little piqued. She was accustomed to being recognized even without the name. "Doesn't the name mean anything to you?"

"No. Should it?"

"I'm a movie star."

"Movie star?" He looked blank. "Houston? Not *that* Lacey Houston?"

"I don't know why you emphasize *that.*"

He shook his head. "An actress! A movie star! Shit, what have I gotten myself into here?" He swung his legs over the edge of the bed and got up.

"What's wrong with being an actress?" she asked, defensive now.

"What's wrong with it?" He shrugged into his robe. "I'll tell you what's wrong with it. Not only are all movie people screwed up, but you live in a fantasy world." He gestured contemptuously. "Lady, I live in the real world. And I want real people around me, not some shadow with no substance."

"Where do you get off saying something like that?" Her anger was running now. "You admitted that you fight for pay. That's the real world?"

"You're goddamned right it is! When you've got a weapon, the other guy has a weapon, and you're going for each other, it's for real."

"To me it's another fantasy, a macho fantasy," she said scornfully. "If men didn't have these fantasies, there'd be fewer wars."

Scowling blackly, he towered over her. He raised his hand as if to slap her, and Lacey steeled herself against cringing. Then he let the hand drop and said in a disgusted voice, "I think you'd better get dressed and get the hell out of here, lady."

He turned away and strode out of the room, the tails of his robe flapping like angry wings.

Lacey sat staring after him for a moment, seething. How dare he talk to her like that! Damn him, she was Lacey Houston!

Then she gave a bark of laughter. Apparently, he dared to talk to her like that because she *was* Lacey Houston.

Her anger drained away and bleak despair

poured in. The tacky scene made her feel like a whore who'd been picked up in a bar and forced to turn a trick for two lines of coke.

Why couldn't she, just once, find a man who didn't consider her unworthy? Against all logic, she felt that she had somehow failed him. No matter what other reasons had brought on her two divorces, there had been times with each husband that she had felt a failure.

Listless, her thoughts dull under the weight of depression, she got out of bed and climbed into her clothes. When she went into the living room a short time later, Ty Medina, still in his robe, stood at the picture window staring out, a glass of vodka in his hand. From the way his back stiffened, Lacey knew that he had heard her. He didn't turn.

She had an almost overwhelming desire to tiptoe. But why the devil should *I* feel guilty? she thought. At the last moment, just as she stepped into the hall, she slammed the door viciously.

Lacey was woozy on vodka the next evening when the phone rang. It was Ty Medina. "Lacey, I'm sorry about last night. I was way out of line, I admit it."

She felt a rebirth of her anger. "You damned well should be!"

"I don't blame you for being pissed. All I can

tell you is that I had a bad experience with another actress a few years back. It was a downer, a real bad trip. That's no reason to take it out on you."

"Why are you calling, Ty?"

There was a brief pause. Then he sighed. "First, I called to apologize. You know, you're a hard lady to track down. I've had one hell of a time getting your phone number. I finally figured out that Cliff Van Horn might have it, but I spent most of the day trying before I thought of him. The fact that I did all that should tell you that I am sorry."

"So what do you think that will buy you?"

"Well, I'd hoped that it would buy me your forgiveness. Secondly, I'd hoped to see you again. Maybe we could have dinner."

Lacey held the receiver away from her ear, staring at it. Cautiously, she finally said, "You can ask me that, after all that abuse? Even more, you expect me to go?"

"I said I was sorry, didn't I? Haven't you ever said things you were sorry for afterward?"

She had, any number of times. Maybe he really was sorry. And he was a charming bastard and better than most in bed.

"Besides, what can you lose?" He said in a perfectly reasonable tone. "Go out with me. If I act like a shit again, kiss me off."

She had to laugh, completely disarmed. "All

right. I'll probably regret it, but I'll risk it."

In her room at The Clinic, Lacey stirred restlessly, pulling out of her reverie.

Regret it? That was the understatement of the decade. She had gone out with Ty Medina, of course, and they had been married three weeks later. It had been a stormy marriage, an utter disaster. Of all the stupid moves in her life — and Lacey was willing to concede there had been many — marrying Ty Medina had been the worst.

After the wedding she had found out that he had lied about his cocaine habit — a common link shared by almost all hard-core addicts. It was possible that he was off the drug when away on his warring forays; she had no way of knowing about that.

The marriage lasted less than a year. During that time Ty was abusive and loving by turns, and it wasn't long before he began to resent being Lacey Houston's husband. Finally, they had a bitter fight and Ty split, heading for another Central American hot spot.

Lacey filed for a divorce. He didn't fight it, and she hadn't heard from him since.

But, she had failed again. She had been rejected again. And when Kurt introduced her to cocaine again, she began to lean more and more heavily on those thin white lines to keep her propped up during the days. And the nights. The end result was that she staggered onto the set of *Heartsong* on the first day, disoriented, unable to speak her lines, completely out of it. Don Sparr, the director, had had enough. If she couldn't straighten up, he would walk. In the end, an agreement was reached between Lacey and the film's producer. The film would go into hiatus during the month or six weeks it would take her to go through treatment. It would be as expensive as hell, yet the only other alternative was to junk the picture, which meant that all the money already spent would go down the tubes.

Lacey had been frightened enough to agree, and she had sense enough to realize that she was getting the best of the deal. If the picture was junked, it would more than likely mean the end of her career. And if she wasn't who she was, one of the top ten box office draws in the industry, she would simply have been replaced. As much as she sometimes hated it, Lacey knew that she would be devastated if stardom was ever denied her.

With a sigh, she got out of bed. The effects of the sedative had worn off, and the room, as nice as it was, suddenly seemed stifling. Was the door locked? She hadn't been specifically forbidden to leave the room. She stepped to the door and turned the knob. It opened easily.

She removed her pajamas and opened the clothes closet. Theodore had brought her clothes in and hung them up for her. She got into a pair of black slacks and a white pullover sweater, then stepped into a pair of flats. She picked up her purse and eased the door open, peering along the corridor. It was empty for the moment, except for an attendant at the desk at the far end of the hall. Lacey remembered that the main entrance was that way.

She turned in the other direction. There was at least one difference between this and a regular medical hospital — all the doors she passed were closed.

At the end, the corridor made a right turn, and then ended at the glass doors to a solarium. It was empty and the doors stood open. Lacey went in. The room was flooded with sunlight; the ceiling and three walls were of glass.

She walked over to the east wall. The desert began just beyond The Clinic grounds and stretched as far as she could see.

Lacey took a cigarette from her purse and then realized that she was without matches. She simply stood, cigarette between her fingers, staring out.

"May I?"

With a start, she whirled around. A slim man dressed all in brown stood immediately behind her. He was in his early forties. His hair was black and full, combed straight back. His features were even, with a nose that brought the word *patrician* to mind. His eyes were a warm brown. In his hand was a cigarette lighter.

He spun the wheel and a tiny flame spurted. "Would you like a light?"

"Thank you."

He held the lighter to her cigarette. Their eyes met and he smiled, showing even white teeth.

"You're Lacey Houston, aren't you?" At her silent nod he said, "I would have recognized you anywhere. I'm a great fan of yours. I'm Jeffrey Lawrence."

Eight

Susan didn't really know what to expect. Noah's invitation had caught her completely by surprise. She had never really cared about seeing the inside of The Clinic, yet the opportunity was too good to pass up. She had always thought — when she thought about it at all — that the inner workings of a treatment center would vaguely resemble those of an asylum, something like what she'd seen in an old movie on television, *The Snake Pit*. Drooling, screaming, hair-pulling men and women wandering around like lost souls.

Instead, she found a well-ordered environment.

She caught Noah's glance, and he grinned. "Isn't quite what you expected, is it?"

She had to smile. "I guess it isn't, no. I suppose I've always had rather weird notions as to what a place like this would be like."

"That's why I wanted to give you a guided tour."

"One thing I do find strange. A guard with a gun?"

"Oh, that's just for show. We've found that it not only gives the patients a feeling of security, but it discourages gate-crashers, and that's important for the celebrities present."

He opened a door and ushered her into a rather large room, furnished with comfortable chairs grouped around a low round coffee table. In one corner was a large coffee maker and a small refrigerator.

"This is probably the most important room in the whole building, something on a par with the operating room in a medical hospital."

She glanced around her. "It looks perfectly ordinary to me."

He was still grinning. "Some of the patients don't think so. They call it The Snake Pit."

This so closely paralleled Susan's thinking of a moment ago that she made a startled sound.

He nodded. "Yes. After the old movie. This is where the patients wrestle their demons. They snap and snarl at one another, and bare their souls. When I'm here, I have to be part referee, part lion tamer, part father confessor, part exorcist. It's the group therapy room. In here we confess to one another, we relate our own horror stories and act out psychodramas. We try to get the patient to open up to the other addicts and alcoholics. If a patient can do that, he, or she, is more than halfway home."

"It sounds fascinating," Susan commented. "I don't suppose you ever let an outsider in? Like a college student auditing a class?"

"Absolutely not –" He caught himself, looking at her keenly. "You?"

"Well, you said you wanted me to see how you work here. What better way?"

"That would be violating a patient's privilege. It would destroy trust in the therapist. And to be effective, that trust must exist between doctor and patient."

"But what if they all agreed to let me sit in on a session?"

Noah looked at her in alarm. "Now wait a minute! You're not thinking of asking for such permission?"

"No, no. Noah, don't worry." She touched his arm lightly. "I'm not going to do that."

"Thank God." Noah relaxed. "Hanks, our estimable director, is already steamed at me for letting you in here at all. If you did something like that, he'd have both our heads."

He began to lead the way out of the room.

"Do all your patients undergo group therapy?"

"Almost all, but now and then it's one-on-one with the therapist."

"Like some of the more famous people? They

don't care to air their weaknesses in front of others?"

"Well, we do have to protect their privacy, if they so desire. But I always strongly recommend group therapy, and only a very few balk."

"I wouldn't mind meeting Lacey Houston," Susan said wistfully. They were out in the hall now, walking along slowly. "I shouldn't think she would object. After Cindy Hodges's column, the whole world must know she's here."

"I would have to ask her," Noah said somewhat stiffly. "Despite her public exposure, Miss Houston strikes me as a rather private person."

"I know this sounds corny, but what is Lacey Houston *really* like? You read so much about her. Every viewpoint seems to be so different —"

Two swinging doors to a side corridor slammed open in front of them, and a young man in a hospital gown burst through. He skidded to a stop, looking both ways along the corridor.

"Billie!" In two quick strides Noah was alongside, seizing his arm in a firm grip.

The young man had a mop of long, unkempt blond hair, which straggled down over his forehead like a veil, through which black eyes peered. Those eyes, burning with a fanatic's fire, fixed on Susan. To Susan, the eyes seemed slightly mad, yet they exerted a hypnotic pull.

The young man started to struggle in Noah's grip. Then an alarm bell sounded and he subsided. With his free hand Noah plucked a two-way radio from his belt and barked into it, "This is Dr. Breckinridge! Turn that damned bell off!"

In a moment the bell was cut off. Furious, Noah snarled, "Who gave the order to turn the alarm on? It's to be used only in an emergency. You've probably spooked everybody in the place!"

"But it *is* an emergency, Doctor," said a tinny voice over the transmitter. "Billie Reaper is loose somewhere in The Clinic."

"No longer. I have him. How did he get out? I left orders for his room to be locked at all times."

"We don't know, Doctor."

"Then find out, dammit!"

Noah refastened the radio onto his belt just as Bud Long came legging it along the corridor. He came to a halt before Noah, panting, his face red.

"For God's sake, Bud," Noah snapped. "How did he get out?"

Reholstering his gun, the guard shrugged. "I don't know. Somebody must have forgotten to lock his door."

Noah frowned at the singer. "You going to

173

tell me, Billie?"

"No way, José." Billie grinned savagely. "The only thing you need to know is that nobody locks old Billie up."

"As far as I'm concerned, you could march right out the front door," Noah said in disgust. "You don't need treatment, you need a keeper. But the way you're dressed —" Noah grinned suddenly "— in a hospital gown, with your bare butt mooning in the breeze . . . what kind of an image would that be for your fans?"

Billie grinned back. "They might like it, man."

"Well, come on, let's go back to your room." Noah glanced over at Susan. "Stay here, Susan. I'll be right back."

Noah began to lead Billie away. Just before Noah took him through the doors, the singer turned his head, tossing his hair back out of his eyes. He winked at Susan.

Through it all she had watched, wide-eyed, a little fearful. This was more like what she had been expecting — a patient running wild-eyed through the halls. She smiled to herself, realizing that Noah was probably furious about it. It certainly wasn't the picture he had been striving to show her.

Alone now, she looked around uncertainly. The hallway was empty. Maybe this was her chance to explore a little. Hesitantly, she went to the end of the corridor. To the right was a solarium, and the doors were standing open.

Susan went in. A tall man and a slender woman stood at the east wall, staring at the solarium door. Susan started toward them.

"What was the alarm about?" the man asked. "A fire alarm? We were wondering if we should get out of the building."

"Nothing to worry about," Susan said, gazing intently at the woman, suddenly realizing that she was looking at Lacey Houston! "Evidently, it is turned on when a patient isn't where he's supposed to be."

"Was someone out?" Lacey Houston asked.

"It's okay, he's being taken care of," Susan said. "Aren't you Lacey Houston?"

"I . . . oh, hell, what's the use of denying it? The whole wide world knows I'm here. Yes, I'm Lacey Houston."

"I'm Susan Channing. I'm delighted to meet you, Miss Houston. I'm a big fan of yours, but then I don't know too many people who aren't."

"You're very gracious to say that, Miss Channing," Lacey said. "This is Jeffrey Lawrence." She smiled ruefully. "A fellow inmate."

"How do you do, Miss Channing?"

Susan transferred her gaze to Jeffrey long enough to acknowledge the introduction, then looked back at Lacey. The actress seemed smaller than she did on the screen, and less glamorous, Susan thought. Of course, the circumstances hardly lent themselves to glamour. Lacey also struck Susan as oddly vulnerable. On screen, she usually portrayed chic, seductive, worldly women. But then, Susan corrected herself, there was always a certain vulnerability lurking just beneath the surface. The actress didn't strike Susan as the prototype of the drug addict. But then, was there a prototype?

"Ah, there you are, Susan!"

Susan turned around to see Noah loping toward them. He nodded to Lacey and Jeffrey Lawrence. "I do hope you weren't alarmed by that bell. It was touched off by mistake."

"I was a little concerned, Doctor," Lacey said. "But Miss Channing was kind enough to explain."

"Oh?" Noah darted a glance at Susan. "That *was* kind of her."

"I'd better get back to my room," Lacey said. "I hope I didn't break any rules, Doctor. I got restless, feeling confined, and had to get out for a few minutes."

"No rules broken, Lacey. You're free to roam about at will. You, as well, Jeffrey. After all, this isn't a jail."

"I'll walk you to your room, Lacey." Jeffrey held out his arm, Lacey took it, and they left the solarium.

The moment they were gone, Noah turned to

Susan. "What did you tell them?"

"Why, nothing but the truth," Susan said innocently. "I just told them that a patient wasn't where he was supposed to be."

"Great," Noah said glumly. "They probably think that freaked-out characters roam the halls at will. Why didn't you stay put, like I asked you to?"

"Why? You afraid that I might see something that I shouldn't?"

"Of course not," he snapped. "Something like that happens rarely around here, although you probably won't believe that. I don't know how it happened today. I suspect the little bastard bribed somebody to leave his door unlocked, although I don't know where he got the money. But I'll find out who, and when I do, heads will roll."

"From what you said earlier, I was led to believe there were no locks here, no one held against his will."

"There are exceptions. The rooms in the detox wing are usually kept locked. This particular patient is a wild man. He was completely out of it when brought in. But he isn't here against his will. He signed himself in —" Noah stopped short, realizing that he was violating one of The Clinic's rules — never talk about a patient, especially to a layman, and a hostile one at that.

"Come on, Susan, it's close to lunchtime," he said. "You've seen enough for one day. We have a small cafeteria in The Clinic for the employees. The food here is as good as any you'll find in Oasis."

Susan took his arm. As they entered the cafeteria, she stopped and looked up at him. "How about the inmates? Are they served the same food?" At his scowl, she laughed "Now, don't come down on me. I'm only using the word Lacey Houston used."

"He's nice, Zoe," Susan said enthusiastically. "He's a little uptight when it comes to The Clinic. But when he's off that subject, he's warm and can be amusing."

It was late afternoon, and they were in the atrium having drinks. Madam was perched on Zoe's shoulder, preening. Smoke drifting up from her small cigar, Zoe studied Susan with some amusement. "Dr. Breckinridge impressed me, as well. But then, I wasn't expecting an ogre. Of course, I'm an old lady, and I'm sure he would make more of an effort to impress you, girl."

Susan's color was already high, but now it deepened. "If you mean did he come on to me, no, he didn't," she said defensively. "But I might not —" She broke off in confusion.

"You might not mind too much," Zoe said

178

dryly. "Is that what you started to say? That might not be such a bad idea, Susan. You should find some fellow for yourself. But never forget one thing. . . ." She leaned forward, suddenly intense. "Our fight isn't with him, it's with The Clinic. Don't ever forget that."

"I won't forget, Zoe," Susan assured her. "I'll keep my priorities straight."

Zoe nodded, satisfied. "Just so you do. Now . . ." She took a pull of her margarita. "Tell me about The Clinic."

"Well, from what I saw, it's a nice place. Clean, competently run. One thing Noah told me is a little surprising. Many of the employees, including some of the nurses, are former alcoholics or drug addicts. He said their own experiences make them invaluable —" The ringing of the phone interrupted her.

Zoe stepped into the kitchen to the wall phone. "Hello?"

A man's voice said, "May Fremont? Is that you, May?"

Zoe's blood turned to ice and she swayed. For a moment she thought she was going to faint. From the crackle on the line she knew that the call was long-distance. She forced the words out, "Who is this?"

"Sam Watson, May. It is *May*, isn't it?"

Zoe closed her eyes tightly, her thoughts winging back. In the beginning, in Nevada, she had needed some political clout, and she had found it in Sam Watson, a mover and shaker behind the scenes in state politics. Sam had done favors for her, and in return, he had been granted free services at the Heavenly Retreat.

A voice out of the past! It could only mean bad news. She longed to hang up, yet she had to know.

"Yes, Sam," she said in a calm voice. "How are you?"

"Getting old, May," the voice said with a chuckle. "If you were still in the business, I'm afraid I could no longer avail myself of the free rides. Pun intended, heh, heh!"

"Sam, how did you get this number? It's unlisted."

"It wasn't easy, believe me. But old duffer that I am, I still have some clout left. And remember, I was the one in the old days who advised you to change your name, to become May Fremont instead of Zoe Tremaine."

"Yes, I remember very well, Sam. Not that I'm not glad to hear from you, but –"

His raspy chuckle interrupted her. "I'll just bet you are. Out of the business, gone respectable, and here comes this old fart out of your, uh, checkered past."

"Sam, what's this all about? I know you didn't call just to hash over old times."

"Hardly, May, hardly." Sam Watson became

serious. "I'm a bit concerned. Somebody has been making inquiries about one Zoe Tremaine. Word came to me in a round-about way, so I thought I'd buzz you."

Zoe went rigid. "Who, Sam? Who is it?"

"That I don't know. Not yet. I'm not even sure if it's through official channels or some private source. I'll try to find out, May, but it will take a while. How about you? Can you think of anybody? You been making enemies?"

"Oh, yes, I've collected a few," she said slowly. Into her mind popped the name Todd Remington. He wasn't an enemy, but could he be behind it? He might have recognized her, but even if he had, why would he dig back into the past?

"The same old tactful May," Sam Watson said. "But one thing . . . Whoever is doing the digging apparently doesn't know the May Fremont name yet."

"Do you think someone will make the connection between the two names?"

"Hard to say. Depends on who's doing the looking. If it's someone with access to police channels, they'll hook the two names up sooner or later. But if it's just a private citizen, it'll be tougher. Can you think of any reason why the cops might be checking on you, May?"

"Not offhand, no."

"Well, I'll nose around some more, see if I

can come up with anything else."

"I'd appreciate it, Sam."

"What the hell, May. I owe you. I had some rare old times at your place in the old days. Just thinking about it makes me *almost* horny, and that's something at my age."

Zoe hung up, her thoughts churning.

One look at her and Susan jumped up in alarm. "What's wrong, Zoe? You're white as a sheet."

Zoe sat down, absently caressing Madam's bright plumage. "Did I understand you to say that you'll be visiting The Clinic again?"

"Noah invited me to come back anytime."

"You met some of the patients, you said. Was one of them Todd Remington?"

"The drunk who caused the trouble at the party?" Susan shook her head. "No, I didn't see him."

"Susan, I want you to do something for me. I knew Todd before I came to Oasis. I'm not sure if he recognized me or not. But I do need to know. It's important. Will you see if you can find out for me?"

"Sure, Zoe." Susan looked at her curiously. "This has to do with your mysterious past, right?"

"Well, yes," Zoe said hesitantly.

"Was that what the phone call was about? Something's upset you terribly."

"Susan . . ." Zoe sighed. "I know you're full of a million questions. I know that I've kept my past a secret, even from you. There is a good reason. I promise to tell you about it eventually. I have a feeling that you'll understand. But I just don't feel up to it right now," she said wearily. "Trust me a little longer. Just try and find out if Rem recognized me at the party."

Nine

"I really appreciate all your efforts, Dan," Thad Dasnell said into the phone.

"It didn't require much effort, Thad, not in this day of computers. And Vegas is essentially a small town. Of course, we can't begin to keep track of all the tourists who pour through the casinos, but I gathered that you're mainly interested in knowing if this Zoe Tremaine was a resident here."

"That's correct?"

"Well, the name seems to be a dead end, and none of the people I showed the photo to registered even a flicker. Of course, it's not the best photo I've ever seen."

"I know, it was taken at a distance with a telephoto lens."

"And I've found no match on the records on the prints you sent me. Have you tried D.C.?"

"Yes, I sent a copy to Washington, but I don't expect to hear for a bit. You know they don't knock themselves out for a small-town force, especially if there's no immediate crime involved."

"Tell me about it. Any reason why you hit on Vegas?"

"Oh, not only Vegas. I've tried Reno and Carson City with the same result. I just had a gut feeling that the woman might have resided somewhere in Nevada in the past."

"Well, I've been a cop long enough to know that a gut feeling often pays off. But it looks like you may have struck out this time."

"I haven't given up yet. I'll keep at it awhile."

"Well, if you get anything more, like a make on her from Washington, get on the horn and I'll dig into it further."

"Okay. And thanks again, Dan."

Darnell hung up the phone and sat for a few moments deep in thought. He had been reluctant to do Channing's bidding and dig into the woman's past, but now that he had started he was intrigued. He was a damned good policeman, he knew that without flattering himself. In the beginning, he had thought it would simply be a matter of sending out a few inquiries, yet so far he'd run into a blank wall. Of course, it had only been a few days; still, there should have been *something*.

Zoe Tremaine was probably an assumed name, and if it was, it seemed likely that there was something in her past that she wanted to hide, and the possibility was high that it was criminal.

Darnell was a dogged, persistent man, and mysteries intrigued him. He hadn't come across one yet that he couldn't unravel, and he was determined that this one wouldn't stump him.

Eventually, he would learn everything there was to know about Zoe Tremaine. What he would do with the information once he had it was a different matter. His dislike of Otto Channing and his distaste for his own involvement with Channing and the mayor grew stronger every day. But if he openly defied Channing, he could wind up with his ass handed to him on a platter.

Well, first things first. He enjoyed doing a good clean job of police work. Once he had all the information, then he would decide what to do about it.

"Bobbie," Governor William Stoddard said, "I'm suffering here. I'm suffering the tortures of the damned. I've never wanted a drink so badly in my whole damned life, and you come at me with chicken-shit stuff! An appropriations bill that somehow got lost in the shuffle. Why wasn't that brought to my attention before I left?"

"I don't know, Governor." Bobbie Reed was speaking from the capitol building of Stoddard's home state, halfway across the continent. "It was an oversight on somebody's part, I agree."

"Well, hell, put it in the mail to me, if you think it can't wait. I'll sign it and ship it back to you."

"Governor, a lot of rumors are flying. People are asking questions. The lieutenant governor was bombarded with questions at his conference yesterday. Are you really off fishing or hunting? One reporter said it was hard to believe, that it wasn't your thing. Another said he had heard you were in a hospital, suffering from incurable cancer."

Stoddard grinned for the first time in ages. "And how did old Darrel take to that? I'll bet that rasped his ass a mite."

"Well, for one thing he came down on me hard after the press conference. He demanded that I put him in touch with you or suffer the consequences. I told him no way."

"And how did he react to that?"

"He blew. He ranted and raved and threatened to have me fired. I reminded the lieutenant governor that I worked for you, not him."

"The next time, tell him that you talked to me and I asked you to pass on Harry Truman's remark, "If you can't stand the heat, get out of the kitchen."

"I already did, or words to that effect."

"Good for you." Stoddard paused. "Bobbie, you didn't call me up to complain about an unsigned bill. You wanted to check on me, right?"

"Well, Governor, it has been three days and not a word from you."

"Bobbie, I'm still alive. And it's good you didn't call before. The only ones I've been talking to, aside from the doctor here, are the pink elephants and green snakes I've been seeing. I've always laughed when I heard stories about the D.T.'s. But take it from me, it isn't funny. I've been seeing things I wouldn't wish on my worst enemy!"

Reed said anxiously, "Maybe I should get you out of there, Governor. I don't much like the sound of it."

"No, I'm in here to stay. I didn't expect a rose garden. I knew it was going to be rough. I just didn't realize how rough. And the doctor here seems to know what he's doing. The worst, he said, is over. Besides, if I leave now, I'd just have to go through it all over again. By the way, Bobbie, the next time you call, don't use my name. Use John Townsend, the name I'm using here. And I don't know how long I'll have a phone in my room. I had to beg for this one. A phone in your room is a no-no —" A knock sounded on the door. "Someone's at the door, Bobbie. I have to hang up. I'll talk to you soon."

He hung up the phone and pulled the covers up to his chin. He smelled foul. He had a vague recollection of vomiting repeatedly during the horrors of the past two days, and of attendants bathing him. But he hadn't had a shower since his arrival here, and he badly needed one. He ran his fingers over the three-day beard on his face. He needed a shave, but that he would do without. It was going to be difficult to avoid being recognized here; his face was fairly well-known. A beard would be a weak disguise at the most, yet it was better than nothing.

The knock came again. He called out, "Come in!"

The door opened to admit Dr. Noah Breckinridge.

"You're polite, Doctor," Stoddard said. "I must say that for you. I seem to remember any number of people barging in here these past two days without knocking."

"That was because you needed immediate attention, Governor Stoddard."

Stoddard winced. "Careful with that title, Doctor. The walls may have ears."

"Sorry. I'll be more careful, Mr. Townsend. Or I'll call you John. We tend to use first names here." Noah was smiling down at him. "But as I was saying, you needed attention. No time to observe the amenities. Now you're better."

189

"Oh? You could have fooled me."

Noah became serious. "Don't you feel better today?"

"Maybe physically, but I took a peek at myself in the bathroom mirror. Jesus, I look like the walking dead!"

"That's to be expected, John. You've passed through a rough time. For one thing, you haven't eaten anything but soup, and very little of that."

"It's not only that." Stoddard scooted up in bed, letting the blanket fall, exposing a muscular, hairy chest. "I feel . . . Well, it's hard to put into words. I feel disoriented, I feel caged."

"That's understandable, many people feel that way at first. From the questionnaire you filled out, I see that you've never been in treatment before."

"That's right."

"And yet, you stated that you have been drinking heavily for years. I'm sure you wouldn't lie about that. When people lie, they tend to go the other way."

"No, Doctor, I wasn't lying. I've always drunk pretty heavily, since my early twenties. I love the stuff. But, up until recently, I've been able to handle it pretty well. For instance, hell, I rarely even suffered from a hangover, no matter how much I drank."

Noah nodded. "Alcohol affects different

190

people different ways. Some people can drink heavily for many years without ill effects – their system seems to be able to handle it. But one thing seldom varies. The older you get, and the more you drink, it takes more and more alcohol to get you intoxicated. Up to a certain age, that is. Eventually, it will get to the point where only a few drinks will do the job. How much have you been drinking these past few months?"

"A fifth a day, on the average."

"I figured as much. I haven't given you a complete physical yet, but from the few tests I have taken, your liver is affected. And with that kind of alcohol intake, probably your kidneys, as well. In short, you've been drinking to the point where it's seriously damaging your health. Do you ever have blackouts, loss of memory during heavy drinking?"

Stoddard avoided his gaze. "Sometimes."

"You're killing brain cells at a rapid rate."

"You're full of good cheer, Doctor. You mean, stop drinking or I'm dead?"

"I don't think you've reached that stage quite yet. Social drinking, if you could limit it to that, wouldn't do you great harm. But there is a stark fact that you must face, John. You're an alcoholic."

"I know that. I'm not stupid."

"Then you also must realize that an alcoholic

must *never* take that first drink. Social drinking is out. An alcoholic never stops with one or two drinks."

"I know, I've heard that," Stoddard said glumly. "It doesn't seem fair that others can do it, and I can't."

Noah smiled slightly. "As my grandmother used to say, 'Being born into this world doesn't mean that life is fair.' It's not fair that one person dies of cancer at forty or even younger, while the next person lives out his or her three score and ten. We have yet to figure out why an alcoholic is an alcoholic. Perhaps it's in the genes. But we can usually find out why an alcoholic drinks. That's what we have to do for you here. Find out why *you* drink like you do."

"Why? Hell, because I like to drink," Stoddard said with a snort.

"That's just a handy excuse. There's far more to it than that."

Stoddard looked at him skeptically. "And just how do you go about finding out why I drink, Doctor?"

"By using therapy. That way you dig deeply into yourself, you find out about yourself for yourself. It can be fear of inadequacy. Deep-seated insecurities. Any number of reasons."

"Inadequacy? Insecurity? Doctor, I'm a governor! I've got all I ever wanted out of life."

"Your position in life, your success, does not

guarantee inner happiness. We've treated a man who was president of our country and many other men and women who are considered to have reached the pinnacle of success."

"This therapy . . . That means sitting down with a bunch of other drunks and talking about myself?"

"That's a part of it."

Stoddard was already shaking his head. "No way, Doctor. I'm not about to bare my soul to others. They'd know I was a politician and would probably figure out who I really was eventually."

"I doubt that very much. And it doesn't necessarily have to be group therapy, although that's preferable. We can do it one-on-one."

Stoddard made a wry face. "In other words, it's like going to a shrink, lying on the couch, prattling on about how I wasn't properly potty trained, how I hated dear old Mom or Dad. Or both."

Noah laughed. "There are similarities, true, but I'm not an analyst. We'll be looking for the root cause of your alcohol dependence. Once we find it, once you recognize it, then you'll be able to deal with it."

"What if you don't find it?" Stoddard flung the words like a challenge.

"I've never failed yet."

"Nothing modest about you, is there, Doctor?"

Noah felt himself flushing. "I suppose that did sound a bit egotistical. But I *am* good at what I do."

"Sorry, guess I was putting you on a little. But if you can cure me, you deserve a pat on the back."

"Understand something, John." Noah held up a cautioning hand. "I can't guarantee a cure. I can dry you out, as they say. That's relatively simple, mainly because alcohol is not available to you in here. And I'm confident of finding the flaw, if you don't object to that word. But the rest is up to you. When you get out of here, alcohol *will* be available, everywhere you go. You will have to decide if the pleasure you derive from its use is worth the damage you're doing to yourself."

"I hear you, Doctor," Stoddard said dourly. "So when do we start?"

"We've already started. This afternoon, we'll move you into the rehab wing. Then I will do a thorough physical. As soon as the results of all the tests are in, we'll commence therapy."

In his room in the rehab wing, Jeffrey Lawrence paced the floor like a caged animal. He was keyed up, on the customary self-induced high he experienced when he was in to a caper.

194

He still didn't know if Lacey's famous jewels were somewhere in her room. They should be, if the rumor that she never went anywhere without them in her possession was true. Yet they had some rigid rules here; she might not be allowed to have them.

The next step was to get into her room and find out if they were there, but he knew that might not be all that easy. It had always been his half-formed opinion that all movie actresses were airheads, but his brief conversation with Lacey had shown him that this wasn't true. She might be erratic, neurotic, a cokehead, yet she was far from unintelligent.

On the surface it would seem to be an easy job, yet he knew instinctively that it wouldn't be. On most jewel thefts he usually picked a time when the premises were deserted. No matter how sophisticated the safeguards and alarm systems, he could usually devise a way around them. But he made it a practice to never make his move with people present.

The initial step in this caper had been taken, meeting Lacey Houston – inadvertently, as it had turned out. He was a little taken aback by the fact that he had liked Lacey on sight. Not only liked her, but was strongly attracted to her. He hadn't expected that.

In the course of his career Jeffrey had met a number of his potential victims; it often helped in the execution of the thefts. Often a person's personality reflected their surroundings. It was possible, for example, to tell after a few minutes' acquaintance, just how cautious a particular individual might be, whether or not they were crafty enough to set up a booby trap – a backup alarm hidden within a conventional alarm system.

Jeffrey sometimes liked the potential victims he met, and sometimes he didn't. In either case, he had never allowed his personal feelings to interfere with the crime. So, why should it be any different this time?

Actually, he never thought of his thefts as crimes. What he did was a job; it was his profession, a profession in which he had served a long and hard apprenticeship.

He had been nineteen when he performed his first job. He had been broke and hungry, after having just been fired – unfairly he thought – from a menial low-paying job.

It happened in a small town on the California coast, north of San Francisco. Leafing through the town's weekly newspaper in search of the help wanted ads, Jeffrey came across an item that caught his eye.

Mr. and Mrs. Thomas Wilkins are sailing to the Orient for a month. Thomas Wilkins is the president of the Farmers' Trust

Bank. Mrs. Wilkins is our leading socialite. Bon voyage!

A banker and a socialite!

To Jeffrey's limited knowledge, all socialites
owned expensive jewelry.

At that point in time, Jeffrey had never stolen
so much as a penny, had never even considered
it. But he was an avid reader of thrillers and
was familiar with the fictional exploits of suave
jewel thieves.

The first step was the easiest. The Wilkinses
were listed in the telephone book. He had been
in the town long enough to be familiar with its
streets, and he found their residence easily. It
was located on a bluff overlooking the Pacific,
on an isolated half acre behind stunted pines
and towering cypresses. The house couldn't be
seen from the road. There was a high concrete-
block fence, with an automatically controlled
gate.

It was after midnight when he scouted the
layout, wearing the darkest clothes he possessed
and a pair of cheap cotton gloves he had
purchased with his last five dollars.

Working his way along the block wall from
the road, he found a high tree, with a sturdy
limb extending over the wall. He clambered up
into the tree and climbed out onto the over-
hanging limb. The top of the wall glittered

with shards of broken glass, but it was a simple act to step from the limb onto the wall, then jump to the ground inside.

Jeffrey landed on dead leaves, making quite a bit of noise, and he crouched on all fours for a few seconds, listening intently. It was entirely possible that the couple owned guard dogs. If so, he was in deep trouble.

But there was no sound, and he finally got to his feet, moving through the trees. Then he was at the edge of a broad sweep of manicured lawn. He paused, studying the house, and he experienced a lurch of dismay when he saw lights in two rooms on the ground floor of the two-story building.

Had the item in the newspaper been correct? Or had the Wilkinses left someone behind to house-sit during their absence?

Jeffrey's shoulders dropped in discouragement, and he almost turned away in defeat. Then a stray bit of information from his reading gave him hope — many vacationers used lights controlled by automatic timers, hoping to discourage burglars. Was that the case here? Jeffrey knew there was only one way to find out.

He whipped up his flagging courage and bolted across the lawn in a weaving run, finally flattening himself against the wall, breathing unevenly.

After a few minutes had passed and all remained quiet, he concluded that he hadn't been observed, so he began to look for a means of entry. His knowledge of burglar alarms was negligible. He knew there were numerous kinds: a beam of light that could be broken by entry through a window or a door; contact points along windowsills or doorjambs.

He slid along the side of the house to one of the lighted windows and peered in. Jeffrey saw an expensively furnished living room, with a small table lamp burning on an end table; the room was empty.

Finally, he figured he had dallied long enough. If there was some kind of an alarm system, his only chance would be to get in, snatch what he could find in a few minutes and make good his escape. The town had a small, lethargic police force, and Jeffrey calculated that it would take at least fifteen minutes for an alarm to be answered. Of course, a loud bell could alert the neighbors, although the nearest house was a block away and it was very late. He would still have a few minutes' lag time.

The room adjacent to the living room was the dining room. He groped on the ground until he found a large rock, then stood with the rock poised.

Taking a deep breath, he smashed a pane of glass and cleared the shards away quickly. The noise he made seemed shockingly loud. He reached in through the empty pane, searching for the lock. To his astonishment he found that it was already unlocked!

Without pausing for second thoughts, he quickly raised the window and hoisted himself over the sill, dropping down into a crouch inside. He strained his ears, but could hear no sound of alarm.

He straightened slowly, waiting to allow his vision to adjust to the darkness. Then he ventured a few steps into the room. Suddenly, he heard the rustle of movement behind him. He started to turn, and froze as something round and hard was rammed into his back. For a moment he thought his heart had stopped permanently.

"Just hold it right there!"

Jeffrey didn't move; he was scarcely breathing. Visions of jail danced in his head. Even worse, he knew he could be shot dead on the spot.

The voice behind him said, "Now, I'm going to step back, and I want you to turn, very, very slowly. Don't make any sudden moves."

The pressure left Jeffrey's back, and he turned slowly.

"Now, let's have a look at you."

A flashlight came on, shining directly in his face. Jeffrey threw up an arm to shield his eyes.

"Hell, you're just a kid!" The voice held a chuckle now. "You're late, kiddo. I was here first." The light went off. "This is your first job?"

Jeffrey worked the word past his dry mouth. "Yes?"

"Figures. Did you ever hear of burglar alarms? That window was wired for bear. If I hadn't disconnected it when I came in, your entrance would have brought the whole neighborhood swarming around. Didn't that occur to you?"

"I thought about it, but I didn't know what else to do."

"So you broke in anyway. No sense, but a hell of a lot of guts, I'll say that for you."

"I'm broke."

"Ain't we all? I found myself on my ass in this burg, otherwise I wouldn't have gone for a chicken-shit caper like this. But I must say I'm surprised by the haul. This Wilkins guy must have a screw loose to leave a bundle of cash in his safe. I guess he thought his alarm system made him safe. Will he ever be surprised when he returns!"

"You've already finished?" Jeffrey asked in astonishment.

"Yep. I was just leaving when I heard you blundering in here like a drunken elephant." The other man laughed.

In the dimness Jeffrey could now make out the slender figure facing him. He was bouncing his gun against his palm. No, it wasn't a gun, it was a flashlight!

"You don't have a gun!"

"Never carry one." That low chuckle again. "First lesson — never carry a piece. Armed robbery is a stronger jolt if you get caught. And there's always the chance of some hotshot trying to take you on. People can get killed that way. The question now is, what do I do with you?"

"You don't have to worry about me telling anyone. I wouldn't gain anything from it."

"No, I suppose not," the other man said thoughtfully. "You hungry, kid?"

"Starving."

"So am I. I never eat the day of a caper. I sort of believe in fasting, you know? Keeps the wits sharper. First, let's get the hell out of here."

He stepped back and motioned with the flashlight. "You first. I don't want to be behind you just yet."

Jeffrey climbed through the window, dropping to the ground. The other man followed him, then carefully closed the window.

"Breaking that window was a dumb move, kiddo. It's what alerted me. If there had been anybody home, they'd have been waiting for you."

"How did you get in?"

"With a glass cutter. Look here."

He took Jeffrey's hand and guided it to a round hole in the pane of glass opposite the one Jeffrey had broken. The hole was just large enough to get a hand through.

"Didn't even know that hole was there, did you?"

"No, I didn't," Jeffrey admitted sheepishly.

"I didn't make any noise, and the hole's big enough to reach in and unlatch the window. Now come on, let's move it. I've been around too long as it is."

As they started across the lawn, Jeffrey felt like a particularly slow student being lectured by an instructor. For the first time he noticed that the other man was carrying a small black bag, much like an old-fashioned doctor's bag.

As they gained the comparative safety of the trees, the man halted. "My name is Mason Bogard."

Jeffrey gave him the name he was born with — one of the last times he ever used it.

Bogard held out his hand and Jeffrey shook it.

"Now let's get something to eat, if there's anything open this late in this burg."

They found a diner open on the highway at the edge of town. They were the only customers, so they could take an isolated booth in the back. The two men ordered hamburgers, French fries and coffee from a bored gum-chewing waitress, and surveyed each other from across the table. Jeffrey saw a slim man in his fifties, with thinning blond hair, cynical black eyes and a thin mouth bracketed with lines of pain.

Bogard chuckled. "Hell, you are nothing but a kid. How old are you?"

"Nineteen," Jeffrey said, ducking his head.

"I didn't start until I was past thirty. I was an accountant before, can you believe that? The guy I was working for was running a scam, and I was so goddamned stupid, I didn't realize it. Naturally, I was the one to take the fall. In the joint I took a fast course in burglary." His mouth got a wry twist. "Do you know how many total innocents are sent to the joint and come out criminals? It's a free school in there. I wasn't sure what I'd do when I got out, but when I found out how tough it is on ex-cons on the outside, I began a career that's run for twenty years. I haven't spent a day in the joint since, and I've lived pretty damned high on the hog."

"How much did you get tonight?" Jeffrey asked, not sure how Bogard would regard the question.

"Not bad, not bad at all." He patted the black bag on the seat beside him. "I was expecting chicken feed, maybe enough to get me to the next town. But this guy had ten grand in cash in his safe and at least an equal amount in gems. By the way . . ." Bogard looked at Jeffrey curiously. "Do you know how to open a safe?"

"I haven't the faintest idea," Jeffrey said rue-fully.

Bogard laughed. "Then you just went in there to snatch and grab, get what you could find and run?"

"Something like that."

"Well, I know how to crack a safe, but usually it isn't necessary. People do strange things with their combinations. They use their birth dates — year, month and day. They use Social Secu-rity numbers, whatever is easy to remember. In Wilkins's desk, I found a copy of his birth certificate. Can you believe that? And the birth date was the combination to his safe —"

He broke off as the waitress came with their hamburgers, and he was silent for a bit after-ward, just staring at his food, a fact that Jeffrey didn't notice immediately, since he attacked his ravenously.

Finally, he took notice. "I thought you were hungry."

Bogard gave a start, and looked up. For the first time Jeffrey noticed that the man's face was drawn, haggard, the bones standing out prominently. "I didn't say that, not exactly. I said that I didn't eat before a caper. It's not the same thing. My appetite hasn't been the best of late, some kind of a stomach upset. Kiddo, how'd you like to go partners with me?"

Jeffrey reared back, startled. "Partners? I somehow got the impression that you were a loner. And why me?"

"In answer to the first, I *have* always been a loner. My wife divorced me when I went to prison, taking our two kids with her. I haven't heard a word from any of them since, haven't the faintest idea where they are. I haven't partnered with anyone because a burglar doesn't need a sidekick. And I learned in the joint that half of those in there made it because someone stooled on them." He grinned faintly. "Or so they claimed. In answer to your second question, you're young and eager, and I'm hardly one to lecture against the evils of a life of crime. I doubt that it would do any good anyway. So maybe if I taught you what I know, it might help keep you out of the slammer for a while. The way you started out tonight, you'll be in jail before the sun comes up. So, how about it?"

Jeffrey thought for a little, devoting his attention to eating again. Was this what he wanted? Tonight, he had needed money and had been driven to it, in a sense. Yet he had to admit that it had been the most exciting night of his life, even if he had failed miserably. The adrenaline rush had been like nothing he had ever experienced. Clearly, Mason Bogard knew the tricks of the trade, or at least a good many. Why not absorb what the man knew and go on from there?

Finished eating, he looked up. "Yes, if you want me."

Bogard grinned and extended his hand across the table. "Good! Now, eat this. I find I'm not hungry, after all." He exchanged his plate for Jeffrey's empty one.

As Jeffrey began eating the second hamburger, Bogard said, "I have one more confession. I'm not in the best of health, so I guess I'm taking you on out of selfish reasons. Don't worry." He held up a hand. "I won't be a burden. I'm not taking you along to prop me up."

Jeffrey worked with Mason Bogard for three years, absorbing all that the older man knew. It wasn't long before he learned that Bogard had cancer. He had been operated on once before he met Jeffrey, and there was another operation not too long after. But true to his word, Bogard never became a burden. When he became too ill to hold up his end, he put himself into a hospital, where he quietly died.

By that time Jeffrey had been anxious to move on. He was grateful for the things the exaccountant had taught him, but Jeffrey knew that simple burglary, housebreaking, wasn't for him. He wanted to become a thief specializing in jewels; he wanted to operate in the rarified atmosphere of perfumed women and tuxedoed men, and after Bogard's death, he quickly moved into that specialty.

Within five years he was the best. He lived high – hand-tailored clothes, expensive cars and lovely women. And all this through just one or two jobs a year.

And now, for the first time in years, he was working on a job while desperate for money. He had learned early in his career that he operated best when he had a cushion, when he knew that he would be all right even if he failed; and this time, he didn't have that assurance. This time he was in hock. If he failed, he would owe forty thousand dollars, and it would not be easy to get.

He had to get his mind off of Lacey Houston. He must stop thinking of her as a desirable, likable woman and home in on one thing – the jewels!

Ten

Susan picked up the receiver of the ringing telephone. "Hello?"

"Susan? This is Noah."

She felt a rush of warmth at the sound of his deep voice. "Noah! How are you?"

"I'm fine. I was wondering . . ." He paused and cleared his throat with a small laugh. "I was wondering if you'd like to have dinner with Howard Hughes?"

"Who?" She stared at the phone.

He laughed again, a touch self-consciously. "Just a little joke, and probably a lousy one at that. I'm referring to Karl Heinman, our esteemed founder. The mystery man of Oasis. I got a call from him last night. He's flying in from somewhere to just have dinner with me, then flying right out again."

"Why you, Noah?"

"I haven't the foggiest. I've never even met the man."

"And I'm invited, as well?"

"Well, no, that's my idea. Maybe I just want some support. I have a gut feeling that it has something to do with opposition to The Clinic and who better than you to lay it all out for him?"

"But isn't Mr. Heinman going to be upset if you drag me along?"

"You know something? I don't give a good goddamn. What can he do, fire me? At this particular moment in my life, he might be doing me a favor. Come on Susan, when will you ever get a better chance to beard the lion? This is your opportunity to jerk his chain."

"Well . . ." She hesitated. Then she said recklessly, "What the heck? If you don't mind, why should I?"

"All right! Pick you up at your place at seven-thirty. The dinner is for eight. At the country club, of course."

"Did you know that I've never even seen a picture of Heinman? He has an uncanny talent for avoiding the press. I don't believe there's ever been an interview with him," Noah commented as he drove his Volvo toward the country club.

"He *is* a mystery man. I don't even know how he made his millions. I've heard all kinds of rumors."

"Billions," he said dryly. "Karl Heinman is a billionaire. And I've also heard many different stories regarding how he made his bucks. One thing I do know, he's a corporate raider. He buys up failing companies, drains them dry then turns them over for a profit. At the moment I understand he's in the middle of taking over one of the biggest oil companies in the country."

"But how did he get started? I've heard that he was born penniless. He had to make his first million somewhere."

"There are all sorts of theories about that. One has it that he made his first fortune dealing in hard drugs, and that he funded The Clinic as a sop to his conscience. On the other hand, I find it hard to believe that a man as ruthless as he's reputed to be even *has* a conscience."

"Some people in Oasis must have met the man."

"A few, perhaps, but I'd wager not many."

"I seem to recall Zoe mentioning that she met him once."

"That wouldn't surprise me," Noah said with a grin. "There probably isn't anyone in Oasis that Zoe hasn't met."

He turned the Volvo off onto the palm-tree-lined driveway leading up to a transplanted Southern mansion. On each side of the driveway the golf course green had the clipped lushness of a carpet.

Noah left the Volvo with an attendant, and he and Susan entered the clubhouse. The interior was impressive – high ceilings and doorways, and a wide curving stairway leading up to the second floor. There was a man seated at a desk just to the right of the stairway.

Noah turned to Susan and spoke in a low voice. "You know, I've never been inside this place. It strikes me that it would be more fitting if they had a crew of slaves working the fans, instead of the air conditioning."

"I used to come here with my parents when my mother was alive."

"That guy behind the desk is looking at me as if I should have used the servants' entrance," Noah said in a whisper.

Susan laughed, eyeing his open-necked sport shirt. "Probably because you're not wearing a jacket and tie. They're mandatory for dining here. I assumed you had both in the car."

"Never wear a tie, I don't believe in it," he said facetiously.

"May I help you?" the man behind the desk asked in a voice that would attract frost.

"I'm Dr. Breckinridge," Noah said in a firm voice. "I have a dinner engagement with Karl Heinman."

The man visibly thawed. "Ah, yes, Mr. Heinman. You'll find him in the Gold Room, Doctor. Turn right at the top of the stairs and go all the way down the hall."

On their way upstairs, Susan giggled. "I guess they make an exception about the jacket and tie when the host is Mr. Heinman."

"And the Gold Room, no less!"

A tall muscular man lounged against the wall outside the closed door to the Gold Room. He straightened as they approached. His long face was expressionless, and Susan thought that his gray eyes resembled a pair of ice cubes.

"What can I do for you?" the man asked.

"I'm Dr. Noah Breckinridge."

The man stared at Susan. "Who's she? I was only told to expect one guest."

"She's with me," Noah said tersely. "Okay?"

"I suppose, but I don't know why I wasn't informed," the man said in a grumbling voice. He opened the door to let them in, closing it behind them.

"For a minute there," Noah whispered, "I thought he was going to frisk us."

Susan was already looking around the room. A table was set for dinner near the big window overlooking the greens. A man sat alone at the table.

She felt a tug of disappointment. Susan had expected some evidence of his eccentricity. The only word she could apply to Karl Heinman was *ordinary*. He had a face with no distinguishing features, a face that could easily be lost in a crowd or forgotten the instant it was out of sight. Both his hair and eyes were a muddy brown. As he stood, she saw he was of medium height and looked almost frail. His clothes appeared to be off the rack, and the tan suit he wore couldn't have cost more than $150. His broad tie was a perfect match for the color of his hair and eyes.

But despite his blandness there was something about him that frightened Susan a little.

Noah paid little attention to Heinman's dress or physical appearance. His first reaction was that there was a feeling of power emanating from the man. Noah had come to recognize it — an arrogance that indicated this was a man accustomed to having his way, no matter what the cost in money or human dignity.

"I assume you're Dr. Breckinridge, or Jake wouldn't have let you in," Heinman said in a high thin voice. "But who's the woman?"

There was no contempt in his voice, it was strictly neutral; yet Susan got the feeling he had little use for women.

"This is Susan Channing, a friend of mine," Noah answered.

"Girlfriend?"

"Well . . ." Noah glanced at Susan with his quick grin. "I hadn't really thought of her that way, but I'm working on it."

"She wasn't invited, Doctor."

"I know, but I thought . . ."

"You thought what?" Heinman asked in that same colorless voice.

"I thought that the reason for this meeting was that you wanted to discuss the growing opposition to The Clinic."

"The opposition?" Heinman made a dismissive gesture. "I care little for any opposition. I founded The Clinic and it's thriving, will continue to thrive. The outcries against The Clinic are like gnats buzzing around a mastodon. So if that's the reason you're here, miss −" he looked directly at Susan for the first time "− you may as well leave."

Susan felt herself flush and started to turn away, but Noah reached over and clamped a hand around her wrist.

"No, she stays. I invited her. And if you're going to ask her to leave, I walk with her. I was hesitant about accepting your invitation, anyway."

For the first time, Heinman smiled, a slight movement of thin lips. "I was told that you were something of a maverick, Doctor. Of course she may remain. I have already ordered dinner for two. I'll order for her, as well."

He picked up a telephone on the small table by the window. "I'd like another hamburger sent up to the Gold Room. Oh, just a second." His glance went to Susan. "How would you like your hamburger cooked, Miss Channing? And what would you like to drink? I ordered milk for the doctor and myself. I do not condone alcohol in any form."

Susan stifled an impulse to suddenly break out in laughter. The best restaurant in Oasis and he ordered hamburgers! Keeping a straight face with an effort, she said, "Medium rare would be fine, and I'll have milk, as well."

Heinman nodded, and repeated her order into the telephone and then hung up. He folded bony hands on the table and stared at Noah. "To continue, I knew you were a maverick, Doctor, when I approved your employment, but then I don't object to mavericks. It shows an independence of thought, and that can be of value, if it doesn't go too far. But I have received a couple of memos from Sterling Hanks —"

Noah interrupted with a snort. "It figures. Hanks writes enough memos to deforest the state of Washington."

Heinman allowed himself a tight smile. "That's true enough, and I am well aware that Hanks is a pompous ass, but he is also a fine administrator. I thought it necessary to stop here on my way to New York to hear your side of it."

Noah shrugged. "My side of it is very simple. I object to the attention being given to the celebrities. The other patients are just as important."

"A very altruistic viewpoint, I'm sure, but unfortunately they aren't the ones who pay the bills. The media attention given to the rich and famous keeps The Clinic operating in the black."

"That's the line Hank gives me," Noah said gloomily. "But when I opted for this field of medicine, I didn't do it to treat people who are so rich and bored that they turn to drugs."

"Let's see if I can make things a little clearer to you," Heinman said severely. "I am not a charitable institution. Many drug treatment centers receive subsidies of one sort or another. Any financial losses accrued by The Clinic must be covered by me."

Susan could keep quiet no longer. "If you feel that way about it, Mr. Heinman, why did you start The Clinic in the first place?"

He looked at her in astonishment, as if he had either forgotten her presence or was appalled at her temerity. Before he could answer, if he even intended to, a discreet knock sounded on the door. It was the waiter with their food.

Heinman could have used the interruption as an excuse not to respond to Susan's question, but when the door closed behind the waiter, he looked over at her. "I will answer your question, Miss Channing, although I feel no obligation to do so since it is none of your affair. But I wish the doctor to understand my motives, as well." He paused to take a bite of hamburger and a sip of milk, then wiped his mouth fastidiously.

"It's not for the reason you may think — that because I reportedly made my fortune as a drug dealer, I opened The Clinic as a repentance for my sins. Oh, yes." His slight smile flickered as Noah grunted. "I've heard that particular rumor, but I can't be bothered denying it. There are always ugly rumors about a man in my position. I made my money the hard way, digging my way out of dirt-poor poverty — by hard work, and the fact I was smarter and a little more ruthless than the people I've dealt with over the years."

He paused to take another bite. "Eight years ago my wife of twenty years died horribly, well before her time. After that I lost it for a time. I drank heavily, and when that didn't give me the forgetfulness I sought, I turned to cocaine, even heroin. After a year I was in bad shape but had sense enough to realize that I had to stop. It never once occurred to me that I couldn't stop, cold, all by myself. It took some time and much soul-wrestling to come to the conclusion that I needed help. Karl Heinman, who had never asked for help from anyone."

He laughed ruefully. "Well, that time I did. I sought help from a drug treatment center and a man very much like you, Dr. Breckinridge. Even with his skilled assistance, it wasn't easy. It took me another six months to finally get the monkey off my back." He smiled. "I suppose that phrase dates me, it's passé today, but it was apt at the time. I haven't touched a drug of any kind, nor a drink of anything alcoholic, since.

"And that's why I established The Clinic, Doctor, to give men like you a chance to perform your magic."

"It's scarcely magic." Noah laughed harshly. "And it doesn't always work. Many of the patients return to drugs, and that's what's so damned frustrating."

"I fully realize that, but you do good work. I've followed your career closely, and I know that you have fewer recidivists than most doctors."

"But I'm still irritated because I must devote so much time to the celebrity patients."

"Without them, there would be no time, no treatment at all for the less fortunate patients. Surely you realize this, Doctor?"

Noah sighed and pushed his plate away. They were finished with their meal now. "Intellectually, I understand, yes, but it still irks me.

And mark this, Mr. Heinman." He leaned forward, suddenly intense. "Sooner or later, there's going to be an incident at The Clinic."

Heinman raised his eyebrows. "An incident?" he questioned.

"Yes, like the two that happened before I started work there. Only it may be worse, much worse, resulting in bad publicity."

"What prompts you to reach such a gloomy conclusion?"

"Because over the past year, two years, some of the patients we've checked in have been pretty, well, *uncontrollable* I suppose is as good a word as any. At one time most of the patients coming for treatment of cocaine addiction, even heroin, were docile once the first withdrawal period was past. Even an alcoholic, once past the delirium tremens syndrome, was too sick to become obstreperous. Unfortunately, that is no longer true. Some who are admitted are so doped up with so damned many different kinds of drugs — cocaine, speed, LSD, angel dust — that they're totally unpredictable, damned near uncontrollable."

"Then I would suggest that it is your job to control them, Doctor," Heinman said quietly, but with a hint of warning in his voice.

As they neared the main entrance to the country club downstairs, Susan began to laugh.

Noah, who was still seething with anger at Heinman's veiled threat, scowled at her. "What's so blasted funny?"

Still laughing, she waved a hand around. "We came to dinner here, the fanciest eating establishment in Oasis, as well as the most expensive, and what does he feed us? Hamburgers, no less! At first I didn't think so, but he's a true eccentric, all right."

"He's an asshole, that's what he is," Noah growled.

"Oh, maybe a little bit of one," she said, still laughing. "But I suppose with his money and power, he's entitled."

"How the devil can I be held responsible for some of the weirdos we get? Some of them are basket cases, liable to fly apart at any time."

She linked her arm with his as they left the posh surroundings of the country club. Although it was dark now, the temperature was still in the nineties. They hurried to Noah's Volvo, which he started before switching on the air conditioner.

"Like that boy in the hall the other day?" Susan asked. "The one who escaped from his room?"

"Yes, like that one, and I wish to hell he wasn't in The Clinic. I tried to talk Hanks into releasing him, once I'd determined how off-the-wall he is, but Hanks said it wouldn't be ethical. We'd already accepted him." Noah snorted. "Ethical, hell! He's thinking about all the neat press we'll get if we cure him!"

"He's famous, then?" Susan asked. "But I shouldn't ask that, should I? Don't you think you can cure him?"

"Actually, *cure* is not a good word to apply to drug abusers. Sure, we can get him off drugs – since he's locked in his room, none are available to him. But the most vital part of treatment with an abuser is therapy. We must dig out the reason, or reasons, behind the abuse, thus revealing them to the patient. My feeling is that this one won't give a damn, and he'll be snorting, or freebasing, as soon as he can after he gets out." He heaved a weighty sigh and looked at her intently. "Susan, please keep all of this to yourself. I shouldn't even be talking about it, but I'm pissed off."

"You think I'll run right to Cindy Hodges with it?" she asked tartly. Then she smiled, taking the sting from her words. "Don't worry, Noah, you can trust me to keep quiet."

"Susan . . ." He drew a deep breath and took her hand in both of his. "I don't feel like going back to The Clinic tonight. They can always get in touch with me through the beeper if there's a crisis. God knows, my colleagues are always teasing me for not taking enough time off. I probably do spend too much time there,

222

in fact, I often sleep there." A wry smile touched his lips, then he sobered, gazing deeply into her eyes. "Susan, come home with me."

She drew in her breath, started to withdraw her hand, then subsided. All of a sudden, the air between them seemed to vibrate with tension, and Susan found herself breathing rapidly, unevenly. She wanted this man, wanted him with every fiber of her being, and there was no doubt that he wanted her. She was no virgin, but she was picky, and it had been a long time since any man had so attracted her.

"All right, Noah," she said simply.

Otto Channing and Mayor Washburn had watched Noah and Susan leave the clubhouse from their vantage point at the entrance to the ground floor dining room.

Washburn looked at Channing in question. "What the hell, Otto?"

Channing nodded. "Yes, that *was* my daughter, Susan. But I have no idea what she was doing here. Or the doctor, for that matter. Neither one is a member of the country club, and the only way they could eat here would be as guests of a member."

Mayor Washburn, losing interest, shrugged. "What's the big deal, Otto?"

"No big deal, but I'm curious."

He started over to the reception desk, with Washburn trailing him. As the man at the desk looked up, Channing said, "How are you, Howard?"

Howard smiled brightly. "Fine, Mr. Channing. And you?"

"Good enough. I want to ask you something, Howard." Channing leaned comfortably against the desk. "That was my daughter who just left here with Dr. Breckinridge."

A tiny frown marred the man's even features. "Your daughter? I didn't realize that, Mr. Channing. I didn't connect the name."

"They must have been the guests of a club member. Who was it?"

The man's face froze. "I am sorry, Mr. Channing. It is against the club policy to give out such information."

"Now look, I am on the board of directors here, as is Mayor Washburn. It was on our say that you were hired in the first place." Channing leaned forward, thrusting his face close to Howard's. "Now, you either tell me who they had dinner with, or it's your ass. Do you read me?"

Howard drew back, his face paling. He swallowed a couple of times and turned his head to look fearfully toward the stairs. In a whisper he said, "It was Mr. Heinman. Please don't let on to him that I told you. He would be very angry!"

Channing didn't respond to Howard's plea. He straightened up, his gaze also on the stairway. Of course Karl Heinman wouldn't be coming down that way, he'd use the rear entrance. "Did you hear that, Charles? Did you know that Karl Heinman was in town?"

"No, but then I seldom do," the mayor said. "When he visits Oasis, he's come and gone before anyone but the person he came to see knows he was here."

"But why in the holy hell would he come here to see Susan and Dr. Breckinridge?" Channing asked in irritation.

"Who knows why Heinman does anything? Why don't you ask Susan?"

Channing scowled at him. "Now you know I can't do that. She refuses to speak to me." He glanced again at the stairway. "I've a good mind to go up there and confront Heinman himself."

"No, for God's sake!" Washbum seized his arm. "Don't do that, Otto. Don't ever do that. No one, but no one, seeks an audience with Karl Heinman. It's always the other way round."

Looking back over his shoulder at the stairway, Channing allowed Mayor Washburn to lead him from the country club.

Noah lived in a condo about a mile east of The Clinic. It wasn't in an expensive area, and

the furnishings were mediocre; but it was suf-
ficient for his needs, considering that he spent
very little time there. At least it was clean – a
cleaning lady came in once a week – but for
the first time since he'd been living there,
Noah wondered how it looked through someone else's eyes. The thought had never crossed
his mind with the other women he'd brought to
the condo; and it made him realize, with some
astonishment, that he didn't consider Susan-in
the words of Sterling Hanks – a "one-night
stand."

Despite her support of lost causes and her
idealistic view of things, Susan was becoming
important to him. He liked her looks, her
intelligence and her sense of humor. And come
to think of it, her opposition to The Clinic
might not be all that unfounded; there were
times of late – as with Karl Heinman tonight
– when Noah was inclined to share her view.

Now he found himself apologizing. "I'm
sorry, this place looks hardly lived-in. Truth is,
I don't live here all that much."

She cast an indifferent look around, then
shrugged. "It looks fine to me. Actually, I
suppose I could be considered unfeminine,
since I really don't care all that much about
where I live. I guess I'm just not a nester. I
have a small apartment, but I spend most of
my time at Zoe's. My apartment is little more

than functional." A melancholy look crossed her face. "I suppose I'm rebelling against what happened to my mother. She was an immaculate housekeeper, almost to the point of being obsessive, and she had a house full of expensive furniture. Little good it all did her in the end!"

"Babe . . ." He touched her shoulder, turning her to face him. "No sad songs tonight, okay?"

He tipped her head back with a finger under her chin and kissed her lightly on the mouth. She returned the kiss with a fervor that took his breath away; and then they were fitted together, his arms locked around her, as they kissed passionately.

Susan was a little taken aback by her instant response to the touch of his lips. Then her surprise was swept away by the tide of emotion his touch evoked in her. Everything outside of the circle of his arms ceased to exist.

Her passion soared higher than she could ever remember, and her fingers clutched at him, digging into his back. A sort of daze enveloped her, and she lost herself in the ecstasy of exploring his lips with her own. She had only a hazy recollection of frantically tearing at his clothing as he undressed her.

And then she was on the bed, naked, looking at Noah, who stood staring down at her. His body was muscular, strong. Susan lowered her gaze, and a shudder passed over her as she acknowledged how much this man wanted her.

Noah noted her focus and he said huskily, "Susan . . . ah, babe!"

She reached out boldly and caressed him with just her fingertips. He made a guttural sound and quickly joined her on the bed.

There was none of the awkwardness of first-time lovers; it was as if they had made love countless times before, as if they were meant to be together.

At the crest of their passion, she wrapped her legs and arms around him fiercely − clinging to the moment as long as possible.

Afterward, as they curled together, she giggled softly.

He raised his head. "It was funny?"

"No, no, you know better, darling. It was marvelous. But I was just thinking . . ." This time her laughter was rich and full. "Do you suppose I could be accused of consorting with the enemy?"

"Are you thinking of Zoe Tremaine?"

She shook her head. "No, not Zoe. Zoe would not only understand, but approve. Zoe is an unusual person. I'm thinking of the others."

"From what I can gather, she is the main-spring behind the whole movement. There wouldn't be all this opposition to The Clinic without her. I really can't understand all the fuss, anyway. As much as I sound off at times,

The Clinic isn't such a blot on the landscape. Nobody would even know that Oasis existed without it.

"That's what its supporters all say. And that's precisely the reason most of us are opposed," she retorted. "We can do very well without all that media attention, thank you."

He looked at her closely. "You told me that your mother died an alcoholic, Susan. I should think you'd be happy to have a treatment center near. If there had been one then, it might have saved her life."

"Near or far, it wouldn't have mattered," she said vehemently. "My father wouldn't have allowed her to go to such a place."

"Yet it is my understanding that he was instrumental in getting The Clinic built. He's certainly one of its biggest supporters now."

"He's supporting it because he believes it will bring money and attention to Oasis," she said bitterly. "For the same reason he's so against the no-growth initiative. It would put the brakes on his wheeling and dealing."

"And you oppose all of his stands. Doesn't that about sum it up?"

His voice was mild, yet Susan felt herself bristle. "No, dammit, that's not the reason! It's because I believe . . ." Her voice died. Because he was right; at least, partly right.

She turned toward him, placing a hand on

his chest. "I don't want to quarrel, Noah," she said in a soft voice, "not after what we've just experienced. I think we should avoid the subject of The Clinic as much as possible."

He looked a little startled, then his quick smile flashed. "I think you're right. We've certainly been getting along famously for the past hour."

He reached out an arm and gathered her to him.

Eleven

Billie Reaper was bored out of his skull, and he was willing to deal with the devil himself for a snort of coke. In short, he was way down, and sinking deeper every minute. His head throbbed, his hands trembled. He had placed a call to Devlin, after practically begging on his hands and knees for permission to use a phone. He had pleaded with his manager to smuggle in some coke, some pills – hell, anything! But the bastard had refused, self-righteously claiming that is was for Billie's own good.

He was sick and tired of people doing things for his own good, especially the ones who grew rich and fat off him. Billie knew now that he was going to fire Devlin; it was the first thing he intended to do once he'd escaped from the place.

Pacing the confines of his room, he paused, gnawing on a thumbnail. He went over the list of his friends and associates; a short list, he

231

suddenly realized. Was there anyone he could call? Offhand, he couldn't think of anyone he could trust not to go running right to Joe Devlin.

He stepped to the bed and thumbed the Call button. His thoughts were still scrambled, and he was operating in some kind of weird time frame; he still hadn't sorted out which attendant was on duty at any particular time. He hoped it wasn't Kathy Marlowe. He had high hopes of jumping her bones before he left here, but he had a strong hunch that she wouldn't serve the purpose he had in mind at the moment.

He paced again, until a key rattled in the lock and the door opened. Billie didn't recognize the attendant — a plump sullen-faced man in his late twenties. The rock star assessed him quickly, shrewdly. The man's blue eyes were weak, watery, and his round face was set in lines of discontent. Instinctively, Billie pegged him for a reformed doper, as were a number of the attendants at The Clinic.

"You're new. What's your name?" Billie asked.

"Jack Newton."

Flashing that charming smile that he used when the occasion demanded, Billie held out his hand. "Hi, Jack. I'm Billie Reaper."

The attendant took the extended hand. "Yes,

I know who you are. The big rock star."

Billie adopted a look of surprise. "What, you don't like rock? You're not that much older than me, man."

Jack Newton thawed a little. "Oh, I like rock just fine, but I find it hard to understand why a man like you, with your money and fame, should –" He broke off, darting a nervous glance at the closed door.

Billie didn't drop his charming smile. "If I have all that, then why am I here? I'll tell you something, Jack, something many people might not believe, but you strike me as the kind of a guy who understands. It ain't easy, being on top. The pressures are hell, and a man has to do a little recreational coke to keep going. Can you dig that?"

The attendant looked uncertain. "Well, yeah, I guess I can see that."

"And it's even more hellacious being caged up in here. Tell me something, Jack. How much bread do you make in this place?"

Jack Newton took an involuntary step back. "Enough."

"Enough? When is enough enough, Jack?" Billie grinned wolfishly. "A couple of grand a month, maybe, out of which Uncle Sam takes a large bite. How'd you like to pick up an extra hundred or two, tax free?"

"I don't follow."

"Oh, I think you do, a bright guy like you. I need something to keep me off the walls in here."

The attendant looked shaken. "You mean dope?"

"Dope, coke, nose candy, give it any name you like, man."

Jack Newton backed up another step. "Oh, no, it would mean my job if I did that."

"Not if you don't get caught. And nobody will ever know but me and thee, man."

The attendant chewed his lip. "Besides, I have no idea where to make a buy."

Billie suppressed a grin, knowing he had him hooked. "Now, a bright guy like you should know how to connect."

The attendant was shaking his head. "It's too risky."

"What's risky? Man, you're not worrying about this piddling job, are you? Taking care of screwups. If something happens, I'll see to it that you get another job, better than this one." He clapped the man on the shoulder. "Just think about it, okay? But not too long. I'm suffering here, really suffering." He leaned closer, winking. "Make a buy for me and I might spare you a couple of lines."

When Jack Newton let himself out of the room, Billie was sure that he had the attendant in his pocket. The thought of making some extra bread, plus the prospect of a few snorts for himself, would be too much to resist. Now, Billie had to get his hands on some money. They had taken his money and all of his personal effects away from him the night he'd checked in. Joe Devlin was his only source. His manager always packed a bundle. When on the road with a band, you never knew when ready cash would be needed. And hell, it was his, Billie's money, anyway. If it wasn't for the Reaper, Devlin would be scrounging for a buck wherever he could.

A few minutes after the attendant left, the door opened again, revealing Dr. Breckinridge. He wore a black scowl, and for a moment Billie feared that Jack Newton had confided in the doctor.

But Noah said nothing at all about the attendant. He had a clipboard in his hand, and he flipped through a couple of pages. "Well Billie, your latest tests indicate you're clean, except for residual traces of cocaine."

"What did you expect?" Billie asked sourly. "I'm a prisoner in here. How could I get my hands on anything?"

"That's the point of all of this, isn't it?"

"The point is, why am I locked up like a prisoner? When will I be allowed out of this room?"

"When we've decided that you can handle it."

"We? Who the hell is 'we'? You have no right to keep me locked up. That's illegal!"

"Not at all. Not only did you sign yourself in, but your business manager, Joe Devlin, signed papers giving us the right to handle your treatment as we see fit."

"Devlin?" Billie stared. "He handles my business affairs, that's all!"

"He's also your legal guardian."

Billie stared, momentarily dismayed. He had totally forgotten the fact that Devlin, under the terms of his managerial contract, had insisted that he be Billie's guardian until the rock star reached twenty-one. And that meant he couldn't fire him for another six months!

Watching the conflict of emotions flicker across the singer's face, Noah's thoughts jumped back to the brief conversation he'd had with Sterling Hanks that morning — the reason for his black mood.

Following the meeting last night with Heinman, and with the billionaire's veiled threat fresh in his mind, Noah had stormed into the director's office. "I want a word with you about Billie Reaper, Hanks."

The director leaned back, smiling slightly. "What about the boy, Doctor?"

"Boy!" Noah snorted. "He may be underage, but he thinks he's running the show here. He's irresponsible, a wild man. He's fighting treat-

236

ment all the way down the line. . . ."

Hanks frowned slightly. "But he's clean now, isn't he?"

"As clean as possible under the circumstances. But once he gets out of that room, he's apt to cause trouble. We can't keep him locked up all the time he's here!"

"We can, and we will, if it becomes necessary. His manager signed a paper giving us full authority to handle Reaper however we see fit."

"How can his manager do that?"

"Because Joe Devlin is his legal guardian, until the boy is twenty-one."

"Doesn't Reaper have any family?"

"Not a soul. At least that's my understanding. His parents were killed in an airplane crash just as Billie was starting his career. And there are no brothers or sisters, not even aunts and uncles."

Noah hesitated. This bit of information threatened to alter his attitude toward the singer. No parents, no relatives at all. Noah had to feel a little sorry for Reaper. He supposed many people would consider these circumstances partially responsible for the rock star's behavior. Aside from that, family support was a vital element in keeping a patient off drugs once he was released from a treatment center.

"Why can't we just let him go, Sterling, now that he's clean? His attitude is counterproductive, and I'd wager anything that he'll go right back to drugs the minute he's out of here."

Hanks steepled his fingers, resting his chin on them. "Now we can't do that, Doctor." Smiling slightly, he opened a drawer in his desk and took out a copy of the *Insider*, flipping to Cindy Hodges's column. "The whole world knows the boy is here. How would it look if we released him prematurely?"

Noah scowled. "Do you read that scandal sheet?"

"Of course I do. Cindy Hodges provides us with a lot of free publicity."

Noah had known that it was futile to debate the issue further with the director, so he had turned on his heel and stormed out.

Now he forced a note of cheer into his voice and said, "I should think you'd be delighted to be finally clean, Billie. Now, it's time to discuss your therapy."

"Therapy?" Billie backed up a step. "That's something for basket cases!"

Noah refrained from making the comment that came so readily to mind. "We have to get at the source of your drug dependency. Otherwise, what you've gone through during withdrawal is all for nothing."

"The reason? I don't need a shrink to tell me the reason, man. I need something to keep me going, to get me up for performing and keep me up. Do you have any idea what it's like facing that mob every night? Wanting to be the best, do the best you can? Man, it's hellacious! But of course you don't know. Nobody but another performer can know."

In that moment, Billie Reaper looked his age, and Noah glimpsed the frightened boy peering out of that face. Again, he felt a tug of compassion. "I know it's a rough trip, Billie, but if you keep using drugs to perform, you're going to kill yourself before you're thirty.

"And cocaine *can* kill, believe me. I know you read about it being the glamour drug, that it's harmless. That's bullshit. Not only can it destroy your nose and cause hallucinations – and you should certainly know about that – but it can suddenly increase the heart rate to a dangerous level or trigger an epileptic seizure so severe as to cause sudden death."

Billie made a gesture to imply scorn, but it didn't quite come off. "What the hell! If I do go, I'll have lived more than most people do in fifty years."

"Other performers manage without chemical boosts, Billie."

"I don't know any. Don't think I haven't read about the golden oldies. Crosby, Sinatra, they used booze. Natalie Cole and Billie Holiday used dope. And look at Elvis. Rock singers have it rougher, anyway. Everybody I know uses. Grass, pills, booze, coke or the hard stuff. Something."

"But it isn't necessary, Billie," Noah said gently. "Usually, it stems from feelings of inadequacy, fear of not being good enough, a fear that it's all luck and could come to an abrupt end."

"Don't give me that shrink crap," Billie said violently. "I don't feel inadequate. I'm the best, man. I've been at the top of the charts a dozen times now. What's inadequate about that, huh?"

Noah suddenly felt weary and disgusted. One of the first things he had learned was that if a patient didn't wish to be cured, it was virtually hopeless. But the effort had to be made. With a scarcely concealed sigh, he continued. "Well, you're here, Billie, and you're clean. For now. And you're due to be with us for at least a month. So, the next step is group therapy."

"Group therapy?" Billie showed a little interest. "That's where all the dopers sit around and tell all their secrets?"

Noah shrugged. "You put it rather crudely, but in essence, that's it."

"Sure, why not? It'll be something to pass the time. Maybe there'll be some chicks, ready to tell about how they can't have good sex without a few snorts of coke. Maybe I can get a chance to show them they don't need coke to have it on with Billie Reaper." His grin was cocky. Then he sobered. "But don't expect me to spill all. I'll listen, but that's it."

Jeffrey Lawrence was a puzzled man. He had come to The Clinic thinking that Lacey Houston would be like all the other stars he'd met — vain and spoiled. He found her to be just the opposite. Although she certainly had every right to be, she was not in the least vain about her looks; she seemed to accept her beauty as a fact of life. And the fame and adulation hadn't spoiled her. There was none of the complaining or whining that might have been expected from a wealthy and pampered woman.

They had taken to meeting in the sun room as often as they could manage. It was usually deserted in the late afternoon, because the desert sun struck the tinted glass full force and most people found the heat uncomfortable.

"I love the heat," Lacey said. She was in a T-shirt and shorts and was stretched out on a lounge chair in the filtered light. She was breathtakingly beautiful. "I soak it up like a lizard."

She turned her face to look at him, those huge eyes vaguely curious. "You haven't asked me the reason I'm in here, Jeffrey."

He shrugged negligently. "I figure it's none of my business. Of course I know, actually," he admitted sheepishly. "I read about why you came here in Cindy Hodges's column. If she has it right."

"Oh, I'm sure she has it right. I'm here to rid myself of a heavy cocaine habit." Her gaze was direct. "Is that what she wrote?"

He merely nodded.

"And before that happened, I was in another treatment center for alcoholism. I'm hoping that Dr. Breckinridge can do the job this time."

Jeffrey said uncomfortably, "Lacy, you don't have to tell me all of this."

"Yes, I do. I want you to know about me." She frowned slightly. "I don't know *why* I feel it necessary you should know, but I do."

"Well, naturally, I'm flattered that you wish to confide in me."

"Although I've only known you for a matter of days, I feel comfortable with you, Jeffrey, and that's something I rarely feel with any man." Her mouth had a bitter twist. "That's probably one reason why I'm what Dr. Breckinridge calls a drug abuser – the men in my life." She leaned toward him, looking intense. "You know, I think he is really going to help me. He's already given me an insight into myself that I've never had before." Then she proceeded to tell him what she had related to Dr. Breckinridge about her life, and the things he had told her about drug dependency.

Jeffrey listened closely, and after she had finished, he knew that she definitely wasn't the type of person he had expected. Her life hadn't been at all easy, and he realized that she had an unsuspected depth of character. Otherwise, she wouldn't have survived as well as she had.

Deep in his thoughts, he didn't grasp something she said. "I beg your pardon?"

"I said, now it's your turn."

It was a question he should have expected. And dreaded. Of course, he had a cover story worked out, the one he had told Dr. Breckinridge in an interview the day he checked into The Clinic; but for some reason he disliked lying to Lacey.

"An exchange?" he asked dryly.

"Well, it's only fair, isn't it?" she said with a touch of defensiveness. "Ordinarily, I wouldn't much care, but somehow it's different with you. With us. Surely you must feel it, as well?"

He simply stared at her, appalled. She was right; there was a strong attraction between them. He had recognized his own feelings, yet he hadn't realized that Lacey felt the same way; and he hadn't guessed the extent of his own attraction until she had voiced the strength of hers. And what would that do to his plans? How could he rob a woman he was falling in love with?

"Jeffrey?" She leaned toward him. "Did you

243

hear what I just said? Or are you shocked at my boldness?"

He managed a grin. "Both, I guess."

"I do have a tendency to sometimes blurt out things when I shouldn't. So if you'd rather, we can just forget I said it."

He reached out to touch her cheek. "No, I don't want to forget about it, but it may take a little getting used to."

"Well, I can live with that." She settled back, stretching out her incredibly long legs. "Now, tell me the reason you're here. Unless it's too painful."

"It hurts, of course, but I'm learning to live with it." He looked off for a moment. "I was a race car driver. Oh, nothing great or famous, so don't worry if you have never heard of me. Few people have. About a year ago I had a bad accident. I wasn't hurt seriously, only a broken leg, but I lost my nerve." Part of this was true. When he was flush and had time on his hands, Jeffrey did play around with racing cars, but he'd never won any important races. To be really good, a man had to work at it. The part about having an accident was pure fabrication. "Anyway, I started drinking after that. For a while there I could handle it, but as time passed and I didn't regain my nerve, things got out of control. About three weeks ago I realized that I was relying too heavily on alcohol and

244

that I had better do something about it, or it was all over for me. So, here I am."

"It must have been hard for you," she said sympathetically. "Not being able to work at your profession. My situation is similar. Heavy cocaine use was affecting my work. The only difference is that I didn't have sense enough to recognize it on my own. It wasn't until the director threatened to close down production that I really faced it."

Jeffrey felt like a bastard, operating under such false pretenses. Looking deeply into her eyes, he saw nothing there but trust and belief. She reached out a hand to him, and he took it.

Noah entered the solarium but stopped briefly, feeling a certain unease at the sight of Jeffrey and Lacey holding hands. He had already observed that they spent a great deal of time together. Personal relationships were forbidden in The Clinic. What could be more distracting than an emotional relationship between two people? But to come down hard on them now might also cause problems.

Yet Noah felt niggling doubts about Jeffrey Lawrence. He liked the man personally, and he could easily see how a woman would be attracted to him. Yet Lawrence somehow didn't quite fit the pattern of an alcoholic. True, he had been saturated with alcohol when he was admitted, but his withdrawal hadn't been nearly as severe as could be expected. It had even crossed Noah's mind that Lawrence had faked his alcoholism just to be admitted to The Clinic. And that, of course, was absurd. What sane man would fake dependency just to get admitted to a drug treatment center?

He raked his fingers through his hair, coughed loudly and started across the room.

Lacey looked around with a start, hastily withdrawing her hand from Jeffrey's grip. She broke into a pleased smile. "Hello, Dr. Breckinridge!"

"Hello, you two," he said pleasantly. "It's time for your session, Lacey."

"Oh, is it that late? I didn't realize. As they say —" she smiled warmly at Jeffrey "— time travels quickly when you're in pleasant company."

Noah met Jeffrey's gaze, and the other man's glance fell away, as though he was embarrassed at being found out, and again Noah wondered about him. "And I'll see you with the group this afternoon, Jeffrey."

Jeffrey simply nodded, his eyes still averted. So far, Jeffrey had participated in three group sessions and had said very little. Noah decided that it was time Jeffrey was put on the hot seat; maybe he'd pick up a few insights into the man. It wasn't something he usually did; he

246

preferred to let the patients take their own time about opening up to the group, but he thought that Jeffrey needed a little push.

"Oh!" Lacey said. "Are you in group therapy, Jeffrey?"

"Yes, I am," he said in a low voice.

"That takes more courage than I have. But then maybe it wouldn't be so bad, with a friend there." He glance jumped to Noah. "What do you think, Doctor?

"Lacey, the decision is yours. Whatever makes you the most comfortable. Of course, you know that I prefer group therapy."

"I think I'll try it." She smiled tremulously. "Would you like that, Jeffrey?"

"Like the doctor says, whatever makes you comfortable," Jeffrey said woodenly. Then he smiled, a smile that struck Noah as forced. "But if you decide to attend, Lacey, it would make me happy."

Patients in drug and alcohol treatment centers react in two completely diverse ways. Some are disoriented in the confined, closely supervised environment, often to the point of hysteria. Others welcome an environment where all their needs are taken care of, where all decisions are made for them by their doctors. Lacey Houston, Noah knew, fell into the latter group. She was quite content to be confined. The outside world had almost ceased to exist for her, and she was reasonably happy in The Clinic. There was an inherent danger in all this, of course. When her treatment was finished and it came time to leave, she would be terrified; for once again she would have to cope with her problems on her own.

Governor Stoddard fell into the first category. Without a drink for several days, he had basically dried out. Withdrawal had been difficult, eased somewhat by drugs, but now he was like an animal caged against its will.

With compassion Noah watched Stoddard pace his room nervously. He hadn't shaved since his arrival, and his face was shadowed by a dark stubble. "I'm so shaky, I'm afraid I'll cut my throat," he'd explained, "even with an electric razor."

Now he stopped, facing Noah. "Doctor, I'm walking on the ceiling in here! I'm almost tempted to sit in on one of your group sessions, even if I risk being recognized. Do you suppose if I continue to let my beard grow and maybe wear dark glasses, I'll be safe?"

"There is some risk, I suppose, John, but you shouldn't be that well-known in California. In any case, most of those in group therapy are too concerned with their own problems to spend much time wondering who's who."

Governor Stoddard turned away, staring

blindly out the window, gnawing his lower lip in troubled thought. Noah knew that the man didn't want to risk being recognized, and he knew that the governor's assistant, Bobbie Reed, would go into shock if he knew Stoddard was even considering attending the open session. Yet it was obvious that Stoddard would be bouncing off the walls if he was confined to this room for a month. And if Noah could believe Reed, Stoddard would also suffer from lack of female attention. The governor had been less than faithful to his wife, Myra, during the course of their marriage, although Reed had made sure the affairs had remained secret. The man had confessed to Noah only for the governor's protection.

"John?"

Stoddard turned away from the window with a start. "I'm sorry, Doctor, I was off somewhere. I've decided to take my chances with the group. At least I'll have people to look at instead of you and four walls. No offense, Doctor."

Rem was feeling reasonably good physically, considering the circumstances. The D.T.'s had triggered fits for several days, but now he was through the worst of it, except for the shakes. He had even been able to eat some breakfast and keep it down. The Antabuse had dulled any craving he might have had for a drink.

But his spirit was about as low as it could get. For several days he hadn't been interested in much except his own misery. Finally that morning he had conned Jack Newton – with the promise of future payment – into smuggling in to him the week's issue of the *Insider*. He had scanned every item in the scandal sheet, read Cindy Hodges's column twice; and although she had mentioned some rock star named Reaper, there wasn't one mention of the fact Todd Remington had been admitted to The Clinic for treatment.

Damn her to hell and gone! She knew that he was in here; he had told her the day she had picked him up. Had he gone through all the agony, gone into hock up to his eyeteeth, all for nothing?

If no one in the industry knew that he was here, if he received no publicity, he had lost the gamble.

Rem, despite his alcoholism, was an optimist and a fighter, and never once had he considered the idea of suicide. But now, now it seemed the solution to all of his problems. Without a shot at a movie role, he had no chance of paying off his debts, and he knew in his heart that he would start drinking again the day he was released. Why not take the easy way and end it all right now?

And then he remembered something — the party Cindy Hodges had taken him to, and the hostess. Drunk as he had been that day, Rem was positive that she was May Fremont. And it was evident from the house, and the party she had given, that she was very wealthy.

It was also clear that she was well-thought-of in Oasis; therefore, it followed that none of the locals knew of her past. What would it be worth to her to keep that past a secret?

Never in his misspent life had Rem committed a criminal act — aside from drunk driving and brawling — and blackmail was certainly a criminal act. But as the playwright put it, desperate situations required desperate means. Besides, if she was wealthy, her money, or certainly most of it, had been made from prostitution; and that was an illegal profession, wasn't it?

What was the name she now went by? He had to rake back through his muddled memories of the past week, but it finally came to him. Zoe Tremaine, that was it.

Telephones weren't allowed in the rooms, but he wouldn't have risked calling from his number anyway. Then he remembered the pay phone he'd seen in the solarium, on the only excursion out of his room. They had taken most of his personal belongings at check-in time, but he had been left with a handful of change.

In his robe and slippers he shuffled down the hall. He walked like an old man, trembling as if afflicted with palsy. He gave vent to a sigh of relief when he found the solarium empty. Leafing through the directory, he discovered that Zoe Tremaine was not listed. Would Cindy Hodges give him her number on the pretext that he wanted to apologize for his behavior at Zoe's party?

Cindy was more than obliging, but after dropping the coins into the phone, he hesitated. Again he leafed through the directory and found a listing for the *Oasis Enterprise*, the town's weekly newspaper.

He dialed the number. When the call was answered, he asked for a news reporter. In a moment a male voice drawled lazily, "Bert Downs here. What can I do for you?"

"Did you know that Todd Remington has checked into The Clinic for treatment for alcoholism?"

"Who the hell is Todd Remington?"

Rem was silent.

"Who's calling, please?"

Rem hung up, resting his feverish forehead against the cold plastic of the receiver. He felt like beating himself over the head with it.

After a moment, he picked up the paper on

which he'd written Zoe Tremaine's number and dialed. It rang several times, and he was beginning to think no one was home when a soft voice answered, "Hello?"

"May Fremont? Is that you, May?"

There was a brief hesitation. "I'm afraid you must have the wrong number. My name is Zoe Tremaine."

"Maybe it is now, but when I first met you in Nevada, it was May Fremont. This is Todd Remington, May. I saw you at your party the other day, remember?"

A soft sigh came over the line. "What do you want, Rem?"

Faced with the abrupt question, Rem was at a loss. He wasn't even sure that he was prepared for blackmail, and even if he was, he couldn't come out with it just like that. "I just wanted to make sure it *was* you and not the booze screwing up my head again. I'll be around this place for a month at least. I thought maybe we could get together and chat about old times."

"Those times are behind, long gone, and I don't care to talk about them." Her voice had turned cold and hard.

"Come on, May, just for old times' sake," he said in a coaxing voice. "What can it hurt?"

"No!"

Rem winced as the phone was slammed

down at the other end.

Zoe was trembling as she hung up the phone. With hands that still shook, she lit a small cigar.

Maybe she had made a mistake in admitting to Rem that she had known him in the past. After all, it was just his word against hers, and who would believe a drunk?

She sighed, knowing that she was not only simplifying but avoiding the issue. Her past, which she had labored so long and hard to keep a secret in Oasis, was in imminent danger of being laid bare for all to see. She was no fool; Todd Remington had more in mind than just discussing old times. At the time she had known him he had seemed an honorable man, but in those days he was riding high — a popular movie star with money to burn. Now he had fallen on hard times. Now he not only was a drunk, but he had to be broke; and she doubted very much that he had changed his life-style when his star had fallen. And she knew from past experience that you couldn't trust a drunk. Years of alcoholism tended to erode moral fiber.

No, she felt it in her bones — eventually, he would come around with his hand out, perhaps asking for a loan to tide him over, for old times' sake; and if she didn't come across, he would hold the past over her head.

The question was, what could she do about it? At the moment, there wasn't very much that could be done.

She could only bide her time, take things as they came. She had dealt with men like Todd Remington all her life. Admittedly, she was a little out of practice, but maybe she could still handle this one.

She sat upright, arranging a bright smile on her face, as she heard a door slam and Susan's cheerful voice call, "Zoe, you home?"

At that exact moment, Chief of Police Thad Darnell had Zoe Tremaine on his mind. He had just received a telex from FBI headquarters in Washington — the fingerprints he had sent them had been identified as belonging to one May Fremont. And she had been arrested on the charge of running a house of prostitution in Denver.

Darnell idly tapped the telex on his desk. He thought it was a pretty good assumption that the charge had been dropped in exchange for her leaving town.

He picked up the phone and punched out the number of the Las Vegas Police Force. In a moment he had his friend, Dan Bartell, on the line.

"What can I do for you, Thad?"

255

"Remember that call I made to you last week about a Zoe Tremaine?"

"Yeah, I remember, and a check of records showed no such animal."

"How about running the name May Fremont through for me?"

"May Fremont? No need to do that." A short laugh rolled over the line. "I knew May quite well. She ran a place outside of town called the Heavenly Retreat. A real class act. But May left here years back. The way I got it, she moved up in the world several notches. She opened a high-class place in Hollywood. But May must be getting up there, somewhere in her seventies now. She should have hung up her knickers by this time."

"Oh, she's retired all right," Darnell said. "At least from the business. She's living here in Oasis."

"I figured that she must be in your town. But why all the sudden interest in her? Surely at her age she can't be causing any trouble. And she must have gobs of dough."

"She's still not too old to cause trouble."

"What kind of trouble, Thad?"

Darnell hesitated. How much should he tell this man? He had known Dan Bartell for a number of years; Dan had served under him for four years in the marines, and he did owe him a favor for the information.

"She's stirring up a small storm here, Dan, spearheading a group opposing growth, civic improvements, things like that."

"One of those, huh?" Dan chuckled again. "And you're seeking a little leverage if needed."

"Something like that, yeah."

"Well, that type can be a royal pain in the ass. Good luck, Thad. Glad I could be of some help."

"Thanks, Dan. Maybe I can return the favor sometime."

Darnell hung up slowly. He had the information that Otto Channing wanted. Now what should he do with it? A year ago, even months ago, he would have gone directly to Channing with it. But things had changed. Or rather, *he* had changed. It galled him to do Channing's bidding now.

He liked and admired Zoe Tremaine, and he knew that Channing would use the information to ruin her in Oasis. Besides, what Zoe and her group were doing wasn't so wrong. They were acting in support of their beliefs. If Zoe had committed a crime, he would not hesitate to come down hard on her. But if he made Channing privy to this information, the man would use it to coerce her, and that would make him a party to a crime. True, Zoe Tremaine had once been a criminal, in the strict sense of the word; but as rigid as he was about the law

257

and its enforcement, he believed that a few of those laws were unjust. The law against prostitution was one of them.

He laughed wryly, thinking back to the crimes he had conspired to commit with Channing and Washburn. Why should he balk at a little coercion at this late date?

Maybe that was the nub of it. He was sick of Channing, the mayor and their little games.

In a sudden decision, he put the FBI telex into the bottom right-hand drawer of his desk, a drawer he always kept locked. For the time being, he would sit on what he knew.

He was flirting with disaster, he realized. If Channing found out, he would try to get Darnell out of the chief's office, and he probably had enough clout to do it.

Maybe when it came down to the bottom line, he would bend to Channing's wishes, but meanwhile it would be worth a secret chuckle or two to watch the man's frustration grow.

Twelve

Dick Stanton ripped the page out of the typewriter, crumpled it into a ball and bounced it off the wall. It fell to the floor, where it joined several other yellow balls.

What crap! God, how he wished he had a drink!

He got up and strode out onto the small balcony of his condo unit. He stared into the distance, watching the heat waves rise off the desert.

Would he never be able to write another publishable word again?

He vividly recalled the letter he'd received from his editor just this morning. It was the letter that had driven him to his typewriter — for all the good it did!

. . . been two years since the publication of *Images of Fortune*, Dick. If we're to keep your name before the reading public, we need a book. How soon they forget!

I know you wrote me, more than once, that you're suffering from writer's block, and since I haven't heard a word from you in six months, I can only assume you're still in the grip of it.

Dick, it's not the end of the world. We can both earn good money by publishing another best seller by Richard Stanton. I had lunch with Kyle Cambridge just last week. He is badly in need of an assignment. He's eager to get to work on another Stanton book. Just give me the word and we're off and flying. . . .

"Shit!" Dick pounded the railing so hard with his fist that for a moment he thought he'd broken a bone.

Nursing his hand, he went back inside, got a soft drink out of the refrigerator and flung himself into the chair before his desk. He sat staring morosely at the typewriter. He was almost tempted to throw it over the balcony and into the swimming pool below. Hell, he might as well; it didn't look as if he'd ever write again.

Kyle Cambridge was a ghostwriter, and a very good one. When Dick had run head-on into a block about a third of the way through *Images of Fortune,* and found himself unable to complete it, his editor had finally talked him into having it ghosted.

In one long-distance telephone conversation, his editor had said, "Damnit, Dick, it's not that much of a disgrace! Other authors encounter the same problem and many of them use ghosts. You'd be surprised if I told you the name of one writer who is consistently on the bestseller lists and yet has all of his books ghostwritten now. He wanted to retire, but his publisher didn't want to see all that loot vanish."

But Dick had stubbornly persisted for four months. Months of pure agony. He tried to write, drank himself into a stupor every night and fought constantly with Ken; but he finally gave in, letting Cambridge finish the book. The ghostwriter had done a creditable job, *Images of Fortune* had made all the lists; but Dick had felt like a shit, and he still felt like one whenever he thought of it.

He was determined that he would either write his next book himself, or it would never be written. But his editor was certainly right about one thing — high living, and the purchase of the condo in Oasis, had just about depleted his finances. He could certainly use the advance.

With a snarl, he rolled his chair up to the desk and punched out a number on the telephone.

After four rings, a female voice said, "Hello?"

"Cindy? This is Dick Stanton."

There was a brief pause, causing him to

wonder if she even remembered him. Then she said, "Why, hi, Dick! How are you?"

"I'm fine, Cindy. I hope I'm not interrupting anything."

"Well, you are, I'm working on next week's column, but I welcome the break. What's up?"

"I was just wondering . . . Would you be free some evening soon to have dinner with me?"

Another brief pause. "Why, yes, that would be nice. But it will have to be next week. I have to finish this damned column first, and I also have a feature article to do."

Dick's heartbeat quickened. "One night next week, then? How about Tuesday? There's not a hell of a lot of nightlife in Oasis, but they do sport one disco. Maybe you'd like to go there after we have dinner?"

No hesitation this time. "I think that would be very nice, Dick. See you Tuesday then. About seven?" She sounded quite pleased at the prospect.

Dick had a silly grin on his face as he hung up. Then the grin slowly died. Could he carry it off? It had been years since he had dated a woman.

He opened a desk drawer and took out his notebook. In his small neat hand he began to write.

Cindy Hodges. A beautiful woman.

Dresses beautifully, carries herself with grace and style. There is an air of the untouchable about her. Have to be careful not to rush matters. She is also witty, a good conversationalist, charming. The charm can be turned off and on at will. Suspect that she could make a formidable enemy. There is a certain aggressiveness about her. But that is all to the good. I could use some aggressiveness in my own character. Perhaps it will rub off on me.

Cindy Hodges was also smiling as she hung up the phone. It was a smile of amusement as she lit a cigarette and leaned back for a moment, wondering why she had agreed to go out with Dick Stanton.

She had known that he was gay from the first moment but that part was all right. She liked dating gay men — they were nonthreatening; and with few exceptions, she had found them to be amusing company. She could use some of that right now.

Recognizing that Oasis, and The Clinic, was a rich source of material for both her column and the occasional feature article she wrote for the *Insider*, she had made the decision to divide her time between Beverly Hills and the desert town. She was earning enough money now to afford two homes, since most of her Oasis expenses would be a tax write-off anyway.

Yet there was one factor she hadn't counted on. Life in Oasis was boring! There were none of the bright lights she had become accustomed to in Los Angeles and New York. She had quickly realized that the three months or so she would find it necessary to be there, could become a drag. There weren't many eligible men in Oasis; it was basically a retirement community. Most of the men were married, and the ones who were not were so decrepit they needed a chain hoist to get out of bed in the mornings.

The only single men she had seen around were pickup drivers and construction workers. Shit stompers, whose main interests in life were football, beer guzzling and bedding any woman they could get their hands on, usually in that order.

With a brisk shake of her head, she went back to her column. She was having trouble filling it this week. No one new or important had checked in or out of The Clinic. She had a pipeline into the place that cost her fifty dollars for every usable item, but there hadn't been anyone of interest since Lacey Houston and Billy Reaper. Her source had informed her that another man had checked in shortly after Lacey Houston's arrival, but the man had checked in under a cloak of secrecy, and so far no clues had surfaced as to his true identity. Cindy's instinct for scandal told her that the man was obviously someone important. If her source didn't come up with an answer soon, she'd have to dig around on her own.

She went through her notes. She had sources of information on both coasts, but none of her informants had produced anything juicy this week. She came across the note she had made about Todd Remington entering The Clinic. She considered it for a few moments, then decided against using it. Who would care about an over-the-hill actor like Remington undergoing treatment for alcoholism? Probably most of her readers wouldn't even recognize the name.

She would have to make do with a few rumors, labeled as such from an unidentified source. There was always the danger of a libel suit from using such rumors, but then the *Insider* thrived on libel suits. The owner thought that a juicy libel suit usually sold enough additional copies to more than cover the expense of defending the tabloid.

Otto Channing barged into Darnell's office without announcing himself. Darnell, busy with paperwork, glanced up in annoyance. "Otto, didn't your mother ever teach you to knock? I'm busy here, can't you see that?"

"I only want a few minutes of your valuable

time, Thad," Channing said with elaborate sarcasm. Without waiting for an invitation, he dropped into the chair across from the desk.

With a sigh, Darnell leaned back. "All right, Otto, what's on your mind?"

"I think you know what I want. It's been days now and I haven't heard a word from you about Zoe Tremaine. You must have a report on her prints by this time."

"Not yet." The lie had escaped his lips unbidden. Darnell sighed inwardly. He was committed now. He still didn't know why he was covering for the Tremaine woman, but there it was. "I haven't called you because I had nothing to report."

"Damnation!" Channing struck his fist against his thigh. "I would have been willing to lay odds that she had a criminal record."

Keeping his face expressionless, Darnell folded his hands on the desk. "Well, it appears that you would have lost your bet, Otto."

"It looks that way," Channing said gloomily. He stared at his locked hands for a moment, then stirred, looking up. "Well, we'll just have to go at her another way then. Use the method I've already suggested."

"Oh, come off it, Otto! I can't arrest someone for spitting on the sidewalk. That's something you only see in the movies about redneck sheriffs."

266

"You can and you will. You're the chief. Make up a charge, if nothing else. And hook my daughter into it, as well."

Without speaking, Darnell stared at Channing in distaste. He didn't like any of this.

"Well, Thad?" Channing said challengingly. "Do I need to remind you of what's at stake here? If this opposition continues, with all the publicity, it's going to scare people away from The Clinic, and Oasis. And the media will eat it up. Media people are like carrion birds, feasting on what they think is rotten, ignoring all the good. And like I said, not only will it affect The Clinic, but if they're successful, it will hamper further growth in Oasis. Already this no-growth measure is causing the developers to hold back. And that will mean bucks out of all of our pockets."

Darnell stared back. Greed, that was what drove people like Channing, Mayor Washburn . . . yes, himself. And the hell of it was, he didn't need the money; he had no family, no one but himself to spend it on. Yet he was tied in with Channing and Washburn. He had wanted power, not money, but to gain that power it had been necessary to go along with them. Now they were like evil triplets, tied together with the same umbilical cord.

He said, "If I do have them arrested on some trumped-up charge, they'll be out on bail before the door clangs behind them."

"I don't give a damn about that." Channing gestured wildly. "I want them hassled. Every time Tremaine, Susan, or any of that bunch opens their mouths, I want them hassled. Do that enough times and they'll back off. I know people like that."

I don't think you know Zoe Tremaine, Darnell thought, or even your own daughter.

"Okay, Otto, we'll do it your way," he said wearily.

It was late afternoon and Zoe was in the cool shade of the atrium, having a drink and a cigar. Madam was perched on the table, pecking sunflower seeds out of Zoe's hand. It was the time of the day that she liked best. Although it was hot, the intense desert heat of midday had somewhat receded. Zoe liked the heat; it was one reason she had chosen Oasis. In cooler climates she always seemed cold, a cold that penetrated her bones. She supposed that many older people had the same reaction — the reason that the so-called Sun Belt was popular with retirees.

She stirred, grumbling to herself. It always annoyed her when her thoughts turned to mortality. She had enjoyed excellent health all of her life, and the doctors assured her that she was in marvelous shape for a woman her age.

But age was the key word, and she was some-times afraid to go to sleep at night, fearful that she would not wake up in the morning. She wasn't afraid of dying, not really, it was just that she had always enjoyed life, especially since her move to Oasis. Who knew what she might miss if she died tonight?

Zoe was not a pessimist; she didn't think that the old days were better than today. Even with the dire headlines in the morning papers, she didn't think the world was going to hell in a hand basket. As much evil as there was in the world, as inept as mankind in general seemed to be, she believed that the world was better now than it had been the day she was born, and would continue to be so, even if civilization slid backward a step for every two steps forward. True, things were far simpler back when she was young, but what was so great about the simple life?

She realized that many people couldn't cope with the complexities of modern life. Hence, the drugs. Hence, The Clinic. But that was their problem, not hers.

She heard the door to Susan's room slam, and she took a sip of her drink. Susan walked through the sliding doors into the atrium. She wore white, even down to the gloves. Madam cawed, eyeing the girl balefully.

Zoe tapped the bird on the head. "Knock it

269

off, Madam." Her gaze went back to Susan. It was rare to see the girl in a dress; usually she was in a shirt and pants, or more likely shorts, this time of the year.

"Virgin white?" she said in her driest voice.

Susan blushed. An endearing trait, in Zoe's estimation. Most girls nowadays had lost the ability to blush.

Susan smoothed the front of the dress. "Well, I'm not a virgin, God knows, but white always seems cooler somehow. You like?"

"I like. Very nice, Susan. I assume you have a date?"

"Yes, with Noah."

Zoe cocked her head. "This is getting to be a regular thing, isn't it, dear?"

"He's nice, Zoe, he really is," Susan said in a rush.

Zoe batted a hand. "Did I say differently?"

"I just didn't want you to think I was being a traitor, joining the other side."

"A traitor?" Zoe raised a quizzical eyebrow. "We're not living in a spy novel here, my dear. Your private life is your own affair. Besides, I happen to like Dr. Breckinridge myself. Just because he works at The Clinic doesn't mean that he's one of the bad guys."

Susan sat down across from her. "Zoe, don't take this the wrong way. I'm not backing off from the fight. I believe in it as strongly as you do. But I've always had the feeling that it's more personal with you."

Zoe sat back, drawing in her breath. "I thought we all had agreed that The Clinic is bad for Oasis, and for much the same reasons."

"Oh, I know." Susan nodded vigorously. "But as I told you at the start, I threw myself into it because my father is on the other side, and that makes it personal for me, to some extent. And I also have the strong feeling that you have a personal reason, one you've never told anyone."

Zoe stared off for a moment. Then she turned back, facing Susan directly. "Yes, I do have a personal reason, a deeply personal one. I could tell you that it's none of your business, Susan, but I think too much of you to tell you that. On the other hand, you caught me by surprise, and it still hurts like hell to talk about it."

"You don't have to tell me, Zoe. You're right, it *is* none of my business. I was just being nosy."

"No, I want to tell you. I *will* tell you. I'll tell you about Cassie."

Susan frowned. "Cassie?"

"Yes, my daughter. . . ." Zoe had to look away. "I was a whore, Susan. First a whore, then a madam, for many years." Finally, she looked at Susan, expecting to see condemnation, steeling herself against it. But Susan

271

merely looked interested.

She said, "You certain you want to tell me?"

Zoe nodded. "Yes, I should have told you before this. More than anyone else, I want you to know. You're as close to a daughter as I have now." She paused as a wrench of sorrow took her. "I want you to know about my other daughter. . . ."

To the best of Zoe's knowledge, no one had known that Cassie was her daughter, except Chloe, Zoe's sister. Cassie had been legitimate, the result of Zoe's one marriage, when she was eighteen years old. Her husband had been a charming rogue, a card shark who worked floating card games in New Orleans, Chicago, New York and other large cities. A year after their marriage he had been caught with an ace in a sleeve holdout and had been shot dead on the spot.

Zoe had been left penniless and eight months pregnant. She had no work experience, for she had married a month after graduating from high school. She was a beautiful woman, with a strong aura of sensuality; so shortly after the baby was born, she turned to the profession where she thought she could make the most money — she changed her name and became a hooker.

She had one living relative, a widowed sister,

who was quite willing to raise Zoe's child for a generous stipend every month – with the condition that Cassie was never to know that Zoe was her mother.

Many times through the years Zoe longed to see her daughter, to speak with her; but she had to be content with yearly pictures as the girl grew up into a young woman, lovely to look at but wild and a little unstable – something that Zoe learned long after the fact. As far as Cassie knew, her mother had died giving birth to her.

Cassie was thirty years old before she found out who her mother was. By that time, she had been married and divorced twice and had been in trouble with the law, once for drunk driving and once for peddling drugs. All of which Zoe also learned about after the fact.

A month after Cassie's thirtieth birthday, Zoe's sister died; and when Cassie went through her effects, she found letters from Zoe, the latest one from the address of the plush brothel in West Hollywood.

Cassie showed up there one evening when the place was roaring. The man at the door wasn't going to admit her, but she kept insisting that May Fremont was her mother. The man finally called Zoe.

Zoe was rocked to the core. She had known about her sister's death, and as much as she had wanted to, she hadn't attended the funeral. And now, here was her daughter on her door-step, and clearly aware that Zoe was her mother. Zoe's first impulse was to turn her away, but she couldn't bring herself to do it.

She told the man at the door to send Cassie up to her office. Waiting, Zoe tried to compose herself, but her thoughts were awhirl, and her pulse rate was dangerously rapid. What was she going to say to the girl? More importantly perhaps, what would Cassie say to her, now that she had learned the truth?

She didn't have to wonder very long. The first thing her daughter said when she walked in was "So my mother's a whore!"

Zoe felt a spurt of anger, but managed to rein it in. She supposed the girl had a right. Of course, she wasn't exactly a girl anymore, even if she was dressed like a leftover hippie — faded jeans, scruffy sneakers, a thin blouse under which her braless breasts moved freely. Her dark hair was cut short and ragged, as if a pair of hedge clippers had been used, and her expression held a cynicism beyond her years. Zoe could see very little of herself in Cassie; she could easily have been someone else's daughter.

"But a high-class one, you must admit," Zoe had answered tightly.

"Oh, I can see that. Any dude would have to

pay dearly for a piece of ass in this joint."

Zoe winced inwardly at the language, but said nothing, deciding to let Cassie spit the venom out of her system.

"What I can't understand is why you never let me know you were alive! All these years I thought I didn't have a mother, until I read Aunt Chloe's letters from you." Surprisingly, her daughter's face twisted, and silent tears begun to run down her cheeks.

"When your father died I was left without a dime, so I became a prostitute."

"That doesn't answer my question."

"Would you have been happy growing up knowing your mother was a whore?" Zoe asked harshly.

"At least I would have known that I *had* a mother," Cassie said with a sob. Angrily, she dashed tears from her eyes. "Did you have to become a hooker?"

"I had no job skills, Cassie, and hooking was the best way I knew to make the money I needed to raise you properly." Zoe's lips took on a wry twist. "Actually, I became a call girl. I know, you can well ask what's the big difference? But it sounds better, you must admit. Then I graduated to madam."

"Oh, well." Cassie brightened, the tears gone. "I suppose I've done things almost as bad" Her gaze became intent. "But you could have married again. Why didn't you?"

"If I hadn't been any luckier than the first time, I'd have been worse off. And after hustling awhile, my opinion of men didn't climb any higher."

Cassie grinned. "I know where you're coming from. My luck with men hasn't been all that good, either."

"You have to understand something, Cassie. . . ." Zoe leaned forward, her voice low. "It wasn't my intention that you should think your mother was dead. But when Chloe learned what profession I had chosen, and when you were old enough, *she* told you that I was dead. She said it wouldn't be right for you to learn that your mother was a whore. And perhaps she was right. Of course, despite the fact she disapproved of where the money came from, she never turned it down. She lived well on my ill-gotten gains."

Cassie laughed. "I know, you don't have to tell me a thing about Aunt Chloe. She was square as a box, and something of an asshole to boot."

Again, Zoe was inclined to scold the younger woman for her language, but concluded that she didn't have the right. Besides, from what she had observed, foul language was the badge of today's youth.

Cassie said, "Maybe you could give me a spot

here. I might be good at it."

For a moment Zoe was appalled, then she saw the glint of humor in her daughter's eyes, and was secretly delighted. At least Cassie had something of her mother in her; she had a sly sense of humor.

"I've heard that the johns in a place like this sometimes have kinky sex demands," Cassie continued. "Maybe they'd go for tricking with the daughter of the madam."

"I'd rather not find out, if you don't mind," Zoe said dryly.

"Oh, Mother, I was just putting you on. I like sex, but if I had to do it with just any dude who wandered in, I think I'd soon get fed up."

Zoe stood up and said unsteadily, "You called me Mother."

Cassie looked startled. "I did, didn't I?"

Then she was up, too, hurrying. Zoe opened her arms and Cassie ran into them, burying her face against Zoe's shoulder, weeping again.

Zoe was swept by a powerful emotion, and she felt tears flood her own eyes as she stroked the younger woman's hair and made nonsense sounds. It was strange to be holding her own daughter in her arms, a girl she had never held and cuddled as a baby. It broke loose a dammed flood of love in her, a love that she hadn't realized existed.

After a few moments they separated, and

both turned aside, as if embarrassed at such an unseemly display of emotion. "What are your plans, Cassie?" Zoe asked, breaking the silence.

Her daughter shrugged. "Oh, I don't know. Hang around for a while, I guess. I've never made the Hollywood scene — it should be interesting. And I'll probably find a job."

"You don't have to rush into anything. And you can stay with me, Cassie. I have plenty of room. Not here, of course. I have an apartment not too far away."

Zoe hadn't been sure if she was making a wise decision. She did have an apartment and there was plenty of room, but she had long grown accustomed to living alone. What few men entered her life were never encouraged to spend the night. How would she react to the intrusive presence of another woman in her apartment?

As if scanning her thoughts, Cassie said with an impish grin, "You sure I won't interfere, with your life-style, Mother?"

Zoe laughed aloud. "I'll try to bear up, girl."

At first Zoe had thought it was going to work beautifully. She loved having her daughter living with her. Oh, there were a few inconveniences. Cassie wasn't the neatest person in the world. Zoe had to get used to stepping over piles of dirty laundry — Cassie had a habit of removing her clothes the instant she came into the apartment, leaving them strewn behind her as she made her way to her bedroom; and she often left the house in the mornings without making her bed. Zoe picked up after her without comment, grimly reminding herself that she was compulsively neat. It was a small price to pay for having her daughter with her after thirty years.

But the fact was that she didn't see too much of Cassie. She came and went at will and often stayed out all night. She managed to refrain from voicing any criticism. Who was she to criticize? And she soon noticed that her daughter was subject to strange moods. One time she would be animated, full of chatter, and the next she would be sullen, retreating into herself. She also didn't eat too well.

Zoe considered herself a gourmet cook; it was a sort of hobby with her. Although she didn't prepare a great many meals for other people, she was always highly complimented on her culinary skills when she cooked.

Finally, after a couple of weeks had passed, and when Cassie had picked her way through an Italian dinner that Zoe had gone to particular pains to prepare, the older woman broke her silence. "Are you sure your health is all right, Cassie? My parakeet eats more than you do."

"I'm fine, Mother," Cassie said listlessly. "I'm

just not into food, never have been."

This should have given her a clue, Zoe later realized. Perhaps her subconscious registered a warning signal, one that she didn't want to admit to herself.

A week later Zoe came home just after dawn and found the door unlocked and a light on in the living room. Irritated at Cassie's carelessness in leaving the door unlocked, Zoe headed for the living room.

The TV was on, the sound too loud, and Cassie was sprawled on the couch, staring blindly at the screen. She turned a drowsy, lax face to her mother. Her mouth was loose and drooling, and her eyes lacked focus.

"What the devil!" Zoe yelled.

Cassie blinked at her, then nodded off, her chin falling to her chest. In angry strides Zoe hurried to the TV set, snapped it off then turned back to the couch. She swung her arm and slapped her daughter across the face.

Cassie's head snapped around, and she stared up at Zoe. "Hi, Mother," she said dreamily.

"What are you on, Cassie?"

"On?" Cassie flapped her arms. "Oh, I'm floating up there somewhere, free as a bird."

She was wearing one of her mother's bathrobes. With a sudden flash of intuition, Zoe rolled up the sleeve on Cassie's right arm. And there it was — the pinpricks of a needle.

"Oh, dear God," Zoe said softly. "What is it, what are you taking?" When she didn't get a prompt reply, she shook the girl roughly. "It's heroin, isn't it? You're shooting up heroin!"

"No big deal, Mother," Cassie said in a slurred voice. "I can handle it."

"Sure you can. Just like all the other junkies I know," Zoe said in a bitter voice. "How long have you been strung out?"

"Oh, off and on. I can stop cold anytime I . . ."

In midsentence Cassie was out, slumping across the couch.

Despair welled up in Zoe as she stared down at her. Her daughter, an addict. She didn't know how to cope. She had seen what drugs could do to her girls, and she had always coped before by throwing them out of whatever house she was operating. But she couldn't do that to her own child!

She stood up, still staring down at Cassie in thought, trying to recall something. A couple of months ago one of her best customers had told her a lengthy tale of being a cocaine addict, and how he had finally broken his habit. He had mentioned something about a drug abuse treatment center. . . .

Then the name came to her.

She went to the telephone book and searched out the name of the center. It was still early, only shortly after dawn, but she called the number anyway, uncertain if she would get an answer at that hour. But the number was answered, and after she had outlined the problem, she received a promise that Cassie would be accepted for treatment. Next, she called a private ambulance service.

Then she went into the bedroom Cassie was using and packed a bag, with a change of clothing and the necessities. Returning to the living room with the bag, she looked down at her recumbent daughter. Doubts assailed her. Was she doing the right thing?

In her troubled life, Zoe had learned that she was always better off if she followed her first instincts. Once a decision was made, it was best to stick to it. Besides, she knew enough about drug addiction to realize that if she waited until Cassie was coherent, she would never consent to being admitted to a treatment center.

Cassie was still out when the ambulance arrived. The two burly attendants got her on her feet, aroused her enough so that they could get her out of the apartment without a stretcher, and started her toward the door.

Cassie, beginning to struggle, looked back at Zoe. "Mother, what the hell is going on?"

"It's for your own good, Cassie, believe me."

Her eyes blazed with naked hatred, but she stopped resisting and went along meekly.

Zoe had to go with them to sign Cassie in. As she hastily shrugged into her coat and gathered up her purse, she was again assailed by doubts. Was she wrong to do this? Yet, what else could she do? From what little she knew about it, reputable treatment centers performed good work, and she was certainly incapable of affecting a drug cure.

She rode in the ambulance with Cassie, but her daughter lay with her head turned away, refusing to speak to her.

At the center, Cassie was taken away as Zoe filled out the necessary forms and paid what monies were required. She was advised by the therapist who would handle Cassie that it would be better if she went back home, better if she didn't try to see her daughter, not until her system was clean of drugs. "Believe me, Mrs. Fremont," he said with a kind smile, "going through withdrawal is hell, both on the patient and the relative. If your daughter recognizes you at all, she'll likely revile you for checking her in. Wait for a few days."

Three days later, the therapist agreed that Zoe could see her daughter. She found Cassie surprisingly docile. Although she didn't greet Zoe with any show of affection, she didn't display any venom, either.

"Have you gone through this before, Cassie?" Zoe had asked her.

Cassie shrugged indifferently. "A couple of times, yes."

"It didn't do much good, did it?" Zoe said tartly, then instantly regretted the remark. "I'm sorry, Cassie, I'm in no position to criticize. But why, why did you get on drugs in the first place?"

Cassie shrugged again. "Why? Because it's a shitty world, as you should know. Besides, everybody does it."

Two days later Zoe had received a call from the therapist. "Mrs. Fremont, your daughter is gone."

"What do you mean, gone?"

"She just walked out."

"But how could she do that?"

"We're not a jail, Mrs. Freemont. We're not prepared to treat people who don't want to be treated."

Hanging up the phone, Zoe was seething. What good were such places if they just allowed their patients to leave at will? Perhaps she was being unfair, but in that moment, she didn't think so.

She waited all day for Cassie to show, then stayed home all evening. Her daughter did not put in an appearance. It was true that her belongings were few, consisting mostly of clothes Zoe had bought for her, but surely she wouldn't just walk away with nothing but the clothes on her back.

By the following morning Zoe concluded that Cassie had done just that. She thought of reporting her missing to the police, she thought of hiring a private detective to track her, but in the end she did neither of those things. After all, Cassie was a grown woman; she had the right to live her life as she saw fit. Later, as Zoe learned more about drug addiction and addicts, she decided that her decision had probably been a mistake. Drug abusers almost never went in for treatment on their own initiative; a family member usually had to assume that responsibility.

Zoe pleaded ignorance — ignorance of how to be a mother, ignorance about drug abuse. Yet this was never quite enough to ease her guilt.

She didn't hear from her daughter for almost two years. Then one afternoon Cassie showed up, emaciated, strung out and pleading for help.

So once again she was checked into a drug treatment facility, a different one this time. After thirty days, she came home clean. She stayed at Zoe's place for two months, spending her time watching television, reading and sleeping; she hardly ever went out.

Then, one morning, Zoe came home and found her gone again. There was a note this time. "I'm sorry, Mother. I can't cut it. I'm bouncing off the walls cooped up in here."

Zoe had thought about getting out of the business before. She had all the money she would ever spend, but she had never really seriously considered retirement. Now she did. It had something to do with the reappearance of her daughter into her life and Cassie's drug abuse, yet Zoe never bothered to analyze her reasons too closely.

Now she began to plan her retirement. Within a few short years she had purchased the house in Oasis, sold her interest in the brothel and moved, reverting to her maiden name, Zoe Tremaine.

She trusted the woman who took over the brothel completely, and she left her Oasis phone number, in case Cassie tried to get in touch. Three years passed, and one night she got a call from Los Angeles. Cassie had been arrested for drug possession and was desperately in need of help.

Zoe went to Los Angeles at once. With the aid of an expensive lawyer and the intervention of a powerful friend in high places, she managed to get Cassie off with a suspended sentence, and released into her custody.

"So I brought my daughter home to Oasis," Zoe said to Susan. "The Clinic had been open about a year then. I had heard only good things about the work they did there, so I checked Cassie in under a false name. No one knew of our relationship – I was just a friend. Ten days after she entered The Clinic, I got a call in the middle of the night. Somehow, Cassie had slipped out. Downtown, on Broadway, she was run over by a hit-and-run driver and killed."

"Oh, Zoe! How awful!" Susan said in great distress. "That girl who was killed was your daughter? I never dreamed!"

"No reason why you should. No one knew," Zoe said dully. "I even buried her under the assumed name. But the thing that really bothers me is that I'll never know for sure whether it was an accident or whether Cassie deliberately stepped in front of that car."

"My God, Zoe, how terrible for you." Susan reached across the table and squeezed the other woman's hand. "That's the reason, then, for your opposition to The Clinic – your daughter's death."

"Yes, I blame The Clinic, just as I blame the other treatment centers I sent her to. They didn't do her one damned bit of good," Zoe said with stinging bitterness. "Oh, I know it may be a little illogical. It could be said, and rightly so, that I failed Cassie as a mother. It could be said that she was a weak person. But it's the way I feel, a feeling going so deep that it makes my bones cold."

Susan was looking at her uncertainly, and Zoe abruptly regretted having told her. How could another person know how she felt about Cassie's death? "You haven't said much about how you feel about my being a whore, a madam, Susan."

"What is there to say? I guess I'm shocked, a little, but then I always knew you were hiding something in your past. And it's your life, Zoe." She smiled suddenly. "It could have been something much worse, like a murder. I've never really given much thought to prostitution. Many people call it a victimless crime."

"You're a nice person, my dear." Zoe patted Susan's hand. "You'd better run along now, or you'll be late for your date, listening to an old gasbag like me rattle on."

"You sure you'll be all right alone?"

Zoe's laughter grated. "I've been all right so far, haven't I? I'm not likely to go around the bend after all these years."

"Well, I . . ." Susan glanced at her watch with a start. "My goodness, I *am* late. Noah will be . . ." She stood up. "We'll talk again later."

"Sure, plenty of time for that."

Susan brushed her lips across the other woman's check and was gone. Zoe made herself a drink, lit a fresh cigar and sat absently stroking Madam while the bird preened proudly.

"Don't worry, Cassie," she said aloud. "I may

288

have failed you before, but I won't fail you again. No matter what happens, I'm not giving up my opposition to The Clinic."

Thirteen

After Todd Remington was released from the detox ward, he was moved into a room in the rehab wing, which was already occupied by a tall slender man who paced nervously back and forth. He finally stopped to stare at Rem curiously.

"Hi," Rem said. "I'm Todd Remington." He stuck out a hand that trembled slightly.

"Jeffrey Lawrence." The man's long-fingered hand had a surprisingly strong grip. "You look familiar to me. Have we met before?"

"Not that I can recall. But then when I'm buzzed out of my skull, my memory ain't all that good." Rem grinned sheepishly. "Ever go to cowboy movies?"

"That's it!" Jeffrey snapped his fingers. "Growing up, I doted on Westerns. I remember seeing you. You always rated up there with Gary Cooper. Even look a little like him."

"Yep. Old Coop and me were often mistaken for each other. Happens even today, long after Coop has gone to that big roundup in the sky."

"They don't make Westerns like they used to."

"Hell, they don't make Westerns, period. Maybe one a year, and that's usually Clint Eastwood."

"It must be tough, starring in a certain kind of movie for years, then they stop making them."

"You learn to adjust." Then Rem made a disgusted gesture. "Who am I kidding? That's so much horse manure. You don't adjust. At least, I didn't. That's why I'm here. I drink to forget." He grinned faintly. "And how many times have you heard that one?"

He looked around the room for the first time. It was almost as spare as a monk's cell — two narrow beds with nightstands, two chairs and two identical bureaus on each side of the door to a clothes closet. But at least it was large enough, with plenty of air and light coming in through the west window.

"Which bed is yours, Jeffrey?"

"I've been using the one closest to the window. I've been in here alone, so I had my choice. But if you'd rather have that one, I have no objection."

"Nope, this will be fine?" Rem slung his small bag onto the bed and sat down with a sigh.

"Did you just check in?" Jeffrey asked.

"No, I've been here several days. Over in the detox wing. They've been drying me out. I came in here bombed out of my skull. You?"

"I arrived about the same time you did."

Rem stretched out on the bed. "This is your first shot at a deal like this?"

"Well, yes. I guess my drinking finally got the better of me," Jeffrey lied.

"You have a ways to go then. I've lost count of the times I've made this scene."

"None of them took?" Jeffrey asked, startled.

"Oh, they took. For a time. But a day, a week, once even as long as a month, and I'd be right back on the sauce again." Rem raised his head, his faded eyes watering. "But I've never given this place a shot. It's always been too expensive for me. I've read nothing but good things about it, and I hope this time the treatment will take. What do you think about it so far?"

"Well, I'm not sure," Jeffrey said cautiously. "It's regimented, I'll have to say that, and I'm not used to that. No books or magazines. You aren't even supposed to make a telephone call. And if you don't make your bed right, or keep your room clean, you get demerits. Enough demerits and out you go. They run it like a military establishment."

Rem nodded. "I reckon it's necessary, Jeffrey. Drunks and dopers need strict discipline. If allowed to break a rule, next they'll be sneaking out to the nearest bar or down to the corner pusher."

"But do they have to treat us like children?"

"You know what they'll tell you if you make that complaint? That a drug or alcohol abuser is a child." Rem grinned. "I don't know as I agree with them, not all the way. But they have a valid point. Look, I'm not defending them." He threw his arms out wide. "Hell, in a few days I'll probably be bitching about the same things. Have you been to any of the therapy sessions yet?"

"Yes. I've been to three or four."

"They ain't pleasant, are they? I've suffered through them at other centers. Every time you get up to speak, you have to identify yourself. 'Hi, I'm Rem. I'm an alcoholic.' It's embarrassing as all hell. Still, it's a lot better than some treatments."

"You do seem to have had a lot of experience."

"You might put it that way," Rem said with a laugh. "I went through one treatment that was pure hell. That was a quickie. Ten days, guaranteed cure. They used Antabuse. Of course, they use it here, but not in the same way."

"Antabuse?" Jeffrey asked curiously. "I've heard about that. How does it work?"

"Well, the place I was in was a small hospital. The cure consisted mainly of duffys."

Jeffrey stared. "What's a duffy?"

"The name comes from an old radio show called *Duffy's Tavern*. You're far too young to remember. In this place, a duffy is scheduled for every second day of your ten-day stay. Wearing only a robe and slippers, you're taken into a small room, which is, in effect, a small bar, supervised by a nurse. It's stocked with the finest liquor available. Glenlivet Scotch, Jack Daniel's bourbon, Beefeater gin, whatever suits your fancy.

"First, you're given an injection of Antabuse. Then you're seated in a chair, and a large, crescent-shaped metal basin is fastened to your belly. Then this jolly nurse says cheerfully, 'Isn't this just the greatest bar you ever saw? How about we start off with a double shot of Jack Daniel's?'

"First, she runs it back and forth in front of your nose so you can get a good whiff, then it's down the hatch. The booze hardly hits bottom before it comes back up again. Then you know why the bathrobe and slippers and the basin. The Antabuse makes you allergic to alcohol, you see.

"But that's not the end of it, no, sir! The nurse keeps pouring, and in about thirty minutes she's poured enough booze down you to get an elephant smashed. By that time you're begging for it to stop. The taste is awful, and the smell alone is enough to make you puke your guts out. And now the nurse is saying, 'Vile stuff, isn't it? Nasty stinking poison!

Here, have another drink.'

"Finally, she takes pity on you and helps you shuffle down the hall to your room. To top it all off, you're forced to drink what is called a butterfly. This is doctored beer, which makes you throw up again and gives you the runs for the rest of the day.

"The next day you're given sodium Pentothal and allowed to rest. I could have kissed that nurse, thinking it was all over. Was I ever wrong! It was simply a day of rest in preparation for the duffy treatment the next day. This went on for ten days. They have to be the most horrible days of my life."

"Did it work?"

"For about a month. For a month afterward I couldn't stand the sight or smell of alcohol. Just a whiff of it made me upchuck. At the end of three weeks, I downed a shot of Jack Daniel's and hustled to the bathroom immediately. But finally, I got over it and was back on the booze again. They claim a high success rate. But not me. I think I'm a hopeless case."

Jeffrey shuddered. "I don't know. I think if I ever went through an ordeal like that, I would never take another drink."

"Maybe you wouldn't. But then maybe you're not a hopeless alkie like me. In that case, The Clinic will probably work just fine for you."

When Lacey learned that she was to have a roommate, she came close to walking out. She loved her privacy. Even as a small girl she had never shared a room with anyone, and she had never even become completely at ease sharing a room and a bed with a husband, or a lover. Usually, after the honeymoon was over, she gently hinted that her partner should sleep in the adjoining room, after they had made love.

One husband — she had forgotten which — had angrily suggested that that was one reason she couldn't hold on to a man, and had left her soon after. Lacey had put it out of her mind; she was a private person and she fully intended to remain so.

But within a few days, Lacey was more than grateful for the presence of a roommate. She had never made a bed in her life, and certainly had never cleaned her room or a bathroom. Bethel Williams, a black R.N., was not only efficient at such matters, but was quite willing to help Lacey learn. She had confided to Lacey that fifteen years of observing people die painful deaths, a failed marriage and a child who had run away from home at sixteen never to be seen again, had turned her toward drugs. As a nurse, she had found drugs readily accessible, and was soon a morphine addict. She had finally been caught stealing morphine by a doctor. Since she had been a fine nurse and otherwise reliable, she had been given a choice – either go through successful treatment or face discharge and the end of her career.

"Before coming here, I knew zilch about cleaning my rooms, and I would have sworn that nothing could ever force me to do it," Lacy had told Dr. Breckinridge during the first private therapy sesion. "Now I find myself not only doing it, but almost . . . almost enjoying it. I've heard that Elizabeth Taylor had to scrub floors on her hands and knees at the Betty Ford Center. Is that true, Doctor?"

Noah had grinned. "I've heard that story many times. I can't really say if it's true or not. But it's a good story, so good that I doubt Miss Taylor would deny it. And I promise you, Lacey, that you won't have to scrub down the halls here."

Today, at their third private session, Lacey was telling the doctor that she usually disliked sharing a room. "But somehow, I don't seem to mind with Bethel. In fact, if I had to be alone now, I'd miss her."

Noah had an occasional mannerism of rubbing the tip of his pen along the right side of his nose as he took notes. He did that now, his gaze intent on hers. "You say this applied to your husbands? And your lovers?"

"Yes, as soon as I could manage to get them

to move to another room without hurting their feelings. Unfortunately, I didn't always succeed in that."

"You strike me as a warm, affectionate person, Lacey."

"I am. At least I like to think so. But that doesn't mean that I want a man with me every minute of the day or night."

"Most people want to be held after making love. They want to go to sleep in a lover's arms."

"I don't. Usually I can't even sleep when someone is in bed with me. And when I do sleep, I wake up with the feeling that the person in bed with me is a complete stranger. Not only that, but I feel threatened, as weird as that may sound."

"Even when you've had too much to drink? Or when you're high on cocaine?"

"It's even worse then. When I wake up sober, or when I crash, I'm absolutely revolted by anyone I find in bed with me."

"Tell me something, Lacy. . . . Was your mother very affectionate?"

"Not to Daddy, not that I could tell. Oh! You mean to me, don't you?" He nodded silently. "Yes, she was, too much so. I guess you could say she smothered me with love. It's an old story, isn't it?"

"It's a classic pattern, yes."

"And you think that's the reason I won't let people get too close to me? Because she was always there, hovering over me, twenty-four hours a day?"

"Your feelings could derive from that, yes, to the point where it's almost a phobia," he said cautiously.

"Can you do anything about it?"

"We'll certainly try. Your positive reaction to Bethel is a hopeful sign."

"You think my phobia, if that's what it is, may have caused me to become a drug abuser?"

"It could have contributed to it. Lacey . . ." He caressed the side of his nose with the pen. "I think it's time you joined in the group sessions. The other day when you learned that Jeffrey was participating, you promised you would. Remember?"

"I know, but . . ." She sighed. "I've just finished explaining how I react to people close to me."

"That's precisely the reason you must join us. How else will you ever overcome this phobia?"

"Oh, I don't mind mixing. I love parties, for instance, with a lot of people around me."

Noah was shaking his head. "That's not what I mean. When you're at a party, even with friends present, you don't have to become intimate. You can always keep your distance. You

299

can't do that with our group. You bare your innermost self. No matter how hostile newcomers are to the group in the beginning, they almost always end up loving one another by the time they're ready to receive their diplomas. A few don't, of course. The failures, the dropouts."

"Love one another? Bare our innermost selves? Oh, my God, Doctor, I simply can't!"

"You must. I'm afraid I must insist, especially after what you've told me here today."

Lacey's shoulders slumped. "All right. If you put it that way."

"Another thing." He picked up a note book from his desk. "This paper I asked you to write, about how it feels to be an addict, about how it feels to hurt people by your behavior, about how you fail them. It won't do, Lacey."

"I'm not a writer, I told you that."

"I don't want you to be a writer. That's one thing wrong with it. You try too hard to be glib, to make fun of your problems. I don't want you to entertain me. I want you to stop being glib, get down to the bone. Be honest with yourself, with me. Write from the gut. Tell me how it feels to be an addict. Tell me how you feel about being in here." He held out the notebook. "Do it over, Lacey."

The worst thing about alcoholism, the very

worst, is loss of memory. At a group gathering, you meet many people, usually strangers, and after a night's heavy boozing, you can't remember names the next day. This is especially bad news for a politician. A memory for names and faces is a politician's stock-in-trade. . . .

Governor Stoddard stopped writing in his notebook and gazed off. Was it wise to identify himself as a politician? True, Dr. Breckinridge had assured him that the contents of the notebook would only be between the two of them, and he swore that the notebook would be shredded once he, Stoddard, graduated. Still, years of being in politics had made Stoddard very cautious about putting anything incriminating in writing. If someone like Cindy Hodges saw this notebook, even if it didn't contain his name, she might make an intuitive guess.

Still looking out of the window, he scrubbed a hand down over the sandpaper rasp of the growth of beard on his face. Dr. Breckinridge had approved of the beard since Stoddard had expressed strong reservations about joining the group therapy sessions for fear of being recognized. The doctor had also said he could supply contact lenses that would change the color of his eyes. Dr. Breckinridge had assured the governor,

301

again, that the likelihood of his being recognized was small. "The people here have enough to worry about with their own problems without playing a guessing game of who's who."

"But I read all the time about such and such a celebrity being in alcohol treatment centers," Stoddard had said.

"That is of course true, but that information gets out *after* they have left here, in most instances. And the ones who usually let it be known are show business people. Some of those even broadcast it when they are admitted." The doctor had smiled briefly. "It seems that being admitted for drug abuse is becoming an in thing among show business folk. I think you have little to worry about, John."

Stoddard had finally caved in and agreed to group therapy when Dr. Breckinridge had insisted that such therapy was one of their most important tools. The governor figured that it would be a waste of time unless he took full advantage. After all, life was booby-trapped with risks.

He gazed down at the notebook. This could also be a booby trap. But what the hell! He had known there would be some risk involved in checking in here.

He resumed writing in the journal and had just finished when there was a knock on the door.

"Come in!"

The door opened to admit Dr. Breckinridge.

"How are you today, John?" Noah smiled.

"Here." He held out the notebook. "I've finished my daily stint."

"Good." Noah sat down. He looked at Stoddard's face closely. "The beard is going to help, and I'll supply you with the colored contacts. I've scheduled you for my group session tomorrow. And there are a couple of other things I must bring up. First, you'll have a roommate beginning tomorrow. He's a dentist from a small town in the central part of the state. I doubt he's ever heard of Governor Stoddard. And the other thing is the telephone. We have to take it out. I've stretched the rules to the limit already by allowing you a phone in here. As I've already mentioned, phones are forbidden. It's just another distraction. If the others were to learn that you have your own phone, there'd probably be a riot."

"You can't make an exception, Doctor? My position is somewhat different from the others. I must be in touch with my assistant every day, in the event of an emergency."

"I'm sorry, I can't allow it. But I do appreciate your position, and I will do this. Pick a certain time every day for your assistant to call, and you may use my office. That's the best I can do for you."

"Well . . ." Stoddard sighed. "I suppose I'll have to settle for that. You know, a telephone is a necessity for a political animal like me." He laughed. "My wife once told me that I must have been born with a telephone receiver growing out of my ear."

"That's another thing that troubles me." Noah was frowning. "You said that your wife doesn't know you're here?"

"That's right, and I don't want her to know. I trust her and generally she's discreet, but if she knew I was here, she'd come running so she could be nearby. And if the press got wind of her being here, someone would be sure to make the connection."

"But that's a vital part of our program, you see. We try to have a spouse, or a close relative, in for the last week of a patient's stay. We give them an extensive briefing in what will be expected of them after the patient graduates. Aftercare is as important as the treatment here, and your wife should be briefed."

Stoddard shook his head. "I'm sorry. I can't risk it, Doctor."

"You're making it very difficult for me, John," Noah said. He was tempted to send the governor packing, but that would mean another hassle with Hanks, and he did appreciate Stoddard's dilemma. "I've broken rules with you that I would never have considered before."

"I know you have, and I appreciate that. I tell you what. I'll give some thought to having her out that last week, okay?" Stoddard knew that he was lying, yet he thought it best to appease this man, whom he liked instinctively.

Noah got to his feet. "You do that, John." He hefted the notebook Stoddard had given him. "I'll read this and give you my opinion tomorrow."

Stoddard grinned. "I feel like a high school student waiting for an A!"

Cindy Hodges received an envelope from her informant in The Clinic in the morning mail. In the envelope were several Xeroxed sheets of paper. She read one with great interest — a copy of a patient's daily journal. Two sentences caught her eye. "This is especially bad news for a politician. A memory for names and faces is a politician's stock-in-trade."

The name on the front page of the notebook was John Townsend, but she knew instinctively that it was false. No prominent politician would check into The Clinic under his or her real name. Now, just who was this one? It might be worthwhile finding out. She would have to give her informant a prod; maybe the promise of a bonus would do the trick.

Fourteen

Zoe gazed out at the rapt faces of some forty women as she finished her speech. "So, in conclusion, I assure all of you that I am firmly behind the no-growth initiative. I have signed the petition to get it on the ballot, and I strongly urge all of you to do the same." She paused, once again scanning the faces. They were in the banquet room of the Embers Restaurant, where the Women's Club of Oasis met. Zoe was the featured speaker for this month's luncheon meeting; her subject – the no-growth initiative, which they hoped would pass in the November election.

"All of you, I am sure, are aware of my strong opposition to The Clinic," she continued. "Perhaps you're wondering what the connection is between the no-growth issue and that place. There is, of course, no direct connection, but both are symptoms of the same disease – the desire to commercialize, to urbanize, to chase after the quick buck. The developers have no regard for our wish to keep at least a semi-rural environment. Most of us came here to escape the hustle, the gridlock traffic, the poisonous smog, of a city like Los Angeles.

"If we approve the no-growth initiative in the November election, it will at least establish roadblocks to further development. And who knows? If we send signals to the heedless politicians who are responsible for the uncontrolled growth of Oasis, perhaps they will move on to some other town; and then we might be better able to fight The Clinic.

"I thank you for your kind attention, ladies."

Zoe sat down to a modest round of applause.

Susan, sitting on her immediate right, leaned over to whisper, "I don't believe you have their wholehearted support, Zoe. Did it ever occur to you that some of these women might be the wives of the greedy developers?"

Zoe nodded composedly. "I'm sure you're right, my dear. However, I'm convinced that most of them are with me. After all, we have more than enough signatures on the petition to qualify the initiative for the ballot. And I think that the chances are very good for passage, if we keep working hard."

"My father and the others can play rough, Zoe. I think they were caught napping, figuring that the petition would never collect enough signatures."

Zoe smiled. "I've been in some rough battles with politicians before. I didn't always win, but I usually held my own."

Susan glanced around the room. There was a rising murmur of voices and the sounds of chairs being pushed back as the exodus commenced. Susan picked up her purse. "Shall we go, Zoe?"

"Might as well."

Outside, the glare of the sun off the parked cars was blinding. As they walked toward the spot where Susan had parked her little car, Zoe put on her sunglasses and stumbled.

Susan grabbed her elbow and steadied her. "Are you all right, Zoe?"

I'm fine. I probably shouldn't have had those two martinis before lunch, however. In this heat, I'll be sweating like a pig."

They got in and Susan started the car, joining the long line of vehicles pulling out of the parking lot.

Zoe hated to drive, and she had not owned a car since moving to Oasis. She either used a taxi or depended on friends, such as Susan.

The restaurant was about two miles from the Tremaine residence. They were only a half-dozen blocks from the Embers when a police siren whooped behind them.

"Is that for you, Susan?" Zoe asked.

Susan was looking up into the rearview mirror. "I don't know. That cop car is right on my tail. But I don't think I did anything wrong."

The siren whooped again. With a sigh, Susan pulled the VW alongside the curb. The police cruiser pulled in right behind her, and Zoe twisted around in time to see a tall handsome young man in the tan uniform of the Oasis Police Department get out and come toward Susan's side of the car. He was blond with blue eyes: a clean-out Nordic type, as were all Oasis policemen. No blacks, no Hispanics for Oasis.

The officer leaned down to the level of Susan's window. "May I please see your driver's license, miss?"

Susan already had her billfold out of her purse. She held it out the window.

"Would you take it out of the wallet, please?"

With a sigh, Susan complied. The officer took it.

"What did I do, Officer? I wasn't speeding and I didn't run any stop signs. There aren't any between here and the Embers, where we had lunch."

"You were driving rather erratically, Miss."

"Driving erratically?"

"And you didn't make a full stop leaving the parking lot before pulling out into traffic."

"Neither did anybody else!" Susan exploded. "I was only one in a long line of cars, and there was no traffic except the cars leaving the lot!"

He glanced up from his study of her driver's license, placed his face close to hers and sniffed. "You've been drinking, haven't you?"

"I had two glasses of wine with lunch, but I'm certainly not drunk, for heaven's sake!"

The officer stepped back. The very model of politeness, he said, "Would you step out of the vehicle, Miss Channing?"

Susan set her lips rebelliously. Zoe touched her on the leg. "Do as the man says, dear. Never argue with an officer of the law. It's a no-win situation."

The officer looked past Susan. "Would you step out, as well, Miss Tremaine?"

He stepped back again so that Susan could get out, then motioned her around the car to the sidewalk, where they joined Zoe.

"May I see your driver's license, Miss Tremaine?"

"I don't have a driver's license," Zoe said. "I don't own an automobile, and I don't drive."

The officer looked skeptical, then held out his hand. "Could I see some identification?"

Zoe dug into her purse for her Social Security card and a check-cashing card. As the officer took them, he thrust his face close to hers. Zoe remembered the two martinis and the fact he knew who she was. She knew what was about to happen and resigned herself to it.

As the officer examined the cards, Zoe gazed

out into the street and saw a line of cars still coming from the Embers. At the sight of the cruiser and Zoe and Susan with the officer, the drivers all slowed, staring at their recent luncheon speaker, who was obviously being interrogated by a police officer. The word would race through Oasis like wildfire. Looking at Susan, Zoe saw that she had also noticed and was fuming, tapping her foot angrily on the sidewalk.

"You've also been drinking, Miss Tremaine," the officer said.

"This is ridiculous!" Susan exclaimed. "Neither one of us is drunk, and Zoe wasn't driving, anyway."

"Being intoxicated in an automobile is against the law. I'm going to have to take you both down to the station for a Breathalyzer test."

"Oh, come on, Officer! Why this hassle?"

The officer's polite facade remained in place. "If you would both get in the unit, please?"

"What about my car?"

"You may lock it and leave it here. You may call from the station and have it towed away."

"Towed?" Susan glared at him. "You mean, we're going to jail?"

"If the results of your tests show your alcohol content is over the legal limit, yes."

"Oh, for God's sake . . . !"

311

"Susan." Zoe gestured. "Do as the man says."

Susan was so upset that she dropped her keys on the sidewalk as she dug them out of her purse. She retrieved them, rolled the windows up in her car and locked the doors. She was still trembling when she got into the back seat of the cruiser alongside Zoe.

The older woman patted her hand. "Easy, my dear. Just go with the flow."

"But this *is* a hassle, Zoe!" Susan said in a choked voice. "Of all the cars coming out of the parking lot . . . He *had* to have been watching for mine especially!"

"You are no doubt right about that."

The officer got behind the wheel, said a few words into his radio and started off. Cars coming from the restaurant were still slowing.

"Everybody in town is going to know we're being taken down to the station," Susan said. "This cretin is making sure of that!"

"Careful of your language, dear," Zoe said dryly. "There is also a law on the books about abusing a police officer. Calling this fine young man a cretin might constitute a violation of that law."

Susan fell silent, seething. She noticed that the officer drove slowly over to Broadway, the main thoroughfare. It was as if they were on parade. And when he reached the police station he pulled up right in front, where everyone on the street could get a good look at them, rather than pulling around to the parking lot entrance where prisoners were usually unloaded.

As they got out of the cruiser, Susan said acidly, "Aren't you going to handcuff us? That would make a much better show for everyone to see."

The officer ignored the remark, motioning for them to precede him into the station. Inside, he ushered them into a room down the hall from the lobby and left them alone, locking the door after him.

Zoe sat down at the table in the center of the room and lit a cigar.

"I don't know how you can take this so calmly, Zoe," Susan said in exasperation. "They're doing this deliberately, trying to blacken your reputation."

"I've long since learned that it's a waste of time and energy to get upset over things you can't control. I'm angry, true, but at the moment I'm helpless."

"I can see my father's hand in this," Susan said darkly.

Zoe frowned at her. "You think he'd really do something like this to his own daughter?"

Susan was pacing the small confines of the room. "You still don't realize that the man's capable of anything, Zoe. We're fighting him, as well as The Clinic, and he figures that by doing this he will weaken our credibility. Surely, you can see that?"

Zoe nodded. "Yes, I suppose he is capable of it —"

She broke off as the officer returned with the equipment for the test. Both women blew into the Breathalyzer. Zoe noticed that the officer was careful that they didn't get a glimpse of the readings.

"Well, young man?" Zoe demanded. "How do we test?"

He didn't look at her. "I have to discuss this with my superiors first. . . ."

"Officer . . ." She drew a deep breath. "I have been remarkably patient, I believe. But my patience is at an end. I demand to see Chief Darnell. Immediately!"

"The chief is a very busy man. . . ."

"Not half as busy as he will be if we don't see him at once. You will both be busy defending yourselves in court when I sue for false arrest!"

"I'll check and find out if he will see you," the officer mumbled, and exited quickly.

Susan applauded. "Good for you, Zoe!"

"Thad Darnell won't be so easily intimidated, dear. He's a tough-minded, uncompromising individual."

"But if we're being hassled, it must be on his orders."

"Perhaps, perhaps not. If your father, as you

314

believe, is behind this, he could have bribed our young officer. Stranger things have happened."

"There's no way those tests could indicate that we had too much to drink."

"That's a given, of course. I've studied alcohol and drug use in depth. The amount of alcohol we consumed during the past two hours would not register more than .02 maximum, far below that of legal intoxication."

The door opened to admit Chief Darnell. He nodded stiffly. "Miss Tremaine, Miss Channing. What is this I hear from Officer Manning about a suit against the city for false arrest? No arrest has been made, ladies. You have only been detained for tests."

Zoe smiled grimly. "I know that, Chief, but the threat worked. It brought you running."

"How about a suit for police harassment, Chief Darnell?" Susan said angrily.

"The young officer was only doing his duty as he saw it. A bit overzealous, perhaps. But no harm was done," Darnell retorted.

"That is not quite accurate," Zoe said. "Quite a bit of harm was done."

"You mean, it might not do your cause any good for it to be known that the strongest opponent of an alcohol treatment center was stopped and tested for alcohol abuse?" The chief was smiling slightly. "Then I suggest that you both abstain entirely when in public."

"What *were* the test results?" Zoe demanded.

"Your blood showed .01 percent alcohol content."

"Approximately my estimate. Hardly enough for a drunk driving charge, is it? Or for being intoxicated in an automobile?"

"Of course it isn't. You're both free to go. I will detail a cruiser to take you back to your car, Miss Channing."

"No thank you, we'll call a cab," Susan said. "We've been seen by enough people riding in a police car for one day."

"No apologies, Chief Darnell? For the inconvenience?" Zoe asked.

He gave her a flinty stare. "I do not apologize for overly zealous officers. I prefer that they be that rather than lax."

"Chief, if this happens again, I will be forced to conclude that Susan is right, that we're being subjected to police harassment. If that is true, there will be hell to pay. I do have some political clout in Oasis, perhaps even enough to prevent Mayor Washburn from being reelected in November. And if that happens, we might even get a new police chief."

Taking Susan's arm, Zoe sailed out of the room, brushing past Darnell.

Thad Darnell stared after them, not intimidated in the least by her threat. He knew that she had tried to defeat Charles Washburn in the last election and had failed.

But his respect for Zoe Tremaine had increased. A madam she may have been at one tune, but she had graduated unscathed from the profession and was a worthy opponent in any battle. He always preferred to do battle with an enemy he respected: it added an element of excitement.

"All right, gang," Noah said, gazing around at the eight people gathered in The Snake Pit. "For the three of you who have just joined our little group, we're on informal terms here, and we address each other by first names only. I will introduce our three new members. This is Lacey." He indicated her by a nod of his head. "That is Rem sitting across from me, and that is John."

Noah was pleased that the group had expanded. Lacey, although understandably nervous, seemed to have reconciled herself. Todd Remington was clearly strung out from detoxification, and Governor Stoddard was slumped in his chair, one hand up to the side of his face, as if to hide it.

Noah quickly ran through the names of the other five members for the benefit of the three newcomers. They included Al, the dentist who shared the governor's room; Bethel, the black nurse who bunked in with Lacey; Jim, an airline pilot in his early fifties; Karla, a druggist; and Jeffrey Lawrence.

Lawrence was a puzzle that Noah had yet to solve. The day he'd checked in the tests indicated that he had consumed several drinks prior to arrival, but he had been far from drunk, and he showed few of the signs of the true alcoholic. When Noah talked to him, he had the feeling that the man was evasive; and yet he was here and unlikely to have checked himself in if he wasn't alcohol dependent.

Noah decided to see if he could rattle Lawrence's cage a little. "Well, Jeffrey, suppose we put you in the hot seat today? You haven't had your turn yet."

Jeffrey looked startled and, Noah was pleased to see, somewhat rattled. "Well . . ." Jeffrey squirmed. "I'm not sure what's expected of me."

"First, announce yourself to the group. I realize everybody already knows your name, but it's a customary procedure."

"Hello, everybody. I'm Jeffrey."

Noah was shaking his head. "That won't do at all. Try – 'Hi, I'm Jeffrey, and I'm an alcoholic.'" Noah stared at him intently. "You are, aren't you?"

Jeffrey experienced a flash of anger and worked to keep his face impassive. What was this man trying to do to him? "Of course, or I wouldn't be here, would I?" he said. He glanced at Lacey, catching her gaze. "Hi, I'm Jeffrey. I'm an alcoholic."

"Hi, Jeffrey!" came the chorus.

"Excellent!" Noah said heartily. "Now, why are you an alcoholic?"

"Why? Because I drink too much," Jeffrey said with a self-conscious laugh.

"Gang?" Noah said, looking around at the group.

"Bullshit," Jim, the airline pilot, said. "You're being a smart ass, Jeffrey. Alcoholism is no joking matter."

"I'm sorry. Of course it isn't," Jeffrey said uncomfortably. "I'm not sure why I drink too much. I guess that's one reason I'm here, hoping to find out." He gazed around at the faces, wondering if they were swallowing his lie. "I'm a race car driver, under a lot of pressure. I started to drink to relieve that pressure. Somehow it escalated until it got out of hand. I knew that it was only a matter of time before the tests at the track caught up to me." He was thinking fast now, trying to make his story sound plausible.

"Did your parents drink, Jeffrey?" Noah asked.

Jeffrey seized the opportunity. "My father did. He was an alkie from the word go. He used to beat up on me when he was loaded."

"Strange," Noah said musingly. "There's nothing about that in your file, and you never mentioned it during our interviews."

"I was ashamed to admit it." Jeffrey hung his head. "What are we hearing, gang?" Noah asked.

"More horseshit," Karla said.

"He's on the pity pot," Al, the dentist, added.

"You do sound full of self-pity, Jeffrey," Noah said.

His gaze was penetrating and made Jeffrey feel even more uneasy. "I guess it does sound that way," he mumbled.

"What caused you to arrive at the decision to come here, Jeffrey?" Noah asked. "I have never been quite clear about that. Your file is rather skimpy."

Again, Jeffrey improvised. "I had an accident after I left a bar one evening. I hit a car parked at the curb and came close to totaling it. Luckily, I wasn't injured and even luckier that the car was empty."

Noah eyed him keenly. "There is no mention of such an incident in your file. Nothing about a drunk driving charge."

"Oh, I wasn't arrested," Jeffrey responded, his eyes lowered. "I was afraid to call the police. It was a hit-and-run. My car wasn't damaged enough so that I couldn't drive it away. If a drunk driving charge got on my record, no race car owner would ever hire me again."

"And how did you feel about that?"

"I was ashamed of myself. That's the reason I didn't tell you about it before, and that's the main reason I decided to do something about it."

Noah looked at him steadily, then finally nodded, switching his attention elsewhere. "All right, gang. Who else wants the hot seat today?"

"Hi, everybody. I'm Al, and I'm a doper."

"Hi, Al!" several voices sang out.

Jeffrey leaned back, obviously relieved that the ball had moved to someone else's court.

Billie Reaper paced the narrow confines of his room, his nerves twanging like a tuning fork. He was badly in need of a jolt. Anything — coke, pills, any goddamned thing! If he didn't climb on the white horse soon, they'd be scraping him off the walls.

They wouldn't let him near a telephone anymore. They'd stripsearched him when he'd been checked in and had taken everything on his person, including all of his money. But Joe Devlin, wearing his perpetual smile, had wheeled his way in yesterday.

"Shit, Billie," Devlin had said. "It's hard to get in to see you. It's almost as if you were in a cell on death row!"

"How do you think I feel?" Billie snarled. "Hell, man, it's *worse* than being on death row. At least there I might know when they're due to put me out of my misery. I'm going out of my skull! And it's all your fault, Joe. You dumped me in here."

"Billie, Billie. It's for your own good, you know that. You were out of it, kid. Strung out like you were, it's a wonder you didn't kill yourself. Or somebody else."

"I feel like killing *you*." Billie advanced on him, hands like claws.

Devlin backed up against the door. "Now Billie, all I have to do is rap on this door. There's an attendant right outside."

"Then get me out of here!"

"I can't do that, Billie. Kid, your whole career hangs on this gig. The whole world knows what happened at Irvine. I'm up to my ass in canceled bookings. Even the record company is threatening to break your contract. But the word is out that you're here, in The Clinic . . ."

"And I'll bet I know who let it out. *You*, asshole."

". . . and I've managed to muffle some of the clamor for your head by telling them that you'll be a changed man when you get out of here. Kid, there's no stigma anymore about going in for drug abuse. Hell, graduating from a place like The Clinic has become glamorous. Look at Liz, Liza, Bob Mitchum. Nobody thinks the less of them. But if you don't stay the course, you're nowhere. They won't trust you ever again."

Billie knew that Devlin was right, and so he backed off. "Then leave me some bread, man."

"What do you want money for in here?"

"Never mind that! There are things that I need."

"How much?" Devlin asked warily.

"Ten big ones."

"A grand? Come on, Billie, I don't have that much on me."

"Don't hand me that. You always walk around flush. Now hand it over, or I'll raise a fuss. Besides, it is my money.

"If I do, you'll promise to stay the whole month?"

"Yeah, yeah. I'll stick it out, but be sure and bring some more bread the next time you drop in."

Devlin peeled off ten hundreds and reluctantly handed them over. He made a mental note to ask the staff why Billie would need the money, then he rapped on the door. Billie peered over his manager's shoulder, wanting a glimpse of the attendant. To his delight, it was Jack Newton.

Behind Devlin's back, Billie motioned with his head. Shortly after the attendant had escorted Devlin out, a key sounded in the lock, and Jack Newton let himself in.

"You read all those papers yet, Billie? I need to get rid of them before someone finds them and they start to figure out who smuggled them in."

"Sure, Jack. Just a see."

Billie opened the drawer holding his underwear and dug out the brown grocery bag containing the trades and the *Insider*. But he didn't hand them over right away.

"Jack, I need you to do another thing for me."

"More papers?"

"No, something more important than that. I need something bad, man. I'm about to go off the tracks here. I mentioned this earlier. You promised to think about it."

Newton sucked in his breath. "I know, Billie, but I don't know. . . ."

"Anything, I don't care. I'd like some crack, but I don't have a pipe in here. So get me some snow to sniff. Or PCP, angel dust. Whatever."

The attendant recoiled. "I don't deal drugs! Smuggling in a trade paper, things like that, are okay. I need the extra dough. But drugs, no way! Not only would I get fired if I got caught, I'd do time in the slammer!"

"Speaking of dough . . ." Billie peeled two

hundreds from the roll, letting the attendant see the other bills, and waved them in his face. "This is for now, another hundred when you deliver. And of course, I'll pay whatever the buy comes to."

Jack Newton's muddy eyes brightened with greed, yet he was still shaking his head. "I don't have any connections in Oasis. This burg is tight. Chief Darnell keeps a lid on things."

"Must be a connection in the Springs. All the rich users live there."

"But not on the street. Those big shots in Palm Springs make their buys from private connections. You think a movie star would make a buy on the street?"

Billie was rapidly losing his patience. "Then cruise up to L.A., man. Man, you've been a user, you have to know how to score on the streets in L.A. Tonight, after you get off. It's — what? — a four-hour drive up and back? I'll sweeten the pot. An extra hundred if you score for me by tomorrow."

In the end, Newton's greed overcame his caution, and he agreed to score.

Billie waited, pacing the room, anticipating the soon-to-come rush. It was unlikely that they would give him any more urine tests, thinking that he was tucked safely away from any possibility of scoring.

He tensed as a key sounded in the lock, and he hurried toward the door just as it opened. It was the attendant.

Looking both ways along the corridor, Newton said, "Here, Billie. I got a gram for you." He held out his hand, and Billie snatched the glassine envelope from him.

Fifteen

Governor William Stoddard had developed a strong attraction to Lacey Houston on sight. Although he was not a movie buff and had only seen two of her pictures, he thought that neither had done her physical justice. In the flesh, she was something else – a slender but ripe body, white skin that looked as smooth as silk, a cap of dark hair and green eyes a man could drown in. And her breasts were spectacular.

Now, as he, Lacey, Rem and Jeffrey made their way down the hall to the auditorium, where they were to listen to the evening's speaker – a doctor active in Alcoholics Anonymous – Stoddard eyed Lacey covertly. Stoddard recognized that he was very attractive to women, and he knew that Lacey Houston was no prude; he knew of her three marriages and numerous affairs.

But Stoddard wondered if this was the proper place to try to seduce a woman. One of the firmest rules at The Clinic was the one forbidding fraternizing after hours, and sexual relations between patients were strictly taboo. Stoddard smiled wryly. The primary aim here was to avoid all distractions; and what could be more distracting than a heated affair?

But dammit, he was going to be in here for a whole month; and now that he was dried out, sexual desire was stirring in him. He couldn't remember a time, since his teens, when he had been without a woman for an entire month.

Well, he would have to play it by ear, see what developed.

He tuned in on the conversation. The other three were discussing . . .

"I've tried it twice," Rem confessed. "Neither time worked, at least no longer than it took me to find a bar."

"But the only way AA is used here, according to Dr. Breckinridge," said Lacey, "is that we're supposed to follow the twelve steps outlined in AA's 'Big Book.' It's only another tool to be used in rehabilitation, he said."

"Tool! The good doctor is always talking about tools. Sounds dirty to me," Rem said in a grumbling voice. "Pardon me, ma'am. Didn't mean to offend you."

"It's all right, Rem," Lacey said with a flashing smile. "I'm not offended."

"There's something else that bugs me about the program here, something else they've borrowed from AA. Both treatments seem to involve religion – someone's always going on about praying to God for help and guidance."

"Not God exactly," she said chidingly. "They're talking about a higher power."

"Same thing, ain't it?"

"Not exactly, Rem," Jeffrey said. "Not the way I understand it. They espouse no denomination here. All they want you to believe in is a higher power of some kind. Even an agnostic must believe in something greater than himself. Apparently, they believe that a person can't swing it alone."

"Yeah, I know all that. They all say you'll connect before you leave here. One guy told me that he was kneeling beside his bed one morning, and all of a sudden a strong white light flooded the room, and it all became clear to him." Rem snorted. "Now that sounds to me like one of them TV evangelists could reap a fortune in here."

Lacey smiled at him. "Surely you believe in something, Rem."

"I reckon I don't. If there is a God, a higher power, he's certainly never given me a helping hand." Rem was plunged into gloom. "The things that have happened to me are enough to make any man doubt the existence of God."

"How about you, John?" Lacey looked at Stoddard. "What do you believe in?"

Stoddard was a bit slow in picking up on the question. He hadn't become fully accustomed to the name he was using here. "I believe in something, certainly." The governor was actually Catholic who, despite some weaknesses, attended church regularly; yet he wasn't sure what he believed in anymore.

They were at the door of the auditorium now, and the conversation lapsed, much to Stoddard's relief.

In the auditorium, Jeffrey paid scant heed to the speaker at first. He was sitting next to Lacey, and he was acutely aware of her nearness. He had never been so powerfully attracted to a woman before. Of course, she was considered one of the great beauties of the world. Yet it was more than that, much more. She projected a genuine warmth, and he sensed a deep capacity for love.

His thoughts came to an abrupt halt. He was in love with Lacey Houston! For the first time in his life, he was in love.

He stifled a groan. How could he steal from her? He had financed this caper and was in hock to Bernie up to his eyeballs. If he didn't pay off the loan, Bernie would have his scalp; and he would put out the word that Jeffrey could not be trusted any longer. No, it was too late to back away, too late to try another caper.

He had to go through with it; he had no choice.

He hadn't made any progress on his plan. Before coming to The Clinic, he had assumed that Lacey would keep the jewels in her room, but he had learned right from the start that few personal possessions were allowed to remain with the patients, only the bare necessities. Even toothpaste was tested for drugs, and shaving lotion for alcohol content. But just to be sure, yesterday he had managed a quick inspection of Lacey's room. He had slipped off while everyone was at lunch and sneaked into her room — none of the rooms in the rehab wing were locked. There was certainly nothing there large enough to hold a collection of jewels So, where were they?

He couldn't very well ask her point-blank. But since they spent much of their free time together, he hoped she would let it slip during a relaxed moment. He felt like a heel gaining her confidence in this way. But what alternative did he have?

With a sigh, he turned his attention to the speaker, a tall spare man in his sixties. He had announced at the start of his speech that he was Dr. Jonas Carter, an alcoholic.

As Jeffrey began listening, Dr. Carter began discussing the merits of Alcoholics Anonymous. "As I am sure you all know by now, there are no dues for membership in our organization. We exist purely on contributions, coming primarily from people who have recovered from alcoholism through the efforts of AA. We are a strong fellowship among men and women who share their own experiences as well as their strength and hope, to help others recover from the disease. We are not associated with any religious sect or denomination. We do not espouse any politics, nor do we engage in any controversy. Our only purpose is to stay sober and to help others attain that blissful state.

"The majority of those who follow our path manage to defeat alcoholism. Those who do not are those who refuse to give themselves over to our program – they are usually people who also refuse to be honest with themselves.

"Always remember this one unalterable fact. We are dealing with alcohol, which is cunning, very tricky and powerful, far too powerful for most of us to combat on our own."

Dr. Carter continued his speech by listing the twelve steps AA had identified as essential to a full recovery.

"There you have it. It is my belief, that you can conquer alcoholism through the twelve principles. I well realize that it may seem, at first glance, impossible to carry them out. Remember, they are merely guidelines, a striving for spiritual progress, not spiritual perfection."

Dr. Carter smiled. "In times past, strong drink was often referred to as the demon rum. That phrase is passé now. Yet, to those of us who are alcoholics, anything alcoholic is certainly a demon, a demon that we must rid ourselves of. I wish you all success in that quest."

The speaker was applauded enthusiastically. Jeffrey, Rem, Lacey and Stoddard waited for the aisles to clear before leaving the auditorium.

"I reckon I'm wasting my time here," Rem said sourly.

"Rem . . ." Lacey put her hand on his arm. "You must look within yourself for the strength to fight this thing. The speaker said to be honest with yourself."

"If I do that, then I'm in deep trouble," Rem responded. "I've always depended on myself, all of my life, and it worked for a long time. But it ain't working any longer."

The aisle cleared, and they started to move toward the exit.

Jeffrey touched Lacey's arm, holding her back. "Under the circumstances, I can't very well ask you out for a drink, but how about a cup of coffee in the commissary?"

She gave him a measuring look, then bestowed that slow sweet smile on him. "I'd like that, Jeffrey."

Otto Channing had been kept waiting in the

anteroom to Thad Darnell's office for fifteen minutes, and he was steaming. He was unaccustomed to cooling his heels outside anyone's office.

Finally, the door opened and the chief stuck his head out. "Come on in, Otto. Sorry to keep you waiting like that, but I was on a long-distance call."

Raging inwardly, Channing followed Darnell into the office and took the seat in front of the desk.

Darnell sat down, his hands flat on the desk. He said blandly, "What can I do for you, Otto?"

Channing leaned forward. "I'm tired of waiting, Thad. What have you dug up on Zoe Tremaine?"

Darnell studied him carefully, his blank stare revealing little.

"Let me say this," Channing said. "If you haven't found anything we can use to scare that woman off, I'm going to employ a detective agency. And I warn you, if they come up with something, something you haven't come up with, I'll have your ass, one way or another. Depend on it!"

"As a matter of fact, that's what the phone call was all about," Darnell lied. He realized that he couldn't afford to stall any longer. "I was on the phone to a friend of mine in Vegas.

A man in the department there. I sent Zoe's prints from the ashtray to Washington. They're notoriously slow, as I'm sure you know. I just got the report back yesterday, and it claims that Zoe once used the alias of May Fremont. At least that's the name she gave when she was arrested for running a house of prostitution in Denver."

"You see?" Channing said triumphantly. "I told you she was hiding something!"

"But she wasn't convicted. She has never been convicted of anything."

"But she obviously has some kind of a record." Channing frowned. "You just said you talked to a cop in Las Vegas? Why?"

"Yes, I called him on a hunch."

"So, what did you find out there?"

"A May Fremont operated a house outside of Vegas for a time, about twenty years back, called the Heavenly Retreat. Then she left there and opened a classier place on the edge of Beverly Hills."

"Dammit, I was right!" Channing slapped the desk with the flat of his hand. "Now we've got something to hold over her head."

"That was all a long time ago, Otto. And remember, she was never convicted, never served time."

"I don't care about that. You think she'd like the fact she's an ex-madam to get out? It would destroy her credibility, and the kooks following her would desert like rats from a sinking ship!" Channing bounced to his feet. "Thanks, Thad. You came through for me. I won't forget it."

Darnell watched the now exuberant Channing stride from his office. He was disgusted with himself for being a part of such a shabby business, and he felt sympathy for Zoe Tremaine. No matter what she had been, she didn't deserve this. Her life since moving to Oasis had been exemplary.

He even moved his hand to pick up the phone and alert her, then stopped. She would get the news soon enough. Otto would see to that.

Zoe had a bad case of the flu, and had spent most of the day in bed. She hadn't called Susan to let her know, because she knew that the girl would rush over immediately and insist on taking care of her. Zoe didn't want that; whenever she felt poorly, she liked to crawl into a hole and stay there, undisturbed, until she felt better. She had even told Juanita not to come in. She had fed the birds, but she refused to have Madam on her shoulder in case the bird caught her germs. Her throat raw and sore from coughing, she also had to forgo the cigars.

She was sitting in the kitchen, wearing a tatty robe, sloppy slippers and sipping on a hot whiskey toddy, when the doorbell rang.

For a few seconds she considered not answering it. She wasn't expecting anybody; Susan had her own key and never rang the doorbell, so it was probably a salesperson.

The bell rang again, imperiously. It was about time for the mailman, and she received the occasional registered letter from her various investments.

With a sigh, she got up and trudged through the house to the front door, giving little thought to the way she looked. The mailman had seen her in disarray before.

She opened the door to a smiling Otto Channing.

"Oh, for heaven's sake!" Zoe said in her clogged voice. "What do you want, Otto? I'm not feeling well."

"Sorry to hear that, Zoe. I just want a few words with you," he said.

"If it's about the speech I made the other day at the Women's Club, your young officer has already hassled me over it. But then you already know about that, don't you?"

"No, I haven't the faintest idea what you're talking about."

"I just bet you don't. Oh . . . I don't feel like arguing with you, Otto. Come on in, get it off your chest, and leave me in peace."

She led the way into the kitchen. "I'm having

a hot toddy for my . . ." She sneezed violently and sat down at the breakfast table. "There's some beer in the refrigerator, if you want one."

"I didn't come here to drink."

She looked up at him with watery eyes. "Then why *did* you come here?"

"I came here to tell you that your secret is out. I know who you are, May Fremont."

Zoe was still, trying to conceal her shock, but she realized from the smug expression on his face that he knew he had scored. She tried to hide her emotions behind a cough, but the cough triggered a series of wracking spasms. When she finally stopped, her eyes were streaming. She grabbed a handful of tissues from the box by her elbow, wiped her eyes and blew her nose.

"Well? Are you going to deny it?"

"There's not much use, is there?" she said in a strangled voice.

"No damned use at all," he said triumphantly.

"That's all history, Otto, buried deeply in the past. I've been out of the business for over fifteen years."

"It's not buried deeply enough. You know the people in this town. How do you think they'll react to having an ex-madam in their midst, living on the proceeds of ill-gotten gains?"

"You sound like something out of an old-fashioned melodrama, Otto. Nobody cares about things like that anymore."

"You know better than that. Some places, maybe, but not Oasis."

"There are no outstanding charges against me. I can't be arrested."

"Nobody is talking about arresting you."

"Then what are you talking about, Otto?" But of course, she knew; she knew precisely.

"You're to cease all opposition to The Clinic. You're to stop all speeches in support of this damned no-growth initiative. In short, you're to stop interfering in matters that are not your business!"

"And if I don't?"

"If you don't, Cindy Hodges will receive a little note informing her of your past."

"I'm not a celebrity. Why should she be interested in an old lady?"

"An old whore, Zoe," Channing said brutally. "And I think she will be interested. Your activities are news. But if she isn't, it will be easy enough to run off several thousand flyers and mail them to the citizens of Oasis. How do you think your devoted followers will react to the news that their spokesperson is an ex-madam, a whore?"

"Not too well, I expect," she said in a dead voice.

"So? Are you going to pull in your horns, or do I have to carry through?"

"This is blackmail, you know."

"Blackmail?" he said with a sneer. "You're hardly in a position to throw stones. So, what's it to be?"

"I don't have a great deal of choice, do I?"

"No choice at all. But at least, so long as you behave, you can still live here in peace and quiet. That's why you came to Oasis, isn't it? That's what you're always yapping about. You should be grateful that I'm not broadcasting the news anyway."

"All right, Otto. You win."

"Good, *May*. You should have a good strong drink now," he said with heavy irony. "If it doesn't cure your cold, at least you'll feel better for a bit. And you don't have to worry. If you get hooked on the booze, there's always The Clinic just up the road."

As he started out, Zoe said, "How about Susan? How about your daughter? I can't speak for her."

"You're the one everybody listens to, not her. Without you, no one will pay attention to anything she has to say."

Channing left, and Zoe sat in despair. What she had always feared had happened. She stood exposed. She didn't have to wonder about how the news would be greeted if it got out. In spite of her brave words to Channing, she knew very well that she would be ostracized. In fact, she knew she couldn't remain in Oasis if the word spread. And she was too old to pack up and move again.

"I'm sorry, Cassie," she said aloud. "I tried. But I guess it's not to be." She felt her eyes burn, but no tears came.

She drained the cup of toddy, then got up and fetched the bottle. Zoe poured the whiskey right into the cup, drank it straight, shuddering. As soon as the cup was empty, she poured another. What did it matter now? What did anything matter?

Unaccustomed as she was to heavy drinking, it wasn't long before she was drunk — for the first time in her life. She was, in fact, so drunk that she was afraid to get up, afraid she would fall flat on her face.

She giggled. At least Otto had been right about one thing. The whiskey had temporarily deadened the aches and pains of the cold.

Dimly, she heard the sound of a key in the kitchen door. Then Susan loomed over her. "Zoe?"

Zoe looked up blurrily. "Susan . . ."

"Zoe? My God, you're drunk!"

"Right, Sushan. Drunk as . . . a skunk."

Susan sank down into the chair across the

table. "But you never . . . Why?"

And then the tears came, in a flood, and Zoe heard herself sobbing out the story of Otto Channing's visit, something she dimly realized she would never have done if she was sober.

Sixteen

Otto Channing lived up to and beyond his income. He liked expensive cars, expensive clothes, expensive women — an altogether luxurious life-style; and at this particular time in his life his finances were extremely strained. Although the no-growth measure was not yet law in Oasis, the possibility of its passing had put a damper on the enthusiasm of developers, builders and money men. "Wait and see what happens come November," they all said, as much a chorus as if they had rehearsed it.

Channing figured that he would be lucky to make it into November without filing for bankruptcy. But at least now, with a club to keep Zoe Tremaine quiet, he could start to operate again. Maybe he could convince some of the development money that without Zoe Tremaine, most of the steam had gone out of the opposition.

If Zoe and her supporters had their way, Oasis would stagnate and die. The fame of The

Clinic had put Oasis on the map; it had guaranteed the community's prosperity.

The morning after his confrontation with Zoe Tremaine, Channing got to his office early, even before Ethel Burroughs, his secretary-receptionist, arrived. Channing had some calls to make. One reason his cash flow was so tight was because he had taken options to buy on several acres of vacant land on the east edge of town. If he couldn't get some developers interested soon, the options would expire, and he would really be in a bind.

His office was located in a minimall just off Broadway. The mall was new, and he had been instrumental in having it built.

He got on the phone immediately, to a developer in Riverside. "Good news, Waldo!"

"I could use some, Otto," Waldo Reese said. "Things have been kinda slow of late."

"I have defused the agitator who's behind all the opposition to growth down here. Zoe Tremaine, you know, is the one who's behind it all, pushing the no-growth initiative and opposing The Clinic."

Reese's rough voice quickened. "However did you manage that?"

Channing grinned. "Just used my persuasive powers."

"Well, that's all to the good, but it's a little late, I'd say. That damned initiative is already on the ballot. How can I risk going in there until I know for sure that the initiative doesn't pass?"

"Without the Tremaine woman, it will never make it. She's been the driving force all along. Without her, the group will become disorganized, and I'm sure that Mayor Washburn can then swing enough votes to defeat the initiative."

"You really think so?"

"I'm sure of it," Channing said strongly. "I'll stake my reputation on it, in fact."

"All right, Otto. I tell you what I'll do. I'll drive down there tomorrow and we'll talk."

Channing tried to keep the triumph out of his voice. If he could get Reese interested again, he was sure others would fall in line. He said, "Why don't we have lunch at the country club, Waldo?"

As Channing hung up, he heard someone in the outer office. He raised his voice. "Is that you, Ethel?"

In a moment the door swung open. "No, Father. It's me," Susan said, striding in.

Channing gaped at her. This was the first time she had spoken to him since she left home. "Well, this *is* a surprise."

"I'll just bet it is," she said in a dry voice. She gazed around the office — lush carpeting, an ornate expensive desk, leather-covered chairs.

The walls were hung with pictures of the many developments Channing had been associated with, along with a number of pictures of Channing posing with various celebrities and politicians. "You've done well, Father."

"You have to have a nice office if you're going to deal with the big boys," he said with a self-deprecatory shrug.

"And you love to deal with the big boys, don't you?"

He felt a ping of irritation. "What do you want, Susan? If it's money you're after, I'm having cash flow problems right now."

"Money? From you? I wouldn't stoop so low. No, Father, I've come to tell you, to your face, what a prime asshole you are."

Channing was jolted forward, his face flaming, saying in a strangled voice, "What?"

"Doing what you did to Zoe was nasty, even for you. She is the nicest person I know, and you almost destroyed her last night!"

"Nicest person!" He spat out the words. "She's a whore!"

"She may have been once. But then you're a whore, too, and at least Zoe was honest about it. You're a flaming hypocrite, hiding behind platitudes."

"I don't have to take this abuse from you, Susan. You're no longer my daughter. You've made that clear enough!"

She stared at him with loathing. "I'm ashamed that your blood flows in my veins. In fact, I've sometimes wondered . . . maybe you're not my father at all. Maybe that's why Mother drank herself to death and the reason you hated her so."

He shot to his feet. "Now that's enough! I insist that you leave at once."

"Not until I've said what I came here to say. If you want me out before then, you'll have to throw me out, and how would that look to the people in the mall?"

Channing gritted his teeth, choking back his raging temper. "Get done with it then."

"Will it do any good to ask you not to broadcast what you know about Zoe?"

"Not a damned bit of good." He sneered. "Not even if you begged."

"I would not beg, Father. Even if I could bring myself to do so, Zoe would never forgive me if I did. I simply want you to do the decent thing and keep quiet."

"The decent thing! So you and the rest of that pack you run with can continue to disrupt Oasis, to halt its growth?"

Her gaze held his. "I take it nothing will change your mind, then?"

"Don't be an idiot, girl! Of course I won't keep quiet, unless she does. This is the leverage I've been looking for to keep a lid on her." He grinned. "How does it feel to know that your righteous leader was once a whorehouse madam?"

"Then I must warn you, Father, that if you do expose her, I will spread a tale about the reason I left your house and will no longer have anything to do with you."

"Spread anything you like," he said with a shrug. "It won't affect me in the least."

"What if I told everybody that the reason I left was because you raped me, practiced incest on me, after Mother died?"

He reared back in his chair. "That's an out-and-out lie, as you very well know!"

"Maybe I know it, but the question is, will the people of Oasis believe it? You know how most people are. They will believe anything bad. And even if they don't believe it, there will always be some doubt. Do you think that revelation will affect your standing in the community?"

"You wouldn't dare do something like that!"

"Try me," she said composedly.

"How could you possibly consider doing such a thing? To your own father?"

"Because I've had a good teacher, *Father*. I'll do anything in my power to protect Zoe."

"I can't believe I'm hearing this."

"Believe it, Father. I not only will do it, I would take great delight in it."

Shaken, Channing could only stare at her. "Well?"

"I give you my word that I'll keep quiet." He had to force the words out.

"Your word is worthless. But if I even hear one whisper about Zoe's past, I'll start spreading my little tale."

"But wait! What if I'm not the only one who knows?" He was thinking of Thad Darnell. Once he would have sworn that he could control the chief; now, he was no longer so sure. "Someone else could leak the story."

"You will have to see that no one else does, won't you? Goodbye, Father."

She nodded curtly, turned and left without another word.

Channing sat, dazed, feeling as if his world was crumbling around him. After all he had gone through! And now this. Betrayed by his own daughter!

What was he going to say to Waldo Reese at lunch tomorrow? He looked down at the list of names on his desk, names he had been going to call this morning, to tell them that it was safe now to proceed with new developments. In a burst of bitter frustration, he crumpled up the sheet and hurled it across the room.

Dick Stanton hummed to himself as he got dressed — the casual look, but definitely California. Suede loafers with tassels, pearl-colored slacks, a dove-colored shirt that fit his narrow torso like a glove, open just enough to show a bit of the hair on his chest.

He had a date with Cindy Hodges. Dinner at the Embers, and a little dancing afterward.

Dick dashed some after-shave on his face and stood back and looked at himself in the mirror. He was happy about the date, wasn't he? Of course he was.

Yet he was also nervous; he was honest enough with himself to admit that. It had been back in the Dark Ages when he'd had a real date with a woman; not just taking a female friend out for a casual, friendly evening.

He recalled Zoe's cautioning words. "She's a man-eater, Dickie. She'll eat you alive. She's dominating, she's arrogant. Why don't you find a nice warm-hearted girl?"

"You don't understand it, Zoe. If I'm going to go straight, it'll have to be with someone like Cindy, a woman who's a real challenge. I don't think I could make it with a girl who doesn't have any spunk."

"She's a challenge, right enough. I just don't want to see you hurt, is all, Dickie. I really don't understand this push to 'go straight.' At one time I certainly wouldn't have approved of your life-style, but I've come to see, finally, that everyone has to go to their own church."

350

"But Zoe, it's my former life-style that turned me into an alcoholic. That's something I've finally realized. I simply can't come to terms with being gay."

Besides, he told himself now, still studying his reflection in the mirror, I wasn't born gay. No way.

As a teenager he had been after the girls as much as any male his own age. And he had scored often, too; especially with the girls who found the hairy jocks unappealing.

Then had come the stint in the army and a brief tour in Vietnam, where he had met Jesse. Jesse Sims — bright, witty, handsome, charming and gay. They had turned to each other for comfort and solace in the horror of what they were seeing around them. Who wouldn't have undergone a change in that hell?

They had watched their fellow soldiers get caught up in a frenzy of killing, pillaging and raping, and had been sickened by it.

Dick had escaped otherwise unscathed, but Jesse had been killed a week before they were due to go stateside. He had been killed by a sniper's bullet not two feet from Dick. Dick had been devastated, and walked through the rest of his tour in a daze.

Then San Francisco and the gay scene. He had plunged into it at once, for the first year homing in on one-night stands, until he had finally settled down with Ken.

It wasn't long after this that it became popular to "come out of the closet," but Dick could never bring himself to really do it. Ken managed the new openness admirably and had scorned Dick for his reluctance. It was then that Dick's drinking started to get out of hand.

He could blame Vietnam, he could blame his distaste for flaunting his gayness; but in his heart Dick knew that his drinking really sprang from the fact he hadn't totally accepted his homosexuality. He was sure that if he had a normal sexual relationship with a woman, he would be able to control his drinking.

As the doorbell rang, Dick gave a jaunty wave to his image in the mirror and went to greet the taxi driver. He hadn't driven a car in years. His license had been revoked some years back, after three arrests for drunk driving.

Later that night, Dick wrote at length in his notebook.

I believe Cindy is the one, I really do! Zoe is wrong about her. All that glittering hardness is just a veneer, a protective shell hiding a caring, vulnerable woman. True, she has to be ruthless at times — she admitted as much to me tonight. To succeed in her line of work, one can't be too concerned about the feelings of the celebrities she writes about.

And it's also true that I am not too enamored with her profession. When I said something along those lines to her, she laughed that brittle laugh of hers and said that it was a dirty job, but someone had to do it.

Yet, as the evening progressed, she admitted to me that she sometimes hates what she does for a living, but she is good at it and it pays well. She tells me that she always wanted to be a writer. She started a book a few years ago, but was never able to finish it.

And then she said that she hoped that I, being a professional writer, could help her get over the mental block that is keeping her from finishing the book. How ironic! Asking me to help her when I can't even help myself. I told her that I hadn't written anything publishable in years. And then she said that perhaps by working together, we might help each other.

I would like nothing better, although I have never worked with another writer. In fact, I know very few writers. I don't even like writers, on the whole. But aside from any possibility of our helping each other in our work, it would be a great opportunity to get closer to Cindy.

However, I do not dare involve myself with her in a professional sense, not in any manner whatsoever. If I did that, I might reveal myself for the failure that I am, that I no longer *can* write. The fountain of creativity, if it ever existed, has dried up. And of course, I couldn't tell her that *Images of Fortune* was ghostwritten. What would she think of me? She has expressed admiration for my published works. I cannot risk losing that admiration. I simply told her that writing is a private endeavor and should not be shared with another person, as fatuous as that sounds.

It did cross my mind to ask Cindy the subject of her work in progress, but I refrained.

I wonder if she suspects that I am gay? No, delete that. Does she suspect that I was once gay? She certainly gave no indication of it. I have few of the mannerisms popularly associated with gay men. At least, not when I apply myself.

I was particularly circumspect tonight. I did not make any sexual overtures. I was not ready. Once, when we were dancing together rather intimately, I became very aroused. I know that it is not unusual for a man and woman to go to bed together on a first date, even with the AIDS scare. But I am old-fashioned in that respect, and I hope that Cindy recognized that in me and will respect me for it.

I am highly pleased at the way the evening went.

Cindy seemed to enjoy herself. At least, she wasn't averse to my suggestion that we repeat the evening soon, very soon. . . .

Dick broke off writing, struck by a sudden happy revelation. He had put more words on paper than he had in a long time. True, it wasn't a novel, but it was *writing*. Could it be possible that the long dry spell was coming to an end?

If true, he owed Cindy Hodges a vote of thanks!

Seventeen

"Today, gang, we have a new member," Noah announced. "Billie, stand up and introduce yourself."

Billie Reaper stood, grinning around at the semicircle of people. "Shouldn't think that would be necessary. But for the ones who don't know, I'm Billie Reaper."

Noah was a little surprised at Billie's demeanor today. He was clean shaven for the first time in days, and his long hair was combed back out of his eyes. There was little of the sullenness Noah had grown to recognize; instead, he wore that cocky shit-eating grin.

"That won't do, Billie," Noah said. "These people don't care who you are outside this building. It's who you are in here that counts."

Billie looked at him insolently. "So what do I say, teach?"

Before Noah could respond, Todd Remington spoke up. "You tell us your name, and that you're either an alkie or a doper. Just like the rest of us do when we talk to the group."

Billie darkened. "Who the hell are you to tell me what to say?"

"I'm Rem, and I'm a alcoholic."

"Well, I'm Billie, like I already said. But why should I tell you jerk-offs that I'm a doper or an alcoholic?"

"Because that's why you're here." Rem leaned forward, his face tight. "And you're no better than the rest of us, so where do you get off calling us jerk-offs?"

"Look, Dad, don't put me in the bag with the rest of you." Billie leaned down, thrusting his face close to Rem's. "Fuck with me, and I'll take your head off!"

Noah finally interrupted. "That's enough. Both of you back off. Sit down, Billie, and act like an adult."

Billie whipped around, glowering, but after a moment he sat down slowly.

"All right, gang," Noah said. "Let's act out a little drama today. Tell us, Rem, when you're drinking heavily, do you patronize bars?"

"Sure, I ain't one of your solitary drinkers. That's a sure sign of alcoholism, ain't it, Doc?" Rem asked with a slight grin. "And I like a good quiet bar, with the companionship of a bunch of fun guys."

"Drinking buddies, isn't that what you mean?"

Rem flushed. "Yeah, sure, I guess you could call them that."

"Tell us, Rem. Did you ever get into fights in these bars you frequented?"

Rem hesitated. "Nope." He grinned. "I'm a lover, not a fighter."

"What are you hearing, gang?" Noah asked.

"Bullshit!" several chorused together.

Rem looked around angrily. "Now wait just a damned minute!"

Noah said, "You're angry now, aren't you? About ready to hit out at someone?"

"Well, yeah, but I'm not . . ." He said triumphantly, "I'm not drunk!"

Noah glanced down at a file open in his lap. "I have your record here. You have been arrested three times for drunken brawling in a bar, and once for drunk driving, in which it was also alleged that you were truculent and abusive to the arresting officer." He looked up. "Is that true, Rem?"

"Where'd you get all that stuff?" Rem asked belligerently. "You have no right to look up things like that!"

"You gave me the right when you signed in here," Noah said calmly. "You may not remember, but you signed a paper giving me permission." He looked around. "Who wants to play bartender?"

"I will," Al said. "I tended bar to put myself

through dental college."

"How could you do that?" Rem asked. "They don't allow juveniles to tend bar."

"I was a late starter," Al said, unoffended. "I didn't go to college until I was well over twenty-one."

"Al, bring that table over here." Noah gestured across the room. "And a couple of chairs."

Al complied.

"And put the water pitcher and a couple of glasses on the table." Noah beckoned. "Jeffrey, I'd like you to assist us." When Jeffrey Lawrence came up to Noah's chair, Noah handed him a sheet of paper "You're going to play a role in our little psychodrama."

Accepting the sheet of paper, Jeffrey read the lines dubiously, opened his mouth to protest then closed it.

Noah looked over at the table. "Take up your position behind the bar, Al. You, Rem, belly up and order your poison."

"How about my lines, Doc? After all, I'm an actor." Rem laughed shortly. "Although there're some who might argue the point."

"You won't need any lines. You're just supposed to react to what Jeffrey says."

With a shrug, Rem sat down at the table. "I'll have a double Jack Daniel's on the rocks." As Al filled his glass with water, Rem laughed again. "If that was the real stuff, I could give a much better performance."

"Jeffrey, you're on."

Feeling somewhat self-conscious, Jeffrey sat down on the other chair. "I'll have a vodka on the rocks," he said, studying the piece of paper.

Al poured water into his glass. Jeffrey started to raise the glass to his mouth, then stopped, glancing at Rem. "Say, mister, aren't you Todd Remington, the famous Western star?"

Rem looked at him archly. "Yup, that's me."

"I've always liked your films. What's your next and when will it be out?"

"You tell me. I'd like to know, too."

"Oh, I see." Jeffrey tried for a supercilious sneer, which he feared didn't come off too well. "Come to think of it, I haven't seen a movie of yours in years."

"You've sure as hell got that right, friend." Rem thumped his glass on the table viciously. "Another double, buddy."

"Why is that?"

"*That* is the sixty-four-dollar question."

"Well, I guess when you're not hot, you're just not hot."

Rem sent him a look burning with venom. "And just what is that supposed to mean?"

Jeffrey, well into the role now, shrugged elaborately. "Seems to me the remark speaks for itself. You're finished in the movies. You're a has-been, Mr. Remington."

All of a sudden, a roar of rage erupted from Rem. "You son of a bitch, nobody calls me a has-been!" Standing, he seized Jeffrey by the shirtfront and began to shake him. "I'll break your damn neck!"

Alarmed, Noah shouted, "Rem! That's enough!"

Rem didn't appear to hear. He continued to shake Jeffrey, all the while shouting obscenities. Noah jumped to his feet. By the time he had reached the actor, Al had come around the table. Together, they pulled Rem away.

Rem turned a snarling, contorted face on Noah, and for a moment the doctor was afraid that he was going to have to defend himself. Then recognition flashed across Rem's face, and he sagged in their grip, all the anger draining out of him.

"Shit, I blew it, didn't I?" He looked at Jeffrey in concern. "Did I hurt you?"

Shakily, Jeffrey stood back. "No, I'm okay, but you scared the hell out of me."

"I'm sorry, Jeffrey, sorry as I can be," Rem said abjectly. "I don't know what came over me."

"The same thing happened at Zoe Tremaine's party," Noah said softly. "Remember, Rem?"

"Well, yeah." Rem passed a hand down over his face. "I remember something like that. But

I was drunk that night."

"The anger and frustration were already there, ready to explode. Often we use the plea of being drunk to excuse such actions."

Rem shook his head doggedly. "You don't understand. When anyone calls me a has-been, I boil over. Because I *am* a has-been, I reckon I have to admit that. That's why I drink so much. My career has gone with the wind."

"What are you hearing, gang?" Noah asked.

"Bullshit!" came the chorus.

Noah resumed his seat. "Rem, you admitted to me that you always drank heavily, even when you were box-office."

Rem sat down facing him, leaning forward. "But I could handle it in those days."

"A true alcoholic never really handles it. It's just that your tolerance level decreases after a lifetime of heavy drinking."

"I still say that my drinking got too much for me only after my career went bust."

"Rem, I strongly suspect that you are what I call a performance user. At the root of your alcoholism is a feeling of inadequacy, a constant fear that you can never measure up to what your public expects of you. And when your career did, as you say, go bust, that was only proof that you were inadequate all along, a subconscious excuse to drink more and more."

"To use the favorite word around here, bullshit! I don't believe it for a minute." Rem glanced around. "How about you, Lacey? Is that why you became a coke abuser?"

"No fair, buster!" Bethel, the black nurse, interjected. "Don't lay it off on Lacey. Your problem is *your* problem."

Noah started to intervene, to get Lacey off the spot; but then he slanted a look at her and saw that she was not offended, so he kept quiet, waiting with interest to see what would develop.

"It's all right, Bethel. I don't mind, really I don't." Lacey glanced over at Rem. "It's possible, Rem. If anyone had told me that a few weeks ago, I would have hooted. But since Dr. Breckinridge explained it to me, I've thought and thought about it, and I've come to the conclusion that he may be right. It all goes back to my mother, I think. No matter how much success I attained, it was never enough in her estimation. If I would only try harder, I could do better. So, I guess I started to believe her."

Rem gave a snort. "I can't believe I'm hearing this! The doc here must have you hypnotized into believing that hogwash. Hell, I'll bet 90 percent of the women in the world would give anything to be in your shoes!"

Noah agreed. "That's probably true, but it isn't reality we're talking about here, not what we are, or what others believe we are, but how we perceive ourselves."

"Well, you can't blame my folks for making me feel in adequate. They both died before I even made my first movie. They died when I was just a plain old cowpoke up in Montana."

"How did you get into the movies, Rem?"

"A movie company was on location near the ranch where I worked. They hired a few real cowpokes. I was one of them. After the shoot was over, I came back to Hollywood with them to do stunt work on other Westerns. One thing led to another. I got a break or two. A director was looking for a new face. He gave me a test, liked what he saw, and I was in."

Noah thought how remarkably like Lacey's story — a career based on luck. "And then it went sour?"

"Yeah. They stopped making Westerns."

"And you couldn't hack it in other films?"

"That about sums it up."

"Why? Because you weren't good enough? Or *thought* you weren't good enough?"

"You know shit about the movie business, Doc. When you're typecast in certain roles for years, they don't want you for anything else."

"Others have made the switch successfully."

"I don't want to hear about others," Rem said harshly. "Put me down as selfish, but I'm interested in me. Anyway, when the roof fell in,

I started to booze."

"A handy excuse, wasn't it?"

Rem said sullenly, "Believe what you want, Doc."

Noah stood up. "That's it for today, gang." As they started to drift out, Noah raised his voice, "Jeffrey, would you stay for a minute, please?"

Jeffrey lingered behind after the others left, feeling tense and on guard. Dr. Breckinridge was far from stupid, and Jeffrey had to wonder if he had him completely fooled.

"Sorry about that little fracas, Jeffrey," Noah apologized. "You played your part all too well, I would say. I expected Rem to blow, but I underestimated the extent of it."

Jeffrey shrugged. "No harm done."

Noah reached down into his attaché case, open at his feet, and took out a notebook. "This won't do, Jeffrey."

"What do you mean, Doctor?"

"I asked you to dig into yourself, examine your feelings, how it is to be an alcoholic, how other people react to you when you're intoxicated and doing things that might hurt or offend them."

"Well, I haven't had that many episodes," Jeffrey said warily. "I recognized early on that my drinking was getting out of hand. Like I said, I was afraid that I'd get behind the wheel of a racing car while drunk. If I ever did that, it would be a disaster. I'm somewhat different from the rest here, Doctor. They might get drunk or doped up, make fools of themselves, might lose friends or wives, maybe even blow a career. But with me, I could kill not only myself but others. That possibility scared the hell out of me."

Noah was nodding. "All right, perhaps you haven't experienced many alcoholic episodes, but there must have been embarrassing moments with friends."

"Not really. I'm pretty much a loner." Jeffrey had an inspiration. "Besides, I was a solitary drinker. I knew that if I got drunk and disruptive in public, the word might circulate and no one would trust me to drive for them. I've read somewhere that solitary drinking is a symptom of alcoholism. That's another reason I got spooked about my drinking."

"You baffle me." Noah's gaze was direct and disconcerting. "It's rare that I come across an individual who is bright enough, honest enough with himself, to realize that he is an alcoholic, or even dangerously close to being one."

Jeffrey thought of a flippant remark, but held his tongue. The doctor was suspicious enough already.

Noah seemed to be waiting; but when Jeffrey said nothing more, he glanced down at the open notebook, flipping pages idly. "I'm at a loss here. With the others I'd say dig deeper, dig until it hurts, then put it all down on paper for me. But maybe you've gone as far as you can dig. Maybe —" that penetrating stare again "— maybe you no longer need to remain here."

Jeffrey felt a stab of apprehension. He could not allow that to happen; he couldn't leave yet. Choosing his words carefully, he said, "I would rather not take that chance, Dr. Breckinridge. I would like to stay for the full course."

"Certainly, Jeffrey." Noah smiled now. "I was being somewhat facetious. I've never released anyone until they've either received their diploma or refused to be helped. Why don't you try to dig deeper," Noah said as he closed his attaché case and moved toward the door.

Walking down the hall from the meeting room, Jeffrey realized that he was sweating heavily. That had been a little too close, and Dr. Breckinridge could still decide to kick him out any day. And he still had no idea where Lacey was keeping her jewels. He had to find out, and quickly.

Hearing voices from the solarium, he walked in that direction, hoping to find her there.

Governor Stoddard was delighted that Jeffrey Lawrence had been asked to stay behind. Jeffrey hadn't been letting Lacey out of his sight. Now it's my chance, Stoddard thought.

He fell into step beside the actress. "The doctor asking Jeffrey to stay behind reminds me of my school days. When one of us was rowdy, or our schoolwork wasn't up to standard, the teacher would keep us after class."

Lacey looked at him out of those incredible green eyes. "Well, this is something like going back to school, isn't it?"

"I don't follow."

"We're here to learn about ourselves. Or perhaps a better way of putting it is, *relearn* ourselves."

They entered the solarium, which was empty, and Lacey took a lounge chair in the splash of afternoon sun.

Stoddard pulled a chair over next to her. "Would you explain that last remark to me?"

"We're here to learn about why we abuse drugs or alcohol – isn't that right, John? According to Dr. Breckinridge, the root of our problems lies within ourselves, and in the process of rediscovery, we should be able to handle our problems better when we are released from here." She smiled slightly. "We even have homework to do, writing in the daily journal, and you certainly could compare our daily therapy sessions to classes."

"There is a theory that alcoholism can be inherited, that it comes to us in the genes."

Stoddard was thinking of his father, who had consumed a quart a day during the last few years of his life.

"I discussed that with Dr. Breckinridge, and although he doesn't dismiss the theory, he's not sure he believes in it. He says he's known too many abusers who have no family history of drug or alcohol abuse. I know that neither of my parents drank or used drugs."

Stoddard studied her covertly. "It strikes me that you have a high opinion of the doctor. You speak of him in capital letters."

Lacey colored. "I didn't mean to. I admire him, yes, but it seems to me that this whole month would be wasted if one didn't have faith in the people in charge of the program here. Wouldn't you agree?"

Stoddard nodded absently. "I suppose you're right in that respect, but it seems to me they go a little overboard here. Taking most of your personal belongings away. No telephones. No books or magazines, except those related to your problem. Not even any TV, except two hours an evening in the recreation room."

"Dr. Breckinridge explained the importance of few distractions. When he refused to let me keep my jewels in my room, I didn't think I could hack it. But now . . . Actually, this is about the first time I've thought of them in days."

"That's right, I've read about that. It's been said that you never go anywhere without your jewel collection. Did you have them with you when you came here?"

"Oh, yes."

"What did you do, send them back home?"

"No, they're in my Rolls. I had a special safe put in, welded to the car frame. Theodore, my chauffeur, is staying in Oasis, in the Holiday Inn, while I'm here. . . ."

Jeffrey entered the solarium in time to hear Lacey's last few words, and he felt a leap of anger. Didn't she know better than to keep a fortune in jewels in a *car?* And why would she tell a virtual stranger their whereabouts?

But the brief anger was replaced by a feeling of elation. Now he knew where the jewels were, without having to ask her. All he had to do was get them in his hands.

With a new bounce in his step, he strode toward the pair seated by the window.

Eighteen

It was Sunday, a day off for The Clinic's patients, and most of them were in a festive mood. There would be no lectures, no therapy sessions today, and visitors were allowed.

Jeffrey had no visitors; neither did Lacey, Rem nor Governor Stoddard. They were gathered in the solarium, relaxing and talking.

Noah usually took Sundays off, but on this particular one, he turned up at The Clinic. Susan had asked him to let her visit today.

He met her at the side entrance with a kiss. "Some of the gang are gathered in the solarium right now, the ones who have no visitors today. They're bitching to one another about how tough they're having it here."

"Could we join them?"

"I figured you'd ask that," he said with a grin. "If it's all right with them, and if you promise to behave yourself."

"Of course I will," she said in all innocence.

"No railing against The Clinic? At least I see

you're not carrying your camera."

She linked her arm in his. "You have my solemn promise, sir, that I shall behave."

As they entered the solarium, Rem was just beginning a story. Noah and Susan stood silently by, listening.

"When I came to Hollywood as a stuntman, we were lucky to earn ten bucks a day, and were even luckier to get a day's work. Hell, we used to sit around in wire cages in some of the studios, waiting for a director to send out a call for extras or stuntmen. I reckon they thought they had to keep us caged to keep us in hand until needed." Rem laughed heartily. "But what the hell, we still earned more than we did punching cows. Movie producers paid more for falling off horses than we'd ever earned trying to stay on one.

"We had a sort of closed society of our own, with a system of rating. We were judged by the way we rode a horse, held our liquor and used our fists. At night, we'd all play poker together at a place called The Water Hole, drink tequila and mescal in coffee cups, and crease our Stetsons to show those in the know what part of the cattle country we hailed from.

"In some ways, doing stunt work was just as hard and, of course, more dangerous than the work we did back home. Six-horse teams, for example, were just as hard to control from the seat of a speeding stagecoach as they were on the dirt roads of Montana, or any other place in the West.

"By the time I came along, most of the stunts had been devised and refined when the Western was in its heyday. I remember a couple of them very well. Dangerous as hell, for rider *and* horse. One was called the Running W. A pair of wires were attached to hobbles on the horse's front fetlocks, then connected to a ring that the rider held in one hand. Nothing that could be picked up by the cameras, of course. You'd tear along at full gallop, kick your feet out of the stirrups and yank the wires, which would trip the horse just as you jumped out of the saddle." Rem chuckled. "There were a lot of bones broken doing that one.

"A variation of that stunt was called the Stationary W, or the Dead Man Fall. The tripping device was anchored to a buried post at the end of about a hundred yards of piano wire. The rider was thrown from the saddle without any warning at all as the horse was slammed to the ground at the end of its piano-wire tether."

"But the poor horses!" Susan said with a shudder. "Wasn't it hard on them?"

Rem looked around at her with a twinkle. "Sure as hell was, ma'am. We always had a loaded gun or two on the set. You've heard about how cowboys shoot their horses when the horse breaks a leg? Well, that's true. There was always a bunch of horses lost on every Western. There was no SPCA in those days. Of course, I got in on the tail end of it. Stuntmen didn't like to see horses killed, either, so they worked hard at saving them, especially the old-timers like Yakima Canutt."

"Yakima Canutt was a legend, wasn't he?" Lacey asked.

"He was the best, yes, ma'am. He was as much responsible for the success of the Westerns in those early days as the great stars and directors like Duke Wayne and John Ford. I worked with Yakima a few times, and he was all they said he was.

" 'Cause he had the background for it. He was born and brought up on a ranch and was one of the great bronc busters of all time. He was one of the first rodeo stars, in the beginning of rodeo. Yakima was a star in silent Westerns, which many people don't know about. He also acted in several talkies, but usually played the villain and doubled for the hero in the stunt scenes in the same picture.

"You all remember that scene in the movie, *Raiders of the Lost Ark,* where old Indiana Jones was dragged under a truck for a good piece, hanging on to the axle? Folks thought that was one of the greatest stunts ever. Actually, old Yakima invented that stunt, with a stagecoach instead of a truck.

"And you know that slouching walk of John Wayne's? Yakima walked like that. Duke aped him, and that walk made him famous. The two men met when Duke was making B Westerns, and became fast friends, a friendship that lasted."

"I read somewhere once that many of the Western stars started out as stuntmen," Jeffrey stated.

"Oh sure, but some of them had to clean up their act when they became stars. I remember stories about one in particular. A stuntman by the name of Charles Frederick Gebhart. He became a star for Fox Films in 1919, but they changed his name to Buck Jones. Buck was somewhat before my time, in fact he died in the Coconut Grove fire in Boston in 1942.

"At the time he became a star, the image of the cowboy actor had been somewhat elevated. I heard about the rules that the Fox people have laid down for him. His hair had to always be neatly combed unless he was in a fight on-screen. He had to have it cut, washed and oiled once a week to give it the proper gloss. His teeth had to be polished and cleaned by a reputable dentist once a month. And he was told to open his mouth wider when he smiled, so that his teeth would be more visible. He was ordered to pay close attention to his fingernails, seeing that they were not clipped too close and were always clean. He was always to be well dressed in public, and it went without saying that his morals were always to be impeccable. No drinking or whoring around in public."

"Hardly like the heroes of the 'adult' Westerns that came along in the sixties and seventies," Stoddard commented.

Rem chuckled. "Oh, by the time Gene Autry came along, they were squeaky clean. A cowboy never took unfair advantage of the enemy, never went back on his word, never lifted a hand to women or children, old folks or animals, helped everyone in distress, respected parenthood and the law, was pure in thought, word and deed, did not smoke or drink. Or . . ." Rem laughed again. "Hellfire, it goes without saying, never use dope of any kind."

Stoddard broke into the conversation. "I'm not much of a movie buff, but I have read a great deal of American history, as do most . . . If the Westerners in the frontier days followed that set of rules, westward expansion would never have made it past the Mississippi River."

Rem nodded. "That's true. On the other hand, it could be that the looser morals of the stars of the so-called adult Westerns may have had a great deal to do with the fading popularity of the Western."

With a sigh, Rem fell silent, gazing into the distance with a melancholy expression.

Noah took advantage of the lull in the conversation. "I'd like all of you to meet a friend of mine, Susan Channing." He introduced the others to Susan.

Rem's spirits revived. "A girlfriend, Doc?" he asked mischievously. "Since I see you around here at practically any minute of the day or night, I'm surprised you find the time. It would make you more human."

"He's human, Mr. Remington, quite human," Susan said, taking an empty chair next to his.

"Rem, please, honey. Remington sounds like a revolver. Actually —" his leathery face broke into a grin "— the name Remington *is* a concoction of my agent, just because it is the same as the old Remington .44 revolver. The name I was born with is Clyde Puckett. Now, how would that look on a theater marquee?"

"All right, Rem it is. Tell us some more stories about the old movie days, Rem. I'm fascinated."

"What I'd give these days for a whole bunch of interested movie fans like you," Rem drawled. "And I'm full of stories of the old days, right enough. Some people might say I'm just full of it, period. But if you'd care to hear a few, I've certainly got the time. For instance, there was the time I was doing stunt work on a Duke

Wayne picture . . ."

Billie Reaper had a visitor – Joe Devlin.

His manager was his usual cheery self. "You're looking well, Billie. Hale and hearty."

"Don't give me that, man," Billie snarled. "I look like shit. How else could I look in a place like this?"

"It's for your own good, Billie," Devlin said, at his most unctuous. "I've been busy lining up bookings. I've been able to convince most of the bookings that you're going to come back stronger than ever."

"Then you can spare me some bread. Gimme, man." Billie held out one hand, rubbing his fingers together. "A thousand."

"A thousand!" The amount temporarily wiped the smile off Devlin's face. "I gave you a thousand the last time I was here."

"That's right and I need another."

"But whatever for? I still don't understand what you need money for in here." Devlin had forgotten to question the staff about Billie's apparent need for cash.

"Grease, man. To make life bearable in here, I have to grease the flesh. Every time I turn around, some dude has his hand out."

"Maybe if I spoke to the director –"

"No! You speak to nobody. Just give me the damned money. It's my money. You hand it

378

over, or I'll have an audit run on the books the very day I get out of here." He thrust his face close to Devlin's. "It's probably something I should have done a long time ago. I have a gut feeling that you're stealing me blind."

"Now wait, Billie." Devlin backed a step, his eyes flickering. "You've got no cause to say a thing like that."

"I've talked to other rock stars. The ones who have audited the books kept by their managers tell me there are always *some* discrepancies." Billie put on the most evil grin he was capable of and gave a harsh laugh. "You want to take the chance, man?"

"It's possible some money may have fallen through the cracks," Devlin said defensively. "But there's no need to go to all that trouble. Besides, like you say, the money's yours, Billie."

"Then gimme." Again, he rubbed his fingers together. "Ten large ones."

Hastily, Devlin peeled off ten one-hundred-dollar bills, gave them to Billie and quickly took his leave.

Billie was happy to see that the attendant on duty in the hallway was Jack Newton. He caught Newton's eye by waving a hundred-dollar bill behind Devlin's back. Newton nodded slightly.

Waiting, Billie paced the room. The gram of coke supplied by Newton had only lasted two days. Billie had kept warning himself to take it easy, that Dr. Breckinridge hadn't just fallen off the turnip truck. If he got even slightly suspicious that Billie was on nose candy again, he'd order a urine test, and that would be the end of his stay here. And where he had wanted nothing but out in the beginning, Billie had sense enough now, after Devlin's repeated warnings, to realize that the booking agents would back off if he didn't get that diploma in his hot little hand, stating that he was clean. But in the meantime, he had to have a boost every now and then, just to keep him going. Hell, he'd fooled the doctor so far. No doctor was sharp enough to read the Reaper!

As the key grated in the lock, he pasted his most ingratiating smile on his face. Newton darted in, sending an apprehensive glance back over his shoulder.

"Hi, Jack, old buddy. Ready to pick up a few more extra bucks?"

"I don't know, Billie," the attendant said uneasily. "I'm taking a hell of a risk here. If you get caught and they learn I'm supplying you, it'll be my ass."

"Jack, Jack! Don't worry, I'll cover your ass. You think I'd knife a guy who helped me out?" He laughed raucously. "Besides, who's to ever know? We're too smart for them, you and me." He added three hundreds to the one already in his hand. "Here's four bills. Connect with whatever you can out there, and I'll match that for yourself. Easy money, man, easy."

"Not so easy. I was lucky to score the last time. The heat's on in L.A. A couple of big busts went down recently, and everything's tight."

"It doesn't have to be coke. Pick up whatever you can, anything to get me over the hump." He took Newton's hand and folded his fingers over the four bills. "You can do it, Jack. I know you can." Newton took the money, crammed it into his pocket and hurriedly left the room.

Feeling loose just in anticipation, Billie did a little dance. He wished he had his guitar. If he had it, he could play and sing a couple of sets for that bunch in The Snake Pit. Damn, what a hellacious bunch of losers. They needed a little livening-up, and the Reaper was the one to do it!

He thought of Lacey Houston. Now there was a luscious chick. He had been surprised to see how good she looked, considering her age.

He would sure as hell like to get close to that. Maybe the next time he would get old Jack to score a little heavier, and then he could persuade Lacey to snort a line or two with him. She must be hurting about now.

When Susan came in that evening after having dinner with Noah, Zoe was out in the atrium, with Madam perched on her shoulder.

"I had an interesting time at The Clinic this afternoon, Zoe."

Zoe took note of the fact that Susan was starting to speak of it as "The Clinic" now. Was she losing her most ardent supporter?

Tapping the ash from her cigar, she said, "Do tell."

"You can be sarcastic, but it really was fun. I had a chance to talk to Lacey Houston, and she is a very nice person, Zoe. Really she is."

Zoe shrugged. "Did I ever say otherwise? A lot of drug users are no doubt nice people, when they're clean."

"And Rem . . . Todd Remington. The Western movie star who crashed your party and made an ass of himself?"

Zoe went tense. "What about him?"

"Well, he's nice, too, now that he's sober. He's full of stories about the old days in the movies. He kept us all entertained with his reminiscences."

"Did he mention me?" Zoe asked casually.

"No, not that I recall. As drunk as he was that day, Zoe, I doubt that he even remembers the party, much less you." Susan's look turned curious. "Is there any reason he should ask about you?"

"I knew him before. When I told you about

my past, I didn't mention Rem." Succinctly, she told Susan about the part Todd Remington had played in her past.

"But he was so drunk, maybe he didn't recognize you."

"Oh, he recognized me. He called me up a few days after the party. He suggested that we get together and talk about old times. I have a feeling that he wants me to buy his silence."

"He didn't strike me as that sort of person at all, Zoe. Blackmail? I don't really think so."

"Basically, Todd Remington is a decent person. But he's a drunk, my dear, and one of the first things I learned was to never trust a drunk. Also, Rem has always lived high, and he's been on a long slide down. I'm surprised that he even came up with the money for The Clinic. He probably borrowed it somewhere. Even decent people can turn on you when pushed to the wall, and I suspect that Rem's back is against the wall."

"Sometimes you dismay me with that vein of cynicism, Zoe. It must come from your past, seeing so much of the seamy side of life — Oh!" Susan clapped a hand to her mouth. "Forgive me, I shouldn't have said that."

"Why not, child? It's true. I'm a survivor, and to survive you have to always suspect the worst in people. It's easier to be wrong and apologize than to be the innocent and get bloodied."

"I still think you're wrong about Rem," Susan said obstinately.

"If I am, I'll gladly apologize —"

She was interrupted by the ringing telephone. She went into the kitchen to answer it.

"Zoe? This is Mary Lee Bosworth."

Mary Lee Bosworth had recently become a convert to the cause. Like all converts, she was fired by the zeal of an evangelist.

"Hello, Mary Lee. What can I do for you?" Zoe asked.

"I don't know if you know or not, but there is a convention of real estate people in Palm Springs this coming week."

"I may have heard something about it."

"Well, I understand that some of the developers are going to be given a tour of Oasis by Otto Channing. Some of us got to talking and decided that this would be a good time to have a rally. We might even picket against further growth in Oasis, let them know they're not welcome here. But we want you to speak at the rally."

"Oh, I don't know, Mary Lee. I've been a little under the weather this week."

"But without you, Zoe, the whole thing's liable to fizzle. We need you."

"Well, I'll think about it. That's all I can promise at this time."

Zoe hung up slowly, thinking of Otto Channing's threat and the potential threat that Todd Remington posed.

Back in the atrium, Susan asked her who was on the phone.

For a moment Zoe toyed with the thoughts of lying, but she told Susan what the call was about.

"Why did you turn her down, Zoe?"

"I didn't turn her down, I just said I'd think about it."

"You've never had to think about something like that. You're going to turn her down, aren't you?" Susan asked accusingly.

"I probably shouldn't take the risk." Zoe sat down heavily.

"What risk? I told you that I warned my father to keep quiet."

Zoe looked at her curiously. "You told me, but you didn't tell me how you managed to scare him off."

"You don't want to know. But take my word for it, Otto Channing will never breathe a word of your lurid past."

"Don't forget Rem. He knows."

"I can't believe he would use it against you. But say I'm wrong. How would your making a speech against growth in Oasis cause him to move any sooner? He can't be interested in any of that. He may not even learn about it."

"You're right, of course. I'm equivocating."

"And that's not like you, Zoe. Do I need to remind *you* of what's at stake here? You're our leader."

"You're right again." Zoe stood up with renewed resolve. "I'll call Mary Lee back, tell her that I've thought it over and will be honored to speak."

Nineteen

Jeffrey lay tense and wakeful until The Clinic had settled down for the night. Fortunately, Rem slept like the dead, except for his raucous and constant snoring. On their first night as roommates, Rem had bragged that although most alcoholics have trouble sleeping when sober, he could sleep anywhere, anytime, drunk or sober.

A few minutes after midnight, Jeffrey threw the covers back and got out of bed. He was fully clothed, except for shoes. He was dressed in flat black — a turtleneck sweater, black cotton pants and even black socks. And now he put on a pair of black wrestling shoes and went to the door.

He inched the door open and looked both ways along the corridor. It was empty. Closing the door behind him, he walked quickly down the corridor and out the side entrance.

During Jeffrey's initial interview with Dr. Breckinridge, Noah had told him, "Anytime you decide to leave, I won't stop you. Nor will anyone else. You have to *want* to be in here, or the treatment won't work. If a patient walks out, it leaves badly needed space for someone who *wants* to be cured."

But Jeffrey didn't want to be seen, either going or coming. If he was spotted now, he would just have to return to his room. If Lacey's jewels were discovered missing and he was seen leaving or reentering The Clinic, suspicion would fall on him sooner or later.

He had driven down from Los Angeles in a rented Cadillac, and had parked it in the far corner of the small parking lot, in a slot adjacent to the driveway. In the locked trunk of the car was a small kit of burglary tools. The lot wasn't well lighted, a fact for which he was grateful. Although the car had been sitting there for ten days, it started at once, and he breathed a sigh of relief.

Before leaving the parking lot, he gave a quick look around. So far, so good. He hadn't been observed.

Jeffrey headed for the highway through town. He remembered seeing the Holiday Inn on his way to The Clinic. But when he reached the highway, he turned in the opposite direction, toward the center of town. Finally, he pulled into the bus station, at the intersection of Broadway and the highway. It was open and brightly lighted, and three people dozed on the hard benches; but the ticket window was closed and there was no attendant on duty.

He parked the car and walked toward the coin lockers against one wall. Jeffrey put in two quarters and pocketed the key, leaving the locker locked.

Then he drove to the Holiday Inn, parking on a side street. Now came the tricky part. To succeed, he was going to need a certain amount of luck.

The motel was a square horseshoe in shape, with a swimming pool in the center and parking slots which were half-full, around the pool area. The motel consisted of two floors.

Fortunately, there was a side entrance to the parking lot, past an ice-making machine and a cold drink dispenser. Quietly, Jeffrey made his way through the side entrance, remaining in the shadows as he reconnoitered the area.

It was now well past one o'clock, and except for the brightly illuminated office, only two rooms showed a light, and both were on the upper floor. The lot was brightly lighted, but then he had expected that. Lacey's Rolls was easy to spot, three cars down from where he stood, nosed in before a unit. Without question, Lacey's chauffeur occupied that room. A bright light, affixed to the underside of the second floor balcony, glared directly down onto the Rolls.

Jeffrey took a deep breath, debating with himself. This had to be the riskiest job he had ever attempted. If he made any undue noise, it could alert the chauffeur; and he would come running out, undoubtedly armed. And if, for any reason, he glanced out the window, he would catch Jeffrey in the act.

If he had any sense at all, Jeffrey thought, he would simply walk away, get the Cadillac and drive back to Los Angeles. But nothing had changed — he was still in hock for forty grand, and Bernie was an unforgiving debtor. And then, as always when confronted with a seemingly impossible job, Jeffrey felt his adrenaline begin to pump. The challenge was too much to resist.

He returned to the Cadillac, got out his kit and slipped on a pair of surgical gloves before retracing his steps.

A quick glance around confirmed that the area was still clear. Even the two windows on the upper floor were now dark. Hugging the wall, he made his way along underneath the balcony overhang.

To his relief, he saw that a plastic conduit ran up the post to the light. He used the rubber-handled wire cutter to carefully peel away the conduit, exposing the wire. Shutting off the light was a calculated risk. Either the chauffeur, or whoever was manning the desk in the office, might notice the light going out, but he wanted as much darkness as possible.

With a quick cut he severed the wires, and the light blinked out, plunging the area around the Rolls into relative darkness. He held his breath, every sense alert, his gaze darting to the window of the chauffeur's room and to the office. A few seconds passed and no alarm was given.

He moved to the rear of the Rolls and knelt by the trunk, searching for an alarm control with his penlight. And there it was, in the right-hand corner. So far, so good. He tried the keys he had on a ring. Some wouldn't even go into the key slot. But finally, halfway through the ring, one slid in easily. Holding his breath, he turned it gingerly. In a moment there was a faint click. Now he could only hope that there wasn't a backup control located somewhere else.

Jeffrey eased around the Rolls to the driver's side and went through the key routine again. The alarm control had probably been installed in the United States, while the door locks had been installed in England, where the Rolls was manufactured, so he might not be as lucky. In fifteen minutes he had gone through all of the keys, and the door still hadn't opened. He cursed under his breath. He would have to do it the hard way.

He moved around to the passenger side and squatted. There wasn't a great deal of traffic on the highway at this time, but an occasional truck passed. He took out the punch and the hammer, put the punch into position as close to the door lock as possible, and waited, hardly breathing. Finally, he heard a truck coming, the engine roaring. He waited until it was almost even with the motel, then hit the punch with the felt-covered handle – once, twice, and he was through.

He waited again, ears straining, his gaze darting back and forth between the window to the chauffeur's room and the office. His luck was still holding.

With the angled rod he probed the interior of the door panel, found the arm of the door latch and gave a gentle tug. Now was the crucial point. If there was a backup alarm, the caper was blown. But the door eased open soundlessly.

Jeffrey reached in, unlocked the back door and slid onto the back seat. He knew that the back was the most logical place for the safe. At least inside the car he was less exposed.

The rear section of the Rolls was as roomy and luxurious as that of a stretch limousine. There was a small well-stocked bar and a TV set mounted against the back of the front seat.

First, he pulled up the seat cushion. Nothing there. Next, be examined the bar. Nothing there, either. Then he switched his attention to the last item — the TV console. He switched on the On button. Nothing happened. It was possible that the set only worked when the ignition was on.

Jeffrey went over every inch of the housing of the set with the penlight. With a mounting sense of excitement, he saw that the housing was one piece, held in place by two screws on each of the three sides.

He took out his pocketknife and began to work on the screws. It was hard slow work, and he cursed himself for not bringing his screwdriver kit; he didn't want to make another trip to the Cadillac. His time was rapidly running out. He had been here close to an hour now, and his luck couldn't hold indefinitely. Sooner or later someone would notice that the light was out and would come to check.

After what seemed to be an interminable amount of time, he had the screws out. It was entirely possible that an alarm had been rigged to go off if the TV housing was removed. *If* it did conceal the safe. It was another risk he'd have to take.

Scarcely breathing, he lifted up on the housing. It came off easily. And there, nestled where the wires and tubes of a TV should be, was the safe.

He sat back for a moment, taking several deep breaths, and flexed the fingers made numb and stiff by the removal of the screws.

His mind flashed on one of the bits of wisdom Mason Bogard had passed on to him. "People do strange things with their combinations. They use their birth dates – year, month and day. They use Social Security numbers, whatever is easy to remember. So, if you can dig up that information beforehand, you're ahead going in."

In his research of Lacey Houston, Jeffrey had memorized her birth date. When the feeling returned to his fingers, he slowly dialed the year of her birth, going right with the four numbers for the year, and back left for the month and day. Nothing happened.

He reversed the order, and in a moment he heard the faint click of the tumblers. He turned the handle, and the door swung open. Aiming the penlight, he saw three jewel boxes stacked one on top of the other.

With a trembling hand, he took out the boxes and lined them up side by side on the floorboards. With a reverent touch, he opened the lid of the first. A starlike burst of light reflected back from the penlight. He quickly opened the other boxes and looked from one to the other in awe.

Diamonds, a cornucopia of diamonds – mounted in rings, bracelets, necklaces and a number of loose stones.

Truly, a veritable fortune!

He continued to look, rapt, mesmerized by the dazzle and by the magnitude of his haul. . . .

With an exclamation, he became aware once again of his surroundings. He had to get out of there. He closed the safe and dropped the housing back over it. The theft would be disclosed soon enough; there was no need to hasten its discovery by leaving things so that a casual glance inside the Rolls would reveal what had happened.

A quick glance around the area told him that he was still unobserved. With the jewel boxes under his arm, Jeffrey slipped out of the car, hurried to the balcony overhang and made his way through the side exit and to the Cadillac. Starting the car, he drove away, not taking a steady breath until he was several blocks from the motel.

He drove downtown to the bus station. After putting the jewel boxes into a canvas bag, he left the car and carried the bag into the station. He was relieved to see that it remained virtually deserted. He placed the bag in the locker and inserted more quarters from the supply he always kept with the tools of his trade. The limit for each coin feeding was forty-eight hours, which meant that he would have to return every other day to put in more quarters; but if he managed to sneak both out and in tonight, that should present no problems for so long as he decided to stay at The Clinic.

Jeffrey had debated with himself about just driving back to Los Angeles tonight, but had decided to remain until the heat had died down after the theft was discovered. But as he drove away from the depot, he wondered just who was he kidding? All he had to do was return the rented Cadillac, settle up with Bernie, haggle with the fence over the price for the loot and disappear, taking on a new identity.

No, the reason he wanted to stay around was because of Lacey, although he couldn't visualize how it could possibly benefit him. There was certainly no future for them. Even if she returned his feelings, there was no way a relationship could work. A jewel thief and a famous movie star? No way. Still, he wanted to be near her, with her, for as long as possible.

He made it back into his room without incident. Rem was still snoring loudly and apparently hadn't noticed Jeffrey's absence.

Jeffrey undressed quickly and quietly and got into bed. But he couldn't sleep. Usually, after a successful caper, after the extended adrenaline high, he was exhausted and could fall asleep instantly. Tonight, he lay awake until daylight crept into the room. Where was the feeling of triumph he usually experienced after a night such as this?

"I believe it's your turn, today, Lacey," Noah commented.

Lacey gave a start and stared at him. "What do you mean?"

"You haven't taken part in one of our little psychodramas yet. It's time. Let's make you the star."

Lacey looked around at the expectant faces. "Must I?"

"You must." Noah leaned back. "From what you have told me in private sessions, and from what you have told the gang here, you have lost trust in people, starting with your mother. You feel that they have let you down, in one way or another, and managed to hurt you. Because of that, you have lost your trust and have come to doubt that anyone can love you for yourself. Is that about the way you see it?"

"Well . . . I don't think it's that bad." She laughed nervously. "I *do* trust some people."

As she spoke, Lacey's gaze came to rest on Jeffrey, who fidgeted in his seat. He seemed uncomfortable under the implied trust shining in her eyes.

She continued, "For instance, I trust you, Doctor."

"I don't count." Noah smiled slightly. "Your therapist doesn't count. For instance, do you think anyone here loves you? Is there anyone here you can trust?"

"I'm not sure." Again, her gaze went to Jeffrey. "I don't think anyone loves me."

"Do you think anyone here hates you?"

"Well. . ." She hesitated. "Hate is probably too strong a word."

Noah glanced around the group. "Does anyone here hate Lacey?"

"No!" came the chorus, with the exception of Billie.

"I think everyone here loves and understands you, Lacey," Noah said. "I believe that is a part of your problem. I know you had a trying childhood. You think your mother betrayed you. You believe that your three husbands betrayed you. Isn't that true?"

"Yes!" To her chagrin, Lacey felt her eyes burn, and tears ran down her cheeks. "Everyone I have ever deeply loved has turned against me in the end!"

"Then you must start trusting people again. You must see that people love you without reservations, for what you are. And we're going to start today." From his attaché case, Noah took a large white bandana. "Everybody gather around Lacey."

As everyone did so, Noah stepped up to her. "Now, I'm going to blindfold you, Lacey."

She backed a step. "Blindfold?"

"No harm shall come to you, I promise."

With a soft sigh she nodded, and Noah wrapped the bandana around her head, covering her eyes.

"Can you see anything, Lacey?"

She shook her head. "Not a thing."

He took both her hands in his and spoke quietly. "Lacey, listen closely now. You've never thought too highly of yourself — is that correct?"

She nodded mutely, tears still running down her cheeks.

"But all of us here think you are a fine person. You have many great qualities. You are a warm loving individual, and you have worked hard for your success. You may have some bad qualities, but then we all do, and yours are no worse than ours. We love you, don't we, gang?"

"Yes!"

"We love you, Lacey, truly we do," Bethel added.

"And we want to help you. Don't we, gang?" Noah asked.

"Yes!"

"Do you love us, Lacey?"

"I . . . I would like to think so."

"Do you trust us?"

"I —" She broke off, gulping.

"Are you *willing* to trust us?"

"O-okay."

"If I tell you to fall backward, will you trust them to catch you before you hit the floor and hurt yourself?"

Tears still streaming down her face, Lacey slowly nodded.

"All right, now I'm going to count to three. On the count of three, you fall straight back. Are you ready?"

Lacey nodded again, her breath catching in a sob.

"One, two . . . three!"

For a moment Lacey stood without moving, her hands knotted into fists at her side. Then she threw herself backward, holding her body as straight as a board.

Jeffrey had positioned himself directly behind her. As she reached the halfway mark to the floor, he reached out for her. The others had crowded around; several pairs of hands stretched out to stop her fall. Billie Reaper had crowded in beside Jeffrey, and he reached out also, but extended his hands around in front of Lacey where they would touch her breasts. Seeing that the others had Lacey safely in their grip, Jeffrey dropped his hands and reached out to seize Billie's arms and pull him away. They stood toe-to-toe, and Jeffrey's face was so close that he could smell the singer's rancid breath.

Billie's eyes were wide and glaring. He snarled, "Let go of me, man, or I'll tear you apart!"

"Just try it, punk," Jeffrey said harshly. "I saw you trying to grope her. I should break both your arms. . . ."

Then Noah was there, separating them. "I saw what you were doing, Billie. Get out of here — go back to your room at once. I'll deal with you later."

Billie stood glaring, his skinny body as tense as a rod. His lips worked, spittle forming at the corners of his mouth. Then he seemed to deflate, and he turned, shambling away and out of the meeting room.

Remembering Lacey, Jeffrey spun around. The others had just removed her blindfold. She was weeping heavily now, but her eyes shone with happiness.

"I love you! I love you all!"

She clasped hands with one person after another. Lastly, she looked around for Jeffrey, started toward him, then halted. "Jeffrey?"

"He was there, Lacey," Noah said. "Jeffrey was right behind you. He was the first to catch you."

"Oh, Jeffrey!" She ran to him and hugged him fervently.

Jeffrey put his arms around her, his heart beating rapidly. He met Noah's gaze over Lacey's head. Noah returned his look, a large question in his eyes.

At that moment the beeper on Noah's belt went off. He turned away to pick up the phone on the desk. He spoke into it for a moment before hanging up. Wearing a puzzled frown, he walked over to where Jeffrey and Lacey stood together.

"That's it for today, gang. Wait a minute, will you, Lacey?" When the others were out of hearing, he said, "The police are here, Lacey, with your chauffeur."

Lacey tensed, squeezing Jeffrey's hand. "What is it about? Is Theodore in trouble?"

"I have no idea. I suppose you want to see them?"

"Of course."

"If you want to see them here, I'll send them back."

"That will be fine."

Jeffrey, knowing what it was about, started to leave with Noah.

Lacey tightened her hand around his. "No, Jeffrey. Please stay."

He cringed inwardly. He hadn't expected to be present when she was informed that her jewels had been stolen.

"I can't imagine what it can be. Theodore is

a good man, dependable, and he has never been in trouble. Of course, I know that there aren't that many blacks in Oasis, and the police in a town like this keep a close watch on the few there are. Maybe they just want to verify that Theodore works for me."

Jeffrey stood, miserably silent. There was nothing he could say that wouldn't sound like an out-and-out lie.

In a few moments, the door opened and two men came in. One was tall and black; the other man was short, middle-aged, with a cynical face and eyes.

"Miss Lacey Houston?" he asked.

"Yes, I'm Lacey Houston."

He took his wallet out, opened it and showed Lacey his shield. "I'm Riley Benson of the Theft Squad." His thin lips twitched in a slight smile. "In fact, I *am* the Theft Squad. Does this man work for you?"

"Of course. Theodore Wilson. He drives for me. What is wrong, Theodore?"

"I'm sorry, Miss Lacey," the black man said. "Your jewels are gone. I just discovered an hour ago that the Rolls had been broken into. The safe had been opened, and your jewels are gone."

"Oh!" Lacey's eyes widened, but she showed no other signs of distress.

Riley Benson stared at her. "I understand

from your man here that the jewels are quite valuable."

"They are, of course. But they are insured." Lacey laughed. "I suppose that sounds terrible of me, but I was afraid that Theodore might be in some kind of trouble."

"He very well may be. At the moment he is certainly a suspect."

"Oh, no!" Lacey exclaimed. "Theodore would never steal from me. He has worked for me for ten years. He's like family."

"Family have been known to steal before," the detective said dryly. "And obviously, he knew the jewels were there."

"So did other people. It's common knowledge that Lacey Houston never goes anywhere without her jewelry."

"Wasn't it rather foolish of you to leave a fortune in jewels in the vehicle, parked in a motel lot?"

"I suppose." She managed to look crestfallen. "But I wasn't allowed to have them in here with me." She brightened. "And they *were* in a safe."

"Which obviously wasn't all that hard to get into. And that's another thing. . . . Does your man know the combination to the safe?"

"Of course he does. If the car was in a wreck or caught on fire while I wasn't around, Theodore would have to be able to get into the safe, wouldn't he? And that proves that Theodore didn't do it, you see?" she said triumphantly. "The Rolls was broken into, wasn't it? Well, Theodore wouldn't need to do that. He has the keys and the combination to the safe."

"If he did do it, he would be smart enough to make it appear that someone else did the job."

"No." Lacey shook her head. "Not Theodore. I'd trust him with my life."

Detective Benson arched an eyebrow amusedly. "Your life, perhaps but how about your jewels?"

"That, too." Lacey took Theodore's hand, looking into his eyes. "Tell the man, Theodore. Did you steal my jewels?"

The black man did not flinch from her gaze. "I did not, Miss Lacey. If I'd ever had it in mind, there have been many better opportunities over the past few years."

"You see, Detective Benson?" She flashed a look of triumph at the officer.

Benson shrugged. "The case will still have to be thoroughly investigated, and that includes your chauffeur. It's the usual routine. Meanwhile, you must come down to the station and fill out a report, so we can move rapidly on the investigation"

"Can it be done here, Officer?" Lacey made a distracted gesture. "We're not supposed to leave. I suppose an exception could be made in an incident such as this, but I'd rather not ask for special privileges, unless absolutely necessary."

The detective hesitated, then said slowly, "I suppose we can make an exception and fill out the report here."

"Good!" Lacey flashed her brilliant smile. "But first, could we talk in private for a bit? Jeffrey, would you mind awfully?"

"No, of course not. I'm to see Dr. Breckinridge anyway at three. I'll see you later, and I'm sorry about your jewels, Lacey."

She simply shrugged, and Jeffrey left The Snake Pit quickly.

Zoe was feeling better than she had in days when Susan dropped her off before the house.

"I won't be spending the night here, Zoe," Susan said somewhat defensively. "I'll be over in midmorning tomorrow."

Zoe suspected that the girl was spending the night with Noah. She said slyly, "Have a good evening, my dear."

She stood in the driveway, watching Susan's little car chug away. It was the usual hot desert night, but the sky was clear, with a million stars, and a full moon was riding high. She threw her head back, breathing in the dry air, feeling good about herself.

By any measure, it had been a successful rally. She had made a stirring speech, if she did say so herself. Almost three hundred women had gathered in the park across from City Hall to listen to Zoe speak from the bandstand. There had even been a number of men in the audience, and the audience had loosed undignified rebel yells at appropriate moments.

Afterward, a number of women had paraded back and forth for an hour before City Hall, carrying placards that read Developers, Go Home; No More Growth for Oasis; Oasis is Big Enough; Carpetbaggers, Go Home!

It had been too hot in the sun for Zoe to march in the picket line, but she had watched from the shade of the bandstand with Susan.

Once, she had seen Mayor Washburn on the steps of City Hall, standing with hands on hips, trading insults with the marchers. Zoe hadn't seen Otto Channing, but she knew that the mayor would pass on the word.

Afterward, she and Susan had joined several of their supporters for dinner at the Embers, rehashing the high points of the afternoon.

Finally, Zoe turned toward the house, going down the side to the kitchen door. To her dismay, she found the door unlocked. Although Oasis was known to be remarkably crime free, and many citizens boasted that they left their doors open, she had continued a lifelong habit of keeping hers locked. Apparently, this time she had been careless.

Halfway across the kitchen, she knew that someone had been in the house. At first she thought it was just a feeling, then she noticed the faint coppery smell.

With a cry of distress she ran into the atrium, switching on the lights. A scene of carnage greeted her.

The bird cages were all open. Brightly colored feathers were scattered everywhere, and blood splattered the tiles. Corpses of birds lay beneath their cages, brutally hacked to pieces. She ran from cage to cage; all were empty.

Dear God, who could be so cruel? she asked herself.

Finally, she sank down into a chair, weeping bitterly. It was as if her children had been slaughtered.

Then a sound brought her head up. It was coming from behind a hydrangea bush in one corner. Hurrying to the bush, she pushed it aside and saw Madam cowering back into the corner. The bird's eyes glittered in the light. Crouching, Zoe extended her arm.

"Come to me, Madam. It's all right now. You're safe."

Zoe had to coax the bird for a bit before she finally ventured out and climbed onto her arm. Caressing the ruffled feathers with one hand, she carried Madam to the table and sat down with her.

Dimly, Zoe thought of calling the police, but she sat on, caressing the frightened bird, consoling her with a soft gentle voice.

Twenty

Thad Darnell had stayed late at the station. Finally, shortly after ten, he decided that it was time to leave. In the small bathroom off his office, the police chief checked to see that his tie was knotted correctly, ran a comb through his hair and left, making sure that the door was locked behind him.

As he went along the corridor toward the reception area, he heard roars of laughter.

Two uniformed officers were leaning on the front desk, laughing as they conversed with Verne Webster, the sergeant who was manning the phones tonight.

"What's so funny, men?" Darnell asked.

The two officers spun around, sobering immediately. "The sergeant was telling us about a call that just came in," one of them said. "A woman phoned to report that her pet birds had been killed."

"I fail to see much humor in that. For one thing, birds can be damned expensive. Who

410

was the woman?"

"That nutty broad . . ." The officer gulped. "Zoe Tremaine, the one who's leading the group against growth in Oasis."

"No matter who she is," Darnell said coldly, "she is a citizen and a taxpayer, and a crime has been committed."

"Of course, Chief," Sergeant Webster said. "I was just about to send a unit on it."

Darnell came to a sudden decision. "Never mind. I'll cover it. It's not far out of my way going home."

One of the few luxuries Darnell permitted himself in his otherwise Spartan life was the Mercedes. He believed in buying American, but in his opinion the workmanship in American cars had sorely deteriorated in recent years, and he had always admired the Germans for their efficiency.

On his way to the Tremaine house, Darnell thought about Zoe's birds. It was not just a random killing, of that he was reasonably sure. He had observed the pickets before City Hall this afternoon, and had been told about Zoe's speech. He had been expecting an irate phone call from Otto Channing, but it hadn't come. Come to think of it, Otto had been strangely quiet the past few days. And why hadn't he used Zoe Tremaine's past to blackmail her into silence? Or had she just ignored his threat?

The lights were on when he pulled up before the Tremaine residence. He rang the bell and waited. When Zoe finally opened the door, Darnell could see the signs of recent tears on her face. For the first time that he could remember, she showed her true age.

"Chief Darnell," she said with a catch in her voice. "I'm surprised to see you answering a call like this."

"The other units were busy, and I was on my way home," he said gruffly. "What happened here?"

"Come along and I'll show you."

She led him down the hall and into the atrium. "There," she gestured, "Look."

Darnell looked around at the slaughtered birds. While in the marines, he had seen men killed on the battlefield and had become hardened to it. To his way of thinking, death was a part of war. But this, this was somehow more shocking. It was senseless, something a malicious spoiled child might do in retaliation for some slight.

"I came home about an hour ago," Zoe said. "My kitchen door was unlocked, and I —" she choked "— I found this."

She lit a cigar and drew on it, exhaling a cloud of smoke. "What kind of a person would do something like this?"

"Was anything taken?"

She shook her head. "I haven't looked carefully, but I'm sure nothing is missing."

"And you do have items of value in the house?"

"A few things, yes." She looked at him hard. "What does that have to do with anything?"

"Well, sometimes burglars, when they can't find anything to steal," he said uncomfortably, "kill whatever pets they can find."

"But we both know it wasn't just a plain burglary, don't we, Chief?"

She crossed to a table in one corner of the atrium, held out her arm and a large-crested white bird hopped up onto it. Head cocked to one side, the bird eyed Darnell balefully.

"I see they missed one," he said.

"Yes, Madam hid behind a bush over there in the corner."

Darnell stared. "Madam?"

"Yes, like in whorehouse." She gave him a flinty stare. "You're the source of Otto's information about my past, aren't you? But of course you are. I should have known that."

Darnell thought of lying to her, then thought to hell with it. "Yes, Zoe, Otto came to me with an ashtray after your last party, with your fingerprints on it. He and the mayor demanded that I run a check. If I had refused, they would only have used some other means." He cursed himself for the defensive note in his voice.

"Or they would have had your job, right?" She made a weary gesture.

He unbent enough to say, "I want you to know that I don't approve. As far as I am concerned, you've committed no crimes here in Oasis, and I don't think you should have to suffer for your past."

"Thank you for that." She smiled wanly. "But getting back to what happened here, we both know that Otto Channing either did it or paid someone to do it. He's paying me back for the speech I made today."

"I'm sorry, Zoe. I don't *know* anything of the sort. There is no proof that Otto is behind it. I'll check around for prints, but I doubt I'll find anything. But you do have my word that I'll look into it."

"I appreciate that, Chief Darnell."

It was graduation day at The Clinic.

Jim, the airline pilot, had finished out his month, and it was time to receive his "diploma."

Most of the patients were gathered in the meeting room to watch the proceedings and offer their good wishes. Earlier, Jim and his wife, Mary Anne, a slender pretty woman in her late forties, had been counseled about the future and what their expectations should be. Mary Anne had also been briefed on what was expected of her.

Now they stood together. Mary Anne beamed proudly, holding tightly on to Jim's arm, her eyes glistening with tears.

The others gathered around in a circle. With a flourish, Noah handed the diploma to Bethel first. The certificate was a framed sheet of paper, much like a high school diploma, simply stating that Jim Baxter had remained the full four weeks, and that although he would always be an alcoholic, he now had it under control.

"It has been my pleasure to know you, Jim," Bethel said. "May your life from this day forward be happy and rewarding, without the use of alcohol."

Rem was next. "You had been here awhile, Jim, when I enrolled in this here school. But I now consider you an old friend, and I am proud to have known you."

The certificate was passed from hand to hand, with each patient saying a few words of praise and good wishes.

When it was Jeffrey's turn, he said merely, "Good luck, Jim." He handed the certificate to Lacey.

"You're going to make it, Jim. I just know you will!" she said with great feeling.

When it was his turn, Governor Stoddard said, "I sure know the hell you've been through, Jim, and I will certainly pray for you."

Then it was the pilot's turn. He studied the certificate, then looked up with tears streamimg from his eyes. "For the first two weeks I was here, I thought the happiest day of my life would be the day I got out of here and would never again have to stand up and say, 'Hi, I'm Jim, and I'm an alcoholic.' Now I know that I'll have to say and think that every day for the rest of my life, but it doesn't bother me a bit. And I doubt that I would ever have made it without the support of every one of you, and I love you for it. Thank you, one and all."

"Let's all join hands," Noah said.

When they had all linked hands, he said, "Now say it."

"Good luck, Jim!"

"Take it one day at a time, Jim!"

Then the circle broke up, and they all crowded around to shake Jim's hand. A number embraced him fervently.

As they walked away together, Jeffrey said to Lacey, "I guess you can't wait until your happy day comes."

"I'm of two minds about it," she said thoughtfully. "I feel so safe in here, but to be thrown on my own again out there . . ." She shuddered. "I don't know if I can survive."

"You can, Lacey, I'm sure you can," he told her reassuringly. "There is a strength in you that I think you never suspected."

416

"If it's there, I don't know where it's been all these years."

"That's because you've been hurt so many times. The other day, in The Snake Pit, didn't that restore some of your love and trust in other people?"

"That's true. If it will just last. But it gets lonely out there, Jeffrey." She looked at him fixedly. "How about you? Do you think you can make it? Are you going back to racing?"

The sudden switch in conversation unsettled him, and he had to take a moment to get his stories straight. "I doubt it. I think that if I did, I might go back on the sauce again."

"Then what will you do?"

"I really haven't decided yet." He smiled. "Like they told Jim back there, I'm taking it one day at a time."

"Have you ever thought about try the movies? You're attractive, personable, and I pride myself on being a good talent scout."

He made a startled sound. "Acting in the movies? It's a little late for that, isn't it?"

"It's never too late. I've known people who started in the movies in their fifties and sixties."

"You know, it's a strange thing," he said slowly. "I took acting lessons once."

"Why didn't you keep at it?"

"When I saw a thousand others out there, probably better than I'd ever be, I became discouraged."

"Persistence is the key, Jeffrey. It's almost as important as talent, and I sincerely believe you have the talent." She shook his hand. "Just give it some thought, okay?"

Thad Darnell entered Otto Channing's office unannounced.

Channing, on the phone, gave him a startled look. "I'll call you back," he said into the receiver, and hung up. "Well, Thad? To what do I owe the honor?"

"I was driving by and thought I'd drop in for a minute." His gaze was drawn to Channing's right hand, which had several Band-Aids across the back. "I haven't seen or heard from you for a few days. I was wondering what happened with Zoe Tremaine. Did you use the information I gave you?"

Channing shrugged negligently, his glance sliding away. "I decided it wouldn't be the right thing to do."

Darnell stared. "You decided *what?* I don't believe it!" He laughed suddenly. "Of course! You tried your shot and she wouldn't back off. Did you hear her speech yesterday, Otto?"

"I wasn't there, but I heard about it," Channing said sullenly.

"I'll just bet you did." Again, Darnell's gaze was drawn to the strips of tape on the other man's hand. "What happened to your hand, Otto?"

Channing's hand jerked, and he lowered it out of sight below his desk. "I . . . I slipped and fell against the shower door in the bathroom, breaking it. But I was lucky. I wasn't cut seriously."

"Is that how it happened? Are you sure a little bird didn't do that, Otto? Or several little birds?"

Channing drew a quick breath, then glanced away from him. "I don't know what you're talking about."

"No? Zoe Tremaine's birds were killed last night. Let me tell you what I think. I think you learned about that speech she made yesterday, and it made you so mad you went out of control, went out there, jimmied her door open, snuck in and killed her birds. All out of meanness and spite. It was like a slaughterhouse in there. And in the process, one or more of the birds scratched you."

Channing glared at him defiantly. "You can't prove I had a damned thing to do with that. Even if you could, what would the charge be?" He sneered. "Killing a few stupid goddamned birds?"

"*Valuable* birds, Otto. And there's breaking and entering, destruction of valuable property. And I could probably think up a few more charges. You know something, Otto? You're a sick man, and I'm ashamed that it's taken me so long to realize it."

"Don't say that to me!" Channing leaned forward, his face a gray mask. "Are you taking that old whore's side against me?"

"It's my job to uphold the law."

"You hold your job on sufferance, Thad, don't ever forget that. Turn on me and your job is gone. Not only that, but there could be criminal charges."

"If there are ever criminal charges, you and the mayor will share the blame with me. As for keeping my job, I will only go so far to keep it. But I'm still curious about something, Otto. . . . You still haven't told me why you haven't broadcast what you know about Zoe's past. And don't try again to tell me it's out of the kindness of your heart. You don't have a heart."

"That's none of your damned business! Since when did you get religion? But I'll tell you this. . . . That woman is going to rue the day she ever came to Oasis!"

"Just be sure it's legal, Otto, or I'll come down on you. Depend on it. And if I can prove you killed those birds, I'll have you up on charges."

Channing had regained some of his aplomb. "Since when have you developed a conscience, Thad?"

"I guess I finally stood back and took a good look at myself, and I don't like what I see. I've done some things I'm not proud of, but I think that being in cahoots with you and the mayor sickens me more than anything else."

"But it fattened your bank account, didn't it? You took your cut without any qualms that I detected, and you can go to jail for that."

"Don't threaten me, Otto," Darnell said in a soft voice. "I have it all down on paper, all our shady deals, safely hidden away. Don't ever forget that." With that, the chief turned on his heel and marched out.

Otto Channing's whole life was falling into ruins around him, and it was all the fault of Zoe Tremaine. There had to be something he could do!

The phone rang by his elbow, startling him. He picked up the receiver. "Hello?"

Mayor Washburn's shrill voice came over the line. "Otto, what are you going to do about that damned woman? I've had calls all morning about that speech she made yesterday."

"*Me* do something?" Channing snarled. "Why is everything always left up to me? You have as much at stake here as I do."

"You handle things like this, Otto. I'm in the public eye. I can't go around carrying on a

421

personal vendetta, especially against a woman as popular as Zoe Tremaine. It could cost me votes."

"Don't forget who helped you get those votes, Charles," Channing said harshly.

"You think I don't know that, Otto?" A whining note crept into the mayor's voice. "But if she isn't muzzled, she's going to scare the money off. And she may even get that damned initiative passed. If she does, it's going to kill us!"

"You think I don't realize that?"

"I thought you were going to have Thad dig up something on her, something to button her up."

"Nothing's shown up yet," Channing lied. "I'm hoping it will soon."

"It had better be soon. The least you can do, Otto, is keep a leash on that daughter of yours."

Channing's fingers tightened around the receiver, and his heart skipped a beat. "What do you mean? What's Susan done?"

"She's hitting the sack with that doctor, that Dr. Breckinridge."

Channing went weak with relief.

"And how do you think that makes matters look? The Tremaine woman's lieutenant screwing the head doctor at The Clinic? It makes it look like he's on her side."

Channing's thoughts began to race. "You

sure about this?"

"Pretty sure. My driver has an apartment in the same building as Dr. Breckinridge, and he said he saw your daughter slip out of the doctor's apartment at two in the morning. Now, you know they weren't in there playing tiddlywinks at that hour."

"I'll look into it, Charles."

Channing hung up, his mind churning. If this was true, it could very well give him the leverage needed!

He flipped through his Rolodex and finally found the number he sought — an unscrupulous private investigator located in Palm Springs. He had used the man twice in the past and had gotten good results.

Twenty-one

Jeffrey and Lacey stood with a small group gathered around an empty flower urn on the patio behind the rehab building. With some ceremony, Noah stepped up to Karla and handed her a notebook, then moved back to stand alongside Jeffrey. They watched as Rem crumpled up a newspaper, put it into the urn and struck a match to it.

"I'm not sure I understand this," Jeffrey said to Noah. "What is this, some kind of camp-fire ceremony?"

Noah glanced at him in some surprise. "It's time for Karla's burning."

"Her burning? I must have missed something here."

"Its customary when a patient has completed his or her fourth and fifth steps. You've been here almost three weeks and haven't attended a burning yet?"

"Once or twice I saw some people gathered out here, but I didn't attach any significance to it."

Noah smiled. "Your turn will come, Jeffrey."

As they watched, Karla began tearing pages out of the notebook and tossing them into the flames.

"What exactly does it mean?" Jeffrey asked.

"Karla made a complete list of all the wrongs she'd committed while on alcohol in that notebook, she'd confessed them to her god and to another human — in her case, one of the ministers who visits regularly. Now she's burning the list."

"And that makes, her well again? Sounds too easy to me."

"But it works. It's a part of the Alcoholics Anonymous creed, and we use it here. From the AA lectures you've attended here, you should know by now that AA works when other means fail."

"Then why didn't she just stay home, attend AA regularly and save the money she paid to attend The Clinic?"

"In the one month here, you receive more than a year of the benefits of AA, plus additional guidance and counseling."

All of a sudden, voices were raised. "We respect and understand you, Karla. You've heard all the bullshit. You are no longer resentful and angry. Serenity is yours!"

Karla burned the last sheet, tears streaming from her eyes. The others gathered around, congratulating her.

"Like I said, your turn will come, Jeffrey," Noah said. He turned away and reentered the building.

Lacey stepped closer to Jeffrey. "I'm looking forward to my burning." She laughed embarrassedly. "My bonfire will probably be the biggest ever seen here."

He took her arm, and they started back inside. "I hardly think you're that much worse than any of the others."

"I've hurt a lot of people in my time, Jeffrey. Not only have I hurt friends and co-workers, but because of my cocaine sprees, I've caused budget problems with many films. Delays while I got myself straight, scenes that had to be shot again and again because I blew my lines. You can't begin to know, Jeffrey."

She hugged his arm to her. He felt the warmth of her body close to his, and gazing down into her trusting eyes, he felt his conscience ping again.

He cleared his throat. "We have a half hour before The Snake Pit session. How about a cup of coffee?"

"Not coffee, but a cold pop would be nice. I've drunk enough coffee in here to float a rowboat."

In the commissary, she leaned across the table and whispered, "I broke one of the cardinal rules this week."

His eyebrows shot up. "I can't believe it's very serious."

"Well, it's a distraction, and you know how they frown on that here. You remember I wasn't in the solarium this past Sunday?"

"Sure, I missed you, but I thought you had a visitor."

"I did. My agent came to see me."

"I fail to see anything so terrible about that."

She glanced around. They were almost alone in the commissary. "He smuggled in a script. You see, when I graduate I'll finish the picture I was on, but there's only a month's shooting at the most, so my agent is lining up another movie."

"I should think you would want to take some time off after being in here."

She shook her head. "It doesn't work that way. Not with me, at any rate. I have to keep busy. And besides, in the film business you have to read dozens of scripts before you find a good one. I read this one last night, and it's a dandy. It's a comedy suspense, titled *Thieves*. I would be playing an heiress on the Riviera, whose inheritance is almost gone. The character has no job experience and is desperate, wondering what to do with her life. There is a wealthy playboy she could marry, which would solve the financial problem, but she doesn't love him. Then, one night, a burglar breaks into her suite. . . ."

Jeffrey went tense and cold, and it required all his willpower to keep a poker face. He stared intently into her eyes. Did she *know?* Did she even suspect? It seemed incredible that she should, but on the other hand, it seemed equally incredible to expect that it was nothing but a remarkable coincidence.

Lacey continued, "This burglar inadvertently awakens her. He has never killed anyone, and he can't bring himself to kill her. They talk half the night, and he falls in love with her. He offers a solution for her predicament. He can use a confederate, a woman who has access to the homes of the wealthy along the Riviera. She will not be required to actually participate in the burglaries, and so she agrees to work with him."

Jeffrey forced words through a suddenly dry mouth. "How does the movie end?"

"Well, since it's a comedy, it has a happy ending. After several successful jobs, they are in love with each other and decide to give up a life of crime and make another life together. But the thing is, Jeffrey, there is a cute gimmick. The audience never sees him without his mask until the very end. This would mean that an unknown could be cast as the burglar." She smiled slightly. "No male star would accept a role where his face isn't seen by the audience until the end. I think you would be perfect for the role. At least I have enough clout in the industry to insist that you be given a screen test, and I'm willing to wager my diamonds you'd get the role."

"Diamonds you no longer have." He was appalled to hear the words rolling from his lips.

She shrugged. "You know what I mean."

"You'd really go to bat for me?"

"I would be most happy to, Jeffrey."

Could she be devious enough to concoct a story like this supposed screenplay to trap him? He found it difficult to believe. Yet, could he afford to risk it?

"You don't have to decide right this minute. But will you promise to at least think about it?" she asked.

"Yes, Lacey. I'll think about it."

The promise was easy enough to make since he fully in tended to be out of here — and out of Lacey Houston's life — within the next twenty-four hours.

The hour was late, and Noah and Susan were on their way back to Oasis after having dinner in Palm Springs.

They had been riding along in companionable silence when Noah suddenly burst out, "I don't know what the hell I'm doing here! It's such a waste of whatever talent I might possess."

"What brought that on?" Susan questioned, placing a hand on his knee. "You haven't mentioned that in days, darling."

"It happens every time I drive over to the Springs. Oasis is bad enough, but Palm Springs is the Beverly Hills of the desert, the watering hole of the rich and famous. What am I doing treating the spoiled rich?"

"But they need help as well as the less affluent. . . ." She laughed suddenly. "Will you listen to me? Not too long ago I was using that same argument against you."

"And you were right, dammit! I feel like I'm marking time, without guts enough to break loose. That's the trouble with a job like I have at the Clinic. It seduces you, warps you until you lose sight of what's important."

"Don't be so hard on yourself, Noah. You're doing fine work."

"I could do better elsewhere," he grumbled as he turned into the parking lot in front of his building. As he switched off the engine, he turned to her, his sudden smile flashing. "Forgive me, Susan. I have to get these things off my chest and whoever's around has to suffer. But I promise, not one word more tonight." He made a quick crossing motion over his heart.

They got out of the car and walked arm in

arm into his building. As he closed the door after them, Noah asked, "Some music? An after-dinner drink?"

"No, darling. Just you. I need you, I'm hungry for you. You see how shameless you've made me?"

"Nothing could be any more flattering, Susan. Go ahead, stroke my ego."

"Maybe I should stroke something else," she said with a coy laugh.

"Oh, you are a shameless wench."

She fell into his arms, and after a lengthy passionate kiss, they started toward the bedroom, shedding clothes as they went.

They made love wildly on Noah's water bed. At the moment of mutual climax, Noah said hoarsely, "I love you, babe."

"Me, too!" she said as she moaned her satisfaction.

A few moments later, lying in his arms, she said in wonderment, "You know what you said? You said you love me."

"I haven't mentioned that before?" he asked guilelessly.

"You know you haven't," she said, and thumped his chest with her fist.

"Well, it happens to be true," he said, serious now. "I guess it took me a while to realize it. It's never happened before, and I've never spoken the words."

"Not even when you had another woman in your bed?"

"Not even then."

"You know, I believe you." She kissed him softly. "And I love you, Noah. But I can't say it's the first time. I fell in love with a football jock my senior year in high school."

"Puppy love," he said. "Doesn't count."

"I'm glad it's you, Noah. The next question is, what are we going to do about it?"

"Well . . ." He hesitated. "I'm going to have to break my promise not to talk about The Clinic. I don't feel I should make a commitment right now, not with being on the fence about remaining at The Clinic. I certainly couldn't leave the patients I'm working with. I'd feel I was deserting them. You know, that's the damned trouble." He sighed. "Every time a new group comes in, I quickly feel that they're my friends. Even the rich and famous ones. Oh, there are exceptions, like Billie Reaper."

"But by the time they graduate, a new group has already checked in."

"I know." Noah laughed. "That's the nub of it right there. I come to feel that they depend on me, and that's bullshit, of course. I'm not indispensable."

"I can wait, Noah. I'm in no hurry for any kind of real commitment. This is all new to me, too."

"You're very understanding." He tightened his arm around her.

"I just thought of something. Zoe is giving a party next Saturday, and she asked me to invite you."

"Tell her I'll be happy to come."

"You once told me that the patients aren't supposed to leave The Clinic until their time is up. Are any exceptions ever made?"

"Rarely. What did you have in mind?"

"Rem. Todd Remington."

"What about him?"

"Zoe wants to invite him to the party."

"Throw Rem into a party with booze flowing? You know what happened when he crashed Zoe's last party. And I'm not sure he's ready to be exposed to liquor."

"But he'd have to avoid parties for the rest of his life. Especially if he goes back to Hollywood and the movies."

"But by then he'll have finished the treatment."

"I have a feeling about him, Noah. I like him and I trust him."

"I like him, too. Hell, who wouldn't. But trust him around alcohol . . . ? Why him, especially?"

Susan hesitated, then told him something of Zoe's past, which Zoe had given her consent to do. She had said, "If you think you can trust your young doctor, tell him about my past. At least the part concerning Rem. It will hardly matter that one more person knows. But I'd rather you didn't mention Cassie."

When Susan had finished, she waited for Noah to comment scornfully about Zoe and her former profession. Instead, he said, "But I don't understand. If she's afraid Rem has blackmail in mind, why stick her hand in the fire by inviting him?"

"I've been trying to convince her that she's wrong about Rem, and she says the only way to find out, once and for all, is to face him. And she absolutely refused to put one foot inside The Clinic. . . . Can you make an exception?"

"Well, by Saturday he'll only have a week left to go, anyway. I'll talk to him. It might be an experiment."

"I'm paying for results," Cindy Hodges said into the phone.

"I'm trying my best, Miss Hodges," Jack Newton complained. "But I haven't been able to find out any more about this John what's-his-name. There is likely more stuff on him in Dr. Breckinridge's confidential files, but they're kept locked. I can't get into them."

"You must get access to them," she snapped. "You should be able to find a way. I have a hunch about this man. I know he's somebody important – I got that impression from the copy of his journal you got for me. There's a good bonus in it for you, Jack."

"Okay, Miss Hodges," Newton said. "I'll see what I can do."

"You do that. I'll expect to hear from you soon."

Cindy hung up, lit a cigarette and stepped to the window to look out. If Newton didn't start producing better results, she'd have to recruit another spy. During the past two weeks there had been little news coming out of The Clinic; no new celebrity had checked in, and she'd gone to the well too often already about Lacey Houston and Billie Reaper.

With a start, she glanced at her watch. Dick Stanton was due shortly. She had invited him to dinner this evening; something she rarely did with any man. But he was presenting a problem that she was going to have to deal with, and she needed the privacy of her own home to do it.

She had enjoyed Dick's company in the beginning. He was wickedly funny, he was a fun escort, and he was literate – she could talk about books and related subjects with him.

But now he was becoming just like other men – he'd come on to her the past two times she'd been out with him. His behavior had surprised her. She had been convinced from their first meeting that he was gay, and she much preferred gay men, since they represented no threat. Now she was wondering if she was mistaken about him. If he *was* gay, why was he putting the moves on her? Was it because he thought it was expected of him? Was he trying to convince her that he *wasn't* gay? Or was he . . . She gasped in astonishment at the thought. Was he trying to convince *himself* that he wasn't gay?

Whatever his motives, she had to sidetrack him. So far she had been able to fend him off without offending him. Not that she cared particularly if she upset him, but things could become sticky if he kept coming on to her.

Cindy glanced down at herself with a wry grin. She was wearing only a bra and a pair of bikini panties. If Dick was attracted to her, he would really be turned on if he saw her like this.

She turned away to get dressed and to start dinner.

Dick arrived on the dot at seven, dressed casually and carrying a bottle of Chateau Beychevelle '66.

Cindy answered the door wearing a frothy pink dress that swirled around her slender legs and hugged her small breasts.

Dick bowed slightly and held out the wrapped bottle. "Wine for the lady."

Her brows rose. "Why, thank you, kind sir. I wasn't expecting . . ." Her voice trailed off.

He nodded with a slight smile. "I know, people are always a touch surprised. But just because I'm not drinking doesn't mean that I get all holy about it and spoil other people's fun. I love to see others enjoy a good drink or a fine wine. I might envy them their enjoyment, but I don't begrudge them. Nor do I preach."

"I'll put it in the fridge to chill. And I was about to mix myself a martini. Can I get you anything, Dick?"

"A glass of ice tea. I hate the stuff, but . . .? He made a wry face. "What can you do?"

"Then have a seat. I'll be right back." She paused in the kitchen archway. "I warn you, Dick. I'm not much of a cook, and I know you're a gourmet. We're having broiled chicken, baked potatoes and vegetables. I've never . . . Well, I've never had the patience to learn to cook."

"I like simple fare. It's a nice change form the rich foods I often eat." He laughed lightly. "I have to watch my boyish figure."

"Good!"

She went into the kitchen, and Dick sat down on the couch. There was nothing fancy about her condo; it was functional, little more. Cindy had told him that she moved around so much it seemed senseless to really furnish any place to her liking.

In a moment she came back, carrying a full martini glass and a glass of ice tea. "Dinner will be ready in about a half-hour." She sat down beside him. "How's the writing going, Dick?"

"I believe I may have the block licked," he lied. He thought of telling her that the only writing he was really doing was in his journal, but since most of that concerned her, he deemed it unwise. "Have you written anything more on the book you told me about?"

"Not really." She turned toward him, tucking her feet gracefully under her, granting him a brief flash of thigh. "I'm too busy with other things." She took a sip of the martini, gazing into his eyes. "Maybe I'll show it to you, later, see what you think."

"I'd like that very much." He smiled somewhat uneasily. "But I must warn you that I'm a lousy critic. Most writers are."

"But I do value your opinion. You've never told me, Dick — how did you become a writer?"

He looked away from her penetrating gaze and took a drink of the tea. "I just drifted into it. In college I wanted to become an artist. But I soon came to the conclusion, agonizing as it was, that I lacked the talent. Oh, that wasn't only my opinion. Every art teacher I had told me to forget it. I suppose that had something to do with my decision to drop out of college after two years. Then I went into the army and ended up in Vietnam."

She made a sound of surprise. "You were over there? Somehow I can't see you as a soldier. Was it as terrible as everyone says?"

"Worse. So damned bad that it's still painful to talk about." He looked at her now and caught a look of compassion on her face.

"You don't have to talk about it, if you don't care to."

"I'd rather not. Anyway, after I came back to the States, I thought I'd write a novel about the hell that was Vietnam. That was a mistake, and like many first novels, it was bad. It got bad reviews and probably sold about fifteen hundred copies."

"But you kept writing?"

"Oh, yes. One good thing came out of the first book. I found an editor who liked my work, who had faith in me. He urged me to keep writing, and he went beyond the call of duty in helping me. My next book was better and sold reasonably well. Then, my third novel made the lists, including the ultimate one, the *New York Times*."

She frowned prettily. "Let's see, I think I read that one. It was located in the South, wasn't it?"

"Yes, New Orleans. *Fiesta.* The background was the Mardi Gras. I mined my roots for that one."

"You're from New Orleans? You don't have a Southern accent."

"I worked hard at losing it. Of course, I was only eighteen when I left the South. Not that I'm ashamed of my heritage. But in literary circles, they tend to slot you. If you're tagged as a Southern writer, it sticks. That's why I used a different milieu for *Images.*"

"Oh, yes." She nodded. "I loved *Images of Fortune.*"

And what would you say if you knew that a ghost had written most of it? he wondered.

At that moment a buzzer sounded in the kitchen, and Cindy jumped up. "That will be dinner."

He rose also. "Can I help?"

"You can set the table over by the windows, if you like." She smiled engagingly. "That shows you what a terrible cook and hostess I am. Most women have the table set before their guest arrives."

After dinner they returned to the couch. An early Beatles cassette was playing in the background. Cindy had a balloon glass of brandy. She was strangely quiet and was smoking nervously.

Could she be feeling the tension of the moment, also? Dick knew he certainly was. His confidence of before dinner had ebbed, and he was wondering if he should postpone the crucial moment until another evening.

No! If he didn't make the move now, he never would.

Head back against the couch, he turned his face toward her, looking at her taut slender loveliness. He knew that it was time. If he failed now, it would be like his writer's block—it would only get worse as time went on.

"Cindy . . ."

She turned her face to his, her eyes unreadable. "Yes, Dick?"

"I think I'm falling in love with you. You must realize that." He groaned. "I want you!"

"Dick, I don't think . . ."

He closed her mouth with his. A far corner of his brain registered the fact that this was the first time he had kissed a woman on the mouth since his late teens. Cindy's mouth tasted of brandy as he parted her lips with his tongue.

Without taking his mouth from hers, Dick moved his hand under her short skirt, his fingers dancing along the silken smoothness of her legs until he reached the nexus of her thighs.

"No!" With a supple twist, she was out of his

441

arms and out of his reach at the other end of the couch.

He looked at her dazedly. "Cindy, what is it? What's wrong? I thought you wanted it, too."

"Well, you were wrong!" she said through gritted teeth. "I think it's time I showed you something. I'll be right back." She got up and went into the room she used as an office.

Dick sat slumped on the couch, staring after her. What had gone wrong? He had been so *sure!* He felt insulted and . . . yes, humiliated! For the first time in almost twenty years he had made a pass at a woman and had been rebuffed. For a moment he considered leaving, without even a word of goodbye, and to the devil with her! Zoe had been right all along—this bitch only wanted to hurt him.

Yet he stayed. Curiosity held him nailed to the couch. He had to know the reason for this unexpected and brutal rejection.

Cindy returned, carrying several manuscript pages. She held them out. "I promised that I would let you read my book this evening. I think you should."

She wanted him to read the manuscript of a novel in progress? He took the pages automatically. "This is your novel?"

"No, not a novel. Just read, please."

She sat down at the other end of the couch and lit a cigarette. She seemed completely composed, not shaken in the least by the scene of a few minutes ago. As she returned his gaze, Dick was sure he detected a faintly mocking light in her eyes.

He began to read.

I think I wanted to be a girl even before I knew there was a difference between boys and girls. As I grew up, I felt cheated. I should have been born a girl, but God, or fate, played a cruel joke on me, and put me inside a boy's body.

I was born James Holton . . .

It had taken Dick's mind that long to grasp the enormity of what he was reading. No wonder he had been drawn to this creature. . . .

Stunned, he glanced up. "You're a man!"

"Was, Dick. *Was* a man," Cindy said composedly.

"You mean . . . ?"

She nodded. "That's right. I had a sex change operation. Ten years ago. Since then, I've been what I wanted to be all my life." A strange and bitter look crossed her face. "It hasn't quite had the results I had hoped for, but at least it's better than before."

"But if . . . ?" He grow for understanding. "If you had the operation, why can't you. ..?"

"Oh, I have all the proper equipment. Almost," she said with a twisted smile, "but the operation was not a complete success. I can have sex with a man, but there's nothing in it for me. Why should I do it just to give some man pleasure?" She almost spat the words at him.

"But why did you lead me on? Why did you let me think —"

"Lead you on? Come on, Dick!" She laughed harshly. "I knew from minute one that you were gay, so I figured I was safe from any hassle. I still don't know what you were after."

"I wanted to go straight," he muttered.

"Dick, it won't work, you should know that," she said with a sigh. "Why don't you accept yourself for what you are and go on from there?"

"You didn't."

She nodded. "That's true, I didn't, but circumstances were somewhat different."

"I think you're disgusting!" he said. He got to his feet, flinging the manuscript pages at her. "I have no interest in reading the rest of this."

She turned cruel and mocking. "Sticks and stones, Dick. And glass houses. You're fitting all the old clichés?"

He tried to think of a vicious rejoinder, but failed. He stormed out, trailed by her taunting laughter.

On the way home Dick had the cabbie stop at

444

a liquor store, where he purchased a fifth of vodka.

An hour later he was drunk and passed out on his couch.

Twenty-two

Shortly before the afternoon therapy session, Jeffrey went in search of Lacey. She wasn't in the solarium, nor was she in the commissary. He wandered the halls looking for her, but couldn't find her anywhere. He experienced a flare of panic. Could she have packed up and left?

Finally, he saw Bethel, her roommate, in the hall. "Do you know where Lacey is?" he asked.

"There was an important phone call for her a while ago. She went into Dr. Breckinridge's office to take it."

Knowing what the telephone call was probably about, he lingered outside Noah's office until Lacey came out.

When she saw him, her face lighted up with a brilliant smile. She fell in beside him, taking his arm.

"I was just talking to Theodore. And you know what?"

446

"What?" he said, beginning to smile in anticipation.

"Whoever stole my jewels returned them last night! He went to all the trouble of breaking into my Rolls again and putting them back in to the safe."

"I'm glad to hear it, Lacey. You must be delighted."

She was steering him toward the solarium. Inside, she glanced around and looked relieved to find it empty. She guided him over to the corner.

"Of course, I'm glad they've been returned, but for the life of me, I can't understand why a thief would do such a thing!"

"Maybe an attack of conscience?" he said, and then wished he hadn't.

"That could be, I suppose." She lowered her voice to just above a whisper. "Or else he found out my secret."

"Your secret?"

"You promise not to tell anyone? My reputation would be ruined if you did."

"I promise."

"The thief may have discovered that the jewels in the Rolls are all fakes. But even so, I don't know why he would bother to return them."

Jeffrey was staggered. "They're *fakes?*"

"Expensive, but fakes nonetheless."

447

Jeffrey's knees went weak, and he had to sit down. The irony of it all struck him forcibly; he felt hysterical laughter rising in him, but managed to stifle it. All the trouble he had gone to to steal them in the first place, and again last night when he returned them! He could just imagine the look on Bernie Kastle's face if he had dumped a satchel of glittering worthless baubles before him.

He glanced up as Lacey took the chair opposite him. "Then all that publicity about you never going anywhere without your jewels was just hype?"

"Not entirely," she said with a smile. "In the beginning I did, and I still do at times. But in the beginning, the collection was not nearly so valuable. I may be an idiot in many respects, Jeffrey, but that much of a fool I'm not. To leave that much jewelry in my Rolls, even locked away in a safe, would be plain asinine. And, of course, there is no way the insurance company would stand for it. But I was trapped by my own publicity, you see. Everyone knows my jewels go where I go, so I had to keep up the pretense."

"Then that's why you didn't seem too upset the day your chauffeur and the cop came to tell you they'd been stolen?" he said slowly.

"Of course. That's also why I asked for a few minutes alone with the policeman. I told him that the jewels were fake, that he needn't bother with an investigation, and that of course no claim would be filed with the insurance company. Jeffrey —" she leaned across to take his hand "— I hope you'll forgive me for misleading you. I've lived so long with the lie that it has become second nature to me."

"Me forgive *you*? It should be . . ." Again, he had been on the verge of blurting it all out. Perhaps someday, but not now; it was too soon. "There's nothing to forgive, Lacey."

"Have you thought about trying for the part in the movie I told you about?"

"I've thought about it, and I've decided to take a shot at it."

"Great!" She squeezed his hand tightly. "I'm looking forward to working with you. You can help me stay clean. We can help each other." Her eyes were deep and warm. "I think you're the first man I've ever met who I can really trust."

"Don't be too hasty, Lacey," he said awkwardly. "You don't know me . . ."

"I know you quite well." Her gaze remained fixed on his.

"You've thought that before, remember? About other men."

"This time I know I'm right." She glanced at her watch with a start. "Good heavens, it's time for the session. We're going to be late." She jumped up.

He also stood. "You go along, Lacey."

"Aren't you coming?"

"No, I think I'll skip The Snake Pit today."

"Dr. Breckinridge isn't going to like that," she said with a frown.

"I don't really have to go, Lacey. I know —" he held up a hand "— you don't understand. But I really don't. I'll explain it to you someday."

"You mean that you're not really an alcoholic, don't you?" she said without censure.

Lacey continued to surprise him with her perceptiveness. "Something like that, yes."

She surprised him again. Without a word, she stepped close, leaned up to kiss him softly on the lips, then turned away and without another word left the solarium.

He looked after her, his heart hurting for love of her. Was it going to work for them? He knew that she loved him; she didn't try to hide it. But could it work, a relationship between an ex-burglar trying to become a movie actor and a world famous star? Well, he could only give it his best shot.

Right now he was going to have to think of some story to tell Bernie Kastle to keep the fence from breaking both his arms and legs.

Governor Stoddard was also the recipient of an

unexpected telephone call, which he was taking in Noah's office.

"Myra, how did you find out where I was?" he asked. "Bobbie, of course. He's the only one who knew. I'll have his ass for this!"

"Don't blame Bobbie, William," Myra Stoddard said in a strained voice. "Junior was ill, and I thought you should know."

Stoddard tensed. "Is Bill okay? What's wrong?"

"It wasn't as serious as I thought. Just strep throat and the flu. But I thought it was much worse until the doctor came a little while ago. But why did you lie to me? After all the years we've been married, don't you think you can trust me?"

Stoddard sighed. "It isn't so much a matter of trust, dear. I guess I was ashamed to have you and the kids know that I was just a plain drunk."

"I knew you drank too much, but I never dreamed it was that bad."

"Well, it was. I knew I had to get straightened out for the coming campaign. I thought I could get through it, and you'd never be the wiser."

"But it does come down to a matter of trust, doesn't it?" his wife said with a catch in her voice. "You were scared that I'd let it slip that you were going through treatment for alcoholism. Weren't you?"

"All right!" he said in sudden anger. "You've never been closemouthed, Myra, you have to admit that. And for this to get to the media would ruin me."

"I realize that I'm a little gossipy, William," she said in a hurt voice, "but I've never let anything slip that was important."

"Well, I still think it would have been best if you hadn't learned about my being here. But now that you do know, don't say zip to a soul, not even to the kids. I don't want them to know."

"Are you all right?"

"I'm fine. I'm off the booze, and I feel better than I have in years."

"How much longer will you have to stay there?"

"I have just a little over a week to go."

"Perhaps I should fly out there to be near you."

"No! For God's sake, Myra!" He paused to quell the rising panic and modulated his tone. "Some snoop would be sure to spot you. Everyone knows about The Clinic here. If you were seen in Oasis, the media would immediately suspect that I was here. No, you stay there, Myra. I'll be back before you know it."

"I feel that I should do more," she said in a small voice. "And I also feel somehow responsible. Isn't the wife partly to blame?" Her voice

452

had taken on a self-pitying tone.

"No," he said harshly. "My drinking had nothing at all to do with you."

"You're sure?" she asked doubtfully. "Is that what the doctors claim?"

"I haven't discussed our private life with the doctors. Goodbye, Myra. I'll be home in about a week."

He hung up abruptly, in a black mood. Myra was a devout Catholic, brought up to believe that a wife lived only for her husband and children. In the beginning of their marriage, Stoddard had viewed this as ideal, but it had paled over the years. And in the recent past she had started blaming herself when anything went wrong.

"Dammit, I could sure use a drink," he said aloud, then looked around quickly to see if he had been overheard.

Was Myra partially to blame for his heavy boozing? No, he couldn't honestly say that she was — she was merely a convenient excuse. Anyway, he was glad she wasn't coming to Oasis.

A glance at his watch told him that it was almost time for The Snake Pit session. He now looked forward to joining the group; he liked to observe Lacey Houston. Unfortunately it hadn't taken him long to learn that there was no way a seduction could take place under the tight strictures of The Clinic. But maybe he could keep in touch with her after they both graduated; he felt that he could trust her to keep quiet about his stay there. If she learned that he was the governor of an important state, she might be willing to play. He had learned that political power was a heady aphrodisiac.

Stoddard left Noah's office and headed toward the therapy session, humming under his breath.

Billie Reaper had just finished the last of the PCP. Angel dust was the only thing Jack Newton could score for him the last time. At least that's what the jerk-off claimed. Well aware that PCP was a little scary, Billie had used it sparingly. The rock star had just cleaned up the last of it – he wanted to be bright and lively for the daily Snake Pit session. Besides, Newton had promised that he would score some coke for him tonight.

By the time he strode down the corridor toward the meeting room, the angel dust had already worked its magic. Billie was floating several inches off the floor, at once removed from reality and the world around him. He was ready for anything the doctor and the others could dish out today. He was due for the hot seat, and he strongly suspected that today would be the day.

454

Well, let them have at him. He could handle whatever came his way. They would see that they couldn't mess with the Reaper!

Noah was a few minutes late for the afternoon session as he hurried along the corridor. He caught up with Governor Stoddard just outside the meeting room.

"Well, John? Was that your wife on the phone?"

Stoddard glanced at the ceiling. "Yes, that was Myra. My son was ill, and she managed to worm my whereabouts out of Bobbie Reed."

"Nothing serious, I hope."

"Just a bad case of the flu."

"Did you ask her to come out next week?"

"She doesn't want to come." Stoddard still didn't meet Noah's glance. "She doesn't want to leave Junior."

"I'm sorry about that. It would be much better, for both of you, if she could be here to be briefed."

"Well, hell, Doctor, I'll manage." Now he looked at Noah with a faint smile. "I let the booze get the best of me all on my own, so it's only fitting I should handle this alone."

They were at the door now. Noah paused with his hand on the knob. He shrugged. "Well, it's your life, John."

He pushed the door open, and they went in

together. The others were already there, seated in a semicircle. Noah took his usual seat, facing them, leaning his attaché case against his leg.

"Good afternoon, gang."

He received a chorus of "hi's" in reply. Even Billie Reaper greeted him brightly.

Then Noah raked another glance over the group. "Wait a minute. Someone's missing. Where's Jeffrey? Does anyone know why he's late?" His gaze rested on Lacey.

Lacey squirmed then said in a rush, "He's not just late, Doctor. He said he wouldn't be here today."

Noah frowned. "Did he tell you why?"

Lacey hesitated, remembering what Jeffrey had told her — that he didn't need the sessions. She didn't know why he was here under false pretenses, although she had a strong suspicion. Yet it wasn't her place to tell Dr. Breckinridge that Jeffrey Lawrence wasn't an alcoholic, and certainly not in front of the group. "He told me that he had some . . . he had something important to do," she replied.

"I fail to see what can be more important than these sessions," Noah said, still frowning. "However, I shall take that up with him. Well . . ." He brightened, reaching down into his attaché case for several notebooks. "As you know, it's my custom, to discuss your daily journals with each one of you in private, but you've all done exceptionally well so I thought I'd return them to you here, today. You've got the hang of it now. As the saying goes, or use to go, you're letting it all hang out. And that's good. I'm proud of you."

He handed the notebooks out, one by one. Except Billie Reaper's, which had been blank yesterday. He had made about a half dozen entries since coming to The Clinic, and those had been close to incomprehensible.

"And here's yours, Billie. No entry for yesterday, which seems to be par for the course."

"I'm a singer, not a writer," Billie said cockily.

"Well, we're not into singing in here. The object of these journal entries is to bare your emotions."

"I get paid for that, onstage."

Noah sighed, holding back his annoyance with an effort. "In that case, I think it's time you were put on the hot seat. If you refuse to write, let's see how you do at talking. Stand up, Billie. You're on."

Billie stood up. He swayed slightly, his eyes fever bright as his gaze jumped from face to face. Noah experienced a faint tick of alarm, but it went away as Billie surprised him.

"Hi, I'm Billie, and I'm a doper."

"Hi, Billie!" came the chorus.

The singer looked at Noah and winked. "How'm I doing, Doc?"

"You're doing fine, Billie. That's an important first step."

"And you said I wasn't cooperative, man."

"All right, let's see just how much," Noah said with a slight smile. "You just admitted that you're a drug abuser."

Billie grinned. "It's what you wanted me to say, ain't it?"

"But do you truly believe it? And when you leave here, will you leave drugs alone?"

"Sure, man. No big deal," Billie said piously.

"What are we hearing, gang?"

"Bullshit!" sounded the chorus.

"If you don't stay clean, Billie," Noah said, "you're a dead man. You were close to it when you came in here."

Billie stared. "Don't screw with my head, man. Coke doesn't kill you. No way!"

"You're wrong," Noah said flatly. "It's a myth that cocaine doesn't kill. There have been several recent deaths from the drug. A number of athletes, for instance."

"Sure, man, but they overloaded," Billie said with a dismissive gesture. "A gram at once, that's too much."

"Recent research has proven that regular cocaine users develop a sensitivity to the drug, to the point that smaller, or even the usual doses can be fatal. And pay attention, Billie. Cocaine overdose victims do not die peacefully. Death is caused by an overstimulation of the central nervous system, followed by a collapse of either respiratory or heart function, and sometimes both. A fatal attack comes on suddenly and without warning, and it resembles a violent grand mal epileptic seizure. I suspect that you experienced such a seizure at Irvine Meadows. You were lucky to have survived. The next time, you may not. A heavy cocaine binge can bring about a fatal heart attack, severe arrhythmia, an embolism or a massive and fatal stroke."

Billie's narrow face had gone pale and he moved back a step. "You're just trying to scare me, man!"

"I sincerely hope so." Noah gestured suddenly. "Lie down on the floor, Billie."

Billie stared. "What?"

"Lie down on the floor. On your back. You said you wanted to cooperate."

With a shrug, Billie stretched out on the floor.

"Now close your eyes and cross your arms over your chest."

Billie complied.

"We are several months into the future, or perhaps a year. You are dead. You're lying in your casket, the best one available, and people you have known are filing past." Noah got up and stood over the prone youth. "This is Dr.

Breckinridge, Billie. I am deeply sorry for your sudden death. But it was not unexpected. You were warned. I had great hopes for you at The Clinic. And here's your manager, Joe Devlin." Turning, Noah gestured to Governor Stoddard.

Stoddard stood over Billie, his script in hand. "You should have listened to us, Billie. You didn't have to do so many concerts, work so hard that you had to snort cocaine to keep going. We didn't need the money that badly."

"Shit, man!" Billie's eyes flew open. "Joe Devlin would never say something like that. Who do you think keeps me working so hard?"

"You're not supposed to speak, Billie," Noah scolded. "You're dead. Close your eyes. Now, your latest girlfriend is next." He motioned to Lacey.

Lacey stood over the prone figure. "Honey, I loved you so damned much. We had a good life together when you were straight. Why didn't you give it up? If you had listened to . . ."

With a snarl, Billie jumped up off the floor in one supple movement. "So you're my girl, huh, bitch? I'll show you how dead I am!"

He seized Lacey in his arms and pulled her against him. Spit flew from his mouth as he sought her lips.

Lacey gave a little scream and tried to pull free, but she was amazed by the strength in his scrawny figure.

460

Alarmed, Noah took a step toward the struggling pair. "Now, Billie, behave. This isn't going to get you anywhere."

"Stay back!" His eyes wild, Billie turned Lacey around in his arms and began to back away from the group. "Me and the big movie star here are going down the hall to my room!"

All of a sudden, Noah realized what was behind the sudden mood swing — Billie was high on something, dangerously high, out of control. A fine damned doctor I am, he berated himself. I should have realized.

He couldn't imagine how the singer could possibly have gotten his hands on a dangerous substance in The Clinic, but that wasn't important right now. The important thing was to stop him before he harmed Lacey.

Even as he was thinking it, Noah had backed up to the wall, pressing against the button that alerted Bud Long, the guard at the front entrance, that something was wrong. Noah hoped it still worked; he'd never had to use it. He could only hope that Long knew what the signal meant.

All the while, Billie had been backing toward the door, with Lacey held tightly against him. The men of the therapy group, recovering from their surprise, had fanned out and were advancing on the singer. Rem and Stoddard had the center positions.

"Now, son," Rem said in a soothing voice, "you don't want to do this. You'll only get hurt and in trouble. . . ."

"Stay back, pop," Billie said. "All of you! If you rush me, the movie star here is the one who gets hurt." He clamped a hand around one of Lacey's breasts and squeezed cruelly. Lacey cried out sharply.

"And that's only a small sample," Billie snapped. "So back off."

"Do what he says," Noah called out. "He's dangerous."

"Listen to the doc," Billie said with his cawing laugh. "I'm a mean mother."

The advancing men slowed and came to a stop.

There was the sound of hurrying footsteps in the corridor outside. Alerted by the noise, Billie planted his back against the wall just to the right of the door, Lacey still held in front of him.

The door burst open and a panting Bud Long charged into the room. He skidded to a stop, his glance going to Noah. "What's wrong, Doc?" He didn't even notice Billie.

Before Noah could frame a response, Billie had snaked out a hand and snatched the pistol from the holster of the left-handed guard. His other arm still around Lacey, Billie waved the pistol menacingly. "Now, I'm backing out of here with the starlet. You all stay put. One head stuck out this door and . . . someone will pay!"

Holding the door open with his foot, Billie backed out of the room and then walked backward down the hall, his gaze riveted on the door to the meeting room.

"Billie," Lacey choked out, "you are being foolish. You're only going to get into trouble. Bad trouble."

"What's that, movie star? You worried about the Reaper?" he said in a taunting voice. "Ain't that sweet now. Long time since a chick worried about the Reaper."

"I don't want to see anyone get hurt."

Billie laughed maliciously. "Anyone gets hurt, babe, it's going to be you."

Billie was really flying now. He seemed to float three feet off the floor, and things, awful things, danced on the edges of his vision. His paranoia increased. The door to the meeting room edged open, and Billie fired the pistol in that general direction. The bullet thudded into the ceiling above the door, which slammed shut immediately.

Billie laughed again and moved his arm up to tighten his hold on Lacey's throat. He hurried backward, dragging her with him.

Lacey's breath was cut off. She clawed at the arm locked around her throat, to no avail. Her lungs began to burn, and black dots flashed before her eyes. She was rapidly being choked to death.

Jeffrey had just returned the rehab wing from a stroll around the grounds, when he heard the sound of a shot. He experienced something that he later thought must have been a psychic flash. Lacey! Lacey was in some kind of danger!

Without hesitation, he started along the corridor at a dead run. Other people were running toward the sound of the shot, but he outdistanced all of them. In a moment he spun around the corner and was in the section of hallway leading to The Snake Pit. He slowed as he came upon the weird tableau – Billie Reaper backing down the corridor, waving a pistol in the air.

And then Jeffrey saw that he had a woman clutched against him and was dragging her. Jeffrey's breath caught as he glimpsed a cap of dark hair. Lacey!

He began moving again, slower this time, every nerve alert. As he advanced and Billie backed up, the gap between them narrowed.

Jeffrey considered his options. Did he dare tackle Reaper? There was always the danger that the gun might go off, and Lacey would be hurt in the process.

Then the decision was made for him. The

door to The Snake Pit opened and Reaper raised the pistol, pointing it at the door. Without further thought, Jeffrey acted. Taking two quick steps, he seized the gun arm in both hands and twisted.

He shouted, "Lacey! Run!"

He exerted all his strength against Reaper's arm, twisting again. The pistol was shaken loose, clattering against the corridor wall. At the same time, Lacey tore out of Reaper's grip. Losing her balance, she fell headlong, skidding across the floor.

Reaper turned a contorted snarling face toward Jeffrey. The boy's eyes were wild and his face distorted.

Warily, Jeffrey let go of Billie's arm and took a step back.

"Don't screw with me, man! I'll take your head off!" Billie screamed. He aimed a fist at Jeffrey's face.

Jeffrey's left hand came up, blocking the blow easily. Adrenaline and anger pumping, Jeffrey doubled his right hand into a fist and drove it into the singer's belly. Billie bent forward, gagging, and Jeffrey brought his knee up. It struck Billie in the face, crunching his nose. Blood sprayed, and he flew backward, crashing against the wall and sliding slowly to the floor. His hands came up to his face, and he stared at the blood on his hands in horror.

Then everybody was there, crowding around. "Take the little creep to his room, Bud, and lock him in," Noah ordered crisply.

Bud Long stooped to pull Billie to his feet and then led him away. The singer was moaning now, tears and blood running down his face.

Jeffrey had already turned away to where a dazed Lacey was sitting propped up against the wall. Squatting, he touched her cheek with gentle fingers. "Lacey, are you all right?"

"I . . . I'm fine, I guess." She smiled tremulously. "A little in shock, maybe." Her smile turned tender, and she took his hand in hers and kissed it. "My hero," she said with shining eyes.

Jeffrey went red in embarrassment. "Oh, I hardly think that word applies."

"Well, I do. It's too bad a camera wasn't turning. It could have been your screen test. You would have passed with flying colors."

"How about we go have a cup of coffee?" He stood, pulling her up with him. "I need something to steady my nerves. I should think you would, too."

Noah watched Jeffrey escort Lacey down the hall as he stood with the therapy group, who were chattering in excited voices as they rehashed the events of the past fifteen minutes. He noticed a slender blond woman hurrying toward them along the corridor. There was something familiar about her, but he knew she wasn't connected with The Clinic. With Bud Long away from the front door, anyone could just walk in.

As she stopped before him, he noticed that she had a small tape recorder in her hand.

"Who are you?" he demanded.

"I'm Cindy Hodges. . . ."

Dismay seized him. This was all he needed! And how did she get here so fast? He knew she lived only a few blocks from The Clinic, but even so . . . Somebody tipped her! She had to have an informant inside The Clinic! He would have somebody's head for this!

"You have no business here, Miss Hodges. I must insist that you leave now. . . ." he said angrily.

But he didn't have her attention. She was staring behind him, and now she pushed past. Looking around, Noah saw Governor Stoddard, face averted, edging away.

"Don't I know you?" Cindy yelled. "But of course! You're Governor William Stoddard!"

Twenty-three

Zoe Tremaine's party was subdued in comparison to the recent events at The Clinic. The resulting publicity had been quite heavy, and Zoe couldn't help gloating; but she kept it to herself, considering that it would be in bad taste to do otherwise.

If Dick Stanton had been there, he might have livened things up, but he wasn't present. As always, Zoe had called Dick to ask him to help arrange the party, but this time he had begged off.

On the phone he had told her, "You'll have to get along without me this time, Zoe. I'm feeling terrible." His voice had sounded clogged, without its usual lift. "If I came, I'd only be a drag. The way I'm feeling, I'd be about as much fun as a funeral director."

"How can I have a party without you, Dickie?"

"This time you'll have to," he'd said, and hung up without even saying goodbye, which was totally unlike him.

Zoe had considered going over to his place and checking on him, yet she knew that he was subject to volatile moods that plunged him into fits of depression; and at those times he was impossible.

So she and Susan had had to do it all. Actually, the girl hadn't been too much help, since she was worried about Noah. She had told Zoe that Noah blamed himself for what had happened, and she hadn't even been sure that he would show up for the party.

He still hadn't shown up, which kept Susan rushing to the telephone every few minutes in an effort to track him down, so far without success. The other guests had all arrived, and Zoe could finally relax for a few moments.

She made herself a drink and found Thad Darnell at a table in the atrium. She sat down with a sigh. The chief was nursing a beer.

Darnell glanced around. "I see you've replaced some of your birds."

"I purchased a few last week. I don't suppose you've been able to learn anything about who killed the others?"

Darnell stared down into his beer glass. "Not really. There were no prints left behind, as I've already told you." He hesitated, then looked her straight in the eyes. "As a cop I shouldn't be telling you this, but I saw Otto the morning after it happened. His hand was bandaged. I'm certain in my own mind that one or more of your birds bit or clawed him, although he claims otherwise. But I have no actual proof, Zoe. Nothing I can pin on him."

She nodded. "I was sure it was Otto, but I was also sure that you couldn't nail him for it. But thanks for trying, Chief."

He raised and lowered his shoulders. "I just wish I could have done more. . . ."

Just then Susan came through the door, beaming. "Noah made it, Zoe. And look who's with him."

Trailing Susan and Noah was Todd Remington. He approached hesitantly. "Hello, May . . ." Too late, Rem realized his mistake.

"Hello, Rem. It's all right. The chief, Noah and Susan know about May Fremont."

Puzzled, Rem stared at Darnell. "Chief?"

"Yes, Rem," Zoe said with a faint smile. "Todd Remington, I'd like you to meet Thad Darnell, chief of police of Oasis."

Darnell stood, hand extended. "I'm happy to meet you, Mr. Remington. I've always been a big fan of yours."

"It's my pleasure, Chief." Rem took Darnell's hand and shook it, looking over at Zoe. "And he knows about you?"

"He knows, Rem," she said quietly. "Now come along, there's someone else who wants to meet you."

Just before they entered the family room, Rem stopped her with a hand on her elbow. "May – Dammit, I don't know what to call you!"

"I'd prefer Zoe, Rem. After all, it *is* my real name. I assumed May Fremont when I went into the business."

"All right then, Zoe. About my phone call sometime back . . ." He shuffled his feet in embarrassment. "I was in the process of drying out and didn't really know where I was coming from. I spooked you, didn't I?"

She nodded without speaking.

"Of course I did. You thought I was going to hit on you for some hush money, ain't that right?" He scrubbed the back of his hand across his mouth. "Sometimes I think the booze has left me with a wet brain. But I reckon if I'm to be truthful, some such idea was in the back of my mind." He took her hand. "But now that I'm in my right mind, more or less, you have nothing to fear from me, Zoe. No matter how strapped I am for money, I'd never stoop that low."

"I'm glad, Rem. I must admit that I was afraid you would try to blackmail me. Susan kept trying to convince me that I was wrong."

He grinned crookedly. "She's sweet, that Susan. A real nice little gal."

"She's all of that," Zoe agreed. "Now come along, I wanted to introduce you to someone."

But just inside Rem reached out a hand to stop Zoe. "Just a minute."

He headed for the bar, and Zoe felt a lurch of dismay. She let her breath go with a sigh as he said to the man she'd hired to tend bar, "How about a Coke, young fellow?"

When Rem turned around, he began to smile as he caught her expression. "Reckon you thought I was after bourbon, huh? Nope. Right now I don't even want a drink. Now I'm not saying that I have it whipped for good, knowing my past history, but I'm on top of it for now."

She linked her arm with his and led him into the living room toward a group gathered around the piano, where a young man was playing and singing softly. She touched the shoulder of a tall lean man with a shock of snow-white hair. "Ward?"

The man straightened up from leaning on the piano, turning a weathered face to her. "Yes, Zoe?"

"I'd like to introduce you to Todd Remington. Rem, this is Ward Bancroft. Ward is an independent producer. He has a vacation home here in Oasis."

"Mr. Remington, I was delighted when Zoe told me you'd be here tonight." The producer wore a broad smile. He threw an arm around Rem's shoulder. "Let's go out by the pool where we can have some privacy. I have a Western in preproduction. It has a role in it that's right down your alley. It's only a supporting role, but it's a strong part . . ."

He started Rem toward the door, talking all the while. Rem looked back over his shoulder at Zoe, wearing an expression of awed amazement mixed with more than a touch of gratitude.

Zoe winked at him.

In the atrium Noah and Thad Darnell were in deep discussion. "I found the guy who tipped Cindy Hodges to what was going down the other day at The Clinic," Noah told the chief. "An attendant by the name of Jack Newton, an exjunkie. Believe it or not, he confessed. I warned Hanks that it wasn't good policy to hire somebody who'd been a user unless we were damned good and sure they had been clean for quite a time. . . ." Noah gave a disgusted shake of his head. "Anyway, it turns out that Newton has been feeding the Hodges woman inside information for some time. And not only that, he's been supplying Billie Reaper with whatever drugs he could come up with."

"What did you do?" Darnell asked.

"Sterling Hanks ordered me to tell him to take a hike, of course."

"You should have called me. If he's been pushing out there, we could put him behind bars."

Noah was shaking his head. "Hanks didn't want it to get out that one of our own has been pushing drugs. In fact, I probably shouldn't even be telling you this, but I'm so damned fed up."

Darnell nodded. "Well, if he's gone, he's out of my jurisdiction. How about the singer, this Reaper guy? Did he go berserk on coke? That's a little unusual, isn't it?"

"Not so unusual. He did it before, at Irvine Meadows. But it wasn't cocaine this time. It was angel dust. PCP is dangerous stuff. His head was already screwed up, and the PCP was enough to send him over the edge."

"What's going to happen to him?" Susan, who had only been listening to the conversation, asked.

"Right now he's locked up in the detox wing. And he's out of there as soon as possible," Noah said grimly. "His agent is sending someone to pick him up tomorrow."

"You should have called me," Darnell said. "He stole a gun from your guard, didn't he? We could get him on an assault charge, maybe even with intent to kill."

474

"If I'd had my way I would have been happy to turn him over to you, but Hanks wouldn't have it. Placing Billie under arrest would only result in additional bad publicity. I'm quoting Hanks now, of course. I don't much care."

"A felony was committed, in both instances," Darnell said with a flinty stare. "In the strict letter of the law, you people should have called us so we could have taken your employee and this singer into custody. You're not a law unto yourself out there, you know."

Noah raked his fingers through his hair. "I can't argue with you about that, Chief. Reaper is still there, if you want to arrest him. Just so you know, Lacey Houston doesn't want to press charges."

"What the hell!" Darnell's shoulders lost their starch. "So long as it's confined to The Clinic, why bother?" He didn't feel it necessary to add that he had received word from both Otto Channing and Mayor Washburn to keep hands off of the whole matter.

Susan saw Zoe coming toward them, small cigar fuming. She sat down, smiling at Noah. "You might be interested in knowing, young man, that Rem made a stop at the bar inside."

Noah went tense. "Oh, hell! Maybe I'd better —"

He started to rise, and Zoe put a hand on his arm. "No, Doctor, it's all right. I'm sorry, I couldn't resist. But there's no cause for concern. He just ordered a Coke."

"Thank God!" Noah said with a sigh of relief. "I'll admit that bringing him here had me uptight. I have enough on my conscience without being responsible for Rem's downfall by bringing him around alcohol too soon."

"Darling, I wish you would stop blaming yourself for what happened." Susan touched her fingers to his cheek. "You can't be held to blame if a character as unstable as Billie Reaper goes off the tracks."

"I'm a doctor, dealing with drug abusers every day. I should have recognized that he was on something. It's my business to know . . ."

"Oh, shit!" Susan said, looking past him. "Zoe, look who's here."

Coming toward them across the atrium was an obviously agitated Juanita, with Otto Channing and Mayor Washburn trailing her.

"I am sorry, Señora Tremaine. I told these men it was a private party, but they would not take no for an answer."

"It's all right, Juanita," Zoe said, motioning for her to go. "You men taken to party crashing now? Perhaps you're insulted that you weren't invited? Your not being invited wasn't an oversight, believe me."

"We're here on business," Channing said stiffly.

"Business?" Zoe's look burned. "I have no business with you."

"I have something here that I think you should listen to, both you and my daughter. Especially my daughter."

Zoe arched an eyebrow. "Susan?"

Susan stared daggers at her father. "I don't know why we should bother, but if it will help get rid of uninvited guests, let's do it. Ask Mr. Channing what he has to say, Zoe"

"It's not what I have to say so much as what this has to say." Channing took a tape cassette from his pocket. "And considering what's on the tape, we should have privacy."

"We can use my study," Zoe said, getting up. "I have a tape player in there."

"I'll come with you, Zoe," Darnell said, also getting to his feet.

"It's none of your business, Thad," Channing said unpleasantly. "What are you doing here, anyway?"

"The chief is my guest," Zoe said, taking Darnell's arm. "And whatever is on this tape, I have the feeling that he should be present."

Channing shrugged. "Suit yourself."

Zoe had converted a bedroom off the hall into a small office-study for herself. After they were all inside the room, she closed the door and held out her hand. "Let me have the tape, Otto."

"No! Just show me your tape player."

With a shrug, Zoe showed him. Channing snapped the tape into the player and turned to his audience with a smirk. "This needs no introduction. It's self-explanatory, as you'll all see." He snapped on the player.

At first there was only a humming silence. Then could be heard the sound of a key in a lock, then the slamming of a door, and a man's voice said, "Some music? An after dinner drink?"

"No, darling. Just you. I need you, I'm hungry for you. You see how shameless you've made me?"

"Nothing could be any more flattering . . ."

A gasp came from Susan. "That's us, Noah!"

"You son of a bitch, you bugged my apartment!" He started toward Channing with his fists raised.

Thad Darnell stepped between them. "Easy, Doctor, easy. I'll handle this." He stepped to the tape player, snapped it off and took out the cassette.

"That's only a copy, Thad. I have others. You really should listen to the rest." Channing laughed coarsely. "It gets better, much better."

Zoe said, "What do you expect to gain from this, Otto?"

"That should be obvious. How do you think your gang of supporters would react if they knew that your lieutenant was bedding down The Clinic's head doctor in secret, all the while you're being so damned sanctimonious about The Clinic being in Oasis?"

"We expect you to keep your mouth shut from now on, or copies of this tape will be spread all over town," Mayor Washburn stated.

"And it also means you cease your opposition to the no growth initiative," Channing added.

"You're a great pair," Susan said in disgust. "There's nothing you wouldn't stoop to."

Her father glared. "You're a fine one to talk, after what you threatened me with."

"Like I said, *Father*, I had an excellent teacher."

"This discussion is at a dead end. You're not going to use this, Otto." Darnell held up the tape.

"Tell me why not," Channing said darkly.

Zoe spoke up. "For a very simple reason. The chief and I have discussed this. He signed affidavits going into great detail about some of the shady deals he has been involved in with you and the mayor. So, if the two of you don't back off, those affidavits will be mailed to the newspapers."

Channing glared at the chief. "You wouldn't dare! You'd be putting your head on the block, as well."

Darnell nodded gravely. "True enough. But

I'm prepared to do it, if it becomes necessary. If you lie down with crooks, you have to expect to get dirty."

"So I would say it seems to be a Mexican standoff, wouldn't you?" he said with relish.

Mayor Washburn had gone quite pale. "I don't believe you, Thad. You're bluffing!"

Darnell smiled tightly. "But are you willing to take that chance?"

From the dejected expressions on the faces of both men, Zoe knew that they were not willing to take the risk. In a harsh voice, she said, "I'd thank you to leave my house now. And I would suggest that you consider relocating, Otto – and you, Mayor, should have serious doubts about running for office again this fall. Your political career is at an end. I intend to see to it!"

Otto Channing and Mayor Washburn took their leave without another word. As their footsteps faded down the hall, Zoe turned to the chief. "Thank you, Thad, for your support."

He grinned faintly. "I really don't think you would have needed it. You're one tough lady, Zoe." Then he sobered. "It's been on mind for some time, but I came to a firm decision in the past few minutes. I'm handing in my resignation."

"That really isn't necessary," Zoe said swiftly.

"We've heard the last of those two. They won't have the guts to cross me again."

"Oh, I'm sure you're right about that. But I'm not fit to serve. I haven't been for some time, but have managed to avoid thinking about it."

"Well, it's your decision, but I want you to know that you've earned my respect."

"Thank you for that. I feel honored."

Zoe heaved a sigh, then brightened. "I think this calls for a toast."

As they made their way across the atrium, a loud drunken voice could be heard from the family room.

Zoe frowned. "Now what?" She increased her stride.

In the family room she was greeted by the sight of a disheveled unshaved Dick Stanton, hanging on to the bar in an effort to remain standing.

"Oh, no!" she cried in dismay. "I should have realized what was wrong with you when I called."

Dick turned around, almost fell and clutched at the bar at the last instant, peering at her with bleary eyes.

"Zoe! My dear Zoe!" he said in a thick voice. "I knew you would be hurt if I didn't . . . did not come to your party."

"Oh, Dickie! How could you after all this

time? What brought this on?"

He picked up the glass of vodka from the bar. "I salute you, Zoe." He took a swig, although most of the liquor ran unnoticed down his chin and onto his shirt. "I should have lisst . . . listened to you. You were right about that bitch. Heart of ice." Tears streaked down his cheek. "Not only that, but not a . . . not a . . ."

His eyes rolled back in his head, and he began to fall. From behind Zoe, Noah sprang forward to catch Dick in his arms.

"He's out cold. Shall I take him to The Clinic, Zoe?" Noah smiled grimly. "We have a vacancy."

"He's absolutely terrified of that place," she said in great distress, close to tears. "For now, take him into my bedroom, and we'll talk about it later."

Noah bent slightly, slung Dick over his shoulder and followed Zoe across the atrium and down the hall to her bedroom.

It was late, and all the guests had departed, except for Noah. Juanita and the bartender were in the last stages of cleaning up.

Zoe, Susan and Noah were having a nightcap in the atrium. Zoe sat with Madam perched on her shoulder.

"How is Dickie?" Susan asked.

"He's still out," Zoe replied. "I just checked

on him a moment ago."

"He really should enter The Clinic, to be dried out, at least," Noah said. "If not The Clinic, some other treatment center. Or even into a hospital."

"I know, I know." Zoe brooded, drawing on her cigar. "But someone will have to sign him in, won't they?"

"Well, yes. Doesn't he have any relatives?"

"Not that I know about. Except for Susan and I, Dick doesn't even have any close friends."

Susan leaned forward. "Can't you give him private therapy, Noah?"

"I suppose I could, if he's agreeable," Noah said thoughtfully. "From what you have told me about him, I would venture the opinion that he has to come to terms with his homosexuality. If he can do that, he will be taking a giant step toward curing his alcoholism."

"Well, I'll be damned if I will be responsible for signing him into that place," Zoe said forcibly. "Forgive me, Noah."

Noah gave a slight shrug. "Nothing to forgive, Zoe. I know how you feel."

"No, you don't. Not the full extent of it. Perhaps someday I'll tell you the whole story. But aside from personal reasons, The Clinic is like a mirage, ephemeral and illusory. Many of the patients are never permanently cured. Even you will admit that, I'm sure. They will return again and again, if not to that place, then to another just like it, seeking the mirage of rebirth."

"Of course, you're right," Noah was forced to agree. "Governor William Stoddard is a case in point. He left The Clinic the day Billie went berserk, knowing that Cindy Hodges was going to expose him in her tabloid. Just today he called me to tell me that he was retiring permanently from politics. He was drunk, he admitted it." Noah sighed heavily. "But what other alternative is there, Zoe? Alcoholism and drug abuse must be treated."

Zoe drew on her cigar, framing an answer, then paused as the front doorbell rang. "Now who the devil can that be at this time of the night?" She raised her voice, "Juanita, will you get that, please?"

Juanita's voice floated out to them. "*Si, señora.*"

A few minutes later, Juanita ushered a man through the atrium doors.

Noah uttered an exclamation of surprise and got to his feet. "Mr. Heinman!"

Karl Heinman nodded stiffly. "I apologize for coming unannounced like this, but I was informed at The Clinic that you were attending a party here."

"This is Zoe Tremaine, our hostess. Zoe, may

I present Karl Heinman? And you know Susan."

"Miss Channing." Heinman inclined his head slightly, then bowed to Zoe. "Again, my apologies for intruding on your party."

"No apologies necessary. Besides, the party's over." Zoe studied him closely, curious about this seldom seen, almost mythic figure. She had to admit that she was not particularly impressed. "Would you care for a drink, Mr. Heinman?"

"I do not drink, ma'am." He looked at Noah. "If I could have a few minutes of your time, Dr. Breckinridge?"

"Of course." Noah motioned. "Please have a seat."

"Perhaps we should talk in private."

"These are my friends." Noah gestured carelessly as he sat down. "Anything you have to say, sir, you may say in front of them."

"As you wish." Karl Heininan seated himself gingerly. "I did not learn of the deplorable incident with the singer until early this morning. I flew in as quickly as I could get away."

"Yes, it was rather . . . well, messy."

"I have been conferring with Sterling Hanks."

Noah sat back, smiling slightly. "And exactly what did our esteemed director, Sterling Silver, have to say?"

"A great many things, Doctor. He offered

485

numerous excuses, none of which were satisfactory."

Noah nodded gravely. "Yes, he is good at that."

"I have asked for his resignation, Doctor."

Noah sat up. "And how did he react to that?"

"I gave him no choice," Heinman said strongly. "His resignation is effective as of the end of next week."

Noah let his breath go with a whooshing sound. "This is an interesting development."

Heinman looked at him intently. "His position must be filled immediately. I am here, Doctor, to ask you to become The Clinic's director."

The time has come to get off the fence, Noah thought. He looked at Susan sitting beside him and took her hand in his. "I appreciate the honor, Mr. Heinman, but I am also leaving The Clinic."

Susan's face broke into a wide smile.

Heinman frowned. "Have you thought this over carefully? You'll be throwing away a great deal of money and prestige."

Noah squeezed Susan's hand. "I realize that, sir, but I feel that it's time for me to use my talents, such as they are, in some other setting. At any rate, I want to take some time off. You see, I'm thinking of getting married. That is, if the lady I have in mind is willing."

Heinman rose abruptly. "Of course, it's your decision. Good night to you all."

Before Zoe could rise to see him to the door, he was gone. She gave Noah a rueful smile. "He doesn't understand, you know. It is unthinkable to him that anyone would turn down the money and power that would accompany that position."

"I know," Noah said with a broad grin as he pulled Susan close. "I feel sorry for the poor bastard, don't you?"